RED WOLFF

BY

K.T. MINCE

"Red Wolff," by K.T. Mince. ISBN 978-1-60264-171-6.

Library of Congress Control Number on file with Publisher.

Published 2008 by Virtualbookworm.com Publishing Inc., P.O. Box 9949, College Station, TX 77842, US. ©2008, K.T. Mince. All rights reserved. No part of this publication may be reproduced, stored in a retrieval system, or transmitted in any form or by any means, electronic, mechanical, recording or otherwise, without the prior written permission of K.T. Mince.

Manufactured in the United States of America.

To

Judy, wife, partner and soul mate. For putting up with me and
encouraging me while I wrote this book.

To

The men and women of the military who go in harms way against a
vile enemy.

To

The tens of thousands of cops who protect us everyday, mostly from
ourselves.

And To

My friend, Jill Angel, the real *Red Wolff.*

PREFACE

This is a story about a small town in rural Northern California, a revenge seeking Islamic terrorist, and a strong willed woman cop.

Red Wolff is the fictional name of a good friend and former colleague. Being a woman, being gay, and being a cop, especially on the California Highway Patrol, was not always an easy road.

The stories about the Highway Patrol, the locations, policies and procedures, police work, and people involved are true. With apologizes to Joe Friday, only the names have been changed to protect the guilty.

While I earnestly hope what follows never happens, in today's world you can't dismiss it out-of-hand. After all, who ever thought Islamic terrorists would fly commercial airliners into buildings?

If it does, well, if it does, fortunately, there are people like Red Wolff.

CHAPTER ONE

LATE AFTERNOON, FRIDAY, JULY 1ˢᵗ

The solitary man standing at the edge of the scenic overlook drew no attention from the half-dozen or so other people who were admiring the view of the small coastal town less than a mile away. The jagged rocks below, with the Pacific Ocean waves crashing against them, and the towering Redwood trees that ringed the entire coastline and surrounding hills, painted a majestic portrait of this remote location.

It was midsummer, and the rural North Coast of California was a favorite destination for vacationers, especially older couples without children, and people from around the world who came to stand in awe at the base of two thousand year old, 300 foot tall Redwood trees.

Emil Lagare slowly brought the new high-power binoculars up to his eyes. The binoculars, like almost everything else he would need for his mission, had been purchased in Oakland, several days prior. As he slowly rocked the focusing tab from side-to-side, the town of Crescent City came into vivid focus. Holding them steady to his eyes, elbows tightly locked to his sides to prevent excess movement, he slowly began to pan from the highway to the left toward the center of town.

He had seen it all before, two months earlier, in Syria, on the videotape made by the imam. Even though the quality of the video was excellent, nothing compared to actually doing personal reconnaissance, to understand the terrain and help finalize the tactical plan. This lesson, "Know the battleground," had been constantly reinforced by his instructors.

Now, as he panned the binoculars across the town below, the voice of his mission's architect, in Arabic, narrated the videotape in his mind. "The only road in and out of town is Highway 101. It runs north and south along the coastline. The road is mostly one lane in each direction with an occasional short additional lane to allow passing. The highway south of Crescent City is very winding and

1

requires great concentration to negotiate," the narrative voice added emphasis to the reference about winding.

As he continued to study the small town below, Emil Lagare began to recognize landmarks and buildings he had first seen in the video. The boat harbor, with its' twenty to thirty small commercial fishing boats and sprinkling of personal pleasure boats, two seafood restaurants, a short wood and concrete pier, and the harbormaster's one story office.

At the entrance to the harbor there were parking grounds for motor homes. "Ten dollars a night, or fifty-five dollars for seven nights," the narrative continued in his mind. Emil Lagare thought to himself that the imam who had actually taken the video had done a thorough job on his scouting mission six months ago.

Now, as the late afternoon shadows began to cast themselves across the parking area of the scenic outlook, most of the other sightseers were heading back to the highway to continue on their journeys or into the town below to find a motel for the night and a fresh seafood dinner.

Emil Lagare stopped his binocular scanning of the town below and briefly looked over his shoulder in response to the sound of cars starting and multiple doors being opened and closed. Glancing at his watch, he knew he should expedite his long distance reconnoitering of the town and check into the motel where the imam had made a reservation in his name.

As he went back to scanning the town below he cursed to himself that it had taken almost a full two hours longer than he had allotted to travel from Oakland to Crescent City. Part of the delay in getting to his destination had been the volume of traffic he encountered on the freeways after he left the mosque in Oakland. He'd seen and driven in heavy traffic before, in Paris, in Rome, and in Cairo, but nothing in those cities compared to the miles of cars, trucks, and buses he had encountered this morning. Strange, he thought to himself at the time, in European cities, drivers would be laying heavily on their horns and dashing from one lane to the other and back again in an effort to get to their destinations a few seconds earlier. Here, the drivers for the most part sat passively in their lane of traffic, moving slowly forward a few car lengths at a time, stopping again, sitting a few seconds, then moving forward again. It occurred to him that the heavy traffic he had endured was part of the exodus from the cities to the country on what his instructors told him was an American "three-day weekend."

Taking the route prescribed by the imam, he finally reached a location where traffic lightened to a point he could actually drive 65 miles per hour. He now found himself making excellent time as the road was two lanes in each direction allowing him to easily pass slower moving vehicles. Not even the numerous underpowered, oversized, boxy motor homes, almost every one of which was towing a small passenger car, being driven by older men with older women in the passenger seat, slowed his progress. Occasionally, he encountered a large lumber truck carrying two or three huge freshly fallen Redwood trees to one of the few remaining mills still in operation along the "Redwood Highway."

Passing through Eureka, the largest city along the coastal highway north of the San Francisco Bay Area with a population of 30,000 or so, he'd stopped briefly for fuel and bought several pieces of fruit in the small market attached to the gasoline station. His instructors had called them "convenience stores." They explained such stores had a wide variety of merchandise, and Americans were willing to pay a higher cost for these items rather than have to travel a longer distance to a major shopping location.

After leaving Eureka, the road abruptly changed to one lane in each direction, with constant curves, up and down undulations in the road, and few opportunities to pass. Here the highway snaked through immense stands of Redwood trees. Giant ferns bordered the road, and tree branches intertwined above, forming a canopy over the highway which created stretches of road where there was a perpetual lack of sunlight on some portions of the pavement. Now the motor homes and logging trucks he had easily passed several hours earlier became great lumbering rolling roadblocks as they struggled up small hills and around curves at 15-20 miles per hour.

Trapped as the fourth car behind a thirty foot Winnebago towing a Ford Explorer, there had simply been no opportunity to pass. Six slow, no, six agonizingly slow miles later, the motor home took a turn-off. Emil Lagare reflexively pressed down on the accelerator, making the mid-sized American made rental car jump forward, pushing him slightly back in his seat. He did not know American cars had such acceleration. While absent mindedly contemplating the engine performance of his rental car, he suddenly realized he was traveling 85 miles per hour and quickly overtaking other vehicles on the road. Instantly he eased his foot from the accelerator and the car's speed rapidly reduced to the legal limit.

Stay at the speed limit, he thought to himself. You have come this far, and being stopped for a traffic violation this close to your target could lead to the unraveling of the mission.

Emil Lagare's mind flashed back to his training and the Commander's Handbook he had memorized. Rule Number Three, under the section on the use of Disguises and Knowing Local Customs, "Don't draw attention to yourself, either by word or deed." Surely, he thought, his instructors would be less than pleased at his recent, although brief, lapse of attention.

Two hours behind his self-appointed time schedule, he easily found the turn-off to the scenic overlook. Signaling carefully, he made the left turn from northbound Highway 101 and drove the quarter mile to the overlook parking lot. Retrieving the new binoculars from the rental vehicle's trunk, he spent almost forty-five minutes surveying the scene below. Now, as the sightseers began to leave, and the tallest of the Redwood trees began to block the sun, Emil Lagare turned his attention back to identifying the buildings and locations previously video recorded by the imam.

After he finished viewing the town in the distance he walked to the edge of the outlook, stood against the four foot high guardrail, and looked down at the ocean three hundred feet below. The sea looked angry to him. The Pacific Ocean was a much darker blue than the Mediterranean Sea he swam in as a boy. The ocean had a cold and foreboding look, the waves crashing against the rocks sending a salt laden clear mist up into the air. He wondered for a moment if it was an omen. He quickly put the thought out of his mind.

Satisfied he now had a real time visual image of Crescent City, Emil Lagare headed back to his rental car. It was almost 5:30 as he backed out of the parking space and headed out of the scenic overlook, back toward the highway. Positioning the car to make a left turn, northbound back onto the highway, he stopped and waited as traffic passed in both directions.

One more car approached on the northbound side, traveling about 35 miles per hour in the same direction he wished to go. As he waited for the car to pass, he caught the brief glint of red and blue as the late afternoon sunlight, filtered by the Redwood trees, reflected through the plastic covers of the emergency roof lights on the police car. Instinctively, Emil Lagare felt the shudder that runs through most people worldwide when they see a police car. Unlike most people who knew they were doing nothing wrong and such reactions were foolish, he felt the head-to-toe tingling that accompanies those who actually had something to fear from the police.

He noted the police vehicle was mostly black, with a white roof and a white front door mounting a large gold star. The words "Highway Patrol" curved above the star. As it passed at a ninety degree angle to his vehicle, the officer looked in his direction and the two made eye contact. A woman, Emil Lagare said half-disgustedly to himself.

4

He remained stopped for an extra minute, until several vehicles finally approached and passed his location heading in the northbound direction. Satisfied there was now a sufficient buffer between him and the police car, he again checked to ensure traffic was clear, and turned left, heading northbound, into the town of Crescent City.

———————

Emil Lagare drove well within the speed limit, as the highway curved and twisted and began to slope downward. Within several minutes his car broke clear of the last of the Redwood trees and he found himself on the crest of a hill at the top of a long downgrade. At the bottom of the hill lay the town of Crescent City.

As he drove down the hill into Crescent City, Emil Lagare realized why this town had been chosen by his superiors. It was the remoteness that made it ideal. Almost four hundred miles, and six to seven hours driving hours north of San Francisco, it was a difficult location to reach quickly. The one highway leading in and out of the town had natural bottlenecks that could be easily exploited. Its remoteness also meant outgoing communication from the town would be difficult. The lack of good communication would mean any organized response by the American authorities would be delayed, giving him more time to carry out the plan. When the American authorities did learn what was happening, it would take even more time for them to analyze their intelligence, develop a response plan, and finally react. By that time, his mission would be well underway.

Emil Lagare had a good feeling about the plan, the mission, and the terror he and his team would wreak upon the Americans in this small town. Yes, this would be a Fourth of July the Americans would remember for a long time he thought. "Allah Akbar," *God is great,* he said to himself.

CHAPTER TWO

The giant Redwood trees bordering both sides of Highway 101 were blocking the late afternoon sun, throwing long shadows across the road. Driving northbound, back into Crescent City, after meeting with the officer assigned to the south part of the county, California Highway Patrol Sergeant Erin Wolff marveled at the scenery. How different and peaceful this was from working in Los Angeles. It was the start of a three-day Fourth of July weekend, yet traffic was still light and flowing smoothly. That would all change by tomorrow she knew, as hundreds of vacationers flocked to the town to camp, fish, or relax on the beaches around Crescent City.

"95-S-3, Humboldt," the communications operator's voice came over the radio speaker mounted below the dashboard in the black and white Ford Crown Victoria patrol vehicle.

Without moving her eyes from the road, in a practiced motion that came from years of experience, Erin Wolff brought the patrol vehicle's radio microphone from its mounting clip on the center of the dash with her right hand, holding it close to her mouth. "Humboldt, S-3, go ahead."

"S-3, 10-19, see 95-L," the voice droned in a flat tone.

"10-4," the sergeant replied. It was after six on a Friday evening and she wondered to herself what the boss was doing at work so late, and why he wanted her to return to the office.

———

Sergeant Erin Wolff was a sixteen year veteran of the CHP. By anyone's measure she was a good highway cop, and great sergeant. The officers who worked for her respected her decision-making, her fairness, and her coolness under pressure. Mostly however, they respected her ability to supervise by leading, not pushing. She was a natural leader and saw the stripes on her sleeve as a responsibility, not an entitlement.

Standing just over five feet six inches and weighing one hundred thirty-five pounds, she had a relaxed easy manner about her. When she walked she seemed to stroll in a way that made it look like her arms and legs were never working in unison, giving her a gait that was hard to miss. She always had a half-smile on her face that seemed to say "I know something you don't." Her most striking feature, however, was her lion's mane of hair. When in uniform, regulations stated a female officer's hair could be no longer than the bottom of the shirt collar. As a result, she always kept her hair pinned tightly in back, letting it down only when not in uniform. Given the strawberry-blond color of her hair, it was easy to see how she'd been tagged in the CHP Academy with her nickname, "Red."

In her sixteen years on the job Red Wolff had worked most of her career in Southern California. She started as a rookie in downtown Los Angeles, working freeway patrol. She quickly established herself as someone who eagerly assumed more than her share of the workload, handling calls on adjacent beats, never getting badge heavy with the public, and never backing down from a confrontation. Five years into her career she took the promotional test for sergeant. Putting her typical enthusiasm into the promotion process, she spent several hours each day after work studying CHP policy manuals, Penal Code, case law, supervision, labor relations, and dozens of other mundane details a CHP sergeant was expected to know. Her efforts paid off when she placed number two out of more than three hundred competitors statewide.

Red Wolff proved herself to be just as good a sergeant, as she was an officer. She established herself as a "no-nonsense" supervisor when it came to what she expected from her officers. Every officer knew when you worked her shift you were never late for roll call, you made sure your uniform was clean, you answered your radio promptly, and you took care of business on patrol. In return, every officer who worked for her knew when the "shit hit the fan" Red Wolff was the one sergeant they wanted on their side. In return for their loyalty, she did the little things for her officers that separate great sergeants from the rest. She made it a point to meet every one of the officers on her shift at least once a month for dinner, spending time talking about personal matters, in addition to business. She never hesitated to help officers when personal problems arose, and she was not afraid to grant officers special time off when necessary. When she sensed morale might be a little low, or as a reward for her shifts' performance, she would hold after work barbeques in the back parking lot cooking hamburgers and hot dogs for her crew.

In every respect Red Wolff was a great sergeant. She also happened to be gay.

The radio message had come from the communications center located some eighty-five miles south in the town of Eureka. "Humboldt Dispatch" as it was known to everyone, served three separate CHP commands along the Highway 101 corridor, from Garberville to Crescent City, a distance of over one hundred fifty miles. Each command was given a radio identifier prefix that helped route calls to the proper patrol officer on a specific beat within each command. Supervisory and management personnel were given radio call signs corresponding to where they were assigned. Crescent City's radio prefix was "95," and Erin Wolff was "S-3," or the third of three sergeants assigned to that office. "95-L" was the call sign for the lieutenant who was the commander of the Crescent City office.

"Humboldt, 95-S-3, at the office," Sergeant Erin Wolff called via the radio.

"10-4, S-3, at the office," came the monotone reply.

Unlike police or sheriff's stations, CHP offices are only open Monday through Friday during normal business hours. The rest of the time the offices are closed and function only as a place where officers change into uniform, meet for briefings, and write reports. Since the CHP does not have its own jail facilities, it is quite common for offices to be locked and empty for hours at a time.

Parking her car in the almost deserted lot she used her key to unlock the front door of the building. Once inside she could see the lights were on in the lieutenant's office.

The California Highway Patrol was created in 1929. Prior to that, each of the fifty-eight California counties had their own "County Traffic Squads" to enforce laws on the roads within that county. In 1929 all of the County Squads were brought under state control. From its beginnings as one squad per county in 1929, the CHP had grown, as California's population and roadways grew, to have one hundred fifty separate commands by the 1990s.

For almost fifty years the California Highway Patrol was a male's only organization. It was not until state law changed in 1974 that the first women were allowed to become officers. The first female officers were hired as a "Test Project" to determine if they could perform all of the duties of a CHP Officer.

Old perceptions, even older veterans, and outdated attitudes were some of the many obstacles the first female officers had to overcome. Doubts about female officers could be heard from the Mexican Border to the Sierra Mountains. "They're not strong enough to arrest suspects, they'll cry at accident scenes when people are hurt, they won't be able to work when they're on their periods."

The wives of male officers posed an additional obstacle for the first female officers. All over the state officers' wives went to supervisors demanding their husbands not be assigned to work with a female. "I don't want my husband working with a female because it will be dangerous for him, a woman can't protect my husband in a fight, and a female partner will be a distraction."

The test project ran for two years. As expected, female officers proved they could handle the job just as well as their male counterparts. Of the initial test project group of females, some did excellent, some performed poorly, and some resigned because the job was not for them. Others stayed for thirty years. Their experience virtually mirrored that of new male officers.

As for male and female officers working together, the results were predictable. Like any occupation where men and women find themselves in close proximity for long hours romances occurred, divorces happened, and jealousies arose.

In the end, women found themselves accepted, sometimes grudgingly, sometimes openly, and at other times indifferently into the CHP family.

Still, law enforcement work was not the type of job that easily attracted women. Though the CHP targeted its recruiting to encourage more women to apply, only about fifteen percent of the eight thousand officers were women by the turn of the new century. Even fewer were sergeants, lieutenants, captains, or chiefs.

Erin Wolff was the youngest of four daughters of a career navy enlisted man. Born in Virginia when her father was stationed there, she'd moved nine times by the age of sixteen as the navy transferred her father from duty station to duty station. Always more of a tomboy than her sisters, she was constantly active in sports, and when her father was stationed in Japan she developed what would become a lifelong interest in the martial arts. She was never all that interested in boys. Instead she spent countless hours mastering the then newly emerging world of computers. She was also a brilliant student achieving a perfect straight "A" average in high school. During her senior year she successfully competed for an appointment to the Air Force Academy, and three weeks after graduation, shortly before her eighteenth birthday, found herself reporting to Colorado Springs.

Coming from a military family, most of the discipline and attention to detail comprising the daily life of an Air Force Cadet was a piece of cake for Erin Wolff. She handled the hazing and constant stress by developing a half-smile which would drive her upper classmen crazy. It would become her trademark in the future. Academically she had little trouble maintaining a high class average, and after her first year at the academy she set her sights on becoming a fighter pilot.

Today the idea of a female fighter pilot hardly rates a second thought. In the mid-1980s, however, women in combat roles was an idea whose time had yet to come. All of the services were grappling with the expanding role of women in the military, and more precisely where the line was between combat support and actual combat.

As difficult as it was determining where women fit into the modern military, determining where they fit into the service academies was even more so. Of the four service academies, the Air Force Academy had the hardest time assimilating women into their ranks. Much of the blame for this lay with an upperclassmen system which used harassment and hazing to focus unwarranted amounts of attention on underclassmen, especially women. Attrition rates among female cadets were nearly double that of their male counterparts, and those who would not resign, often found themselves the subject of physical threats. The lion's share of blame for such activities, however, lay with the academy cadre's practice of turning a blind eye to the harassment, and senior officers who wrote off such things as "Boys will be boys."

It was during Thanksgiving weekend of her second year at the academy when Erin Wolff first confronted "The System." Most academy activities shut down in the early afternoon the day before Thanksgiving, giving both cadets and cadre a head start on a four-day weekend. Cadets who could, took advantage of the opportunity to head home for the holiday by grabbing a space available seat on an air force plane, or booking a commercial flight. Others headed for Denver just to get away for a while, or to the ski slopes for some relaxation.

Cadet Erin Wolff's father was now stationed at Pearl Harbor, a distance she decided was just too great to travel in only a few days.

Instead, she opted to remain at the academy along with about twelve hundred other cadets. Besides, she had reasoned, she could visit her parents during the Christmas holidays when she had ten days off, and she could use the time alone to relax and catch up on her sleep.

Thanksgiving Day was uneventful. She slept late, skipping breakfast, and then went on a long run by herself. Running had always been one of her favorite activities, a chance to push herself physically and to think. The traditional turkey dinner with all the trimmings served in the cadet dining hall was excellent, and following dinner she'd gone back to her room to listen to classical music.

Friday morning she woke early, and though it was one of the few opportunities she had to sleep in, decided to hit the weight room. The weight room was just off the main portion of the academy's physical training facility. Every conceivable type of weight training equipment was available, from Universal machines to free weights. There was also a large rubber mat area where cadets could stretch or use six foot wooden broomstick like poles to twist and bend.

Entering the weight room she was surprised to find two male cadets already there using the dumbbells. She recognized both as seniors, although she could not recall either of their names. Suppressing her disappointment that she did not have the room to herself she headed for the free weight section of the room and began loading a barbell to do bench presses. Erin Wolff was exceptionally strong for a female. She had a disciplined weight lifting routine. She worked her arms and shoulders on Mondays and Thursdays, her chest and back on Tuesdays and Fridays. Her routine called for her to do four sets of twelve repetitions of each exercise, increasing the weight by ten pounds on each set.

After taking off her warm-up jacket and sweat pants, she started with one hundred thirty pounds, and quickly pumped out the first set of bench presses. As she added five pounds to each side of the barbell for her second set, she noticed the two male cadets watching her and whispering to each other. By the time she laid down on the bench to begin her heaviest and last set of bench presses, both male cadets were within fifteen feet of her, watching.

"That's a pretty big load, need a spot?" asked the larger of the two, offering to help her steady the barbell.

"No thank you sir," she replied respectfully as she lay under the bar and pushed it up slightly off its support rack.

Lowering the bar to her chest, she began pushing it up and lowering it in a smooth motion, inhaling as the bar came down, exhaling as she pushed it up. On the sixth repetition they were on her.

They timed their attack perfectly. As she lowered the bar, the larger male, who was standing near her head, used his body weight to pin the bar down against her chest. The other, who was standing at the foot of the bench, began yanking at her gym shorts with both hands trying to pull them down.

Erin Wolff wrapped both her legs around the underside of the bench and struggled to free herself.

"Come on bitch," the larger of the two snarled. "Time to earn your wings."

The smaller of the two men continued pulling at her gym shorts, but she maintained a vise like grip on the bench with her legs. Frustrated by his inability to remove her shorts, he momentarily relaxed his grip and stood.

In a movement so fast it was almost a blur, Erin released her legs from the bench and brought them both up and toward her head. The larger man, still bent over holding the weight bar down on her chest, never saw it coming. Bringing her feet and knees together, she unleashed a violent kick upward dislocating the larger male's jaw. He immediately released his grip on the bar and fell to the floor writhing in pain.

Erin used both hands to push one side of the weight bar off her chest and wriggled from beneath it. Jumping to her feet she found herself face-to-face with her other attacker. Outweighed by over sixty pounds, and a full six inches shorter, she strategically retreated backward as the male cadet brought his hands up and advanced upon her.

From the corner of her eye, she spotted one of the six foot wooden poles standing against the wall. Grabbing the pole, she pointed it toward her attacker, and moved her feet into a defensive stance. He did not know it, but the man advancing on her was in deep trouble.

Erin Wolff had been studying Aikido for three years. As a martial art, Aikido focuses not on punches or kicks, but on fluid motion, speed, defensive blocks, and twisting an opponent's joints until they lock. The basic premise of this style of self-defense was your opponent is at their weakest at the moment they attack. What she especially liked about Aikido was all of the moves done while in hand-to-hand contact, could also be done using a "Jo" or five foot wooden stick. She'd spent countless hours practicing "Jodo," the Aikido style of Japanese stick fighting.

The wooden stick Erin held pointed at the second male cadet was longer than she was used to, but the extra foot would not prove to be a detriment. When her attacker closed within eight feet, she slid the stick forward in her left hand like a pool cue, her right hand supplying the power. In a lightning fast thrust, the end of the stick caught him in the indentation between his chest and right shoulder. The force of the blow stopped him dead in his tracks and spun him partially around. Howling with pain and anger, the male cadet swung with his left arm in an attempt to connect with her head. Using the pole, Erin Wolff deftly blocked the blow downward to her left. This movement, along with her attacker's momentum, caused him to stumble forward, his head following the rest of his body. Stepping back with her left foot, Erin Wolff pivoted slightly to her left. She brought the wooden shaft up horizontally, just above her head, and spun it one hundred eighty degrees with her hands, like the rotor blades of a helicopter. The centrifugal force generated by the spinning shaft caused a resounding crack when the other end of the pole struck the left side of the male cadet's head. Had she not moderated the force of the blow, she could have split her attacker's skull open. As it was, he would have a huge bruise and a terrible headache for the next week.

Recovering from this strike, she resumed a defensive posture and watched both men as they lay on the ground. Without another word, she dropped the wooden pole, grabbed her clothes and left the weight room.

She immediately reported the attack to the duty officer.

Disappointingly, The System closed ranks around her attackers in the ensuing investigation. Both men denied any involvement in the attack. They claimed to have been off the academy grounds at the time of the incident and their injuries were the result of skiing accidents.

The larger of the male cadets, whose jaw she had dislocated, was the son of an active duty air force major general. The other cadet was the son of a city alderman from Philadelphia. No charges of any kind were ever brought against either man, and both would go on to graduate the following June.

Not only did The System protect her attackers, but Erin Wolff now found herself subjected to "The Treatment." Her classmates began to avoid her company and others spoke to her only in an official capacity. Even other female cadets minimized their contact with her, lest they themselves become subjected to The Treatment.

By the end of her second year at the academy, Erin Wolff was virtually alone among four thousand cadets. Taking stock of her situation, she realized she could not endure two more years of the isolation she was being subjected to. She also came to the realization she would never become a fighter pilot. If she survived the next two years, the best she could hope for was to fly transport aircraft, and even that was a long shot. More than likely she would graduate and find herself in some type of administrative or logistical support assignment. Neither prospect held much appeal.

One week later she resigned from the Air Force Academy.

———

Some people might find themselves lost, bitter, or unsure of what to do next. Former Air Force Academy Cadet Erin Wolff faced none of these problems. At twenty years old she had the self-confidence and drive to begin forging a new path for herself. Using her accumulated savings from two years at the Air Force Academy, she moved to San Diego enrolling as a junior at San Diego State majoring in communications systems. With the experience she'd gained at the Air Force Academy, and her natural self-discipline, she easily completed the bachelor's program and began to seek her master's degree.

San Diego was a great place to go to school. It was warm most of the year, and with beaches and ocean sports nearby, Erin Wolff found herself happy and content with life. She joined several women's sports teams and for the first time in her life began to explore her sexuality.

She'd known she was gay since her teenage years. It was not something she could share with her parents, especially her father. Growing up in the late seventies and early eighties, being gay was still not something openly discussed, and "Gay Pride" was about fifteen years in the offing. Erin Wolff did the high school dance routine, dated casually, and giggled with her girlfriends about boys.

Her first and only gay experience occurred when she was sixteen while her father was stationed in Japan. It happened on a Saturday afternoon after her father picked her up following a soccer game on the navy base. On their way home to base housing he dropped by his office where he was the Chief Petty Officer in charge of maintenance on ship borne guided missiles. On this day he was dropping by to ensure the weekend maintenance crew had a handle on the guidance problem with one of the missile systems.

Her father left her in his office with a young female sailor who was the maintenance office typist and clerk, while he went to the maintenance area to talk with the repair crew. The female sailor engaged her in small talk and their eyes met several times in a way that stirred emotions in Erin Wolff that had, until now, remained dormant. After about a half-hour, while she was sitting at one of the vacant desks in the office waiting for her father to return, the young sailor moved softly behind her and placed a hand on her shoulder. The touch of another woman sent electric shocks throughout her young body. The experience was uncharted territory for her, yet, much like a teenage boy trying to steal his first kiss, she knew instinctively what to do. Swiveling in her chair, she stood. She and the young sailor moved into a corner of the office where they could not be seen.

Erin had only been kissed by a few boys on her occasional dates or at parties. She was not prepared for the deep, all consuming first kiss with another woman. She responded, almost involuntarily to the young sailor with deep kisses and the kind of touching her mother had warned her about with boys. Touching another woman's breasts and having her own breasts fondled, even through her clothing, sent an excited shudder through her from her toes to her scalp. The encounter lasted less than a minute but it confirmed what she had always known deep in her heart about her sexuality.

The young sailor's thirteen month tour of duty in Japan was almost over and Erin Wolff took whatever opportunity she could to meet with her. Once they even managed to meet off base and spent the afternoon at a local hotel in town where, for the first time, she was able to completely experience the thrill of sexual contact with another woman.

Erin always kept the secret of her sexuality tightly to herself. After her lover was transferred, she contented herself with memories of their time together. She would not have another experience with a woman for over three years.

Before the Clinton Era policy of "Don't Ask, Don't Tell," being gay was grounds for dismissal from the service. There were plenty of gay men and women in all branches of the military, but they conducted their personal lives in great secrecy. There was always the fear if they were discovered they would be discharged.

It was into this environment Erin Wolff found herself thrown when she entered the Air Force Academy in 1987. During her two years at the academy she suppressed any thought of becoming involved with another woman, focusing her energies on surviving the tough cadet curriculum. Not that there weren't opportunities. Since her first encounter when she was sixteen, she'd become adept at recognizing the signs and signals of other gay women. A certain way somebody looked at her, a comment made with double meaning thrown out to see how she responded, a lingering touch, or unnecessary acts of being helpful as a reason to be around her.

Though internally she longed for the touch of another woman, she rebuffed these gestures. With other female cadets, or in mixed company, she kept a tight rein on her emotions and never revealed any intimate details about herself to others. Even so, in the regimented academy atmosphere her classmates whispered, and rumors circulated. Rumor had it Erin Wolff was gay.

Erin always suspected many of her classmates and the academy staff had guessed her secret. She also suspected her attempted rape, the lack of any real investigation, and her subsequent treatment by the academy system, had been driven by the fact she was gay. Right up to the day she resigned from the academy, she never complained about the events of the past year, nor did she ever reveal the truth about her sexuality. Even in her written resignation, she listed "Personal Reasons" for why she was resigning. "Fuck 'em," she muttered to herself as she left the academy grounds for the last time in the rear seat of a taxi, not looking back.

Now living in San Diego and free from any restrictions or concerns about her sexual preference, she immersed herself in a gay lifestyle. She had several lovers over the next three years, including one long term live-in relationship. She also experienced the joy and pain which comes with any relationship, including a painful breakup with her lover after almost two years. All-in-all she was living a good life, but still felt empty. She needed to find a meaningful career path that would provide her with a sense of purpose.

It was during spring semester of her first year of graduate school when things began to fall into place. Between her first and second classes of the day she had an hour break. She wandered to the student union to get a cup of coffee. On this particular day there was a job fair in progress. Computer companies, the automotive industry, hotels, telecommunications organizations, and almost every other conceivable type of private industry had booths set up. There were also booths for the armed forces, and several California law enforcement agencies. Erin got a cup of coffee and began to wander through the dozens of booths.

Erin Wolff bypassed most of the booths, picked up a brochure from one of the nationwide telecommunications companies, and smiled to herself as she strolled by the booths for the army and air force.

She paused momentarily at the booths for the Los Angeles Police Department and San Diego County Sheriffs. She moved close enough to hear the white male recruiter talking to several young male students, extolling the reputation and toughness of LAPD. Moving on she spotted the booth for the California Highway Patrol manned by a young blond female officer and an older black male officer. She approached the booth and picked up a brightly colored brochure with the shadows of a male and female officer on the cover and the outline of California in the background. The brochure was entitled "Watching Out for California."

"Hi, how you doing?" inquired the black officer with a toothy smile.

"Just looking," Erin replied, somewhat taken aback by the officer's deep voice and friendly greeting.

"Cool," the female officer chimed in as she moved next to her partner officer. "We've got dozens of different jobs, and with the CHP you can work anywhere in the state."

Intrigued, Erin Wolff now began to look seriously at the brochure she held in her hands, then engaged both officers in a series of questions about the testing process, types of job assignments, salary, promotional opportunities, and working conditions.

In an upbeat manner the officers responded to each of her inquiries, throwing in little extra bits of information to enhance their answers.

Interested, but hesitant, she finally said to the officers, "I'm gay."

"So?" the female officer replied.

CHAPTER THREE

About the same time Sergeant Erin Wolff was returning to the Highway Patrol office to meet with her lieutenant, Emil Lagare was checking into his motel. The motel had a small office that also sold soft drinks, beer, water, snack food, and cigarettes. Registering under his true name, he used a credit card for payment, bought several bottles of water and left the office. He had no fear in using his real name, as he knew he was in the United States legally, and to his knowledge, no authorities suspected the purpose of his trip. Besides, he knew once his business in this town was concluded, he would not be leaving.

Parking the rental car in front of the door to his motel room, Emil Lagare removed two large, soft-sided wheeled suitcases from the trunk, and entered the room. For the first time in over ten hours he relaxed mentally. Almost immediately, the dull ache in his upper shoulders and neck caused by the long hours of driving and the constant thoughts of his mission began to fade. After washing his hands and face, he removed his shoes, but instead of praying as would have been expected of a devout Muslim this time of day, he layed on the king-sized bed and brought his right forearm across his eyes. His thoughts raced wildly from his mission to the many tasks he had yet to accomplish this day. His mind then locked onto the series of events that had brought him to this remote location.

Emil Lagare was 25 years old. Born in Beirut, to a French-Catholic father, and a Muslim-Lebanese mother, he had the privileged upbringing that his father's wealth provided. His father's import business flourished, even through the many Israeli incursions into the southern parts of his country, and the years of civil unrest that accompanied various factions vying for control of war torn Lebanon.

18

For the most part, Emil Lagare's family was apolitical concerning the unrest in Lebanon during the early years of his life. Although a predominately Muslim country, there were nonetheless plenty of people, Muslim or not, who were eager for the liquor and cigarettes his father imported from Europe and America. During this period, his mother raised him on the fringes of the Muslim faith. Although his mother was a devout Muslim, she was not fanatical in imposing her beliefs on young Emil, respecting that he had a Catholic side also. His father's frequent business trips, however, meant little or no Christianity was taught in the household. Emil's mother did ensure he said his daily prayers as required and she instructed him in reading the Quran. Emil's mother considered herself a liberated woman. She did not adopt the dress of Muslim women by wearing the headscarf known as a Hijab, or the Abaya, the long outer robe and pants, a practice that often turned heads and was the subject of gossip. Likewise she did not push her son toward growing a beard as a sign of being a devout Muslim or insist he cover his head, as was the norm among other boys his age.

During his teenage years, when not in school, Emil traveled extensively with his father during business trips throughout the Middle East and Europe. Visiting Saudi Arabia in 1995, Emil had his first encounter with fundamentalist Muslims who preached a brand of Islam that espoused violence as a method of battling the influence of democracy and what was seen as western decadence. The dominant theme of these groups was a hatred of Jews and a corresponding hatred of the United States for its support of Israel.

Through travels with his father, Emil cultivated his natural gift with languages and soon was fluent in not only Arabic from his mother and French from his father, but also English and Italian. The dual citizenship afforded by his French and Lebanese heritage gave him passports issued by both countries, and made travel across international borders simple. It was during these trips he developed a love of architecture and decided this would become his life's work. Upon graduation from secondary school he applied to and was accepted into France's prestigious School of Architectural Engineering at the University of Paris.

By 1999, the year he left for the university, Emil Lagare was a handsome and confident 18 year old. Tall and thin, he had a light olive complexion and a full head of straight black hair. He inherited the erect bearing of his father and the flowing grace of his mother, to accompany the easy broad smile he flashed continually.

Upon his arrival in Paris, Emil discovered the city had a significant Muslim population. Most were from Morocco, Saudi

Arabia, Syria, and Iraq, and worked in many of the menial service jobs the French, with their growing affluence, would not do. For the most part, the Muslim population of Paris created a city within a city. Store signs were in Arabic, shops owned by local Muslims sold food from their homelands, and small coffee bars served the strong dark brew sweetened with milk, the favorite beverage of the men in the Muslim community.

Throughout his first two years in Paris, Emil lived in a small flat near the university. He found the atmosphere around the campus to be intoxicating as he mixed with fellow students from not only France, but Germany, Italy, Spain, and other Muslim countries. Even though the students he associated with were all majoring in architecture, the coffee bar and study group discussions often found their way to politics and the world events that unfolded daily in nearby Eastern European countries, breakaway republics of the former Soviet Union, and the Middle East.

It was at one of these coffee shops in early 2001 where Emil Lagare first met Yusef al-Mashtal, a Saudi national, who was visiting the imam of the local Paris mosque. Al-Mashtal had a small group of Muslim students, all male, surrounding him as he spoke passionately about the son of a Saudi industrialist who had declared war on the United States. Dressed in a Jubba, the traditional loose fitting long outer robe, with a heavy black beard, he spoke passionately of this man's organization in Afghanistan and the Muslim fundamentalist government controlling the country that gave him sanctuary.

While most of the other students were enthralled with al-Mashtal's dialogue and nodded in agreement with his diatribe against Jews, the United States, and other western democracies, Emil remained reserved and let little of his thoughts or emotions show. Over the next several weeks Emil saw and heard al-Mashtal speak on two other occasions, once again at the same coffee bar, and once at a gathering in the mosque. On both occasions Emil remained in the background listening, showing neither agreement nor disagreement. Al-Mashtal noticed Emil on these occasions, and as he spoke he looked directly at the young student.

As the meeting at the mosque began to breakup, al-Mashtal made a point to approach Emil and invited him to a coffee bar near the mosque. Curious, but with his senses alerted, Emil agreed.

The coffee bar was still crowded, even though it was well past ten, and much of the city had retired for the night. Muslim men stood at the long wooden bar or huddled around small tables arguing politics with their heads surrounded by thick clouds of cigarette smoke as they sipped their coffee. Al-Mashtal found a vacant table on the patio facing the street and both men sat. A tired looking middle-aged woman took their order and shortly two small cups of hot black coffee appeared on their table.

"So," al-Mashtal began. "You are not impressed by what you heard me speak of this evening." It was a statement, not a question.

Somewhat taken aback by the directness of his statement, Emil paused for several seconds before replying, "My father taught me to be cautious in business and religion."

"A son should always heed the advice of his father," al-Mashtal replied with a smile. "Especially a father who lives both in the Christian and Muslim world."

Again, Emil was taken off guard by this man's words indicating he knew about his family. Recovering quickly, Emil merely nodded agreement.

Realizing his last statement may have triggered something in the young man, al-Mashtal said, "Fear not Emil, I only know of your family from inquiries I made about you after I first saw you at the coffee bar several weeks ago. Wherever I travel and meet with my brothers, I always try to find out where they are from, especially the ones I have not yet won over to our cause. And I am right that I have yet to win you over, am I not?"

Emil sat silently for several seconds, his mind mulling over al-Masthal's words. His French-Christian side telling him he should abandon any further contact with this man, his Lebanese-Muslim side inexplicitly drawn to him. Looking directly into al-Masthal's cold, black, lifeless eyes, Emil finally responded.

"You speak of a war against America, of carrying the struggle to the shores of our enemies, and of ridding Islamic countries of the influences of the west all in the name of Allah," Emil said. "Why, however, do you speak of these things here? Shouldn't the struggle begin in our own countries first? In my country, war has been the only constant in my entire life as Muslim fights Muslim, Christian fights Muslim, and Muslims fight Jews."

"An astute observation," al-Masthal responded. "But the struggle has begun in our own countries, long ago, and has spread much farther than our own borders. Did you think the bombing of the American embassies in Africa, or the attack on the American warship in Yemen last year were the acts of isolated fanatics? No young Emil, these were organized and planned acts carried out by dedicated members loyal to our leader and our cause."

"And precisely what has this to do with me?" asked Emil.

"Ah," smiled al-Masthal. "Direct and to the point, just as the imam said you would be. Worldwide, there are millions of Muslims, countless thousands are ready to take up arms and sacrifice themselves for the glory of Islam. Up until now they have not had a rallying point or leader to focus their efforts in striking back at our enemies."

Emil sat passively as al-Masthal continued.

"Now, unknown to most of the world, or even to most Muslims, there is an organization called al-Qaeda, *The Base*, which has the means, the funding, and most importantly, the will to strike out at those who have sought to oppress us for these many years. Very soon a small band of our brothers will carry the struggle to the very door step of America. Then the whole world will know of al-Qaeda."

As al-Masthal continued to speak, Emil leaned slightly forward, as if inexplicably drawn to his voice.

"Why do you speak of such things to me?" asked Emil.

"Because "The Cause" always has need of bright young men who can think, who can lead, and who have the ability to mix easily with other cultures," al-Masthal said.

Emil thought for several seconds and then spoke, "Surely you don't believe that I am the type of person who would strap five kilos of explosives to my body and blow up a bus, do you?"

"Yes, I do believe you are that type of person. Maybe not now, but in the future. However, The Cause has plenty of people ready to become martyrs by blowing up buses and themselves for Allah. The Cause seeks you out now to prepare you for the time, and the time will come, when you will be called upon to do your part in the struggle." There was great emphasis in al-Masthal's voice when he said, "and the time will come."

Emil, his Lebanese side quickly boiling to the surface, replied emphatically, "I do not see such a time ever occurring." At the same time he stood, reached into his pocket and put a wad of Francs on the table for the coffee.

Exactly the response I was told to expect, al-Masthal thought to himself as Emil stood and prepared to leave. "I meant no offense young Emil. Please, one more moment of your time."

"A moment only," said Emil, still standing.

"The world will be a different place in six months," said al-Masthal looking up at the young student. "Events across the world will bring true believers to our cause. The time will come when you will seek me out, and you too will become a true believer. When you are ready, the imam will know how to reach me."

With that, al-Masthal also stood and the two embraced lightly, then each turned to go their separate ways.

True to his word, the world was a different place in six months. On September 11th, hijackers crashed airliners into the World Trade Center towers in New York, and another into the Pentagon. In Paris coffee bars that evening, excited Muslim men danced, and in the crowded shops, Muslim women let out high-pitched yodels with their tongues.

Over the course of the next three years American troops attacked and toppled the Taliban government in Afghanistan, and shortly thereafter, an American led coalition invaded Iraq, ending the regime of Saddam Hussein.

Through all of this Emil remained focused on his education and in spring of 2004 he graduated with his degree. Now 24 years old, he returned home to Beirut while exploring job possibilities in the Middle East and Europe. While he had changed into a taller and even more confident young man, some things remained the same. Beirut remained a war torn and dangerous city. Rival Islamic groups vied for power, and frequent attacks on Israel were planned and executed from the city.

His parents' home was somewhat removed from the center of the city, as his father preferred living closer to the docks where much of his goods were off-loaded and stored in warehouses along the shore. Built on a slight rise, the house had a 180 degree view of the Mediterranean, with open fields between the house and the warehouses two miles in the distance. As such, they seldom had any fear of reprisal attacks by the Israeli's when an extremist group attacked across the border into one of the many kibbutzims in Northern Israel.

In November of that same year, Palestine Liberation Organization Chairman Yasser Arafat died, and the resulting power vacuum sent many rival militant groups into competition for control of his political organization. From Lebanon, the terrorist group Hezbollah saw an opportunity to increase its political standing by executing a series of attacks on Israel. Timed to coincide with Hanukah, Hezbollah carried out three attacks within Israel, two at kibbutzim where schools were attacked, killing seventeen children, and a third attack by a bomb planted on a bus crowded with vacationers returning from the seaside. Eleven adults and four children were killed in this attack.

As usual, the Israeli response was swift and lethal. Emil Lagare had seen the American made Israeli F-16s on several prior occasions when they made reprisal attacks on Beirut. This morning, their screaming General Electric engines pierced the sky just after sunrise as they began their bombing runs from over the ocean, diving low toward the city to deliver their deadly precision guided bombs into buildings suspected of being Hezbollah headquarters. Even though his home was several miles from the location of the bombing, the explosions still shook the ground and the plume of smoke rising from the destroyed buildings was clearly visible. Then, as the jets turned in a wide arc over the city and headed south back toward Israel, Emil heard another ominous sound.

The dull "whup whup" sound of the two bladed helicopter rotors was a sharp contrast to the loud whining sound of the engines on the fighter jets now rapidly moving out of sight. The first of the four Cobra attack helicopters popped up from sea level a mere 500 yards from the warehouses along the docks. Manufactured by the Texas based Bell Corporation, the Cobra, although somewhat dated, was still a deadly attack helicopter. In short order, the other three Cobra's also rose behind their leader, and almost in unison they began to climb to 700 feet as the gunners started to acquire their targets. There were several dozen warehouses adjacent to the docks. Like the two warehouses owned by Emil Lagare's father, most were engaged in legitimate commercial enterprise, importing food, exporting fine leather products, and storing the items which made a large city run. One of the warehouses, however, had long been suspected by Israeli intelligence of being both the barracks for Hezbollah fighters, and the location of a large cache of weapons and explosives. The flight leader launched his 14 rockets into the warehouse then banked his helicopter sharply to the right to provide a clear field of fire for the next helicopter. Flying in column, the next two helicopters unleashed their rockets and also banked to the right. The pilot of the fourth Cobra, whose job it was to assess the damage and, if necessary, destroy any remaining targets, banked his helicopter slowly to the left as both he and his gunner surveyed the scene below. Sitting in tandem, with the gunner forward and slightly lower than the pilot, both crew members had more than 180 degrees of unobstructed vision. When the gunner called "Target, seven o'clock, enemy in the open," the pilot instinctively turned his craft to the right and moved his rotor control slightly forward to give the helicopter a nose down, tail high attitude. The pilot could now see two pickup trucks, each mounting a machine gun, rapidly speeding away from the burning warehouses toward the city, and twenty-five to thirty men, many carrying AK-47 assault rifles, running from the warehouse into an open field.

As the pilot adjusted his flight path slightly, the gunner quickly selected the appropriate weapons system for the targets he faced.

Foregoing the rapid fire machine gun and the armor piercing rockets, he chose instead one of his two high explosive multi-purpose rockets, armed the weapon, input the range to target data in the weapons computer, aimed at the lead pickup truck, and fired. The two foot long rocket leapt off the launch rail and trailed fire as it sped toward its target. The weapon chosen by the gunner was especially lethal to light armored vehicles and personnel. Designed as an "air-burst" weapon, the rocket remained eighty feet above the ground until it reached its intended target. An explosive charge then ejected the nine sub-munitions contained in the rocket body just above the lead pickup truck. Each of the sub-munitions contained three point two ounces of Composition B explosive and one hundred ninety-five small metal fragments. As these bomblets descended, they self-armed, then detonated sending metal fragments in a wide arc in search of a target. As the smoke cleared, the pilot and gunner saw the first pickup was completely destroyed, along with its' three man crew. Fifteen of the men who were running toward the field lay dead near the smoking hulk of the vehicle.

By this time, the men running and the crew of the second truck realized there was no escaping the deadly attack from the helicopter. They began to stand their ground, returning fire. Sensing, rather than feeling that he was under fire, the pilot threw the helicopter into a sharp right turn and began to position his aircraft for another attack. As the pilot maneuvered the Cobra into firing position, the gunner quickly read his laser display range to target indicator and input the data into the arming system of his second rocket. In the stress of the fight, and with the Hezbollah fighters now finding the range, the gunner inadvertently entered 3000 yards rather than the correct range of 300 yards into the weapon's onboard guidance system and fired the second rocket.

Emil, along with mother and father were sitting on the veranda of their home having their morning coffee. With a commanding view of the Mediterranean, the veranda provided a relaxing atmosphere to begin the day. When the first of the fighter jets was heard coming from the ocean toward the city, all three walked to the edge of the veranda and watched as the attacking aircraft began their bombing runs in the distance. They were still at the veranda's edge when the first helicopter unleashed its' weapons on the warehouses some two miles away. Emil's mother screamed when the warehouses burst into flames, then disintegrated from the secondary explosions caused by the detonation of the munitions stored inside.

Both Emil and his father recognized the danger simultaneously when the fourth helicopter fired its first rocket at the pickup trucks and men fleeing directly toward their home. They both felt the shock wave when the rocket's sub-munitions exploded, even though it was still over a mile away. Now, as the helicopter made a tight turn and began its' second run at the remaining men and vehicle, Emil and his father each grabbed his mother by an arm and began to run for the safety of the house.

It was already too late. The errant rocket raced over its intended target and straight for the house on the small rise. Seconds before the three running figures reached the door from the veranda leading to the safety of the main house, the nine sub-munitions in the rocket were ejected from the rocket body and tumbled down. They exploded within microseconds of each other, spewing almost two thousand small metal fragments at a tremendous velocity in a wide arc before them.

Twenty-seven fragments ripped into his father's back and left side. One fragment severed his spinal cord killing him in mid-stride. Emil, who was in a half-crouch while he pulled his mother by her right arm, felt the burning sting of six fragments as they tore into both legs, dropping him instantly to the ground. Although he was in a great deal of pain, his legs feeling like they were on fire, Emil was still conscious enough to roll onto his back on the tile deck of the veranda. Looking up, he could see his mother still standing, as if frozen in place, a quizzical look on her face. She then pitched forward and fell face down almost on top of her son. Emil could feel the warm blood from the neck wound spurting out each time her heart pumped. He could see she was trying to form her lips to speak, but the words would not come. The blood continued to drain from her body, Emil trying to stem the flow with his hand, while screaming for help. His efforts were futile. She died in his arms within a minute.

Lying on his back, with his dead mother partially atop his body, his mind cloudy from the leg wounds now sending messages of pain to his brain, Emil looked up to see the Cobra helicopter hovering over the veranda while the pilot and gunner surveyed the damage they had wrought. Looking directly at the pilot, his eyes invisible behind the tinted face shield of his helmet, Emil's last conscious thought before passing out was to avenge this day.

Although Emil's leg injuries were not life threatening, he spent the next two days in the hospital. His parents' funeral was scheduled for the third day. After the funeral, Emil returned to his parents' home where, thanks to the efforts of his father's trusted business manager, repairs were already underway to the veranda and the side of the house impacted by the rocket. For the next five days, Emil said and did little. His legs were still painful from the wounds caused when the metal fragments of the sub-munitions drove themselves deep into his flesh. The doctor advised his injuries would take time to heal, but he would suffer no permanent disability. His family's servants moved quietly around the house and out of respect, stayed out of sight for the most part, appearing only to serve Emil his meals.

During these five days Emil sat for endless hours on the veranda where his parents had been killed, staring out toward the ocean in the distance. While to the servants this almost catatonic state seemed a natural reaction to the death of his parents and the trauma he himself had suffered, another dynamic was playing itself out in Emil's mind.

Sitting on the veranda, Emil took stock of his situation and contemplated his life. His father's business was highly successful and had left him financially secure. For the most part, his father's business manager ran the day-to-day operations, so there was no urgent need for him to become directly involved in the family business. Likewise his parents' home was completely paid for, and except for the salary paid to the half-dozen servants, it represented no financial drain. His own efforts to find employment as an architect had proven fruitless, and he had no prospects of securing a position. As Emil sat and dwelled on these factors, a deeper emotion constantly pushed its way into his thoughts, the need for revenge.

Exactly three weeks after the attack, his leg injuries now healing rapidly, Emil Lagare made legal arrangements for his father's business manager to have full operating control of the company, and for the servants to care for the house for one year. He then booked a first class ticket to Paris.

———

Arriving at Charles de Gaulle Airport in the early afternoon, Emil used his French passport to easily clear customs. Outside the terminal, he walked the line of parked taxicabs until he found a driver who appeared to be from the Middle East and spoke to him in Arabic. The driver, who was Syrian, put Emil's one small suitcase in the trunk and rapidly pulled away from the terminal curb to the sound of horns blaring and curses from other drivers at the front of the queue. Though traffic was moderately heavy, the driver covered the fourteen miles into Paris in less than twenty minutes, stopping in front of a hotel that catered to businessmen from the Middle East.

Fifteen minutes later, after checking into his room, washing his face and changing shirts, Emil was back in a taxi heading for the Muslim section of the city. It had only been six months since he graduated and the Muslim part of Paris looked exactly the same to him. Streets teemed with women wearing traditional long outer garments and head scarves, carrying shopping bags filled with food for tonight's dinner, Muslim men with heavy black beards filled the coffee bars and vendors haggled with customers on the street.

The taxi dropped Emil in front of the mosque. He paused for a few seconds on the sidewalk surveying the scene in both directions, knowing, if he entered the mosque, it would start him on a dangerous journey. Emil turned and walked into the mosque without hesitation.

Evening prayers were just ending when Emil walked through the entrance. Dozens of men were moving from the main prayer room into the hallways, talking and putting on their shoes. Emil stood with his back to the wall while the crowd thinned and within a few moments he spotted the imam talking to some of the last men to leave the prayer room. The imam bid these last stragglers good night, then, in the shuffling gait of an old and tired man, headed for his small office. Emil approached him.

"Good evening imam."

The imam stopped and looked up. He did not immediately recognize the tall young man who spoke to him. However, within a few seconds, recognition flashed in his eyes and he smiled, "Emil, it has been far too long." He extended his arms and grabbed the young man's shoulders. "What brings you back to Paris?" the imam asked.

Bending slightly at the waist to get closer to the imam, Emil spoke in a hushed voice, "I wish to contact Yusef al-Masthal."

Without changing expression, the imam looked about the room, replying in an equally low tone, "It is not wise to speak of such things in the open. Come to my office." He gestured as he spoke and began to shuffle toward the back of the mosque.

Once in the tiny office the imam motioned him to a wooden chair and closed the door. "One can never be too careful when speaking certain names, even in a mosque. Now, why is it you seek Yusef?"

Emil related the incident involving the death of his parents and his meeting with Yusef al-Masthal almost four years prior when he was a student. He then added al-Masthal's statement that he could be contacted through the imam.

Expressionless, the imam said nothing for several seconds, then remarked, "So, you are seeking revenge for the death of your parents, not to join our cause against the enemies of Allah."

"Yes," replied Emil. "For revenge."

"I'm sorry Emil, I cannot help you. The need for personal revenge has no place in our cause. Now, I must attend to other matters. Go home and seek your revenge through some other means."

Stunned by his abrupt dismissal, Emil left the mosque and stood in silence on the sidewalk watching the early evening vehicle and pedestrian traffic. Hailing a cab, he returned to his hotel, his mind unable to comprehend what had just happened.

Once back in his hotel room, Emil dropped his tired body into an overstuffed arm chair and stared blankly out the window. The events of the past three weeks, the flight from Beirut, and his disappointing meeting with the imam, had drained his youthful energy and left him suddenly exhausted. As darkness fell about the city, Emil sat in the shadows of his room, his mind unable to focus.

In this half-asleep state, Emil's mind at first could not tell if the knocking on his hotel room door was a dream, or real. As the knocking persisted, Emil shook the fog from his brain and snapped awake. He stumbled in the dark as he fumbled with the light switch on a table lamp on his way to the door. Opening the door Emil found himself looking at a tall well dressed clean shaven man. Still coming out of his half-sleep state, he did not recognize the man until he spoke.

"Greetings, Emil Lagare. So, as I predicated many years ago, the time has come," a smiling Yusef al-Masthal said.

Now fully awake, Emil found himself unable to speak and stepped into the hallway to embrace al-Masthal, then motioned him into the room. Once inside there was none of the usual small talk that might be expected from two people who had not seen each other in over four years.

Yusef al-Masthal spoke first, "My deepest condolences on the death of your parents and for the wounds you yourself suffered young Emil." Acknowledging his comment with a slight bow of his head, Emil waited for al-Masthal to speak again.

"And now the imam tells me you seek vengeance on those who committed these acts." "Yes," Emil replied. "But the imam...."

With an abrupt hand gesture, al-Masthal cut him off in mid-sentence. He smiled slightly as he spoke. "Imam's have their reasons to fight, and others of us have our reasons. The need for revenge can be a powerful motivator." Pausing for a moment, he continued. "However, as with anything else, vengeance must be harnessed and channeled to ensure maximum results."

Emil remained silent, looking into al-Masthal's black eyes, waiting for him to continue speaking.

Al-Masthal looked directly at Emil and spoke deliberately. "You have many talents and abilities that would be useful to our cause, Emil Lagare. First, however, some education in Islam and The Cause are needed. Then, training in the methods of fighting our worldwide war against Jews and western decadence. And lastly, if you are good enough, training as the commander to lead a mission to wreak destruction on our enemies."

"Yes, yes," Emil said, nodding enthusiastically. "I'm willing to undergo whatever training or hardships are necessary to have my revenge."

CHAPTER FOUR

The testing process for the CHP took almost a year. The number of steps Erin Wolff had to go through dissuaded many people from even considering, let alone completing the process. Only three of every one hundred applicants who started the process ever made it to the CHP Academy. First a written test, then an oral interview panel, a physical agility test, visual acuity and color blindness test, medical examination, psychological examination, and finally a background check. During the year long process, Erin continued in school and finished her masters' degree program.

In June of 1990, Erin Wolff, now twenty-three, received an appointment to the CHP Academy.

For the second time in four years she was again being referred to as a "Cadet." The CHP uses the word "cadet" rather than "recruit" like police departments to refer to its trainees at the academy.

The CHP's training academy is located in Sacramento. It was where every CHP officer began their career. Reporting the first day Erin Wolff found herself back in a regimented atmosphere. Male and female Academy Staff Officers, in their "Smokey the Bear" campaign hats were everywhere, yelling, pointing, and yelling some more, successfully doing their best to rattle the one hundred twenty-five new cadets in their first hour at the academy. "Line up here," "Hurry up," "Stand at attention," "Say yes sir or yes ma'am when you speak," they yelled. Erin Wolff took it all in stride, having been through the same type of thing her first day at the Air Force Academy. It only took about fifteen minutes before one of the male staff officers noticed the half-smile on her face as she stood in line. Moving like an angry cat, the staff officer was on her in an instant.

He got right in her face, the brim of his campaign hat making contact with her forehead, "What are you smiling at cadet?" he bellowed.

"Nothing sir," she replied.

"Then get that grin off your face," he growled angrily.

"Yes sir."

Jesus Christ, Erin Wolff thought to herself as the staff officer found another cadet to torment, what have I gotten myself into?

The rest of her first day evaporated into a blur of forms, orientation lectures, an academy tour, dorm room assignment, and issuance of cadet uniforms

In the early 1990's the average CHP cadet was twenty-four years old. Very few had been in the military, and only a handful had prior law enforcement experience. Almost all of them had some college education. Sixteen of the one hundred twenty-five cadets who reported at 7:30 the first day were women. By 5:00 that afternoon, four male and two female cadets had resigned.

Academic classes commenced the next day. Class consisted of four two-hour sessions a day with an hour for lunch and an hour for dinner served at the academy dining hall. Cadets were required to be back in the classroom by six for ninety minutes of study hall, after which they returned to their dorm rooms to shine shoes, iron uniforms, and make a phone call before lights out at ten.

On Friday of their first week cadets receive an orientation on the academy's physical training program. The first part of the orientation is in the classroom. That morning, Erin Wolff and the remaining members of her class, now down to one hundred twelve cadets, stood at attention in their classroom waiting for the arrival of the Physical Training Instructors. Between the horror tales they'd been told about the PT orientation, and their own anxiety, it was possible to smell the fear in the classroom.

There were four members of the PT staff, three officers, one of them a woman, and a sergeant. The door to the classroom burst open and they strode inside. Each of them was slim, not overly muscular, with short hair, and scowls on their faces. Dressed alike, in long legged blue nylon stretch pants, blue tight fitting exercise shirts, and running shoes, they were indeed fearsome looking.

The classroom part of the orientation took thirty minutes. The sergeant instructed them on the rules of the gym, and how to use magic markers to print their last names on the back of one of the five white academy logo T-shirts they were issued on their first day. "Hurry up, get those shirts marked," the PT instructors growled as they passed between the rows of seated cadets. The tension in the room was thick as the cadets, unsure of what was in store for them, rapidly marked their shirts as they had been instructed. Once every cadet had marked one shirt they were given ten minutes to return to their dorm rooms, change into PT gear, and report to the gym floor.

Thus far there had been no yelling, no punishment push-ups, and no name calling by the PT staff as they had been led to expect.

The yelling started as soon as they entered the gym. The PT instructors were running here, running there, yelling at the cadets to line up in alphabetical order, ten rows of twelve cadets each. Confusion reigned as cadets tried to find their proper place in line, facing the stage at the front of the gym. Once they were in proper order, an instructor appeared on stage and demonstrated the first exercise.

"The first exercise is Side Twists, done in this manner. Arms extended and level," the instructor demonstrated as he explained. "When I say "Ready Exercise" you will begin to the left. I will count one, two, three, you will reply with, one. Do you understand?"

"Yes sir," came the loud reply in unison from the class.

"Side Twists, ten repetitions, ready, exercise," barked the instructor.

What happened next was a choreographed part of the orientation. The instructor on stage began by twisting to his left and counting "one."

Most of the cadets on the floor twisted to their left, while about a dozen twisted to the right, mirroring the same direction the instructor twisted.

"Stop, stop," yelled the sergeant. "He said to your left," as he got in the face of one of the cadets who, out of confusion or fear, twisted in the same direction as the instructor on stage.

Other cadets had taken the sergeant's yell to stop as a signal to drop their arms from the extended position at their shoulders.

"Get your pencil arms up," yelled the other instructors at those cadets.

The sergeant told the instructor on stage to begin again.

"Side Twists, ten repetitions, ready exercise," the instructor barked again.

What happens in the human brain under stressful conditions is sometimes unexplainable. Instinctively, the brain is telling the body to twist left, but the body rebels and has a mind of its own.

Once again the instructor on stage twisted to the left yelling the count of one. This time, three of the same cadets who had done it wrong the first time, did it wrong again and twisted to the right, mirroring the same direction the instructor twisted. Three other cadets, who had done it correctly the first time, did it wrong the second time.

"Stop, stop," yelled the sergeant.

Now as part of the ritual of physical training orientation, the sergeant and the other two instructors on the gym floor pulled large black magic markers from inside the waist band of their nylon pants.

"Oh my God!" yelled the female instructor as she got in the face of a male cadet who had twisted the wrong way. "How are you going to find your way to an emergency call if you don't know left from right?" She then used the magic marker to put a large black "L" on the back of the cadet's left hand.

While the three instructors on the gym floor were focusing their attention on those cadets in need of special instruction on "Directional Determination," the remainder of the class stood with their arms outstretched. Soon, their shoulders began to ache. The ache quickly turned to pain, and the pain to agony. The entire gym floor became a sea of cadets attempting to hold their arms up, while twisting and bending, trying to find a position that eliminated the pain in their shoulders. The total time they had their arms up was less than a minute, it was sufficient, however, to cause almost all of them to break into a sweat, beads of moisture starting to run down their faces.

And on it went for the next forty-five minutes. From one exercise to another, push-ups, sit-ups, leg-lifts. Instructors yelling at specific cadets for failure to perform exercises properly, identifying them by the name printed on the back of their T-shirt.

"Johnson, you can't even do one sit-up, how do you get out of bed in the morning?"

"The people of California are paying you to do push-ups Jennings, you're cheating the taxpayers!"

"Keep your legs six inches off the ground Rodriguez. Are we going to have to assign a sergeant to you for your entire career to make sure you do your job correctly?"

Following the last exercise most of the cadets were completely spent, dripping with sweat, and panting to catch their breaths. Erin Wolff was sweating, but for the most part she survived the workout without a problem.

The sergeant now told the cadet class to exit the gym and line up in company formation on the service road for their orientation run.

Sacramento is brutally hot in the summer. By eleven o'clock the temperature was approaching ninety-three degrees heading for a high of one hundred four. The CHP Academy is surrounded on two sides by levees holding back the Sacramento River. The humidity is even more oppressive than the heat as a result of being in a bowl, directly adjacent to the river,

The run, which was slightly more than a fast one mile walk, combined with the workout they had just endured and the heat, immediately began taking its toll on the cadet class. Within the first quarter-mile, six cadets had stopped running and were walking far behind the rest of the formation. Two instructors were trailing the formation, running from cadet-to-cadet, half-pushing, half-dragging them along, yelling at them the entire time.

Following the run, the class was brought back into the air conditioned gym, told to get back in their positions on the gym floor, and sit down. The sergeant and his instructors trooped up and down the rows of seated cadets, checking for signs of heat exhaustion.

The PT staff, along with being infamous for their first week workouts, were also the chief assigners of nicknames to cadets. Beginning at the front of the gym they walked down the rows of cadets assigning an occasional nickname. Most of the nicknames were just a way to shorten the name of a cadet so it would fit on the back of their T-shirt. Others were to differentiate between two cadets with the same last name.

As it happened there were two Wolff's in this cadet class. Besides Erin, there was a white male cadet who spelled his name Wolfe. He was a former school teacher from San Francisco, almost thirty years old, making a career change. He was terribly out of shape.

When the sergeant got to the male cadet Wolfe, he told him to include the word "Old" above his name on the back of all his gym shirts.

The strawberry color of Erin Wolff's sweat soaked hair shone through brightly in the artificial light of gym floor. Put the word "Red" above your name he told her. The nickname would stick forever.

The sergeant mounted the stage and addressed the entire class in a loud and unfriendly voice. "What a pitiful demonstration! All of you were told months ago about the physical training at the academy. You were told to start getting yourselves in shape to handle this training program, and to prepare yourselves for a dangerous, physical job. Most of you did nothing, and now you'll have to work extra hard to make it through this place. Today was just an orientation. Physical training begins for real at zero five hundred hours on Monday morning. I suggest some of you take the weekend to reevaluate why you are here, and if you really want to be a California Highway Patrol Officer."

With that the class was dismissed, told to shower, and go to lunch.

In the first month following the PT orientation, twelve more male, and three more female cadets would resign. Some resigned because they found the training too hard, but most simply came to the realization the CHP was not the career for them. Others resigned because they found they could not handle being told by the academy staff they had bad breath, or body odor, or despite having a college degree, they could not spell, or that being late actually had consequences. Being held accountable for their own actions for the first time in their lives was simply not for them.

In the next five months, seven more cadets would resign when they failed to successfully pass the driving portion of training.

The six months of academy training was a breeze for Erin, now known to her classmates and instructors as "Red" Wolff. Daily early morning PT followed by classes in law, the Penal Code, the Vehicle Code, arrest procedures, report writing, enforcement tactics, felony stops, response to crimes in progress, narcotics, and emergency vehicle operations were just a few of the over one hundred different courses that make up the cadet curriculum.

Physically and academically Red Wolff was near the top of her class in everything. Her natural intelligence made the classroom academics easy, and she found herself constantly sought out by her classmates for help. Physically, she could outrun most of the men in her class and could do more pull-ups than all but two of the strongest males.

As promised by her recruiting officer, being gay at the CHP Academy did not pose any problems. All California state agencies had been mandated by law for the past ten years to ensure discrimination based on sexual orientation did not occur. CHP management took great pains to implement and support this law at the academy, and CHP offices throughout the state. Instructors at the academy are handpicked and the assignment was considered a step toward promotion. Every once in a while, however, an instructor would make an inappropriate remark, usually thinking they were being funny. That instructor would find themselves working graveyard shift in Barstow within the week.

There were two other gay women in Red Wolff's class and although they were not subjected to any discrimination from the academy staff, their sexual orientation soon became the subject of gossip, both among the staff and their classmates. They became known to their classmates as "The Gay Caballeros" because they were always together, at lunch, working out in the weight room, or going on liberty together. Still, other than something to gossip about, their being gay was never an issue at the academy. She would soon find out the academy was not the real Highway Patrol, and management's support had its limits.

Graduation Day at the academy is a festive time. The actual graduation starts at ten, but families and friends arrive early to tour the academy grounds, demonstrations of high speed driving are put on, and lots of high ranking "brass" are around. Following speeches and awards, each cadet, dressed in their formal uniform, marches across the stage in the gym to receive their badge from the Commissioner of the Highway Patrol while proud families snap photographs. Erin Wolff's whole family was there.

By three in the afternoon it's all over. Following the ceremony, reunion and pictures with family, and lots of hugs between classmates, the newly minted officers' change into civilian clothes, clean out their dorm rooms, load their cars, and head for wherever.

New officers receive their first assignment based on the "needs of the department." For most of Red Wolff's class this meant Los Angeles, although a handful went to the San Francisco Bay Area, and two went to remote desert locations. As probationary officers their first assignment would be for one year. Once off probation they could, if they wished, transfer to wherever their seniority would take them.

Red Wolff, and twelve male officers from her class, were assigned right in the middle of downtown Los Angeles.

Walking into the lieutenant's office, Sergeant Red Wolff could see he was talking to a man in a fashionable suit, Cole-Hahn shoes, and an expensive tie. Definitely not from Crescent City she thought to herself. Although she did not know him, she knew from his haircut, his demeanor and bearing, he was a cop.

The Highway Patrol is fairly informal when it comes to using name and rank when addressing one another, especially among those who have worked together for any length of time. Since transferring to Crescent City over a year before, she'd always called the commander of the office by his first name. Lieutenant Bob Collier had been the commander in Crescent City for nine years. He'd worked in Los Angeles, the Bay Area and the desert, while he promoted his way up through the ranks. He enjoyed the small town feeling of Crescent City and was three years from retirement. Since she didn't know who the visitor was, she shifted to formal mode. Walking into her commander's office she said, "You wanted to see me lieutenant?"

"Hey Red," he responded in his usual low key manner, remaining seated at his desk.

"Red, this is Sergeant Mike Waters from the Governor's Protection Detail in Sacramento. He's here to discuss security measures for the Governor's visit on July Fourth, and to scout out the venues."

"How's it going," she said, extending her hand toward the visitor. It was a statement rather than a question.

"Great, a pleasure, I've heard a lot about you," he replied with meaning in his voice that was not lost on her or her lieutenant.

"Red, Mike here will be staying in town tonight. Can you meet with him tomorrow to show him around town, take him to the places the "gov" will be going, and then firm up the security arrangements between us, the PD, and the sheriff's?"

"No problem L.T."

"Fine," the male sergeant acknowledged. "I'll meet you here at 0900."

Red Wolff paused for about thirty seconds after he left the office before she turned back to her lieutenant and said, "Who was that pompous ass?"

"It's a new Highway Patrol, Red, there are a ton of guys like him now, full of themselves and willing to cut your heart out to get promoted. Take it easy with him tomorrow, and with any luck, we won't have another Governor's visit to Crescent City for the next hundred years."

Smiling, she laughed, "Okay Bob, go home and have a nice weekend, I'll see you on the Fourth."

Leaving the lieutenant's office, she headed down the hall of the deserted building toward the office she shared with the two other sergeants assigned to Crescent City. As it happened, one of her fellow sergeants was on vacation and the other was off due to an injury sustained when his patrol car was rear ended. She would be the only sergeant for the next week.

Turning the lights on, she grabbed a stack of reports and other paperwork turned in by officers from the previous shift and began to browse through it. As she reviewed the paperwork, she monitored the constant radio traffic between her four field units working that afternoon and the communication center. An accident on 101, a request for a tow truck to help a stranded motorist at the Oregon border, a registration check near the airport. As an experienced supervisor Red Wolff had a mental picture of where all her units were and what they were doing. She also listened to the scanner which monitored the radio traffic from the local police and sheriff's units who were being dispatched by their own radio system located at the sheriff's department. Although the officers from the three agencies were on different radio systems, they could talk directly to each other through a method known as cross-banding. They would transmit on their own radio, and listen to the response on their in-car scanners which were programmed to the police and sheriff's frequencies.

It took about an hour for her to review all the paperwork. Noting the time, she turned the lights out in her office and made her way back to her patrol car, making sure to lock the front door behind her as she left.

Back in her vehicle she picked up the radio mike and pushed the transmit button, "Humboldt, 95-S-3, 10-8."

"10-4, S-3, 10-8."

Now that she'd advised the communications center she was back in service, Red Wolff headed for a prearranged lunch break with one of her officers.

There are not a great many places for officers to go to get a quick and inexpensive meal in Crescent City. As a result, many officers either bring their lunch and eat in their patrol vehicle out on their beat or go home if they are working close to where they live.

On this particular Friday evening she'd chosen a local coffee shop where, if they were lucky, there just may be a couple of prime rib sandwiches left over from the prime rib dinner special served the night before. At $7.50 it was a great deal. Truck drivers may know the best places to eat, Red Wolff thought to herself, but cops know the best and cheapest places.

Pulling into the parking lot of the coffee shop, she could see the officer she was going to meet for dinner had already parked his patrol car in the very back of the lot. The patrol car was backed into a stall with a six foot block wall behind it. The officer was still sitting in the car.

As she backed into the slot next to the other patrol vehicle, Red Wolff thought to herself, just like he taught me years ago, always have something at your back so nobody can sneak up on you. She had a half-smile on her lips as she reminisced about her friend and mentor.

Sergeant Red Wolff notified the communications center that she and her officer were out of service for lunch.

Once they were both out of their cars, the male officer looked at his sergeant, shook his head, and jested, "After all these years you still can't park worth a damn."

"Screw you Silva," came the lighthearted reply. "You're buying."

Ray Silva was the best cop she'd ever met. Tall, slim, with a full head of silver gray hair, he had a relaxed manner about him, but at the same time he had an aura of authority that came from thirty-two years of experience as a CHP Officer.

They had been friends for over sixteen years going back to the time in Los Angeles when Red Wolff was a brand new rookie officer.

CHAPTER FIVE

In agreeing to al-Masthal's terms, Emil Lagare knew he faced many challenges both mentally and physically. Yet, he was not ready for the indoctrination in Islam he was about to undergo.

Within two days of his meeting with Yusef al-Masthal, Emil found himself in Egypt living in the unlit backroom of a rundown mosque on the outskirts of Cairo. Here, under the watchful eyes of a strict and fiery imam, Emil spent every waking hour reading the Quran and being quizzed on its passages. He ate simple meals, alone, and slept on a thin straw mattress.

After daily prayers, and during the discussion groups with the young men of his mosque that followed, the local imam preached a combination of hate for Jews and a corresponding hate for America. The imam spun an intricate web linking Israel and the United States to the oppression of Islam, the occupation of Palestine, the overthrow of the Taliban, and the war in Iraq. His calls for true believers to take up arms against these enemies always met with resounding cheers of Allah Akbar from his audience, and already twelve men from his mosque had answered the call and were fighting in Iraq.

For the first time in his life, Emil Lagare found himself growing a beard as directed by the imam, a sign of devotion to Allah. The stubble itched his faced and he was thankful there was no mirror for him to view the slow and agonizing process. He was also forced to forego his western style pants and shirt, in favor of a traditional Dishdasha, the long loose fitting neck to ankle white gown. Topping off his attire he wore a Kufi, the round brimless Muslim hat which covered the top and sides of his head.

Accompanying his studies of the Quran and the constant questions by the imam as to their meaning, there were continuous lectures on the role of women in Islamic society and their subservience to men in all things. Coming from his background, his western education where women were equals, and the heavy influence of his mother, these concepts caused him a great deal of

41

inner conflict. Still, his burning need for vengeance helped him tolerate these conflicting values and overrode his discomfort.

Slowly, without realizing it, Emil Lagare was changing. After three months of living with the imam, he was able to recite whole passages from the Quran. The words he now spoke when referring to Israel or the United States had a vitriolic quality to them, and even his interaction with women had changed.

Pleased with the progress of his charge, the imam spent the next thirty days reinforcing the previous lessons, while adding massive doses of geopolitics, Islamic fundamentalist style.

By early April, Emil Lagare, now with a full beard of dark black hair, dressed as any one of the other passengers, and with a radical brand of Islam in his soul, found himself on a rickety boat crossing the Red Sea with pilgrims heading for Mecca. Arriving in the port of Jeddah, he found passage through customs to be nothing more than showing his passport to a bored inspector. He then headed for the bus station where, using money given to him by the imam, he boarded a crowded bus bound for the two day trip, which took him through Jordan and eventually to Syria.

Once he arrived at the Syrian border, Emil found customs there equally easy to pass. The bus continued on to Damascus where he began walking to the memorized address given him by the imam. Carrying only a small satchel, the walk was not as much tiring as it was long. Over two hours later he arrived at a small apartment building and found the proper flat. Following the customary greetings and thanks to Allah for his safe arrival, Emil Lagare was given food and a place to sleep. The next morning he found himself in an aged Toyota four-wheel drive truck, heading for a training camp deep in the Syrian Desert.

The camp was sixteen miles off the main highway leading from Syria to Iraq. Located in a remote valley with high rock walls on three sides, the camp was in such a desolate part of the country Emil felt he could have been on the moon for all the starkness of his surroundings. The dirt road that left the main highway was little more than a rock strewn path, save for the ruts beginning to form from the tire tracks of the vehicles that traversed the road twice a week bringing supplies and trainees to the camp.

As soon as he arrived in camp, Emil was instructed to report to the supply tent where he was issued American army desert camouflage fatigues, boots, a Kevlar composite American "fritz" type helmet, a floppy brimmed hat, and a razor.

Once he stored his meager personal items, changed into uniform, and shaved as instructed, Emil reported to the large tent dominating the center of the compound. The tent, square, with a peaked roof, had its side flaps rolled up revealing several tables, maps on easels, two computers, a small refrigerator, and five large standing floor fans to move the hot dry desert air. A diesel powered generator hummed noisily behind the tent supplying electricity for the entire camp.

As he approached the front of the tent, Emil found his way blocked by a large weathered looking man dressed in the same type of American uniform he had been issued. This man, however, had an American made M-16 rifle hung by its sling across his chest. The man instructed Emil to wait outside.

As Emil waited outside what he determined to be the command tent, he noticed for the first time there was a complete lack of other activity at the camp. No other people were visible, and except for the drone of the diesel generator and the wind whistling through the valley, no other sounds could be heard.

Within the open sided command tent Emil could see several men seated at a table viewing a video monitor and pointing out locations on a map. Their discussion was calm and measured as they regularly stopped and rewound the video to review certain items on the tape. While Emil could not specifically make out the scene on the screen, it appeared to be of a town near the water and a great many tall green trees.

Focused on the distant video monitor, Emil failed to notice the tall man who approached him from behind. "A long way from Paris, young Emil," the voice said, startling him back to his surroundings.

Turning, Emil found himself staring into the black eyes of Yusef al-Masthal. As usual, the face was expressionless.

"Yusef!" cried Emil in surprise. "Yes, it is a long way from Paris. In many ways."

"And are you the same person you were in Paris, Emil?" al-Masthal inquired.

"That person died long ago on a patio in Beirut," replied Emil shaking his head. "He was reborn a true believer and committed to The Cause."

Yusef al-Masthal smiled at Emil and clasped an arm around his shoulder. "Come Emil," he proclaimed, directing his young convert into the tent. "It is time to meet your destiny."

Once inside the tent, al-Masthal introduced Emil to the camp's commander and another man in charge of foreign operations.

Yusef al-Masthal began. "For now, Emil, all you need to know is you have been selected to command an operation within the United States. The mission is dangerous, but it will be an unexpected and bold strike which will confound our enemies and spread fear across their nation."

Emil sat passively as al-Masthal continued. "Since the destruction of the twin towers in New York, the Americans have greatly improved their airport security systems and made the cockpit doors of their aircraft virtually impossible to penetrate. Likewise, their intelligence services have become adept at uncovering our operations both in the United States and other countries. Therefore, our operations section was charged with developing and planning a mission that will avoid detection, cause destruction, and shake the American's belief in their security."

When al-Masthal concluded his statement, he nodded to Qassim Saleh, the Chief of Operations and Planning.

Qassim Saleh was a rather bookish looking man. Short, and a bit on the pudgy side, his hawk nose and round face gave him more the look of a merchant in a bazaar, than a strategist plotting death and destruction in America.

"I lived for six years in Chicago and another nine years in San Francisco," Saleh began. "During this time I traveled extensively throughout the United States. For the past four and a half years we have been planning and attempting operations directed at major population centers and cities with recognizable landmarks. Just as we have been planning these operations, the Americans have been able to thwart our efforts. We have decided, therefore, to shift the focus of our operations to a small target. Such a shift in strategy will be totally unexpected. It will also have the added element of causing panic throughout an entire segment of the American population who have, up to now, considered themselves immune from attack."

Saleh spoke directly to Emil. "We have eight weeks before this operation is slated to commence. This means five weeks of intense training in firearms, explosives, communications, and driving. Following that, two weeks of rehearsals, and one week for you and your team to make their way to the designated target area."

Emil listened intently, attempting to discern more about his mission from the scant details provided by Qassim Saleh. "When will the rest of my team arrive?" he asked.

"Six are already here. The other eighteen will arrive over the next two or three days. For now, you have all the information you require," Saleh responded in a tone indicating no further questions would be entertained. "You will follow the guard outside and begin training immediately."

In any military boot camp, training is conducted under the watchful and often harsh eye of a drill sergeant. The training for Emil Lagare and his men was no different.

Muhammad Attiya was a naturalized American citizen. Born in Saudi Arabia, he immigrated to the United States with his parents when he was eleven years old. Only an average student, he found English difficult and his grades suffered accordingly. He did manage to graduate from high school in 1995, but found it difficult to locate anything other than menial jobs. Six months later, much to the disappointment of his parents, he joined the American Army.

Army life agreed with Muhammad Attiya. Trained as a weapons specialist, he became an expert in all of the American Army's infantry weapons. Promotions followed quickly, and by 2001, he was a sergeant assigned to a weapons platoon in Germany. In Germany for the first time since childhood, Attiya found himself living in close proximity to large populations of Muslims. Whenever he was off-duty, Muhammad Attiya spent his time frequenting the many coffee houses in the Muslim district of the city near his base. Coffee house conversation often revolved around the oppression many Muslims felt in Germany and other European countries, and the growing conflict in the Arab world. Although never a strict Muslim himself, Attiya was quickly drawn into the social and political world surrounding the local mosque.

Here, for the first time in his life, Attiya heard the fiery words of imams who preached a brand of Islam entirely different from any he had heard before. By September 11th, 2001, Muhammad Attiya was deeply under the influence of the imams and their interpretation of the Quran.

As the world situation changed, Sergeant Muhammad Attiya found it increasingly difficult to separate his military duties from his new found political and religious ideologies. On-duty, he often expressed his Muslim political views to his fellow troopers, which included the destruction of Israel and favorable references to the Taliban government in Afghanistan. As would be expected, none of his comments sat well with the army or with other soldiers. When Attiya's unit began preparations for deployment to the Middle East, he openly refused. The court marshal that followed found him guilty of violating numerous sections of the Uniform Code of Military Justice. He was sentenced to eighteen months in a military prison in Kansas and a Dishonorable Discharge.

Following his discharge, Attiya cashed in the seven years worth of U.S. Savings Bonds he'd accumulated through payroll deduction and bought a ticket back to Germany. As an American citizen he had little trouble entering the country. Once back in Germany he reconnected with the many Muslim friends he'd made there. Germany was only a brief stopping off point for Muhammad Attiya and he quickly found himself recruited to train young Muslim fighters in Syria. Over the next two years Attiya helped train over seven hundred fighters who had joined the jihad against the Americans in Afghanistan and Iraq. Now, for the first time, he would be training fighters who would carry the war to America itself.

For the next three weeks, Emil and the twenty-four members of his team, trained intensely under the strict and demanding eye of Muhammad Attiya. All of the team members trained as a group with American infantry weapons, the M-16 rifle, the Beretta 9 millimeter pistol, and the M-249 machine gun. All training was conducted in American Army uniforms.

In addition to becoming proficient in firing weapons, they also spent countless hours marching in formation, executing the American Army Manual of Arms, and saluting in the American fashion. Many of the team members found the repetitive marching, halting, and left and right face turns boring. Soon grumbling could be heard from some within the ranks.

Emil Lagare exerted his authority as commander immediately. He severely chastised the grumblers, reminding them their only purpose was to perform the training exercises as ordered.

The training continued non-stop from before sun up when the desert temperature was in the low thirties, through the heat of the day when the wind whistling down the valley super-heated the dry desert air to well over one hundred degrees. The setting sun brought no respite from training, as night exercises with American night vision goggles were conducted, while the temperatures fell rapidly, chilling team members to the bone.

As physically demanding and long as each training day was, they were even longer for Emil. Each night after the evening meal and cleaning his weapons, Emil studied his copy of The Commander's Handbook. This eleven volume, 7,000 page manuscript instructed him on his responsibilities in carrying out his mission and the trust that had been bestowed upon him. Additionally, the handbook detailed actions and statements to avoid that would draw attention to himself such as saying "Allah Akbar," or "Allah be praised." The handbook also explained that while engaged in a mission, he was granted special dispensation to violate the Quran's prohibition against drinking alcohol and eating pork, and exempted him from saying his prayers five times daily.

In addition to weapons and marching exercises in which all team members participated, specialized training was conducted by four teams of six men each. One group practiced martial arts style attacks designed to overpower an opponent. A second group drove large tractor-trailer trucks and large three-axle trucks without trailers. The third group worked on explosives and incendiary devices, while the last group worked on communications systems.

Emil's team consisted of a diverse cross section of devout and idealistic Muslims from across the Arab Islamic world. Of the twenty-four men on the team, seven were Saudi, five from Iraq, four each from Iran and Syria, two from Egypt, one from Libya, and one was Palestinian. In addition to the common bonds of Islam and the Arabic language, each spoke at least passable English. Eleven of the team members had fought against the Americans in either Iraq or Afghanistan. All of the Iraqis were former members of Republican Guard who chose to shed their uniforms and fade away rather than stand and fight an obviously losing battle against American firepower for Saddam Hussein. None of the team members were known terrorists, had criminal records, or were on "watch lists" that would alert American immigration authorities as they entered the United States. At the insistence of Muhammad Attiya, no facial hair, including moustaches, was allowed, and every team member shaved each morning.

By the fifth week Emil and his men were a highly trained and cohesive group. As training continued, each team member honed their specific skills to a fine edge and increased their weapons proficiency to pinpoint accuracy.

Only their marching skills kept them from looking like a freshly minted American basic training platoon nearing boot camp graduation. Every army develops a marching style that makes it readily identifiable. The British Army marches with a stiff backed style, accentuated with arms swung in a long high arc. The American Army marches in a more relaxed motion that is almost a swagger, arms swinging only six inches to the front. Likewise, the Republican Guards had a style which stressed a more stiff legged movement, and a stiff arm swing. It was this marching style that two of the former Republican Guard members reverted to periodically during the team's many marching practices. Only drill instructor Muhammad Attiya's constant screaming and threats of additional marching forced the two errant team members to focus on marching in the American style.

At the start of the sixth week of training, Emil met again with Qassim Saleh and Yusef al-Masthal, the man who was responsible for his long journey, physically, mentally, and spiritually, to this location. For the first time since he arrived in camp, Emil found himself back in the command tent.

Yusef al-Masthal spoke first. "You and your team have done well, Emil. I have observed your leadership skills and how you have come to command not only the respect of your men but also how they have come to trust you."

"I am blessed by Allah to have such dedicated and skilled team members," said Emil. "I know they will carry out whatever mission they are assigned without hesitation."

"Yes," replied Yusef al-Masthal. "They will perform bravely and will enter heaven as martyrs."

"As will I," Emil answered matter-of-factly referring for the first time to his impending death.

Yusef al-Masthal said nothing, staring at Emil with those cold, lifeless black eyes.

Qassim Saleh spoke next, "Let us sit and I shall provide you with an overview of your mission. We will then explore each facet in greater detail."

When they were seated around a large video monitor, Saleh began. "This mission has been in the planning stages for nine months. Only four of our brothers know the exact location, date, and details of the plan. Yusef al-Masthal and I are two, our agent in the United States, who is to be your contact there is three, and a financial benefactor in Saudi Arabia, whose name it is not necessary for you to know, is the fourth. This night you become the fifth. The mission is designed to take advantage of the American holiday celebrating their declaration of independence from the British in 1776. The Americans refer to it as The Fourth of July. On this day, many patriotic events occur across the country. Almost every town and city in America, regardless of size, holds a parade with marching bands, local military units, political leaders giving speeches, and a community gathering where children play games and much food and alcohol is served. In the evening, at first darkness, fireworks displays occur." Qassim Saleh paused at this point to allow Emil Lagare to absorb this first bit of information.

Sensing that Emil understood, Saleh continued. "As it is a national holiday, almost all businesses and government offices are closed. This year, the fourth day of July falls on a Monday. As such, the Americans will celebrate what they call a three-day weekend. These three-day weekends provide the Americans with an extra day away from work. Accordingly, many will take advantage of this by going to the ocean, to the forests, to amusement parks. Others will travel to visit relatives or friends by vehicle or commercial airlines. As it is summer in America, most schools are not in session, and families will be traveling with their children. The result is a day, or, in this case, three days, when roads are crowded, air travel is delayed, and most importantly for your mission, their guard will be down. This is particularly true with regards to their military. Many units will have minimal staffing, and the ability of these units to mount a swift and coordinated response will be severely limited. It is this combination of national holiday, three-day weekend, and the resulting lack of ability for the Americans to mount a rapid response we have planned your mission around." Saleh paused again and studied Emil Lagare's face for signs of his comprehension.

Satisfied Emil was following his opening explanation thus far, Saleh resumed speaking. "As you recall from our first meeting, I told you your mission would be directed at a small target, someplace the Americans would not expect, a place where their security measures would be lax. Nine months ago, our agents in America were given instructions to seek a target easier to attack than a major population center. We provided specific criteria on the type of target, remoteness, precise events occurring at that location, proximity of active duty military bases, a National Guard armory, and the size of local law enforcement. Twenty-seven locations were videotaped by our brothers in America posing as tourists, holy men on sabbatical, or families with children on vacation. The videotapes were sent to Germany without a narrative voice over. Once the tapes were received in Germany, they were reshipped to Damascus where they were given to me. When I received the tapes, a coded e-mail message was sent to the original source of the video who then provided a return e-mail containing a description of what was on that specific tape. In this way, if either the tapes or the messages were intercepted by our enemies, the two parts were never together, making it virtually impossible for them to discern our plan. Once both parts were in my possession, they were reviewed by Yusef al-Masthal and me. Seven locations initially met the criteria. Two were eliminated because American military bases were within five hundred miles. Four more in the central part of America were eliminated as it was desirous to strike a location on the Pacific Coast to show the Americans that no location in their country is safe."

"This is the location that has been selected," Yusef al-Masthal now spoke for the first time, pushing the play button on the remote control. The large video monitor glowed to life and lit the tent with a green hue.

"This is the California town of Crescent City," Saleh began. The screen filled with a distant shot of the town, blue ocean on one side, and green tree covered hills on the other. "It is located four hundred miles north of San Francisco. This video was taken by the imam of the mosque in Oakland, California, a city just across the bay from San Francisco. I know Imam Nasr Ahmed well. During my nine years in San Francisco, we met continually and I was a member of his mosque. He will be your contact in America. He is trustworthy and loyal to our cause. He has a vast support network capable of supplying all of your logistical needs. The town and surrounding area has a population of fifteen thousand. There is a Coast Guard patrol boat stationed in the harbor, but the closest military base of any consequence is the Marine Base at Camp Pendleton, almost one thousand miles away. Key to our plan, the town has a National Guard Armory. The troops assigned to this unit are part of an infantry battalion recently returned from duty in Iraq. Approximately one hundred of them will participate in a local parade the morning of July fourth. Following the parade, at a community gathering, the California Governor will present medals to the soldiers. Because the Governor will be present, we anticipate there will be extensive television coverage of this event, another key element in our plan."

The videotape shifted from the panoramic scene of the town from a high vantage point, to one shot from inside a moving vehicle. Qassim Saleh's voice narrated as the video continued, "This is the main road into and out of the town. It is called Highway 101. Here the vehicle is traveling north into the town. The harbor is on the left. The Coast Guard cutter can be seen tied to the pier. As you can see, only a chain link fence separates the ship from the street."

The video image then cut to the front of a large one story building with glass front doors leading into a lobby. "This is the community center and beachfront park," Saleh continued. "It is here in the park the medal ceremony will be conducted." The video continued to show the park and the hollow interior of the community center. Saleh explained the main room could hold up to one thousand people.

At this point, Saleh paused the tape and referred to the large detailed street map on the easel. "Here is the overlook from which the initial scenes of the video were taken," he said pointing to the map. "And here is the community center and the adjacent park."

One by one, the videotape showed the significant locations in Crescent City. The airport, the police and sheriff's departments, the hospital, radio station, and the highway leading through the center of town. At each location, Qassim Saleh paused the tape and Emil's attention was directed to the map where that location was pinpointed.

It took three days for Qassim Saleh and Yusef al-Masthal to explain the entire operation to Emil Lagare. As each phase of the mission was explained, it was cross-checked on maps, and when available, the tape was played to familiarize Emil with the actual size and location of the site. The scope of his mission was immense and Emil marveled at the in-depth planning, intelligence, and logistical support dedicated to this operation.

The details, all of which Emil Lagare had to memorize as he would carry no written documents, were staggering. First, travel plans from camp to the United States for himself and the twenty-four members of his team. Then the financial matters, knowing how and where additional money could be obtained if necessary. The transportation arrangements for each team member from different points of entry into America to Oakland, and then transporting his team from Oakland in four different vehicles to converge on Crescent City, California within hours of each other. Lastly, contact persons, communications, contingency plans if some members of the team were denied entry into the United States. All of these issues had been carefully analyzed by Qassim Saleh and his planning staff.

By the end of the seventh week in camp, Emil Lagare had a firm grasp on the entire operation and the intricate details of how it would be carried out. Prior to the beginning of training, the decision had been made by Qassim Saleh and Yusef al-Masthal that only Emil Lagare would have knowledge of the entire operation, and his men would know only in general terms what their tasks would be. They would not know where and when the operation was to be conducted. Team members would be provided with instructions on where they would travel to in America and the name and telephone number of a contact person. The entire scope of the operation would only be revealed to team members by Emil Lagare once they arrived in Crescent City. This precaution would ensure if any team member was arrested and interrogated by American authorities they could not disclose information that would endanger the mission. An extra day before the commencement of the mission had been planned into the timetable allowing team members to actually visit the locations where they were to conduct their specific portion of the operation.

After seven long and arduous weeks, the team's training was complete and preparations were made for individual members to depart. The night before the first group was to leave, a small celebration was held in the camp's dining hall. A video camera was set up in the corner of the tent to film the festivities.

Yusef al-Masthal addressed the entire team praising them for departing on a glorious mission that would bring much honor to themselves, their families, and The Cause against the hated Americans and their Jewish allies. At the end of seven weeks, each of the twenty-four men and their leader already considered themselves martyrs who were doing Allah's work, and knew they soon would receive their reward in heaven. In turn, each of the team members rose and spoke to the video camera, giving a short speech praising Allah for the chance to die in His service, thanking his parents for giving him life, and denouncing the enemies of Islam.

The following day, the first group of four was driven by truck to Damascus where, according to their instructions, they boarded airplanes bound for three different European cities. From there, they either boarded another aircraft bound directly for an American city, to another European city, or waited, as instructed, for another team member to join them. In this manner, all twenty-four soon to be martyrs found themselves entering the United States from Europe, from Canada, or from Asia.

Emil Lagare traveled from camp to Damascus, then on to Beirut. In Beirut he visited the offices of his father's lawyer where he made arrangements for the ownership of his father's business and home to be transferred to relatives. Then he hired a taxi and traveled to the cemetery where his parents were buried. Telling the driver to wait, Emil walked to the gravesite where he spoke in hushed tones to his parents.

Beginning slowly, Emil first addressed his father, "Father I depart today to avenge your death and to bring destruction on those who caused the death of my mother." Turning slightly to address his mother, Emil said, "Mother, I understand now the tenets of Islam you tried to teach me, and I swear by Allah your death will be avenged."

The feelings of emotion within Emil Lagare tore at his heart, his soul, and his spirit as he looked down at the headstones on the graves of his parents. Try as he might, no tears came. He turned and walked slowly back to the waiting taxi. His mission had begun.

From Beirut, Emil flew to Paris, spent one night in the hotel at the airport, then boarded an Air France flight to San Francisco. The flight left Charles de Gaulle Airport at 10:15 in the morning and took just over eleven non-stop hours to reach San Francisco. Because of the many time zones he crossed, it was one in the afternoon when he landed. Using his French passport, clearing immigration took only minutes. As planned by Qassim Saleh, the fact that Emil Lagare appeared on no "watch lists" virtually assured he would have no trouble entering the United States.

Upon clearing immigration, Emil Lagare walked the long concourse of San Francisco International Airport following the exit signs to the street. Once outside, he found himself on the upper level of the terminal where taxis and shuttle buses jetted in and out of small curbside parking spots, horns blared, and pedestrians walked in front of moving vehicles with seeming impunity. As instructed, Emil now followed the signs to BART. The Bay Area Rapid Transit system was San Francisco's equivalent of a subway system. Sleek, white, bullet-shaped electric trains, each with three to six passenger cars, arrived and departed every few minutes. Built in the mid-1980s, the system had only recently expanded to include service to the airport. Arriving in the passenger terminal, Emil Lagare stared at the route map painted high on the wall and the bewildering fingers painted in red, yellow, blue and green representing the destinations of each line. Emil knew he wanted to take the "Blue Line" to the Oakland Civic Center.

Having negotiated the Paris subway system for years as a student at the university, Emil recognized the automated ticket machine and began to fumble with his wallet to retrieve the bills necessary to feed the machine and obtain enough automated credit on a ticket to make the trip. Although a seasoned European traveler, Emil had never before handled American money. Unlike most European money, color-coded to differentiate between denominations, all American money is the same greenish color, only the numbers in the corners and the face on the front of the bill are different. As Emil shuffled bills in his hand, he could feel the pressure of being noticed. Several patrons were now in line behind him and he could hear their impatient comments as he remained confused by which bill to slip into the machine.

"Can I help you?" the polite, but firm voice offered from his right side.

Turning to his right, Emil's throat immediately tightened. He found himself staring into the face of a blue uniform clad BART policeman. Unable to speak, Emil's first thought was to run. He felt his body tingle from his feet, across his thighs, up his back, to the top of his ears.

Finally Emil found himself able to form the words, "I wish to go to Oakland."

"No problem." The policeman's voice relaxed slightly as he realized Emil was foreign. "It costs about four dollars to get to downtown Oakland. Do you have a five dollar bill?" He pointed to Emil's wallet as he spoke.

Flipping through the bills in his wallet, Emil found one with the number five in the corner and pulled it from his wallet.

"Come on," said a voice impatiently from behind Emil. The policemen turned his head slightly, stared the man down, then returned to helping Emil.

"You put it in this slot and punch in five dollars. The machine will give you a ticket good for five dollars worth of rides."

"Ah," Emil exclaimed, his confidence suddenly returning. "Just like the subway in Paris."

"Is that where you're from?" the policemen inquired with a smile on his face.

"Yes," Emil replied confidently, using his prearranged cover story. "From Paris, I'm here on holiday."

"Well, you have yourself a nice holiday. The turnstile is right over there. The next train to Oakland is in seven minutes."

"Thank you for your assistance," Emil smiled as he walked to the turnstile.

"You're very welcome." He watched the young man head toward the platform. "Fucking Frogs," the policemen muttered to himself.

Inserting the cardstock token into the automated turnstile, Emil Lagare pushed the three pronged rotating gate with his leg and entered the platform area. Within minutes the train arrived. Given the time of day, each of the five cars on the Oakland bound train was less than half-full. Entering the second car Emil easily found a vacant seat with no other passengers nearby. The doors closed automatically and the train accelerated rapidly out of the airport. His first obstacle was now behind him.

Emil Lagare stared out the large picture window of the car. The train ran both at ground level and over elevated sections as it made its way north fifteen miles from the airport toward San Francisco. The BART right-of-way roughly parallels Highway 101 and Emil could clearly see traffic on the freeway and surrounding city streets. The area from the airport to San Francisco is almost completely urban, the tracks passing through industrial locations, residential areas, city streets with shops and businesses, hotels, car rental agencies, and parking lots which serve the airport.

It was a workday and by this time, the afternoon commute had begun. Emil could see stopped traffic in both directions on the freeway, city streets crowded with passenger vehicles, large commercial trucks, and people on foot heading in every direction. After making two more stops, the train began a slow descent until it entered a tunnel and began its subterranean journey under San Francisco Bay.

It took eleven minutes for the train to traverse beneath the bay and emerge on the Oakland side. The speaker system announced arrival at the Oakland Civic Center just before the train slid to a stop.

Once off the train, Emil went to a bank of phones in the station where he dialed the memorized number given him by Qassim Saleh before he left camp. The phone was answered after two rings and Emil, speaking in Arabic, utilized a prearranged code phrase. Several seconds of silence passed before the person on the other end of the phone told Emil to exit the station and wait on the street. Within ten minutes Emil found himself in the front passenger seat of an American made sedan heading away from downtown Oakland.

South of Oakland's civic center, with its distinctive big city atmosphere, the landscape changes into part residential, part commercial. After a short drive, the car pulled into the parking lot of a small strip mall. There were two restaurants, one Chinese, the other Kansas City type barbeque, a printing shop, liquor store, and a 99 cent variety discount outlet. At the far end of the mall Emil Lagare could make out the store front of the Oakland mosque with Arabic and English writing over the doorway.

The driver, a young man of about twenty, who had yet to say a word, motioned for Emil to follow. He entered the front door of the mosque. After spending the last hour in the bright afternoon sun, it took Emil Lagare's eyes several seconds to adjust to the artificial light inside the mosque. He stood just inside the door. From there he could see the approaching figure of an older man dressed in the long traditional robe of an imam.

"The blessings of Allah upon you," the imam greeted Emil.

"And upon all who serve The Cause," Emil responded as instructed.

Pausing for a moment, the imam spoke again, this time with the second part of the verification code, "How is my friend Qassim Saleh?"

"As skinny as a Palm tree in an Egyptian oasis," replied Emil Lagare with a blank expression on his face.

Having received the correct responses to both his questions, the imam now broke into a broad smile and with a jovial laugh offered, "Qassim Saleh is as fat as a pregnant Camel in a Damascus marketplace! Welcome, Emil Lagare." He clasped his arm around the younger man and drew him into the interior of the mosque.

"We have been expecting you Emil," the imam began once they were behind the closed doors of his office. "All preparations have been made, all equipment secured, and every member of your team has arrived without incident. They are all here at the mosque. It is somewhat crowded with so many people here, but much easier to maintain secrecy."

"And the vehicles and local drivers?" asked Emil.

"Again, all arranged. I personally selected the four young men who will drive the vehicles. Each is a true believer. All of them have deep ties to The Cause through parents or other relatives, and each will follow your orders to the death."

"Excellent. It is as Qassim Saleh told me. You are a man of extraordinary resourcefulness and a true believer in our mission. When can I see my men and meet the new members of the team?"

"Immediately if you wish."

The imam escorted Emil to the rear of the mosque where one of the large prayer rooms had been converted into a temporary barracks.

There were mats and blankets on the floor and most of his men were either lying down or sitting in small groups in the few chairs available. The sight of their commander brought all of the men immediately to their feet. There was much laughing and shaking of hands as the team members greeted their leader and praised Allah for his safe arrival.

After several minutes, the high spirited greetings began to die away and Emil turned to the imam, "Imam Nasr Ahmed, as part of my orders I must speak to my men alone."

"Certainly, young commander, I will leave you now. Evening prayers begin in just over an hour. As instructed, to reduce questions about your presence here, you and your men will remain secluded in this room until the faithful have left the mosque for the evening. Dinner will be provided shortly thereafter."

"Thank you, imam, for your hospitality, and for your understanding," Emil acknowledged with a slight bow of his head as the imam turned and walked out of the room.

One of the concerns the planners of the operation had was getting twenty-four Arabic looking men through immigration points into the United States. To maximize each of the team members' chances of clearing immigration without arousing suspicion, each man had traveled alone. The men were selected for this operation for their specific skills and ability to speak English, as well as the lack of anything in their backgrounds that would bring attention from foreign intelligence agencies, or would cause their names to appear on "watch lists" at immigration checkpoints in Europe or the United States. Each man arrived on a flight which landed late in the shift of the immigration personnel working at the port of entry, and timed to coincide with numerous other international flight arrivals. The planners hoped the combination of large volumes of people crowding immigration checkpoints and fatigue from working a long shift, would deter customs and immigration officials from focusing on a lone Arabic man. Every man was traveling on his real passport and gave a different destination within the United States.

Once clear of the immigration checkpoint, each took an additional flight to the actual destination they had told immigration. From this destination city, they spent one night at a hotel adjacent to the airport and booked a final flight to Oakland the following day.

To ensure the secrecy of the operation and that no team member had generated any undo suspicion, Emil Lagare gathered his team and questioned each of them about their flights and any problems they had encountered clearing immigration. Amazingly, none of his men reported any problems and several reported only a cursory examination of their passports at airports in Florida and Los Angeles. His team had arrived intact, and to the best of his knowledge, without arousing the suspicion of American authorities. Thanks be to Allah, he told himself.

Following evening prayers the crowd of local Muslims cleared the mosque within an hour and the large door to the room where Emil and his men waited rolled back. Imam Nasr Ahmed appeared with four young men and plates of food. Following the meal and prayers of thanks, the imam introduced Emil to the four new members of his team.

All four were in their late teens or early twenties, dressed in blue jeans and expensive running shoes. Several wore black Oakland Raiders team jackets. While none of them would have gone unnoticed in Beirut, Damascus, or Cairo, here in Oakland they would not even get a second look.

The use of local Muslims to supplement Emil Lagare's team had been the idea of Qassim Saleh, the mission's planner. While Saleh knew there was an element of risk in relying on men who had not trained with the rest of the team, he had faith Imam Nasr Ahmed would choose only the most loyal and trusted of his followers for the mission. Saleh knew it would be necessary to use local men to rent the type of vehicles needed to transport all twenty-four team members and their equipment in as few vehicles as possible. Experience had shown rental car companies would not rent vehicles to drivers without a major credit card, something only the team leader possessed. He also knew that driving on California's freeways took some measure of experience, something none of the team members, not even their leader possessed. Most importantly, however, local Muslims were familiar with how to do the myriad of things that went along with functioning in America on a daily basis. Everything from how to purchase fuel at an automated pump, to how to buy food in a market, to how to respond to even the most innocent of questions from clerks or other travelers they may come in contact with. Also, if they should have unexpected contact with the police, or become involved in an accident, the local Muslims' knowledge of how to act, or what to say would be invaluable. Lastly, the local Muslims could be used as "muscle men" to supplement the team's activities once the mission began. Qassim Saleh realized the value of these local men was worth the risk.

Emil Lagare knew his new team members had each received weapons training as part of the weekend retreats sponsored by Imam Ahmed's mosque. These weekend outings involved renting motor homes from any of the several dealers in the greater San Francisco Bay Area. Once a month it was not unusual to see five or six large Winnebago type motor homes parked in front of the mosque on a Saturday morning. Each motor home would transport three or four young Muslim men on the two hour trek into the delta region of Northern California. Here, in the swampy farm land of levees and corn fields, training was conducted in the use of handguns, shotguns, and hunting rifles. These weapons had been legally obtained by various members of the imam's mosque from gun dealers throughout the Bay Area. After filling out the mandatory paperwork and waiting the requisite ten days as prescribed by California law, the imam's followers brought the weapons to the mosque where they were held for the weekend retreats. Training was provided on several different types of handguns, including the Beretta 9 millimeter semi-automatic pistol used by the American military and several types of revolvers and pistols used by American police forces. After three such retreat weekends, the imam's followers were proficient and deadly in the use of these weapons.

It was time to sleep now. Tomorrow, Thursday, would be the last day for him to inspect equipment, cover details with each of his four teams, workout last minute logistical items, and prepare himself mentally for his mission.

As previously planned, the four local Muslim youths remained overnight at the mosque with Emil Lagare and the rest of his men. While Imam Nasr Ahmed had personally selected these men and their loyalty to the The Cause was unquestionable, it was simply more prudent to have them remain at the mosque where there was less chance of a misspoken word unraveling the entire mission.

Emil slept soundly beneath a thin blanket on the mosque's wooden floor. He awoke to the sounds of his team members talking and eating breakfast which consisted of yogurt, fruit, and warm bread freshly baked by a local Muslim woman. They sipped thick dark coffee provided by their four local Muslim brothers who had joined the team yesterday.

Following breakfast, Emil Lagare said his morning prayers then met with Imam Nasr Ahmed. He was eager to set about the many tasks of the day.

After the customary morning greetings and small talk, Emil Lagare brought the conversation to the work ahead, "Time is short."

"Yes," replied Imam Ahmed. "We will begin immediately."

Leaving the mosque, Emil and the imam were driven by one of the local Muslim men who was now part of his team to a nearby self-storage facility. Using the key pad, the driver opened the electronic gate and drove into the yard. The driver stopped in front of one of the several dozen roll up garage doors and turned the engine off. All three men exited the car and the young driver used a key to open the pad lock securing the door.

As the door rolled up, Emil could see many large cardboard boxes filling the ten by twenty foot storage unit. All the boxes had been opened and neatly restacked.

"I believe we have everything Qassim Saleh ordered," stated the imam. "The last of the items arrived only this week. We inspected every box. Every item is here."

"Excellent." Emil opened several of the boxes and began to inspect the contents. "When can we move these boxes back to the mosque so each of my men can be issued their personal equipment?"

"A truck will arrive shortly and the boxes will be taken back to the mosque. There you can see to the needs of each man," came Imam Ahmed's response.

When the boxes were brought back to the mosque, Emil Lagare gathered his team and distributed the specially ordered equipment. For the next several hours each man familiarized himself with his personalized equipment. Once satisfied with their individual items, they were repacked in the boxes and the boxes separated by team.

Emil Lagare, with his twenty-four original team members and his four new American Muslims remained in the mosque for the rest of Thursday. The time was devoted to reviewing plans, studying maps, and integrating the new members of his team with the men he had trained with in the desert. By late afternoon Emil Lagare felt he and his team were as ready as possible.

After the evening meal Imam Nasr Ahmed spoke to the entire group reaffirming they were doing Allah's work and soon the eyes of the world would be on them and their mission.

Emil Lagare watched his men as the imam spoke and noted each was immersed in deep personal thought. It was good they were leaving tomorrow, before the boredom of seclusion in the back of the mosque eroded their finely honed edge.

Friday, July 1st, dawned as a slightly overcast summer San Francisco morning. Within a couple of hours the marine layer would burn itself off as the interior valleys of California heated into the one hundred plus degree range pushing the light cloud cover back out to sea.

All the men were up early and their eagerness was apparent. By 6:30 they had eaten, said their prayers, and shaved. Before 7:00, team members were loading equipment and large cardboard boxes into the vehicles waiting outside, while Emil Lagare and Imam Ahmed watched. The sight of four large motor homes parked outside the mosque at the beginning of a weekend and young men loading equipment onboard, was not unusual for passersby. It was something they saw every month.

7:30 was the designated time for the first vehicle to depart, followed by another vehicle every fifteen minutes. Emil Lagare, traveling alone in a non-descript rented compact car, would be the last to leave. After the last motor home left, Emil Lagare sought out Imam Nasr Ahmed.

"My sincere gratitude for all your assistance," Emil thanked the imam. "You shall surely be rewarded by Allah for all you have done."

"My reward will be the success of your mission young Emil Lagare. May the sword of Allah be in your hands as you strike a blow at our enemies," Imam Nasr Ahmed humbly replied, his eyes turned upward.

With that, Emil Lagare entered his vehicle and made his way onto the busy early morning streets of Oakland.

———

The slamming of a car door outside his motel room brought Emil Lagare out of his half-sleep. In his tired condition, he was slightly disoriented. He could hear the voice of a man telling someone to bring the suitcase from the trunk and the sound of another car door slamming closed.

The voices began to fade away, then the door to the room next to his slammed, causing his entire room to shudder. Swinging his feet off the bed he sat upright, wiping the sleep from his eyes. Glancing at his watch he noted he'd slept for less than a half-hour. Over ninety minutes of sunlight remained for him to explore the town of Crescent City. There was still much to accomplish this day.

CHAPTER SIX

Eight days after graduating, Red Wolff and her classmates reported to the Central Los Angeles Area of the CHP. Central, as it was known around the Highway Patrol, had more officers than any other CHP office in the state with one hundred forty-five personnel. It was one of ten Highway Patrol offices in the greater Los Angeles Basin. Located under the crossroads of two elevated freeways, it was a large temporary building that had been there since 1969, the year the Highway Patrol took over responsibility for the downtown L.A. freeway system from the Los Angeles Police Department. Because of its location, it was always noisy from the thousands of vehicles passing in all directions over and around the office and dirty simply because it was located right in the middle of downtown.

Six months of academy training was just the beginning for new officers like Red Wolff. The real training began once they started their "Break-in" period. Break-in consisted of three fifteen day periods with three different Field Training Officers, or FTOs in police jargon.

For her first fifteen days Red Wolff was assigned to afternoon shift, working from two until ten. Her FTO introduced her to writing citations, clearing collision scenes, making traffic stops, responding to calls for service, driving, learning the beats they were working, and making arrests. She made lots of the normal rookie mistakes, but was quickly picking up on everything her FTO was teaching her.

Just like the academy, Red Wolff had little trouble with her break-in period. After her first fifteen day period on afternoon shift, she was assigned a different FTO on the graveyard shift, working from ten at night until six in the morning. For her last break-in period she was assigned to day shift with another FTO. She learned different ways of doing things from all three of her training officers. Each of them pressed her hard to ensure she could perform the required job tasks, and could safely do them by herself.

One of the things each of her training officers cautioned her about was that break-in simply could not expose her to everything she needed to know, or every type of situation she might encounter. During her forty-five days of field training, Red Wolff spent a great deal of time behind the wheel driving, but had not been involved in a high speed pursuit. Nor had she been involved in a felony arrest, encountered a suspect with a gun, or had the occasion to deal with a violent individual.

Nonetheless, after forty-five days of break-in, she'd met all the standards expected of a new officer and was ready to either work by herself on day or afternoon shift, or partner with another officer to work graveyard.

In Central Los Angeles, officers were assigned to a shift for three months at a time by seniority. Consequently, almost everyone working the graveyard shift was a new officer like Red Wolff, or maybe an officer with a couple of more months on the job then they had. It wasn't the blind leading the blind, but it was close.

While most senior officers in Central preferred to work day or afternoon shift, a few always signed up for graveyards. Ray Silva was a kind of legend in Central. With twelve years on the job, he was one of the most experienced officers in the entire office and had the seniority to work any shift or beat he chose. He'd been assigned to Central right out of the academy and even though he could have transferred to almost any place in the state, he chose to stay in Los Angeles. He always worked graveyard, enjoying the freedom to drive without the impediment of commute traffic, as well as the cool night air, as opposed to the choking, eye-stinging smog of the day. But mostly, he enjoyed the type of work that came with working Los Angeles at night.

Tall and lean, with a full head of salt and pepper black hair, he had a large toothy grin and a mustache that was still solid black. The first generation son of Portuguese immigrants, he had a deep olive complexion and people often mistook him for Hispanic, a notion he would quickly correct in anyone who made that mistake. He did not speak Portuguese and his Spanish was limited to what he picked up on the job. He had always wanted to be a Highway Patrolman ever since the day a CHP officer came to his elementary school in Crescent City to give a safety talk. In his eleven year old mind's eye, that officer was about eight feet tall, with gleaming brass, and a shiny leather gun belt. After a lack-luster year at the local junior college, he joined the army for three years and did a tour in Vietnam. After the army he returned home to Crescent City, working on his dad's fishing boat while simultaneously going through the testing process for the CHP.

Most cops never fire their weapon in the line of duty except at the range. There are lots of times, of course, when an officer pulls their weapon in high-risk or felony situations, but seldom do they ever have to resort to actually using it. Likewise, officers often find themselves in physical confrontations when they try to take suspects into custody, but these seldom produce deadly results.

In his twelve years on the CHP, Ray Silva had been involved in two shootings, both justified. In the first, he stopped a vehicle driven by an ex-con who, unknown to him, had just held up a convenience store, or "stop and robs," as cops called them. The CHP teaches its officers to make right side approaches to stopped vehicles rather than approaches on the left side. This protects the officer from passing traffic, and gives them a better view of the interior of the stopped vehicle. As he approached on the right side, he could see the driver looking over his left shoulder, but could not see the driver's hands. When the driver finally realized where the officer was, he wheeled to the right, leveled a large caliber handgun at him and fired. Ray Silva sensed the gun before he saw it and had already slipped his Smith and Wesson .40 caliber semi-automatic pistol from his holster. Milliseconds before the ex-con pulled the trigger, Ray Silva had already fired two rounds through the right rear window of the stopped vehicle. Both rounds found their mark causing the ex-con's one shot to go into the roof of his car. The ex-con died in the driver's seat within twenty seconds.

Ray Silva's second shooting was equally dramatic. Responding to a call of a naked pedestrian on the freeway at three in the morning, Ray Silva and his partner arrived at the location to find a naked man standing in the middle of four lanes of traffic. He knew immediately what he was dealing with. For whatever reason people on the hallucinogenic drug PCP always want to take their clothes off. The man was holding a large hunting knife swiping at passing traffic. Activating the revolving red and blue roof mounted lights on their patrol car; they stopped in the middle of the freeway trying to prevent any traffic from passing. Ray Silva called for backup and yelled at his partner to get flares out to try and help block traffic.

In a city where the automobile is a necessity, everyone drives. This includes the thousands of immigrants from all over the world who did not grow up with cars and multi-lane freeways. The middle-aged Taiwanese woman had only been in the United States for three months, but she had a valid California Driver's License. On her way to work, she was not sure what the flashing red and blue lights or the bright orange colored flares meant. Slowing to thirty miles per hour, she could see someone in uniform off to her right waving his arms at her. Continuing to slow down she wondered why the police car was stopped in the middle of the freeway with all of its' lights flashing. Returning her gaze to the front, she saw a naked man standing directly ahead of her. Slamming on her brakes, she came to a complete stop and, for whatever reason, rolled the driver's side window down. The man was at the door in an instant, slashing at her with the knife. Ray Silva and his partner didn't have a choice. Both fired at the same time. While his partner's round shattered the driver's side rear view mirror, his round caught the man under the right arm pit, causing him to drop the knife. It did not, however, stop him from trying to attack the woman in the car. Rushing the wounded man, Ray Silva and his partner tackled him and pushed him to the ground. While they were wrestling the naked man on the ground, the frightened woman sped away. She was never located again. Suspects on PCP, besides wanting to take their clothes off, often display super-human strength. Although the suspect was small and had sustained a direct hit from Ray Silva's service weapon, it took all of the strength of both officers to finally twist his arms behind his back and handcuff him. He continued to struggle on the ground and would have bled to death had Ray Silva not applied direct pressure to his wound while his partner held him down with a baton across the back of his neck.

Working graveyard shift, it is not unusual for a two officer unit to make four or more physical arrests every night. A physical arrest meant actually handcuffing a suspect with their hands behind their back. Handcuffing someone who was going to jail was not only CHP policy, it was for the officers' safety as well. Many arrestees are initially compliant with an officer's instructions, but as the reality of going to jail sets in, some become extremely violent.

That's the way it happened the night Ray Silva and his partner tried to arrest a driver for a narcotics violation. It started out as a simple stop for speeding on the Harbor Freeway about midnight. The speeding vehicle pulled to the right shoulder, and Ray Silva made a right side approach. As soon as the driver rolled down the right side window he could smell the burning marijuana coming from inside the vehicle. Signaling to his partner by touching his nose, his partner approached quickly on the driver's side, opened the door and asked the driver to exit.

Once out of the car, the driver was directed to the right shoulder. Both officers noticed at once that the driver they'd stopped was huge. Easily six and a half feet tall, he was also extremely muscular, and agitated about being stopped. It was obvious to Ray Silva the driver was under the influence of drugs and in no condition to continue driving. It was also obvious to him the more talking they did, the more agitated the suspect was becoming. As he started the process of handcuffing the driver, he got one handcuff on his right wrist before the suspect spun around, causing him lose his control hold. Flailing his arms, the suspect charged at both officers. The one handcuff, secured firmly to the suspect's right wrist, now became a deadly weapon as it narrowly missed Ray Silva's head several times. As his partner called for backup, Ray Silva found himself pinned with his back against the side of the patrol car by the increasingly violent suspect while freeway traffic whizzed by less than two feet away. Unable to draw his baton or mace, he found himself trying to fend off the suspect's blows with one hand, while at the same time trying to keep the suspect from pulling his weapon out of his holster with the other. After calling for backup, his partner jumped immediately into the fray, grabbing one of the suspect's hands and trying to twist it into a control hold. The suspect just shook him off and went back for Ray Silva's gun. Trying again, his partner managed to get a full control hold, but this time the suspect twisted, lifted him completely off the ground, and threw him onto his back in the traffic lane where he hit the back of his head on the pavement. The suspect then went back to pummeling Ray Silva. Luckily for his partner, the driver of the closest passing vehicle saw what was happening and managed to swerve, avoiding the fallen officer. Dazed, he managed to crawl out of the lane and into the rain gutter on the side of the pavement. Realizing he was now on his own, and was fast losing a fight that could mean his life, Ray Silva momentarily stopped fighting for control of his weapon with his right hand, and used all his remaining strength to bring the heel of that hand up into the base of the suspect's nose. The loud crack as the suspect's nose broke could be heard even over the din of the freeway. The suspect released his grip on Ray Silva's gun and staggered backward into the traffic lane adjacent to the shoulder. It was almost like a Roadrunner and Coyote cartoon when the large, flat front end of the passing Peterbilt semi-truck and trailer struck the suspect. He never knew what killed him.

Ray Silva was a loner by choice. As one of the most senior officers in Central, the sergeants left him alone and his reputation kept most of the newer officers at arms length. Still, he was never hesitant to help anyone and always jumped in when he saw someone doing something dangerous, or about to make a major screw up. He kept his off-duty life to himself, and even officers who'd ridden with him for three months in a patrol car knew very little about him. Those who didn't know him took his quietness as being aloof. The few officers who did know him recognized it as being shy. His supervisors encouraged him many times to take the sergeants test which he always declined to do, saying simply he didn't want the responsibility.

Whether it was a fluke, fate, or just the luck of the draw, rookie officer Erin "Red" Wolff, just off break-in, ended up as the partner of veteran officer Ray Silva.

The first day of the new quarter was a Thursday. Red Wolff got to the office about nine that evening, changed into uniform, checked her mail slot for subpoenas, reports, and messages, then went into the briefing room to wait for roll call.

There were about a half-dozen officers already in the room, mostly all new officers like her, relegated to graveyard shift by virtue of being low man on the sign-up list. Sitting by himself, at a table near the back of the room, was her new partner.

Summoning all her courage and inner strength, she walked up to Ray Silva to introduce herself. She could see he was watching her as she approached.

"Hi, I'm Erin Wolff," she extended her hand.

Surprisingly, he stood up and firmly shook her hand looking her in the eye. "Ray Silva, looks like we'll be working together."

"Yeah, I guess you got stuck with me," she responded almost sheepishly.

"They call you Red don't they?"

"Yes sir," Red Wolff said automatically.

"Look, this isn't the academy, you're off break-in, and we have three months together. Call me Ray. What name do you want me to use for you?"

"Call me Red, I don't think I'll ever shake the name," she smiled at her new partner.

"Okay Red, grab a chair and let's talk."

Red Wolff sat next to her partner as more officers began to fill up the briefing room.

Ray Silva turned to his new partner and began talking in a low tone. "We're both officers, supposedly that means we have an equal say in what we do and how we do it. One of us has some experience, the other doesn't. The whole idea of what we do every night is to go home safe at the end of the shift. Everything else we do, make arrests, write tickets, help people, whatever, is secondary to that. Your primary job is to keep yourself safe. Your second job is to watch my back. Those are my jobs also, to watch out for me and to watch out for you. First off, I want you to take that name tag off your uniform shirt. I know regulations say you have to wear it, but there is also a regulation that says you shouldn't get killed. If we ever get in a situation where someone gets a gun on one of us, we call each other by the others last name as a warning. If you have a name tag on that says your last name is Wolff, and you call me Wolff as a warning, the bad guy will figure it out and pop a cap into you. Also, I won't give up my gun to save your life and I don't expect you to give up your gun for me."

Erin Wolff sat next to her new partner not knowing what to say.

"One other thing, if something ever happens to me out there, I get shot, or run over, or beat up, don't worry about me. You call for help, then focus on catching the suspect. When you do, cancel his ticket." Ray Silva's words were plain and matter-of-fact.

"Any questions so far?" he asked. "No, okay briefing is about to start."

Red Wolff's mind was spinning, who is this guy and why am I working with him, she thought to herself?

Roll call, beat assignments, and the latest briefing items took about fifteen minutes, then all of the officers grabbed their gear and headed for the parking lot.

Ray Silva had already grabbed a set of keys from the keyboard. "I'll start out driving tonight, you can start tomorrow."

"Sure," Red Wolff answered, her head still in a daze as she followed her partner to the parking lot.

Their first couple nights working together were nothing out of the ordinary. A couple drunk driving arrests each night, two minor fender bender collisions, one major accident investigation, and a handful of citations. At different times, Ray Silva gave his new partner advice on where to stand during a stop, or warned her to watch for passing traffic. The little conversation between them was strictly job related.

Partners split their activity fifty-fifty. One partner writes the first ticket of the night, the other writes the next. They do the same thing with drunk driving arrests and collision investigations. That kept their workload and monthly statistics, fairly even.

Right out of the office on their third night together, with Ray Silva driving, they stopped a car driving on the freeway with no lights. When there are narrow or no shoulders on the freeway, standard CHP practice is to use the patrol vehicles P.A. system to direct a violator off the freeway at the next exit. Red Wolff used the patrol car's loud speaker to get the driver headed toward the freeway exit. Once off the freeway and safely on city streets, the vehicle was ordered to stop at the curb.

"Your "outs" for the ticket," Ray Silva chuckled to his partner, indicating it was her turn to write a citation.

"Thanks." There was a half-smile on her face.

As both officers exited their patrol car, the violator got out of his vehicle at the same time.

The driver was a young black man in his late teens or early twenties. Dressed in dark colored slacks and long sleeved white shirt, Ray Silva could see he wasn't a "gang-banger." While he strode casually up to look into the violator's vehicle, Red Wolff directed the driver to the sidewalk and engaged him in conversation.

"How you doing tonight sir? We stopped you because you're driving without any lights. Can I see your license please?"

The driver patted the pockets of his trousers and then mumbled, "These don't be my pants."

Somewhat taken back by the thought the young man could be wearing someone else's pants, Red Wolff paused momentarily, then asked, "So where's your license?"

"It be in my other pants," the driver replied.

Ray Silva saw nothing unusual during his visual inspection of the young man's car. He stood off to the side and watched the on-going exchange between the driver and his new partner. He'd seen it a thousand times before. He knew from experience the young black driver either never had a license, or if he did, it was suspended, or he had a warrant out for his arrest.

Red Wolff changed tactics and asked the driver for some form of identification, which of course he could not produce. Increasingly frustrated by her inability to get anywhere, she glanced at her partner who was standing off to the side behind the driver.

"Say "Homes," I see a wallet in your back pocket, why don't you take it out?" Ray Silva said, injecting himself into the conversation for the first time, shifting his speech into "street-talk" mode.

Slowly taking out the wallet, the driver thumbed through the items inside, skipping over several pieces of identification as both officers watched.

Ray Silva saw the tell-tale green upper border stripe of the California Identification Card the driver had conveniently thumbed passed.

"Let me see the I.D. card," Ray Silva told him.

In the ensuing conversation, Red Wolff determined the young man never had a driver's license, that he had two outstanding warrants for minor traffic offenses, and he was on his way to work at an all-night coffee shop.

Red Wolff instructed the driver to wait by his car then turned to her partner. "What do you think we should do?"

"I know what I'd do. The question is what are you going to do?"

"Well, to do things right, I need to arrest him on the warrants, impound his car, and take him to jail."

Ray Silva paused for a full five seconds as he looked at the young black man, then back at his new partner.

"Yep, that's doing things right," he said, pausing again.

Looking Red Wolff dead in the eye, he continued, "Time for Career Decision Number One. You can be the kind of cop who does things right, or you can be the kind of cop who does the right things. This kid's not the sharpest knife in the drawer, but he's trying. Booking him on the warrants will take us off the road for a couple of hours and the jail will release him with a notice to appear in court before you complete the paperwork. If we impound his car it will cost him over a hundred bucks to get it back, which by the look of him he can't afford, and to top it off, he'll probably get fired for missing work tonight. If you book him, you did things right. If you let him go, you get nothing. If you let him go, and the sergeant finds out, you could get fired. You have about thirty seconds to make a decision. Your call."

Two minutes later they were back in their patrol car heading for coffee. They rode together in silence.

Do things right, or do the right things, Career Decision Number One. What a strange one this guy is, Red Wolff thought to herself as the city continued to pulsate around her.

"Do you want to tell me what that was all about?" she asked as they stood drinking coffee by their patrol car in the parking lot of an all-night donut shop on Sunset Boulevard.

"Look Red, you've got three months into a thirty year career. If you spend every minute attempting to cure the ills of society, a screwed-up legal system, and all of the social injustice in the world you'll make yourself crazy. Have you ever read any Wambaugh?"

"No, who's he?" she replied.

"Joe Wambaugh was an LAPD detective who wrote a bunch of mostly fiction books in the seventies about cops. There was an old-time veteran in one of his books who said you only needed three things to be a good cop. Common sense, compassion, and a sense of humor."

"So what's that got to do with the stop we just made?"

"What useful purpose would it have served to arrest that kid? He wasn't a danger to anyone and the people of California aren't any worse off because he didn't spend the night in jail."

"Aside from the fact I could get fired for letting him go, why was it a career decision?" she asked.

"Because from now on," Ray Silva responded, "you'll look at everything from the perspective of just how much ability you have to impact the lives of people by what you do."

Sipping her coffee, Red Wolff stared over the rim of her paper cup at her partner. "Just so I know," she questioned, the cup just below her lips, "how many career decisions are there?"

"Three," Ray Silva stated without hesitation or emotion.

"What are the other two?"

"Finish your coffee, let's go back to work," he told her in a manner clearly indicating to Red Wolff the conversation was over.

After work Red Wolff went home and slept fitfully for a couple of hours before heading to the mall near her apartment. At the mall bookstore she bought three Wambaugh books.

The next couple of weeks were filled with arrests, accidents, writing citations, and doing the day-to-day tasks that go along with working graveyard shift.

Red Wolff honed her skills at high speed driving, safety tactics when making stops, and dealing with the myriad of people who frequent the night in Los Angeles. She learned she had to develop different ways of dealing with various types of people. For the average working person, a friendly matter-of-fact style worked almost every time. For those self-important people driving fancy expensive cars, she realized they considered being stopped an inconvenience and handled them accordingly. Dealing with non-English speakers, of which there were thousands, patience and learning a little Spanish was needed. For "gang-bangers," those gun toting members of the hundreds of street gangs in Los Angeles, constant vigilance, and a tough, take-no-shit approach, was necessary.

After their first month together, Red Wolff and Ray Silva were clicking as partners. There were still incidents she had not experienced before for which she needed her partner's guidance. And he still corrected her when she was not doing something safely. But all-in-all she was gaining confidence every night and felt comfortable that she was holding up her end of the partnership.

About halfway through their second month she experienced Career Decision Number Two.

They got the radio call just after eleven of an injury accident, eastbound on the Santa Monica Freeway near San Pedro Street. On any given Sunday night there was still considerable traffic heading eastbound even at that hour as thousands of cars are heading home from the beach towns. As traffic approaches the East Los Angeles Interchange, the number of lanes decreases and traffic slows. Rear end accidents are fairly common.

When they received the call they were on the Santa Monica Freeway, a couple of miles away, heading in the opposite direction. Red Wolff was driving. Accelerating smoothly she moved rapidly through traffic and positioned herself to take the next off-ramp in order to turn around. The off-ramp was about two hundred yards long and clear of any other traffic, but the signal at the bottom of the ramp was red. Activating the rotating red and blue roof lights, she began to decelerate as she hit the siren switch. As the patrol car approached the intersection, Red Wolff's attention was focused, as she'd been instructed by her partner on cross traffic coming from the left. Traffic on her side was light and stopped in response to her emergency lights. While Red Wolff was watching for traffic coming from her left, Ray Silva was watching for traffic coming from the opposite direction. "Clear right," he said loudly to ensure he was heard over the siren. As soon as she heard her partner's assurance there were no cars coming, Red Wolff ran the red light at forty-five miles per hour, smashed down on the accelerator and turned the steering wheel hard to the left, sending the patrol vehicle into a four wheel broad slide across the intersection. When the slide stopped, the rear tires bit into the pavement and the patrol car lunged forward. She now accelerated rapidly positioning the patrol car to negotiate the right hand turn that would take them onto the eastbound on-ramp to reenter the freeway. Red Wolff kept her foot buried on the accelerator as the on-ramp curved to the right, causing great billows of black smoke to rise from the tires as they screeched in protest.

By the time she hit the end of the on-ramp, Red Wolff had the patrol vehicle doing well over seventy miles per hour. Without looking, she reached down and killed the rotating lights and siren.

Ray Silva taught her that unless it was absolutely necessary, never to use the lights and siren on the freeway when responding to an emergency call. Too many drivers, he told her, simply didn't know how to react when they saw red lights behind them. Instead, she glanced over her left shoulder, saw a small opening between cars, and headed for the fast lane. The patrol vehicles speedometer was steady at one hundred ten miles per hour as she expertly wove between vehicles.

About a mile from where the accident was reported to be, both officers could see brake lights and a long line of traffic backed up across all six eastbound lanes.

"Grab the shoulder," Ray Silva instructed.

Without responding, Red Wolff slowed to about twenty and guided their full-sized Chevrolet Caprice onto the right shoulder. Traffic was at a dead stop in the three right hand lanes, stop and go in the others.

Arriving at the scene, Red Wolff pulled the patrol car off the shoulder and positioned it to block the two right lanes, activated the emergency lights, advised the communications center they were "10-97," and exited the patrol car.

It was Red Wolff's outs for the collision investigation. As she grabbed her report writing equipment, Ray Silva began to lay a flare pattern. Within a minute he heard his partner on the radio calling for an ambulance and a tow truck.

Collision scenes are always chaotic no matter when they occur. At night, however, they take on a surrealistic feel. When people walking around the scene pass in front of headlight beams they cast long shadows down the roadway for several hundred feet, rotating red and blue emergency lights bounce off passing cars, and thick, acrid, white sulfur smelling smoke rises from the emergency flares. Add to this, smashed cars, broken glass, radiator water, injured victims, and crying children. It requires an officer to quickly take charge and restore order.

The Highway Patrol's protocol at a collision scene is to first provide emergency medical aid to injured victims, gather the minimum required information to conduct an investigation, then clear the traffic lanes.

As collisions go, this was a relatively minor incident. There were only two cars involved, a mid-sized late model Buick sedan with a family of three, and a full-sized seventies Chevrolet with only the driver. Red Wolff could easily see what had occurred. The Buick was stopped in the far right lane due to heavy traffic. The Chevrolet had not been able to stop in time and rear ended the Buick. Though the Chevrolet was in the process of braking, it still hit the stopped Buick at about thirty miles per hour. The front of the heavier Chevrolet, with its solid frame construction, caused major damage to the rear of the newer model Buick with its mostly plastic body.

Had they all been wearing seatbelts, everyone would probably have walked away from the collision with only aches and pains. Unfortunately, the small girl in the Buick had been asleep in her mother's arms in the front seat when the collision occurred. The force of the impact sent the little girl into the windshield where she suffered a laceration to her scalp.

Red Wolff quickly took charge of the scene. Using a compress from the first aid kit, she applied direct pressure to the child's head wound. She knew from her training head wounds tended to bleed a lot, but unless there were internal injuries, the girl would be fine. As soon as the ambulance arrived, she relinquished medical duties to the paramedics and turned her attention to the drivers.

The driver of the Buick was a middle-aged black man. Red Wolff copied his information onto her report form and obtained his statement about the accident. Within a few minutes, a tow truck arrived and began hooking up the Buick to haul it off the roadway. The driver of the Chevrolet was a Hispanic male in his early twenties who did not speak English and did not have a driver's license.

The paramedics stabilized the young girl and within a couple of minutes were ready to transport her to the hospital. Having obtained all the information she needed from the driver of the Buick, she advised him to go with the ambulance. The ambulance left the scene, followed shortly thereafter by the tow truck pulling the Buick.

The Chevrolet sustained only minor damage to the front end and was drivable. While Ray Silva extinguished the flares, Red Wolff, through hand signals and the little Spanish she knew, directed the driver of the Chevrolet to drive his car off the freeway at the exit a quarter-mile ahead. Both officers jumped back in their patrol car and followed him off the now clear and open freeway.

The east end of the Santa Monica Freeway is elevated as it runs through a primarily industrial part of Los Angeles. The area is home to garment manufacturers, trucking companies, and machine shops. At night this location is virtually deserted, the streets dimly lit by the occasional low power, yellow sodium overhead light. Even the din of the freeway, only a few yards away, is muted.

The driver of the Chevrolet stopped once on the city street that parallels the freeway. The patrol vehicle stopped directly behind. The driver got out of his car and was directed to the sidewalk by Red

Wolff. While she tried to converse with the driver, Ray Silva did his usual cursory inspection of his vehicle.

In Spanish, the driver of the Chevrolet told Red Wolff his name was Hector Morales, he did not have a license, and the car belonged to a friend.

After completing his inspection of the car, Ray Silva stood back and watched the interaction between his partner and the increasingly cocky driver. Something didn't feel right about the driver to Red Wolff, but she was unable to determine exactly what that was. She ran the driver and his vehicle through the computer. Both came back clear.

Walking over to his partner, Ray Silva asked, "Mind if I talk to him?" Even though he was senior, officers did not interject themselves into the actions of their partner without asking.

"Be my guest," she replied.

Ray Silva walked up to the driver and stood squarely in front of him. After a number of years on the job, most officers develop a way of walking, talking, and interacting with people that radiates self-confidence, experience and "street-smarts." "Command Presence," is not something that can be taught. Officers either developed it, or they didn't. Ray Silva had it. Red Wolff didn't have it yet, but with a little more seasoning, she would.

"What's your name?" he asked in English.

"No hablo Ingeles," the driver replied.

"What's your name?" he asked again, this time more forcefully.

The driver, his cocky demeanor now fading fast, replied again, "No hablo Ingeles."

Ray Silva carried his flashlight in his left hand. Issued by the state, the flashlight was about a foot long, made of high strength aluminum with a rechargeable battery. It weighed just over a pound. Holding the flashlight by the head, he placed the long end of the light on top of the driver's head about three inches above his hairline.

"Speak English mother-fucker," he said softly.

"No hablo Ingeles."

Cocking his wrist slightly, Ray Silva raised the flashlight about an inch off the driver's head, then let it drop. The flashlight made a quiet thud as it hit.

"Speak English mother-fucker," Ray Silva said again, louder, with more emphasis in his voice.

"No hablo Ingeles," came the response again.

Red Wolff was frozen in place. Nothing in her training prepared her for what she was seeing. Instinctively she knew it was wrong, but she could not move or speak.

Cocking his wrist Ray Silva brought the flashlight up once more, this time about three inches off the driver's head. Again he let it drop, the weight of the light causing it to make a more audible sound as it made contact.

"Speak English mother-fucker."

"Hey man, don't hit me no more with that flashlight," the driver whined in the slow lyrical street English of East Los Angeles.

It took only ten more minutes for Ray Silva to gather the information his partner needed to complete her investigation. The driver "found" his license in the trunk of his car and gave a statement about what happened in the accident. Ray Silva ran his correct name through the computer and he came back with a suspended license, but no warrants for his arrest.

"Let's go partner," he told Red Wolff as they got back in their patrol car and headed for the hospital, leaving the driver standing on the street next to his car wondering what just happened.

———

They made the short ride to the hospital in silence. At the hospital they contacted the young girl's mother and father. They told the officers their daughter was in the emergency room. She needed a couple of stitches, but she was going to be fine.

"I'll drive so you can work on your report," Ray Silva told his partner when they left the hospital.

"Okay," Red Wolff replied in a voice just above a whisper, her eyes fixed straight ahead.

They drove in silence, the occasional radio calls between other units the only sound within the patrol vehicle. Ray Silva used the quiet deserted streets to cross from the east side of the city, through Chinatown, then north on the Pasadena Freeway to Dodger Stadium. The main stadium entrance was uphill, twelve lanes wide, leading to the parking lot. In the off-season, or late at night, it was the perfect place for officers to park and write reports. Ray Silva positioned the patrol car with the rear end up against the side of the hill and killed the engine.

"Okay, let's get this over with," Ray Silva started. "You're trying to figure out what just happened."

"You're damn right!" Red Wolff exclaimed angrily. "I didn't sign up for this. I thought we were supposed to help people and enforce the law, not hit them."

"Who says we didn't help people tonight?"

"Who did we help?" Red Wolff's tone was angry and incredulous.

"Well, that little girl in the hospital and her family for one. At least now they'll have the correct name of the guy who hit them and the name of his insurance company."

Red Wolff paused for a moment to digest that thought, then continued, "But our job is to enforce the law, the courts are supposed to administer justice."

"Red, you're still a true believer. I'm not. I've seen too much, and seen how the court system fails everyone. People don't go to court to get justice; they go to court to get injustice. Think about it, the average person hardly ever has contact with the police, or the courts. Sure, they might get a ticket now and then, or be involved in a civil matter, but for the most part the justice system is not even on their bubble. Little assholes like our buddy tonight thrive on the fact the courts and jails can't handle the sheer volume of people who find themselves in the system. Drug dealers, murderers, thieves, drunks, they all go to court to get their injustice. If there was justice, they would get long sentences. They know the system will allow them to plea bargain their charge down to a minor offense. That guy knew we wouldn't waste time taking him to jail to find out who he was and even if we did, the worst that would happen would be the courts giving him probation for driving with a suspended license."

"So what's the answer?" Red Wolff asked, staring out the windshield into the city lights of L.A. in the distance.

"There isn't one Red, the system is broken, and it won't get fixed until people hurt bad enough. When they hurt bad enough they'll demand more jails, more cops, more courts, and they'll elect the politicians to do it. Until then, it's Career Decision Number Two time. Yeah, what I did tonight was wrong, no question. The only thing I hurt on that guy though, was his pride. He tried to run a scam and got caught. You have to decide whether you turn me in to the sergeant, or whether you go through your career recognizing that Lady Justice sometimes needs a little help."

"That's an awful lot to digest. What if he comes to the office and files a complaint?" she asked.

"He won't, his pride won't let him," Ray Silva replied, starting the patrol car and heading back onto the freeway.

After a couple of minutes Red Wolff spoke again, "So how'd you know he spoke English?"

From the Harbor Freeway, Ray Silva took the Sixth Street exit and headed into the seedy part of downtown. The bus station takes up the whole block at Sixth and Main Streets. The station is lit up all night, and there is a constant flow of night people up and down the street. Many are new arrivals just off the bus, some are homeless, others looking to work a scam, or panhandle a little money. By and large, however, they're all young Mexican males. Most are illegal, just across the border, looking for work.

"Look how they're dressed," he told Red Wolff, "Blue jeans, heavy work shirts, winter jackets, dirty baseball caps, backpacks, big brown paper bags with their possessions. Most of them have fairly long hair and their demeanor is submissive, eyes down, shoulders hunched, mostly trying to look invisible. Now think about that guy tonight. Khaki pants pulled up high around his waist, a sleeveless white T-shirt, a black Fedora with the rim turned down, classic East L.A. "low-rider" dress. His hair was buzzed and he stood in an arrogant way with his arms folded across his chest trying to stare you down. Do you think one of those guys in front of the bus station would dress or act like that?"

"How come I didn't pick up on the difference before?"

"Because you didn't know what to look for," he told her. "Red, you've got the makings of a good cop, but it takes a while to put it all together. Give it some time."

"Anything in addition to the way he was dressed?" she asked.

"Oh yeah, when I checked out his car I turned on the radio. It was tuned to Huggy Boy."

"Who the hell is Huggy Boy?"

"He's a local D.J. who plays fifties and sixties Doo-Wop music. Only low-riders and old guys like me listen to it. If our guy didn't speak English, he would have been listening to a Spanish station.

"Why didn't you tell me he spoke English at the scene?"

"You didn't ask."

"You're an asshole Silva," she laughed, as he guided the patrol car back toward their beat.

The rest of their three months working together were fairly uneventful. More drunks to arrest, two fatal accidents, a major freeway closure involving an overturned gasoline tanker, drug possession arrests, gang-bangers with guns, and a couple of high speed pursuits. Red Wolff experienced the full range of things that go along with being a highway cop in L.A. She also spent a great deal of time, unsuccessfully, trying to draw her partner into conversations about his personal life. She wasn't being nosy, it was simply the kind of conversation you had with your partner to find out more about them.

When it came time to sign up for the next quarter, it was a natural Red Wolff and Ray Silva would decide to work together again. They made a good graveyard team.

CHAPTER SEVEN

As Ray Silva already knew, and Red Wolff was finding out, being a California Highway Patrol Officer was not a hard job. It is sometimes dangerous, no question. But for the most part, if officers did things the way they were trained, the job was easy enough. Easy enough to have time to mind other peoples' business.

The average Highway Patrol Officer has above average intelligence, and they find out soon enough the job can get boring without some intrigue and controversy.

Antonio "Tony" Martinez fit that description perfectly.

An eight year veteran, he'd worked in Central his entire career. Born and raised in Los Angeles, he was handsome in the Fernando Lamas way. He was light skinned, tall and thin, with a Latin charm he exploited constantly. In his tight fitting motorcycle breeches and black riding boots, he cut a dashing figure in uniform, a fact he also exploited constantly. He went through women like a full-sized American car went through a tank of gas.

Most officers who'd worked with him for awhile knew he was a snake. More specifically, he was a lazy snake. Always the last to answer his radio for a call, he showed up at incidents willing to help, but never in time to be the lead investigator. He'd also cut a wide swath through the female officers in Central. New female officers fell for his smooth line and charm, even though he was married.

In an era before cell phones were small, cheap, and readily available to everyone, Tony Martinez carried two pagers, one for everyday use, and one for his girlfriends. He was married before he came on the job, so his wife believed everything he told her about his work activities. It was not unusual for him to "have" to go to Sacramento numerous times a year for training he told her, or to receive a page which meant a "callout" at night.

Being gay had not been an issue for Red Wolff throughout her break-in period or her first three months on graveyard with Ray Silva. It was such a non-issue between Red and her partner, it hadn't even come up as a subject of conversation.

Tony Martinez made it an issue. Although he was a snake, he still had a small following of fellow motorcycle riders who he manipulated in his conversations at coffee or lunch breaks.

It was subtle at first. A condom in her mailbox, a pink ribbon taped to her locker, or the word "queer" written next to her name on the shift sign-up schedule.

Red Wolff and Ray Silva had worked a routine graveyard shift on Thursday night. He'd completed all his paperwork, and gotten out of the office to head home by 6:20. She had court that morning which meant sticking around the office until it was time to drive to the court building. It was just a traffic ticket and she was done by 10:30.

Ray Silva was at his usual place in the briefing room Friday night when Red Wolff came in. He could see immediately she was mad. Grabbing a chair next to her partner she sat down hard and didn't speak.

"What's up Red?" he asked.

"Nothing!" came the reply in a tone that meant something was definitely on her mind.

"What?" he asked again.

"Later."

After roll call they headed for the parking lot to check out their vehicle before driving to their beat.

"What's going on Red?"

"Let's go over to my car," she said pointing to her personal vehicle, anger in her voice.

She spoke as she opened the trunk. "This morning when I got back from court, I found this in the front seat," pointing to a twelve inch long rubber dildo.

"Damn, did you tell the sergeant?" her partner asked.

"You fucking right I told the sergeant, who told the lieutenant, who told the captain, who laughed and said, boys will be boys. Then he wanted to know if it was mine, or if maybe some other female put it there. He said he didn't have enough information to formally investigate, and the asshole didn't even want the God-damn thing as evidence."

"Look Red, this sucks, but there isn't much you can do about it except file a complaint over the captain's head. Let's keep our eyes open and see if somebody sticks their head up. One thing about the jerk-offs in this office, they can't keep their mouths shut for long."

Still fuming, Red Wolff agreed, and they went to work.

Ray Silva was right, it didn't take long for someone to stick their head up.

It was a busy Friday night, Saturday morning. By the end of their shift, Red Wolff had a drunk driving arrest and a possession of drugs for sale arrest reports to finish writing. Ray Silva had a major injury collision involving three cars and a drunk driver report to complete.

On graveyard it's possible for the passenger officer to write some reports while their partner drives. Other reports simply need to be written without distraction or the motion of a moving car. Red Wolff and Ray Silva returned to the office about five that morning to get a jump on the reports they had to finish.

Weekend mornings around a CHP office have a different feel than weekday mornings. Because the business office is closed on weekends, there are fewer people around. The civilian office staff, automotive service technicians, the officers who work office support jobs and management are all off on the weekends. The front part of the office is blacked out and the shutters closed. The only comings and goings are during shift change.

Both officers stowed their gear in their respective locker rooms and headed for the large debriefing room. The big center table in the middle of the room had ample space for twenty officers to do their reports. Officers were beginning to trickle in for day shift and both the graveyard and day shift sergeants were in their office. Red Wolff and Ray Silva had completed a good deal of their paperwork by the time the officers in the other seven graveyard units made their way into the room.

As usual, there was the initial banter between officers about this arrest or that accident, but soon everyone fell into completing their required paperwork, activity logs, and reports. A couple of officers finished their reports quickly and headed for the locker room to change clothes and go home.

Day shift briefing finished about six and most of the officers left the office to begin their day. A couple of day shift officers filtered into the report writing room to restock on report forms, or to complete unfinished paperwork from a previous shift. One of those officers was Tony Martinez.

He sat on the opposite side and opposite end of the big center table from Ray Silva and his partner. The room was fairly quiet except for the sound of paper rustling, or the occasional conversation between partners. The graveyard sergeant stuck his head in the room on his way home and told his troops he would see them tonight.

Shortly thereafter the day shift sergeant came by on his way out to patrol, reminding the dozen or so officers in the room that the last person to leave needed to be sure the back door was closed and the gate to the parking lot was locked. After the day shift sergeant left everyone in the room went back to their paperwork.

"Hey Silva, I heard your partner found a present in her car yesterday," Tony Martinez smirked with a tone in his voice designed to elicit a response.

Red Wolff started out of her chair only to be restrained by her partner's arm across her chest. "I told you someone would stick his head up. You're on probation, let him talk," Ray Silva told her in a hushed voice.

The lack of a response emboldened Tony Martinez. "I see you two are signing up to work together again. You changing teams Silva, or you going to switch hit?"

The two made eye contact for several seconds, then Tony Martinez turned his gaze back to the paperwork he was doing.

Ray Silva didn't have a temper. Everything he did was calculated and controlled. Slowly he got up from his chair and walked around the table toward the other officer.

Tony Martinez caught Ray Silva's movements in his peripheral vision but kept his head down, pretending he didn't see the approaching officer. That was a mistake, because he also didn't see Ray Silva pull his service weapon from his holster. The next thing he felt was the hard steel barrel against his temple.

"Okay Martinez, time to put your "cojones" on the table. You've got two choices. You either apologize to my partner, or sit there and let your "machismo" override that pea brain of yours, in which case I will kill you stone dead." Ray Silva's voice was calm, and deliberate.

Tony Martinez tried to squirm away from the barrel of the gun against his head, but Ray Silva only pressed it harder into his temple.

Tony Martinez was a snake, but he wasn't a stupid snake. Without hesitating, he apologized to Red Wolff. He then picked up his gear and hastily left the office.

About half the officers in the room went back to writing their reports, the other half deciding that the reports could wait, grabbed their equipment and left the room also.

"What the crap was that?" Red Wolff demanded.

"Come on Red, we'll finish the reports tonight. Let's go get a beer."

The Shortstop was a cops' bar near Dodger Stadium. It was almost exclusively the domain of LAPD officers. Open at six a.m., it catered to patrol officers who worked the night shift in the morning hours, and detectives and administrators who worked normal business hours, in the evening.

Ray Silva was known by more than a few of the LAPD officers in the place. Grabbing two beers from the bartender, he found the table where his partner was seated. As soon as he sat down she spoke.

"Ray, I don't need you to fight my battles for me."

Raising his hand to cut her off, he looked directly into her eyes and interrupted. "It wasn't your battle to fight, it was mine."

"You're not gay, I am," she replied, loud enough that a few officers at adjacent tables looked their way.

"Your being gay was only a small part of what just happened. What it was really about, is Career Decision Number Three."

"What are you talking about?" she asked, totally confused.

"Look Red, assholes like Martinez are with us always. They look for people to bully, for people who won't stand up to them. They love to stick their noses into other peoples' business and create issues where they don't exist. They get away with it because nobody ever stands up to them."

"I can stand up for myself," she said firmly.

"I know that Red, but he wanted to see if I would stand up for you." Ray Silva put strong emphasis on the word "I." "Besides, do you know what they call a probationary officer who gets into a confrontation with another officer?"

She shook her head no.

"Unemployed."

"So why did you stand up for me? And why isn't my lifestyle an issue for you like it seems to be for a lot of the jerk-offs we work with?"

"You've been trying for months to draw me into conversations about my personal life, what I did before the Highway Patrol, girlfriends, my family. Red, I've always made it a habit to never let people get too close. To answer your questions I'll have to tell you about Billy Walker."

Red Wolff sipped at her beer as her partner began his story.

"First, you have to understand the context of the times. When I grew up there was no such thing as being gay or lesbian. There were fags, queers, homos, and dykes. Words like "alternate lifestyle" didn't exist. Men who liked men were feared and steered clear of so they didn't make you their next target. They were thought of as sissies and fair game to beat up. I was nineteen when I went to Vietnam. I'd been "in-country" for about two months when this FNG got assigned to the squad I was in."

"What's an FNG?" Red Wolff asked.

"Fucking New Guy. Anyway, his name was Billy Walker. He was almost twenty-six when he lost his student deferment and got drafted. Hell, he was older than everyone in the company except the first sergeant. He only weighed about a hundred thirty pounds, and was really effeminate looking. The guys in the squad immediately pegged him as a fag, and they hounded him unmercifully. And before you ask, so did I. At base camp one night, he got beat up pretty bad by two guys who didn't want a queer in their tent. And no, I didn't beat him up, but I didn't try to stop it either. Two days later our company got helicoptered from base camp to a fire base on a remote hilltop. We did missions into the jungle everyday looking for the enemy and never found shit. On our third night, the North Vietnamese began probing our perimeter. They probed for two nights. I was assigned a fighting hole with Billy Walker. With two men to a hole, one guy can sleep a couple of hours while the other stands watch. I was too scared to sleep, so Billy Walker and I talked. You following all of this?"

She nodded yes, and signaled to the bartender for two more beers.

"So, I told Billy I was sorry he'd gotten beat up and that I hadn't done anything to help him. He just smiled and said it was okay. A couple of minutes later Billy shifted position in the hole and his arm accidentally brushed against mine. I thought he was making a move on me so I instinctively pulled back. Billy just laughed, and told me I wasn't his type. Then he told me something I've never forgotten and something I've always tried to live by ever since. He told me that being gay or straight, black or white, tall or short, smart or dumb isn't what you really are. He said, "You are, what you do, when it counts." He no more than got those words out when the shit hit the fan. It was obvious it wasn't a probe. The NVA rockets and mortars came first, then you could hear them at the perimeter wire. There were hundreds of them, and they were all coming at our squads' position. The sergeant called in supporting artillery fire and everyone was firing as fast as we could, but they just kept coming. Our squad machine gun was in the hole next to us, about five meters away. They took a direct hit from a mortar round and both of the guys were killed. The M-60 was the only real firepower our squad had. The next thing I see is Billy Walker running to the hole where the machine gun was. There are bullets flying everywhere, noise, and the NVA are inside the perimeter wire within a few yards of our position. All of a sudden, the machine gun starts back into action. I looked over, and there is Billy Walker, all one hundred and thirty pounds of him, standing at the top of the hole, firing the machine gun from the hip, yelling "Come on you cocksuckers" at the North Vietnamese. He kept on standing there, firing and yelling. It seemed like a long time, but it was probably only a minute or so before he'd broken the back of the NVA attack all by himself. The next morning we counted forty-three dead North Vietnamese in front of his position. Anyway, ten seconds after he stopped firing, he caught a burst from an AK-47 in the chest that blew him back into the hole. He was dead before he hit the ground."

Ray Silva stopped relating his narrative as his eyes got watery and he took a drink of beer. Red Wolff watched as he continued.

"The little fucker saved all our asses that night. I tried to get the first sergeant to put him in for a medal but he wouldn't do it. He was an old-timer, from someplace like East Bumfuck Mississippi or Alabama. He said, "There wasn't no fag, gonna get no medal, in his company." A couple of weeks later, back at base camp, somebody fragged him while he was on the shitter. He got a butt full of shrapnel and a trip home."

"What does fragged mean?" Red Wolff asked.

"It means one of his own men tried to get him. In the case of the asshole first sergeant, somebody tossed a grenade into the latrine while he had his pants down."

Red Wolff searched her partner's eyes to see any trace of whether Ray Silva had been that somebody. His eyes remained impassive.

"So, that's the story of Billy Walker, and why I did what I did this morning. It's also Career Decision Number Three. This career decision doesn't involve telling the sergeant, it only involves what Billy Walker said, that you are, what you do, when it counts."

"You could get fired for what you did," Red Wolff said to her partner.

"Maybe, let's wait and see how it plays out."

They finished their beers in silence.

Just before they were ready to leave, Red Wolff looked at her partner and asked, "How do you know when it's Career Decision Number Three time?"

"You'll know."

Nobody reported the incident between Ray Silva and Tony Martinez to a supervisor. But everyone was talking about it, and eventually, management heard about it too. A formal investigation was initiated.

Since he was the supposed victim, the first to be interviewed was Tony Martinez. He denied any knowledge of the incident. As the suspect in the investigation, Ray Silva was interrogated by a sergeant and lieutenant. He also denied anything had happened.

There were ten other people in the room when the incident occurred. It's an amazing fact of police work that so many trained observers can see or hear nothing. Everyone who was in the debriefing room was interviewed. Each was asked what they saw or heard. The answers the investigators got ran the gamut from, "My attention must have been diverted," or "I was on the phone," or "I was picking up my pencil from the floor and didn't see anything." In the end nothing in the way of disciplinary action ever came of the incident.

The incident did, however, have an unexpected benefit.

Motorcycle officers park their motors in the back parking lot of the office when they attend briefing and when they are writing reports. When they do, they leave their riding gloves on their motorcycles. Three days after the incident, Tony Martinez left his motor in just such a way while he attended roll call. When briefing was over, he lingered around the office, as usual, finding reasons not to go immediately to work. When he did finally head for the parking lot, he followed his usual routine of sitting on the motorcycle, putting his helmet on, then lastly pulling his gloves on one at a time. When he slipped his hand into his left glove, he found an obstruction which caused him to push harder. When he pulled his hand out, he found somebody had filled his glove with dog shit. Tony Martinez was finding out that being a jerk-off had its consequences.

Two days later he made a stop on a car for speeding. The car had three gang-bangers inside. When the driver couldn't produce registration, he ran the plate on the vehicle. The vehicle came back within seconds as stolen. He immediately gave his location and called for back-up. Normally, a call for back-up would cause every unit within miles to answer that they were responding to assist. Today, the radio was silent. After almost thirty seconds with no unit answering the call for back-up, the communications operator started calling units to see if they could respond to help. Each unit she called had a reason why they couldn't. Finally a sergeant answered that he was responding, but he had an extended ETA because of his distance from Martinez's location. In situations where an officer has requested help, other officers forego using the radio for routine calls until the situation is under control, or Code 4 in cop talk. The radio remained silent until a female voice was heard to say "Kind of lonely out there, huh?" The suspects in Tony Martinez's stolen car were taken into custody without incident. They never found out who the female voice belonged to. The following day, Tony Martinez put in a transfer request.

Red Wolff and Ray Silva continued as partners on and off for the next three years. Red Wolff's skills and abilities were obvious to her supervisors, and she was tasked occasionally with becoming an FTO for new officers. She was also used as an Officer-in-Charge when a supervisor was not available. She'd become a confident, highly knowledgeable officer, who was respected by her peers and recognized by her supervisors. For his part, Ray Silva remained on graveyard, working with the occasional new officer, but never involving himself much with anything other than patrol work.

Over the years, they became close personal friends and Ray Silva did let her close regarding his personal life. She found out he'd been married briefly early in his career and had an eight year old daughter who lived with her mother in Ventura, about fifty miles north of L.A.

Red Wolff and Ray Silva saw each other once in a while on a social basis, he with his semi-steady girlfriend, and she in the company of a different woman each time. He didn't think anything about it, after all, he told himself, Red Wolff was young. And besides, based on his track record, he was not in any position to judge.

Things of great importance seem to happen in threes. So it was with Red Wolff and Ray Silva. On patrol one night in their third year working together, Ray Silva announced he was transferring. He explained to his partner that his mom was getting older and since his father died, she was going downhill fast. He was going to transfer home to care for her. Over the course of their shift, Ray Silva told Red Wolff about Crescent City, the Redwood trees, the rain, and the small town where he grew up. She was obviously saddened by the news, but she knew from her childhood as a navy brat, transfers happened and even good friends have to go eventually.

That same night Red Wolff told her partner she'd decided to take the sergeants test. Ray Silva wasn't surprised. She was smart, tough, and a good "Highway Copper." He told her she would make a great sergeant and he'd work for her anytime.

The third important thing that happened that night would have lifelong significance for Red Wolff. Late in their shift they received a call of a disabled vehicle blocking traffic. When they got to the scene they found a vehicle stalled in a curve in the right hand lane. Red Wolff jumped out of the passenger side of the patrol vehicle to talk to the lone occupant of the stalled car, a female in her late twenties, while Ray Silva turned on the emergency lights and stayed behind the wheel. Red Wolff explained to the female driver that her partner was going to push her vehicle out of the road and all she had to do was steer her stalled car to the shoulder. Using the specially installed heavy steel push bumper, Ray Silva easily pushed the car out of the road as he'd done thousands of times before. They got the lane clear, and even though it was completely off the road, the disabled vehicle was still in a dangerous location, in a curve, with no overhead street lighting.

Red Wolff moved to the front of the car and motioned the female driver to join her. Her partner walked up a few seconds later. The female driver explained she was driving from San Diego to the Bay Area to see some friends when the car just died. She was dressed casually in blue jeans and a light sweater. Ray Silva noted she was clean cut, pretty, with short blond hair, and a nice figure. Her car was no great shakes, an older model Toyota.

Ray Silva saw the small blue Department of Defense decal in the lower driver's side window. The military used these decals to identify service people driving their personal vehicles at the entrance gates to their bases. He also noted the decal indicated she was an officer.

"You in the service?" he asked.

"Not anymore, just got out today," came the reply.

His partner now jumped in. "Well, you're not in a great spot here, want us to call you a tow truck?"

"Sure, I belong to Triple-A."

Red Wolff used the epaulet mike attached to the portable radio on her gun belt to call for the tow truck.

Within a minute, the dispatcher came back telling her the tow truck had been called with an ETA of about twenty minutes.

"Why don't you have a seat in your car, you'll be safer," Red Wolff told her. "We'll stand by here until the tow truck gets you to a better location."

Taking Red Wolff's advice, the female driver got back in her car and the two partners went back to their patrol vehicle.

Red Wolff and Ray Silva sat in their patrol car for a couple of minutes until she told him she was going back up to the disabled car to talk to the driver. Ray shrugged and told her to go ahead. He would work on his reports.

Within twenty minutes the tow truck arrived and removed the disabled vehicle. As soon as the tow truck left, Red Wolff jumped back in the passenger seat of the patrol car. She had a half-smile on her face.

"Why are you smiling like a cat eating shit?" her partner asked.

"I got a date!" Red Wolff replied with a bounce in her voice.

"You mean she was gay?" Ray Silva said incredulously. "How did you know she was gay, and how in the hell are guys like me supposed to tell?" There was mock anger in his voice.

Red Wolff just smiled back at him. "I could tell and guys like you will just have to take your chances."

"Life's a bitch, then you die," Ray Silva moaned, shaking his head as they drove away.

Some days on the Highway Patrol seem to go by in an instant. Others seem like they will never end. Likewise, the weeks go by slow, but the years add up quickly.

Ray Silva got his transfer to Crescent City and Red Wolff was promoted to sergeant. She also got a new partner, not a Highway Patrol partner, but a life partner. The date with the female disabled motorist became a steady relationship.

Mary Jean Snider turned out to have been a lieutenant commander in the navy, a Seahawk helicopter pilot, and a veteran of the War on Terrorism. She'd sustained a permanent injury to her left leg when her helicopter had been shot down on a rescue mission in Afghanistan. The injury rendered her unable to return to flight status with the navy, but she landed a job flying news helicopters in L.A.

They dated for several months before making the decision to live together. Their equally weird work schedules meant they saw each other sometimes only in passing in the mornings or evenings, but their relationship grew, and each knew they had found a partner for life.

Red Wolff had always been active in sports and physical activity. She and her new partner joined several women's softball leagues and with the mild Southern California weather, they had games almost every weekend. The teams were made up of a wide variety of women, some professional, some blue collar, some housewives, some straight, and some gay. Through their involvement with softball, Red Wolff and Mary Jean Snider became more involved in gay activism and gay pride.

Red Wolff also competed in the California Police Olympics. The California Police Olympics are the third largest organized Olympic Games in the world, behind only the World Olympic Games and the Pan-American Games. The California games have every type of event the regular Olympics have, plus many additional competitions. One of the competitions specific to the Police Olympics is called "Toughest Cop Alive" or TCA for short. TCA is eight events, all conducted in one day. The events are a 5 kilometer uphill run, a sixteen pound shot-put, 100 meter sprint, 100 meter freestyle swim, 20 foot rope climb, a bench press, and a 200 yard obstacle course. Competitors gain points for their performance in each event and the one with the most points at the end of the day is "Toughest Cop Alive." There were twenty-three competitors in the women's division. Many were bigger physically than Red Wolff, but none had more stamina and inner drive to win. She beat her closest competitor by over a hundred points. Nobody who knew her was surprised.

When she made sergeant she had to transfer to where there was a vacancy. In this case it was an adjacent CHP office in the L.A. Basin, which meant she didn't have to move, and her partner didn't have to think about giving up her job flying for the news station.

—————

As a newly promoted sergeant, Red Wolff went to the bottom of the seniority list at her new assignment. Consequently, she found herself on graveyard shift again, this time as supervisor to a bunch of new officers like she'd been years ago. New officers present their own set of challenges to supervisors. Being young, new, and aggressive, is a combination that often results in mistakes in judgment, especially when driving. Much of her time was spent filling out reports of patrol car accidents, officers being injured and investigating citizens' complaints because of improper actions by her inexperienced graveyard crew. Still, it was exciting work, particularly at major incidents where she found herself the senior CHP supervisor on-duty making decisions and interacting with supervisors from other agencies.

Over the course of the next several years, Red Wolff worked her way up in seniority among the sergeants in her new office. When an opening came for a motorcycle riding supervisor, she jumped at the chance. The fact she had never in her life ridden a motorcycle was a minor detail.

Red Wolff knew the CHP's motorcycle school in Sacramento was one of the toughest police motorcycle training courses in the nation. With a fifty percent washout rate, the first thing she had to do before going to training was learn to ride a motorcycle.

There were always one or two spare motorcycles parked at the office. Enlisting the help of one of the experienced motor officers, Red Wolff could be found after work every day, riding the spare motor around the parking lot. Almost every motor officer would stop and offer her suggestions, or show her how to negotiate the cone patterns they set up for her, something they would have avoided doing had she not been such a good sergeant and so well respected by her troops. After practicing for two weeks, Red Wolff went to the Department of Motor Vehicles and got a motorcycle endorsement for her driver's license. Now street legal, she borrowed the personal motorcycle of one of her officers and began riding on the streets of L.A. After gaining confidence on city streets, she ventured out on the freeways, and within a few days was comfortable riding anywhere.

Motor school in Sacramento wasn't a snap, but she was good enough to make it through the training. She returned to L.A. and after three weeks of on-the-job break-in by a motorcycle training officer, she was ready to begin her new duties as a riding supervisor.

On a personal level, as a riding sergeant, she was exempt from working graveyard shift, making her hours more compatible with Mary Jean's.

Red Wolff worked as a riding sergeant for the next six years. Life was good. Her relationship with her partner grew solid as they found commonality in the things they liked and friends they had. In the years since she joined the Highway Patrol, management had become more and more intolerant of discrimination based on sexual preference. Incidents that Red Wolff endured early in her career became almost nonexistent. That didn't always mean those in high places approved of gays on the Highway Patrol, it only meant they recognized their obligation to adhere to state law. As a sergeant, she was often sought out by gay officers, both male and female, when they had an issue related to their lifestyle.

Still, Red Wolff and Mary Jean Snider were realists and they knew in a world where they were the minority, certain social mores had to be observed. They appeared together at all the Highway Patrol social functions, Christmas parties, picnics, and Law Enforcement Appreciation Days. They were careful not to flaunt being a couple by holding hands, kissing, or other displays of affection they knew would be the subject of gossip.

Over the ensuing years, she'd only seen Ray Silva once. She and Mary Jean had taken a weeks vacation and driven up Highway 101 from L.A. to Crescent City. It was every bit as beautiful as he had described it many years before when they were graveyard partners. What struck Red Wolff and her partner was the vast isolation of the place, the small town atmosphere, and the low cost of housing.

Ray Silva had purchased a piece of property three miles north of town on a hillside with a one hundred eighty degree view of the ocean two miles in the distance. He'd built a multi-level home with large balconies on the ocean side which allowed him to see Crescent City to the south, and Oregon to the north. Red Wolff and Mary Jean stayed with him for two nights. They ate fresh crab, drank wine, and reminisced about their time working together. The next day they started early on their sixteen hour drive back to L.A.

By 2005 Red Wolff was ready to take the next step up the career ladder to lieutenant. Lieutenant is a lousy rank on the Highway Patrol unless you are an area commander in a small rural county. Most lieutenant jobs involve being an administrator, working for a captain, in a large metropolitan command. The hours are lousy, there is no overtime and depending on the captain, the lieutenant ends up doing all the work, while the captain gets to come and go as they please. Conventional wisdom was, the only reason you would ever want to be a lieutenant, was so you could get promoted to captain.

Still, Red Wolff knew it was the next step in her career, and so, she began studying the hundreds of CHP manuals in preparation for the written test. Out of one hundred forty-five competitors statewide, Red Wolff placed number seven. All she had to do now was wait until the six people ahead of her were promoted and a vacancy opened for her.

Up until 1984, there was a section of Los Angeles County that was an enclave completely surrounded by the city of Los Angeles. West Hollywood was at one time a seedy part of L.A. known for its gambling dens, prostitution, and residents who were free spirits. Over the years, it became a more and more popular place to live, as the newly rich discovered reasonable prices for homes and businesses, and the movie industry discovered its quaint architecture for location filming. It also became a Mecca for people living alternate lifestyles and, consequently, gay activism.

The West Hollywood Gay Pride Parade had been a tradition since 1970. Held every June, the parade drew less than five thousand people in the early days, mostly all gay. Year after year the event grew bigger and bigger and was soon attracting over thirty-five thousand people of all different lifestyles, including families with children and a host of major corporate sponsors.

The California Highway Patrol, like all police agencies, always has a hard time recruiting new officers when the economy is good. In the early part of the new century, California's economy was booming and finding new officers, regardless of their sexual orientation, was always a challenge. Recruiting in the gay community was especially hard given the natural suspicion of gay people toward the police.

The Highway Patrol in Los Angeles has to compete against the L.A. Sheriff's Department, LAPD, and over forty different smaller police departments for the limited number of persons interested in a career in law enforcement. As a consequence, every department tries to find innovative ways to make in-roads into the different ethnic communities in L.A. to attract new recruits. In the gay community, both the Los Angeles Sheriff's Department and LAPD participate in the West Hollywood Gay Pride Parade. These agencies allow gay officers, both male and female, to march in the parade, in uniform, and set up recruiting booths near the parade site.

The Highway Patrol had never sanctioned participation in this event. Part of the reason was political, because as a state agency, any participation could be seen as an endorsement of a gay lifestyle by the Governor, and part of the reason was the Highway Patrol's management.

Every year for three years Red Wolff had requested permission from management for gay CHP officers to participate in this event. Her written request laid out concisely all of the advantages of participating in the parade, recruitment, community outreach, and traffic safety. The request went from the Highway Patrol's headquarters in L.A. to the main CHP headquarters in Sacramento. Each year the request was denied without explanation.

The Highway Patrol is commanded by a Commissioner who is appointed by the Governor. The position is extremely political and only those with the backing of key politicians have a chance at the top job. The Commissioner is responsible to the Governor for what the Highway Patrol does, but at the same time has great latitude in day-to-day operations. So, while the Commissioner adheres to and follows state law in regards to sexual orientation and discrimination, they have the ability to use their discretion on other issues such as participating in alternate lifestyle events.

In the case of the Gay Pride Parade, it was simply a matter of the Commissioner saying, in private of course, "I don't want those fucking freaks marching in a parade in a CHP uniform."

The Highway Patrol officially participated in many cultural and ethnic events, of which there are dozens in Los Angeles County. The Martin Luther King Day Parade in South Los Angeles, the Cinco de Mayo celebration in East Los Angeles, Breast Cancer charity runs, and AIDS walks, were but a few of the events where there was an official CHP presence. Year after year, however, the Highway Patrol was conspicuously absent from the Gay Pride Parade.

Red Wolff made the decision to march in the parade, in uniform, in spite of what she knew could be disastrous consequences for her career. In her mind, it was simply time to force the issue with CHP management.

She shared her plan with several other gay Highway Patrol officers from around the Los Angeles area. Of the twenty or so officers she contacted, six others, four female and two male, marched with her in the parade, in uniform.

Just as she had foreseen, the consequences were swift and harsh. The six other officers were each given thirty days off without pay. Red Wolff was given the same thirty days off and, because she was a sergeant, the highest ranking person to march in the parade, she was removed from the lieutenants' promotional list. It would take several more years and a new Commissioner, before gay CHP officers could march in the parade.

———

While doing her thirty days off, Red Wolff took stock of her life. She was now in her late thirties. She had been on the Highway Patrol for almost fifteen years and she was a sergeant, which she figured she would remain for the rest of her career. She was riding a motorcycle, had a rock solid relationship with her lifetime partner, and for the most part, life was good.

Still she felt something was missing. She'd worked L.A. her entire career and it was beginning to become boring. Los Angeles was growing more and more crowded, crime was up everywhere, traffic was even worse than when she first started and growing worse every year. It was time for a change.

Red Wolff took Mary Jean out for a seafood dinner that night and they discussed their future. Mary Jean indicated she wasn't unhappy with their current situation, but she was game for anything. She said it wouldn't bother her to stop flying her news helicopter and, if they moved, she'd always wanted to write a book.

Where to go became the topic. Red Wolff had six years seniority as a sergeant. That was enough to get a transfer to a few nice places, if there was a vacancy. They began to discuss different locations. Bakersfield? No, too hot. San Francisco? No, too expensive. Monterey? Well, maybe.

Just then the waiter brought their dinners. Both had ordered the Dungeness crab. They looked at the crab, then each other. Crescent City!

It took Red Wolff six months to get her transfer. They made several trips to Crescent City to scout out houses and the town. As it happened, there was a house for sale not far from where Ray Silva had built his home years before.

The transition from a metropolitan area to a rural one takes a while. Things ran slower in Crescent City. Both Red Wolff and her partner had to learn to slow down a little, to accept that there were no malls, no Nordstrom's, and learn how to chop wood for the stove that heated their home. They learned to see the long rainy season as a benefit of living in such a beautiful place and how to shop in Oregon where there was no sales tax. Within a few months, they were settled in and living like local people.

Red Wolff's reputation had preceded her to the Crescent City Highway Patrol Office, but it didn't seem to matter to anyone. All of the officers were experienced and knew their jobs. Her two fellow sergeants accepted her as part of the supervision team and the lieutenant was a good boss. Although the pace was a lot slower, she was happy and life was good again.

CHAPTER EIGHT

Sergeant Erin "Red" Wolff and Officer Ray Silva found a booth in the back of the coffee shop. Both ordered coffee and the prime rib sandwich special.

"What did the "loot" want?" asked Ray Silva, referring to her being called back to the office by the lieutenant.

"Stuff to do with the parade on Monday and the Governor being in town," Red Wolff replied as they ate. "Looks like we'll all be working on Monday to provide security and traffic control."

"No biggie," he tossed back, obvious disinterest in his tone. "We're both off the next two days, and Julie is in town for the long weekend. You and Mary Jean want to get together?"

"Sure, I've got to meet the guy from the Governor's Protection Detail in the morning and show him around town, but let's plan something for tomorrow night," Red Wolff answered.

While Red Wolff and Ray Silva were having dinner, Emil Lagare left his motel room and was driving around Crescent City. Daylight was fading fast and the first signs of the seasonal nighttime fog rolling in could be seen.

As he drove, he mentally recalled some of the details about the town and the surrounding area he had learned in training camp. Del Norte County had a population of about 21,000. The "E" on the name Norte was silent, making it rhyme with the English word snort. There was only one incorporated town in the county, Crescent City, with about 7,000 residents. The town's population swells in the summer with what the Americans called "snowbirds," retired people who live in the hot dry deserts in the winter, and come to the cooler coast in their motor homes during the summer.

Using the visitor map of the town he picked up in the motel lobby and remembering the detailed maps he'd studied in training camp, he was able to easily navigate his way through town. He drove north out of town on U.S.101 toward the Oregon border. Four miles north of town, at the junction of Highway 101 and Highway 199, he found the location pinpointed on the large maps in training camp. Three hundred foot tall Redwood trees bordered the highway on each side, and the lanes narrowed to only one in each direction. Finding a place to turn around he headed back toward town.

Taking the first exit he came to, Washington Boulevard, he stopped at the top of the ramp to survey the location. To his left he could see the back side of the fenced off local Highway Patrol office with several patrol cars parked in the lot. The gate to the parking lot was pulled shut and the office appeared to be closed. It was as he'd been trained, the Highway Patrol did not maintain a twenty-four operation and they were not a threat, as they only patrolled the highways.

Turning right, he proceeded along Washington Boulevard, passing the new hospital on the right and the local Wal-Mart store on the left. There were small tracts of homes on both sides of the road. Continuing west, Emil Lagare drove toward the ocean less than a mile ahead. At the ocean he saw a sign for the local airport, McNamara Field.

He turned right and entered the airport grounds. McNamara Field was a civil aviation airport located on a small peninsula just north of Crescent City. It had a five thousand foot runway which was big enough to allow commercial commuter prop-jets to provide service several times a day. The airport had only one small terminal building, a couple of metal hangers for private airplanes, and a fueling facility. Given the time of day, the terminal was closed as the last commercial flight had already landed. There were a couple of private vehicles parked in the lot, but the airport was deserted.

Leaving the airport, Emil Lagare drove south along the ocean for two miles until he was back in town. He passed several streets before he started picking up street signs with numbers. He remembered from his training that the old part of town was laid out in a grid. The street closest to the harbor was Front Street. After that, numbered streets began and increased from Second Street through Ninth Street. Streets with letter names began at the western side of town near the ocean with "A" Street and continued through the alphabet to "M" Street. He turned away from the ocean on Fifth Street where he soon encountered the county sheriff's department. His training told him the county sheriffs ran a twenty-four operation, but had only seventeen deputies. On most days there were only three deputies working the day shift, three working the afternoon shift, and sometimes only one on graveyard. He knew they always worked alone. Because the size of the area the sheriff's office patrolled was very large, often only one deputy worked around Crescent City, while the other two worked at the far ends of the county. He also knew the county sheriff provided radio communications for both themselves and the local police department.

He parked his car on the street and casually walked through the glass front doors of the sheriff's department. The inside lobby was small, but well lit. Upon entering, he walked the few steps to the front counter where he could see a middle-aged female deputy sitting in an alcove behind a radio console. When she saw Emil Lagare enter the building, she called the cellblock and within moments, a young male deputy appeared. Emil Lagare noted both deputies were in uniform, but neither wore a gunbelt. Acting like a lost French tourist, he asked for directions which the male deputy cheerfully provided. He had all the information he needed.

Leaving the sheriff's department he drove into the center of Crescent City where he soon encountered the main city and county government offices. They also were closed and only a lone city police department vehicle was parked next to the building. Crescent City Police Department he remembered had eleven officers. They worked basically the same hours as the sheriff's department and usually there were only two officers working each shift.

Continuing past the government building, Emil Lagare found himself back at an intersection with Highway 101 as it traveled through the town. Crescent City, as he learned in training camp, was one of the few remaining places along the entire thousand mile length of Highway 101 that the highway actually went through town, rather than around it. Turning right, heading south now on the main highway, he passed several gas stations, motels, a small shopping center, and the bulk of the one and two story buildings that formed the center of Crescent City. In less than a half mile the buildings ended and he was at the entrance to the large park where the July Fourth celebration would be held. The beachfront park was about the size of a football field. It had a large grassy center and was ringed with trees. Adjacent to the park he also saw the large single story community center. Emil Lagare drove through the big, mostly empty parking lot between the edge of the park and the ocean. As he scanned the park he could hear the waves breaking against the large rocks and man-made concrete forms that functioned as a breakwater.

Returning to the main highway he again turned south, almost immediately encountering the local bulk fuel storage and distribution plant on the left. The plant, like everything else on this Friday evening, was closed. A chain link fence gate on rollers pulled across the entrance. As soon as he passed the fuel plant he was at the entrance to the small boat harbor. There were two RV parks along the ocean side of the highway at the harbor entrance.

Both the parks were almost full. There were dozens of large motor homes in each park. There was also a bustle of activity as people were coming and going from the park on foot or in the small cars they disconnected from their RVs. He could see many people barbequing and other groups of people sitting around talking. Most of those, he observed, were older couples. These he deduced were the snowbirds he'd been told about.

Almost all of the dozens of motor homes looked the same. Square, flat-sided, most of them painted white. Emil Lagare drove slowly through one of the RV parks, then the other. He was checking to ensure his teams had all arrived. He would not make face-to-face contact with them tonight, he simply wanted to know they were there. Imam Nasr Ahmed knew almost all RVs looked the same. He had taken the precaution of attaching a small Oakland Raiders decal to the front and back bumpers of each of the vehicles so they could be easily identified. Just as planned, Emil Lagare found two of his team's vehicles in one RV park, and two in the other. Perfect so far, he thought to himself.

It was almost dark by now and Emil Lagare had two more locations to scout. The first was the Coast Guard station in the harbor. Slowly leaving the RV park, he drove into the parking lot at the base of the fishing pier. Parking his car in the lot, as vehicles were prohibited on the pier, he casually began strolling toward the ocean. There were many people walking slowly along, enjoying the fading sunlight, and the mirror flatness of the water in the small boat harbor.

The Coast Guard station he could see was well lit. It was a small compound. There was a twenty foot wide asphalt road leading from the pier to a chain link fence with a roller type gate in front of the compound. Just inside the gate was a one story brick building he knew was the main office for the Coast Guard detachment and just beyond that a small metal boat shed for the rigid hull Zodiac. Sitting at a right angle to the pier was the left side of the cutter. It was just as the photographs and videotape had shown. It was a perfect letter "T." The pier formed the vertical stem of the letter. The cutter crossed the top of the "T."

Emil Lagare had studied the characteristics of the boat, and knew its capabilities. The internet was a wonderful source of information. Still, he wondered why the Americans would provide such valuable data so easily. The eighty-seven foot long cutter had a crew of eleven he knew, it cost three and half million dollars to build, and was armed with two fifty caliber machine guns, plus various small arms. It also carried the latest in communications and electronic equipment.

Back in his car, Emil Lagare headed for his final location of the evening. The last strains of daylight were being overtaken by the coming darkness as he drove past the National Guard Armory. The entrance to the armory was directly off Highway 101. The armory parking lot was lit by numerous tall floodlights that cast shadows on the many light military vehicles, mostly Humvees and trucks in the lot. The armory building was set back from the street and it too had floodlights which illuminated the area around it. The fence around the entire complex was eight feet tall, topped with three strands of barbed wire. There was a guard shack at the entrance gate which was dark and empty. The main gate he could see was the type that had two twelve foot wide sections that swung open on hinges. When both sections were closed, they were held together by a heavy gauge chain and large lock. Intelligence had not been able to determine anything about the security system for the armory or parking lot, but it was assumed there were motion detectors and an alarm system which provided security when the armory was closed since there was no twenty-four hour guard. Not that it mattered, Emil Lagare thought to himself.

It had been an exhausting day. Emil Lagare was both hungry and tired. There were more locations to scout out on Saturday, plus meetings with his men. For tonight he would find something to eat, then sleep.

On Saturday morning Red Wolff met with Sergeant Mike Waters at the closed CHP office as planned, where he explained the Governor's itinerary and the time frames involved. He told her the Governor and six members of the Governor's traveling staff would arrive at the local airport on a small chartered jet around ten a.m. The commander of the Governor's Protection Detail, a CHP captain, would also be on the aircraft. At the airport, three members of the protection detail would be waiting with unmarked vehicles which they were driving up from Sacramento on Sunday. They would drive the Governor to the Fourth of July celebration at the park. Two local CHP units, plus her as the supervisor, were needed to provide escort for the motorcade. Two black and whites would be in front, one black and white at the end.

At the celebration site there would be no reviewing stand. There would be an area at the end of the beachfront park near the community center building where a podium and microphone would be set up. Numerous local dignitaries, the mayor, county supervisors, police chief and sheriff, the Highway Patrol commander, and about thirty other people would be seated in folding chairs behind the Governor. Directly in front of the podium, standing in formation, would be about a hundred National Guardsmen from the local unit that had just returned from Iraq. The public would be allowed to sit or stand all around the troops, but the local police and sheriffs would keep pathways open around the formation.

There would be the standard opening prayer, remarks by some of the local politicians, then the Governor would speak. Following her speech, the Governor would pin a campaign ribbon on the local guard unit's flag and give out a couple of medals. Once the ceremony was over, the Governor may or may not linger to shake a few hands, it varied every time. Either way he said, the protection detail would have full responsibility for the Governor's security. The local CHP officers would be responsible only for guarding the Governor's vehicles and ensuring the path was clear when the Governor was ready to go. He also wanted two local CHP officers, in uniform, to stand on each side of the dignitary section for security.

When the Governor was ready to leave the celebration, they would return to the airport. He also stated because the Governor's visit was a rare occasion in this part of the state, there would probably be television media in town and the Governor may make a few remarks to them. Red Wolff knew the closest television station was in Eureka, eighty miles south.

Once the Governor was "wheels up" Waters told her, she and her officers could go back to their normal duties. Total time the Governor was expected to be on the ground in Crescent City was less than two hours.

After explaining the itinerary to her, Waters asked Red Wolff to drive him to the airport, then along the travel route to the park. He also wanted to see where the closest hospital was, a precaution he told her that was done at every new location in case of a medical emergency.

Once in Red Wolff's patrol vehicle, she started explaining the town and the distances involved between the airport and the park.

"You ever work any protection details before?" Waters asked her.

"Yeah, a few in L.A., mostly motor escorts for the President, nothing ever involving the Governor," she replied.

As they drove from the Highway Patrol Office to check out the airport, Waters told her when the plane arrived, the entire motorcade, led by one of the local marked CHP vehicles, would drive onto the tarmac to pick up the Governor. The Governor would ride in the first unmarked vehicle, along with the CHP captain who would be in the right front seat. Waters said he would ride shotgun in the second vehicle with some of the Governor's staff. The remainder of the staff would ride in the third vehicle with a black and white bringing up the rear.

All of the protection detail, Waters explained, would be in dark colored suits, something, he added as a jab toward the officers he considered as working in the sticks, which would obviously indicate they were not from Crescent City.

What an asshole, Red Wolff thought to herself. All of her officers had fifteen to twenty years experience and they'd all done their time in L.A. or the Bay Area before getting the seniority to transfer to a place like Crescent City. They were the ones doing the everyday job the California Highway Patrol was nationally renowned for, not him and his self-important flunkies guarding the Governor. Red Wolff bit her tongue.

Waters continued, saying they would all be wearing a lapel pin with a colored California State Seal. Different colored seals were used every day as a security measure. They would be wearing a blue colored seal on Monday he told her.

After checking out the hospital and the airport, Red Wolff drove Mike Waters along the route into Crescent City and the beachfront park next to the community center. Waters indicated the community center would be used for the ceremony if it rained. They drove along Front Street which bordered the park, then turned into the entrance.

The community center had parking lots on both sides, with a twenty foot high rock and concrete breakwater behind, separating the building from the bay. There were maybe two dozen cars scattered around the parking lots, people walking around the building, a couple of families with kids using the playground equipment in the park, and some teenagers necking under one of the Redwood trees.

The three cars parked together at the far end of the east parking lot caught Red Wolff's eye. "Crap," she muttered out loud.

"What?" Mike Waters exclaimed, his senses now on high alert.

"Over there, a Del Norte felony in progress, she told him pointing to the three cars.

"What's going on, a drug deal?" he asked anxiously.

"Worse, a fish deal," Red Wolff laughed.

103

"A what?" Waters replied, totally confused, but his right hand reaching for the small frame .40 caliber Smith and Wesson semi-automatic on his hip, concealed beneath his suit coat.

"Sit tight, this will only take a second," she told him as she drove toward the three parked cars. "And relax with the gun."

As Red Wolff maneuvered the patrol car toward the parked vehicles, one of the men hurriedly slammed the trunk of his vehicle closed. One of the other men took the large newspaper wrapped item he had and tossed it into an ice chest in the bed of his pickup truck.

Stopping her patrol car with the driver's side toward the three men, Red Wolff rolled the window down and spoke to the oldest of the three, "What are you doing Joe?" she asked.

"Hi Red, we're just talking," the man replied innocently.

Indian Joe was a legend among law enforcement in the county. Sixty-seven years old, a full-blooded Mi-Wok, he'd lived in Del Norte County his whole life in a small house near the mouth of the Klamath River. He had a lengthy arrest record, mostly Fish and Game Code violations, for illegally selling the Salmon he as a Native-American could legally gill net for personal consumption, but could not sell. He also had several Driving Under the Influence arrests, and a suspended license, not that it kept him from driving. Red Wolff always cut him slack on the fishing violations, but not on the driving. She'd personally arrested him twice.

"You're not selling fish are you Joe?" Red asked, knowing full well he was.

"You know I wouldn't do that Red, I learned my lesson," Joe replied, knowing she knew he was lying.

"And you're not driving are you?"

"Nope," he answered shaking his head.

"Okay Joe. You coming to the parade on Monday?" she asked as she put the patrol car in gear to drive away.

"Never miss it Red, see you Monday," Joe waved as she drove away.

"What was that?" Mike Waters asked, his mind wondering what he had just seen.

"Po-leece work, Northern California style," Red Wolff laughed.

The briefing and tour around Crescent City took almost two hours. It was a little before eleven when they returned to the office. Waters told her he would be taking a commercial flight back to Sacramento that afternoon and he would be back Monday morning by eight. He would meet her and the Crescent City officers that morning and conduct a briefing prior to moving the motorcade to the airport.

They shook hands in front of the closed office and Waters headed for the airport. Red Wolff went inside the building to begin adjusting schedules to ensure there were enough officers to cover routine patrol, plus six officers to work the detail escorting the Governor.

There were twenty-one officers assigned to the Crescent City CHP office, but only seventeen were available to work on Monday. Two were on vacation and another had a broken arm from a collision. An additional officer was in Sacramento for training. She knew on the fourth, because of the parade and the additional traffic due to the long weekend, she would need four officers to work day shift and four more to cover swing shift. She couldn't use the officers assigned to graveyard, as they would have just gotten off at six in the morning and needed to be back at ten that evening. The easiest thing to do was to call in six officers on overtime, the six officers who were off that day. They wouldn't be happy about it, but there was no choice. She started calling officers at home. Ray Silva was one of the calls she made.

Once she had her detail all arranged, she called both the sheriff's office and the police department to talk to their on-duty supervisors to find out how many personnel they had working on Monday. In a small town, cooperation between law enforcement agencies was essential because no one agency had enough people to adequately cover everything. Personnel wise, she learned they were facing the same problems she was, covering routine patrol functions and having enough bodies to provide security for the parade and the Governor's visit. Out of the fifteen deputies on the sheriffs department available that day, seven were working regular shifts and seven were assigned to the celebration. The sheriff and the undersheriff would be sitting in the dignitary section while the Governor spoke. The police department would be assigning four of its' officers to the events surrounding the parade and Governor's visit, while five were working regular shifts. The Chief of Police would be sitting behind the Governor at the park, and one officer would be at the police station. The entire eleven person police department was committed to work on the fourth.

It was four o'clock by the time Red Wolff got everything arranged for Monday. Crappy way to spend a day off she thought as she called Ray Silva for a second time to confirm they were getting together for dinner as they'd discussed the night before.

Emil Lagare slept late Saturday morning. It was almost nine when he awoke. He washed and shaved, put on clean clothes, and ate at the fast food restaurant across the street.

He left the motel driving north on Highway 101. He returned to the National Guard Armory, slowed as he drove by, then pulled into the shopping center parking lot across the street from the armory entrance.

The scene at the armory was quite different than it had been the evening before. The front gate was open and a uniformed security guard was in the guard shack. Inside the armory parking lot Emil Lagare could see activity as groups of uniformed men and women were coming and going from the main armory building to the parking lot, other groups were involved in drill or vehicle maintenance. From his training, he knew this activity was typical of Saturdays and Sundays as the members of the unit performed their obligatory once a month weekend drill meeting.

Fox Company was part of the Forty-Seventh Combat Brigade. It was a light infantry company, composed of citizen soldiers from Northern California and Southern Oregon. The brigade had returned recently from twelve months in Iraq where it had been involved in combat operations against the growing insurgency and peacekeeping duties associated with the mounting sectarian violence.

As a light infantry company, the unit was designed to be highly mobile and was equipped with only small arms. The M-16 rifle and 9 millimeter Beretta pistols were the units' predominant weapons. Each of the nine squads in the company was equipped with two M-249 machine guns. Sufficient ammunition for these weapons was kept at the armory. There were other types of heavier weapons such as mortars, shoulder fired rocket launchers, and anti-personnel mines the company used. These weapons, however, were held at active duty military bases and were only issued when the unit was involved in annual active duty training exercises or actual combat operations.

Emil Lagare diverted his attention to the highway maintenance yard which shared a common parking lot fence with the armory. Cal-Trans is the name of California's Division of Highways. One of the largest of all California state departments, it was responsible for everything from designing and building freeways, to picking up the trash along the roads.

In Northern California, one of Cal-Trans' major responsibilities is to keep the highways open. In locations like Crescent City, where months of rain cause continual rock slides, this is a daunting and on-going job. In many places in Northern California the highways are constructed along the natural gorges carved out by rivers. Steep rock hillsides border the highways in these gorges and rockslides are a common occurrence. Cal-Trans workers clear most of the smaller slides using skip-loaders or bulldozers to simply push the rocks out of the road. Occasionally, however, an enormous rock will fall or an entire hillside will break loose, creating a quarter-mile long, fifty foot high pile of rocks, trees, dirt, and debris. For these events Cal-Trans maintenance yards are equipped with dynamite to blast the roads clear.

As he studied the layout of the Cal-Trans yard, he could see dozens of orange painted vehicles, pickup trucks, dump trucks, caterpillar tractors with bulldozer blades, and smaller skip-loaders. There was a single wood framed building which he surmised was the office and a large metal building in the rear he took to be the repair shop. The gate to the yard was locked indicating no routine activity today.

After finishing his reconnaissance of the armory and the Cal-Trans yard, Emil Lagare headed back into the center of Crescent City where he located the telephone company office. He knew by the large air conditioners in the rear of the building and the many service type vehicles parked in the fenced and closed parking lot, this was the main switching station for all land line telephones in the entire county. It was also where all the lines for security alarms protecting the businesses and government offices fed into.

Referring to the tourist map of the town, Emil Lagare drove to the only radio station in the county. He noted the station was located in an ordinary looking wood frame building with a half-glass, half-wood front door. The station had a small business office lobby which was dark, indicating it was closed.

His last stops before going to meet his men were the three microwave towers for the three different cellular telephone companies that provided service in Crescent City and the surrounding area. Each of the towers was protected by a chain link fence topped with barbed wire.

Satisfied he had toured all of the locations he'd studied in the desert, Emil Lagare headed to the harbor.

Up until this point none of his team members knew what their specific objectives were. This of course had been intentional so if any of his men were detained by American authorities they could not divulge information they did not have. They had spent countless hours in the Syrian Desert practicing their specific tasks by day and night, firing weapons, driving, marching and using explosives, but to what end, they did not know. Today they would find out.

Parking his car in the harbor lot he walked to the first motor home containing his team of drivers. Upon entering the vehicle there were the usual congratulations all around on arriving safely and thanks given to Allah.

With one of the young Muslims from Oakland driving, the motor home left the RV park and headed north on Highway 101. Emil Lagare narrated as they traveled slowly past the fuel facility, the beachfront park, the airport, and the junction of the two highways north of town. He explained the significance of each location and its' importance in the overall success of the mission. He also indicated who was assigned to each specific target. Each time Emil Lagare assigned specific members of a team their targets, there was loud cheering and shouts of Allah Akbar. Returning to the harbor area he told his team about the Coast Guard cutter. The loudest cheers were for the team assigned this objective.

Emil Lagare made three more motor home trips that day, repeating the same process of explaining and assigning specific targets to specific team members.

By four in the afternoon he'd completed his last briefing session to the last motor home full of men. He was tired again and needed some time alone to think and pray. Emil Lagare instructed his teams to maintain a low profile while in the RV park and not to draw any unnecessary attention to themselves. It would be foolish to be discovered now, he told them, when they were this close to beginning their mission. He arranged meeting times with each of the four teams on Sunday at different locations when they would do a final check of their equipment.

Red and Mary Jean got to Ray Silva's house about seven. The sun was still well above the horizon giving the Pacific Ocean a deep blue color. Within an hour the sun would be down, turning the ocean black and the entire western sky a bright blue streaked with golden patches. Even with the sun down it would still take almost forty-five minutes before it actually got dark. The fog beginning to form out at sea would soon be drawn to the shore by the warmer temperature of the land.

Red Wolff gave a courtesy knock on the front door at the same time she was turning the handle and pushing the door open.

"Yo Silva," she called. "Anyone home?"

"In here," came a female voice in reply.

Just inside the entrance, the house opened up into one giant room. The kitchen and dining room were to the left, a step down living room to the right. Almost the entire western side of the house was windows giving a one hundred eighty degree view of the ocean in the distance. The house was cozy and warm from the heat put out by the Ben Franklin wood stove in the living room.

Walking into the kitchen, Red saw Ray's long time girlfriend, Julie Bradley putting the finishing touches on a salad.

"Hi Erin, Hi Mary Jean," Julie Bradley greeted them with a smile. She always used the name Erin, never Red. After the obligatory girl hugs, Red Wolff found the opener and began uncorking the bottle of Kendall-Jackson Chardonnay she'd brought.

———

Julie Bradley and Ray Silva had been seeing each other for about four years. She was slightly over five two, a shapely one hundred fifteen pounds, with short blond hair. She was as physically strong as she was business wise tough. She lived in Marin County, just north of the Golden Gate Bridge, and commuted into San Francisco everyday where she was vice-president of a brokerage company. She started at the company twenty years before as a secretary and worked her way up through an old-fashioned work ethic, and night classes in business economics. As she began to rise in the company, she found herself more and more the lone female in a then male dominated industry. The defining moment in her career had come when she was invited to ride in the cart, while her male counterparts played a round of golf with the company's executives at an upcoming conference. Bullshit, she thought. She bought a set of clubs that night on the way home, and was taking lessons the next day. By the time of the conference, she could out drive and out putt many of the men. Her short game still needed some work. Julie Bradley was an ass-kicker.

Ray Silva met her on one of his many vacation trips to Cabo San Lucas. Cabo was only three hours by air from San Francisco, and it was in the same time zone as California so there was no jet lag.

The town of Cabo San Lucas had grown considerably in the past twenty years, losing a lot of its little fishing village charm to the plethora of glitzy clothing stores and discos that have taken over the town. Ray Silva always stayed at the Sol Mar Hotel, the last hotel on the end of the Baja Peninsula. Because the hotel was on the Pacific Ocean side of the narrow peninsula known as "Lands' End," it was blocked from the bright lights and hustle of Cabo San Lucas just over the hill on the Sea of Cortez side.

He'd seen her for several days lying by herself next to the hotel pool, and eating by herself at the restaurant in the evening. The next day the sun was its usual hot self, but the cooling breeze off the ocean had failed to materialize. Ray Silva could see Julie Bradley's body glistening from the heat. Seizing the opportunity, he bought two Pacificos, the local beer, from the pool bar and strolled over to where she was stretched out on a lounge chair, reading a book.

"You look like you could use this," he said with a smile, extending a bottle toward her, a slice of lime protruding from the open neck.

"Aren't you supposed to ask if you can buy me a drink before you actually buy it?" she said, returning his smile while looking at him over the top rim of her sunglasses. She'd stretched out the word "before" when she said it.

"At my age I can't handle the rejection," he replied with a grin.

Taking the offered beer, Julie Bradley said coyly, "Do lines like that actually work when you're trying to pickup women?"

"The jury's still out on that," he laughed as he sat down next to her.

They spent the next four days together, strolling through Cabo, haggling with shop owners over a dollar on the purchase of a trinket, or going to dinner. She let him buy the first night, but insisted on picking up the check the following evening.

Being the same age, both being divorced with grown children and both being fiercely independent, they found they had much in common. After returning to California, they settled into a steady long distance relationship. A couple times a month one of them would make the six plus hour, nearly four hundred mile drive to see the other. Although they had plenty of opportunities to see other people, both recognized they had a good thing going with each other.

Julie Bradley's curry chicken and broccoli casserole over rice was always a crowd pleaser. Dinner conversation revolved around everyone's work, upcoming vacations, and the women all taking verbal shots at Ray Silva which he shrugged off while giving as good as he got.

Then Mary Jean Snider dropped a bombshell.

"We're having a baby!" she said to Ray Silva and Julie Bradley while Red Wolff looked on.

"What?" exclaimed Julie happily.

"We just found out Monday the artificial insemination procedure worked. Mary Jean is due in March," Red Wolff said proudly.

"Oh Mary Jean, Erin, I'm so happy for you!" Julie Bradley couldn't contain herself. There were more girl hugs all around.

"Is it a boy or girl, what do you know about the father?" Julie peppered the two women with questions.

"We didn't want to know the baby's sex. We know the sperm donor's name is X-2354. He's tall, and has blue eyes. He's a lawyer from Dallas. Best sex I ever had with a man," Mary Jean laughed.

Ray Silva rolled his eyes in mock disapproval. He'd always accepted Red Wolff's sexual orientation, and besides, gay couples having babies wasn't anything new. When he could finally get a word in between all of the excited talk among the three women at the table, Ray Silva smiled and said, "Congratulations, I'm happy for you guys."

Red Wolff knew without even looking he was sincere.

By nine, the conversation had petered out. The combination of wine and the heat from the fire was making everyone sleepy.

As they got ready to leave, Red Wolff said to Julie, "Ray and I have to work Monday for the parade and Governor's visit, are you going to go and watch?"

She was mulling it over when Mary Jean said, "Let's go together Julie, we'll make a day of it. We'll pack a picnic lunch and Ray and Erin can join us when they finish with the Governor."

Julie Bradley agreed.

Both Red Wolff and Ray Silva had the day off on Sunday, a chance to sleep-in and take care of household chores. Mary Jean and Julie made plans for meeting on Monday.

———

As arranged, Emil Lagare met with the first of his teams on Sunday morning in their motor home at an ocean vista point near the airport. Equipment was removed from storage bins inside the vehicle and their individual specific missions again discussed in great detail. As he'd been trained to do, Emil Lagare reinforced in each of his men the importance of their tasks and the rewards Allah would shower on them upon their deaths.

He met with each of the other teams at different locations around Crescent City, repeating the equipment check and the specifics of that team's mission.

Emil Lagare was mentally drained by the time he finished meeting with his last team. He felt he had completed all the things he needed to do in regards to mission readiness. Locations had been scouted, equipment had been checked, and detailed briefings conducted. The spirit of his men was high and he believed all were ready to meet Allah.

He needed time now to prepare himself for his upcoming death.

CHAPTER NINE

Highway Patrol Captain Aimee Gardner was cute as a button and sharp as a tack. Standing five feet tall, and one hundred five pounds, she had mousy brown hair, a Barbie Doll figure, and flirtatious eyes. She also had a quick tongue, sharp mind, and the ability to charm everyone around her. As head of the Governor's Protection Detail she traveled everywhere the Governor went.

At thirty-four she was young to be a captain already, having just over twelve years on the job. Single, she had no shortage of men chasing after her, a practice she encouraged.

Supposedly, because it's a merit based civil service process, there is only one way to get promoted on the Highway Patrol. In reality there are two.

The first method requires having diverse experience, extensive job knowledge, and passing a promotional test. This is the "how good you are" method. It takes longer to promote this way, but it produces good, competent leaders.

The second way to promote is the "how good you look" method. Using this method all you needed to do was look good on paper and have people in high places sponsor your career. There were lots of people in management positions who promoted in this manner. Unfortunately, they knew almost nothing about the Highway Patrol, or how to lead people.

Aimee Gardner had done the Academy and break-in just like everyone else, and had actually spent three months working a beat on day watch, by herself, while assigned to the East Los Angeles CHP office. She quickly realized working patrol could be dangerous, and at five feet tall, sooner or later somebody was going to beat the shit out of her.

Every CHP command has officers assigned inside the office, to administrative jobs that don't require working patrol. Aimee Gardner wangled one of those jobs after working patrol for only three months. In the next twelve years, she would never work the street again. After working an office job for just over three and a half years, she promoted from officer to sergeant and managed to secure another administrative job, this one at headquarters in Sacramento. In her new job she rubbed elbows with, flirted with, and traded quips with, the power brokers who saw to it that after three more years she made lieutenant. Promotion to lieutenant brought another administrative job at headquarters, writing Highway Patrol policy for field operations she knew nothing about. What she did know after being a lieutenant in headquarters, were the internal politics of the Highway Patrol and when the new Governor wanted a woman to head up her protection detail, the CHP brass had no alternative but to comply. Aimee Gardner was their first choice.

Aimee Gardner jumped at the chance. Besides the promotion to captain, she knew the job wasn't dangerous because there were always at least three other officers around the Governor. Additionally, there was a lot of travel involved, and it was a high profile position which would guarantee her promotion in a couple of years to assistant chief.

The Sacramento Governor's Protection Detail, with recently promoted Captain Aimee Gardner in the right front seat of the unmarked dark gray Jeep Liberty, picked up the Governor at her residence at 7:30 in the morning. It would take fifteen minutes to drive from the Executive Mansion, the Governor's home, to the Sacramento Executive Airport in the south part of the city.

The radio call sign for the Governor was CHP 5000. To those who worked her protective detail, however, her code name was "Grandma." She had cultivated that name with the media when she described her politics while she'd been in congress.

She had been Governor since January following her upset victory the previous November over Arnold Schwarzenegger. As an outspoken critic of the Bush Administration and the war against terror, she was swept into office by the same fickle, liberal California voters who turned on Schwarzenegger after electing him in the special election that recalled then Governor Gray Davis.

This Fourth of July obligation was a pain-in-the-ass event for her, but she knew she had to put her money where her mouth was regarding her stated position of opposing the war, but supporting the troops. At least the event was in the morning and she would be back home by early afternoon.

California is the only state that does not have an executive aircraft for its' Governor. Several state agencies, the Highway Patrol included, have small turbo-prop aircraft capable of carrying ten people, but they were never used in favor of renting a Cessna Citation executive jet. Today's trip would cost the California taxpayers $23,000, not to mention the costs in overtime, vehicle movement, and expenses for the protection detail.

CHP 5000 went "wheels up" enroute to Crescent City at 8:10.

———————

While the Governor was flying from Sacramento, five different things were happening around Crescent City.

The first was the overnight fog lingering longer than usual. As a result the morning air was cold and there was moisture on everything. The sky was brightening, however, and the sun would soon break through and begin to push the fog away.

At the National Guard Armory, ninety-seven members of the local guard company were arriving to prepare to march in the parade. Although the company had a strength of one hundred eighty-three soldiers, only a hundred or so lived close enough to make the drive to Crescent City for the parade. Dressed in the same camouflage fatigues, or what the army called Battle Dress Uniforms, they had worn for their year deployment in Iraq, they also wore their rough tan colored leather combat boots and floppy brimmed bush hats. They each carried an M-16 rifle on their shoulders in the sling arms position, and they wore their web gear cartridge belts. Because it was a parade, they wouldn't be carrying any ammunition, and there would be no magazines in their weapons.

When directed by their commander, they mounted trucks and Humvees for the one mile ride to the parade staging area. At the staging area they dismounted their vehicles, fell into company marching formation, and waited for the parade to start.

The annual Fourth of July parade and celebration in Crescent City is a big deal. The parade starts about 8:30 with three patrol cars, one each from the sheriff's office, the police department, and the Highway Patrol leading the way, red and blue lights flashing, sirens blaring, and the officers talking and joking with their friends along the parade route on their patrol cars' public address systems.

Following this came girl and boy scout troops, then a fire engine or two, more marchers from the little league or 4H club. Then the local dignitaries riding in open convertibles, the high school band, trucks from the few remaining logging companies in the county, horses with cowboys, and tractors pulling wagons full of waving kids. The whole town is either in the parade or watching it from the sidewalk.

Julie Bradley and Mary Jean Snider staked out a location near the end of the parade route where they set up folding chairs at the edge of the sidewalk. Each sipped on a coffee drink they'd picked up at the local equivalent of Starbucks.

This year the National Guard Company marched in the place of honor, right behind the parade's Grand Marshal, or in this year's case, five Grand Marshal's, all aging World War Two veterans.

The parade winds through town and ends at the beachfront park where families reunite, BBQs are fired up, and organized games begin for the kids. The festivities last until dark when a fireworks show caps off the day.

At the CHP office, Red Wolff and the six officers assigned to escort the Governor were having coffee and listening to Sergeant Mike Waters give his briefing. The three officers who would drive the Governor's vehicles were also there. Waters told them CHP 5000 was expected to arrive about 9:50. They would leave the office thirty minutes before to be in position when the Governor landed.

They were all CHP officers, but there was a stark contrast between the ones from Crescent City, and those assigned to the protection detail. The local officers were a few years older, except for Ray Silva, who was a lot older. The local officers had a way of sitting or standing that gave off an attitude of bored indifference to the whole operation. The Governor's visit was an intrusion into their routine. In their business suits the protection detail officers on the other hand had a crisp, no-nonsense look about them. They stood straighter and took their jobs deadly serious.

Emil Lagare had spent a fitful night. He was tired, but his brain would not shut down. Visions of his father and mother lying in pools of blood played on the video screen in his mind. The training camp, the responsibilities of being commander, the layout of Crescent City, all flashed and disappeared in his head. Sleep finally came after one in the morning. He'd set the alarm clock in his motel room for 5 a.m. but his mental clock woke him at 4:45.

As soon as he rose, he knelt on the floor and said his prayers asking Allah to guide him this day.

He had arranged for all four teams in their motor homes to meet at a long stretch of beach just north of town at 7 a.m. The road in this area had a wide shoulder and there were often other RVs parked in this location while the occupants strolled the long flat white sand beach. For the first time since leaving Oakland three days ago, the entire twenty-eight members of his team were together again.

Qassim Saleh's plan was based on timing, deception and confusion, not to mention the sheer audacity of an attack aimed at small town America. He knew they could not bring the weapons they would need into the country with them, and trying to obtain them legally through purchase, or illegally on the street, would surely start unnecessary talk. Instead, the plan was to obtain the weapons they needed as the first step in the operation.

One at a time Emil Lagare entered each of the four motor homes. In each of the vehicles there was much activity, none of it frenzied, as his men unpacked boxes.

Except for the lack of a unit shoulder patch, the uniforms being unpacked were exact duplicates of the kind worn by the local National Guard unit. Imam Nasr Ahmed had done his job well. Using sizes sent via coded e-mail from the Syrian training camp by Qassim Saleh, the imam had ordered uniforms complete with boots and floppy hats for each man from the internet. He used three different uniform supply companies to ensure no one order was so big it would cause suspicion.

Once everyone was dressed, other boxes containing communications equipment were opened. The high frequency programmable radios could be set to an infinite number of channels. At about $150 each they'd been easily purchased by Imam Ahmed at four different big box electronics stores in the Oakland-East Bay Area. Emil Lagare personally checked each radio to ensure it was programmed to a common frequency and had a fully charged battery. The plan did not call for an excessive amount of radio communication between teams and a single battery would last three to five days.

The radios also had a scan feature which would allow every team member to hear radio transmissions from local law enforcement agencies. The frequencies of the police, sheriff's, Highway Patrol, and the fire department had been obtained from the internet and programmed into the radios.

Every man wore canvas web gear cartridge belts, again identical to the type issued by the U.S. Army. They also had a large combat type knife in a sheath.

Because each team had a different primary mission, they carried different types of supplemental equipment. The drivers had heavy leather gloves, large bolt cutters, several heavy duty shank locks, and highway warning flares. The explosives team carried wire cutters and electricians tape. Members of the assault team wore bulletproof vests obtained by the imam from one of the many companies selling their products on-line. As part of their equipment, the men on the communications team each had a canvas bag to carry a small electric chain saw and twenty-five feet of extension cord, in addition to bolt cutters and the same heavy duty locks. Everything they needed had been purchased at businesses in Oakland, or through the internet. Nothing that had been purchased, whether viewed by itself, or as a whole, would have raised any suspicion.

By 7:35 all was in readiness. Emil Lagare, now dressed in his American Army uniform, went to each motor home and said a short prayer with the seven men inside. At the first motor home, the one containing his assault team, he directed them to leave the beach and travel to the shopping center parking lot across the street from the National Guard Armory. From there they were to observe and report via radio when the company left for the parade. He knew it would take them less than ten minutes to get into place.

Nine minutes later the team reported they were in position and could see soldiers climbing into trucks. Within a few minutes they called again advising the trucks and Humvees full of troops were leaving the armory. They also reported the gate remained open, with only a sole guard.

Emil Lagare, through his radio, directed the other three motor homes to proceed toward the armory.

From the gate guard shack at the armory, Hal Stephenson watched traffic pass north and south on Highway 101. It had been a good weekend for him pay wise because the holiday meant he got three days work. The extra days pay for working as a security guard at the armory gate because of the Fourth of July parade would come in handy.

Hal Stephenson was a retired school teacher. He'd taught high school English for thirty-five years and retired two years ago to pursue his love of fishing for Steelhead trout and salmon in the nearby Smith River. He was in pretty good shape for a man of sixty-four, following a daily regimen of walking and stretching.

He learned about the Department of Defense Security Guard position from a friend and investigated it further on the internet. The position was perfect for him. It was part-time, usually Saturdays and Sundays, when the local National Guard Company was having its' drills. He shared the job with another person so he only worked two weekends a month. The shifts were long, usually twelve hours a day, but the $13.59 per hour salary was a nice supplement to his retirement pay and social security.

Hal Stephenson saw the first of the four white motor homes as it made the right turn from Highway 101 into the entry of the armory. Looking into the large front window of the vehicle he could see a man in uniform driving and another man, also in uniform, waving from the passenger's seat.

Assuming they were members of the local guard company who were late for the parade, Hal Stephenson waved back as the vehicle stopped directly adjacent to his guard shack. The other three motor homes were stopped on the highway waiting to turn into the armory, blocking the view of any passersby.

The door to the first motor home swung open quickly almost hitting Hal Stephenson. His last thought before he died was why are these two guys pulling me into the motor home and why do they have knives in their hands?

Emil Lagare watched impassively from the passenger's seat of the second motor home. It had started. The old man guarding the gate would be but the first of many to die this day.

As planned, once the motor homes entered the armory parking lot, one of the men in the last vehicle pulled the gates closed. To anyone who cared to notice, it appeared the armory was closed.

It was 8:05 and Emil Lagare knew there was much to do. One of the men from the assault team had taken the six shot revolver and twelve rounds of extra ammunition from the old man guarding the gate. The six men of the assault team, all dressed in American Army uniforms, burst out of the first motor home as it came to a stop in front of the double metal and glass doors at the main entry to the armory building. The doors were unlocked and the team stormed inside.

The interior of the armory building was cavernous. There were offices off to the sides, but the main portion of the building was like a gymnasium. It took several seconds for the eyes of the men on the assault team to adjust to the dim light inside the building. The team did not encounter any troops or other security guards giving the impression the building was empty. Lights were on in one of the offices in the rear of the building and the assault team sprinted that direction.

The lighted office was actually that of the company commander. Seated at a desk inside the office reviewing paperwork was a lone middle-aged man in uniform. It took him a few seconds to comprehend the six men who burst into his office, although they were dressed in uniforms just like his, were not "friendlies." They were on him before he could do little more than stand up. Within seconds he'd been pummeled to the floor by three of the men. One of the former Iraqi Republican Guards, without hesitation, shot him in the forehead with the security guards revolver.

While the assault team was securing the armory building, the other three vehicles discharged the rest of the men at the armory door. Within a few seconds the empty motor homes were moved to the rear of the armory parking lot giving the impression all was normal.

Aside from the lone soldier who was the company clerk, Emil Lagare's men found no one else in the armory. What they did quickly find inside the commander's office was a wall mounted metal key box. Because there was activity around the armory, the box had been left unlocked. Inside were the keys to every lock in the armory and every vehicle. Emil Lagare studied the box full of keys for several moments then removed a set marked "Weapons Room" from its hook.

It only took the assault team a few seconds to open the room where the weapons were stored. Inside the room along one wall they found ten storage racks designed to hold twenty M-16 rifles each, and five racks that each held two M-249 machine guns. More than half the rifles and six of the machine guns were gone, which told Emil Lagare they were probably being carried by the troops in the parade. Along the opposite wall were large bins with hundreds of empty magazines and cases of ammunition. The weapons racks were quickly unlocked by one of the men on the assault team while others were busily loading bullets into the magazines for the rifles and machine guns. Two of the men from the communications team found a large foot locker type chest which contained seventeen 9 Millimeter Beretta pistols, magazines and ammunition.

The M-16s in the armory were the "A-2" type. Unlike the Vietnam era version of the weapon which fired in either the single shot or full automatic mode, the A-2 model was modified to fire either a single bullet or a three round burst. During weapons training in the desert, Emil Lagare's men had been told by their former U.S. Army instructor, Muhammad Attiya, the American military modified the weapons after the Vietnam War to improve fire discipline and for conservation of ammunition. During the same training, Attiya explained the M-249 machine gun. The M-249, he told them, was the most likely Squad Automatic Weapon, or SAW, they would find in a National Guard Armory. The weapon was based on a Belgium design and manufactured in the United States. It had a sustained rate of fire of over seven hundred rounds per minute and fired the same ammunition as the M-16 rifle. The weapon could fire from either a belt of ammunition, or from a two hundred round plastic triangular shaped box magazine.

According to plan, the communications team was the first to be equipped with weapons and magazines. As soon as they were ready, the six men on this team split into three groups of two. One group got back into one of the motor homes, and the second group into another. The third group stayed with Emil Lagare. The front gate was opened momentarily while the two vehicles left the armory, then quickly closed again. With the Muslims from Oakland driving, the two motor homes headed for different targets.

On Highway 101 and around Crescent City, everything appeared normal. No alarms had sounded. The police had not made an appearance at the armory and the sun had finally broken through the morning fog. It was 8:35.

The parade had gotten off to a start about six or seven minutes late, but soon it was possible to hear the sirens of the three patrol cars as they led the parade, and the boom of the drums as the high school marching band played their first number.

Inside the armory, the men on the three remaining teams busily continued loading magazines with ammunition. It was disappointing to Emil Lagare that they did not find any type of explosives in the armory, but there was an alternate plan for this eventuality.

———

In planning the operation, Qassim Saleh had used deductive reasoning to make assumptions about the types of security systems businesses used to protect themselves when they were closed. He knew Crescent City, like most small towns, did not have an exceptionally high crime rate. The police knew who the local criminals were and strangers in town stood out, especially those who might be in the wrong place at the wrong time. Still, he had reasoned, most businesses would have some type of electronic alarm system. It was a simple matter of observing the front doors of these businesses to see if they displayed a decal or sign proclaiming they were protected by this or that alarm company. Qassim Saleh knew whatever type of alarm system they had, it worked through the telephone lines.

After securing the armory, the second part of the plan was to neutralize the many electronic security systems protecting the businesses and government facilities around the town. Eliminating these security systems would also eliminate most of the town's ability to communicate.

The first motor home slowed and stopped directly next to the closed chain link fence gate of the telephone company parking lot. Two men quickly exited and used the three foot long bolt cutters purchased at a hardware store in Oakland to easily cut the shank on the padlock securing the gate. Throwing the bolt cutters back in the motor home, they rolled the gate open just enough for them to enter the parking lot, then closed it behind them. Moving fast, but without haste that could draw suspicion, the two moved to the back door of the building. The door was secured by means of a magnetic lock which required a coded identification card to open. One of the men fired three rounds from his M-16 directly into the magnetic lock mechanism on the door shattering it to pieces. Although the sound of the rounds being fired was loud, they were drowned out by the sounds of the parade. Anyone who did hear them would assume they were firecrackers.

The telephone switching center was completely automated. Through its banks of computers, magnetic switches, and routers, incoming and outgoing calls were processed without human involvement. The system was almost foolproof and worked flawlessly. There was one technician at the switching station twenty-four hours a day to troubleshoot the system should a problem arise and to ensure the huge air conditioners outside the building continued to keep the inside temperature at a constant level so that the electronic equipment did not overheat.

The two men moved cautiously into the building, rifles at the ready as they had trained to do in the Syrian Desert. Moving from the back of the building toward the front, they found all the small offices dark and their doors closed. Moving toward the center of the building, they could see light and hear music. As they entered the large room containing the electronic equipment that was the brains of the local telephone system, they both saw a young man standing with his back to them adjusting something in one of the banks of magnetic switches. One of the men brought his M-16 up to his shoulder and fired two rounds. The young man died without even seeing the man who killed him.

Both men now moved rapidly. As members of the communications team, they had been trained in the workings of telephone systems. Within moments they located the main switches and routers that controlled the telephone system for all of Crescent City and Del Norte County. These components were disabled by smashing them with their rifle butts. As soon as the switches were smashed, red lights began blinking on the wall display next to the computer control station, and all of the land line phone systems, alarm systems, fax machines and computer modems that used a phone line in the county ceased working. They now pulled the electric chain saws and extension cords from their equipment bags and plugged them into wall sockets. Qassim Saleh had opted for electric, rather than gasoline powered saws, simply because electrical power could be found almost anywhere and there was no question about the ability to get them started. The twelve inch bars on the saws cut through the long strands of fiber-optic cables connecting the computers, routers, and switches with ease. Any repair job on the switching station would require a complete rewiring of the facility. When they'd finished cutting, the men dropped the saws on the floor as they would not be needed again.

The men quickly left the building, and were back in the motor home within a minute, but not before they replaced the lock on the gate with one they had brought with them. To anyone who happened by the switching station, everything would appear normal.

As soon as they were back in their vehicle, they radioed Emil Lagare their mission had been accomplished.

Simultaneous with the assault on the telephone company the second motor home pulled up to the local cable television office. Qassim Saleh knew many Americans used cable companies not only for their television, but also to get telephone and internet service. In order to eliminate any communications into or out of Crescent City, the cable company needed to be neutralized also.

The office was in a small single story building at the edge of town. Like most such companies, it had an outside drop box for customers to pay their bills. As the motor home stopped directly in front of the glass doors of the business office, so did a pickup truck with a woman driver and a small child in the passenger's seat. The woman bounced out of the truck, walked quickly to the drop box, and deposited her payment. She left just as quickly, never glancing at the motor home, or knowing how close she came to dying.

Sitting in the motor home, the Muslim from Oakland and the two men from the communications team could see that although the office was closed, with the blinds drawn, it was well lit and there was movement inside the building. They opted for the direct approach. Exiting the motor home, both men approached the door and began urgently knocking. After several moments with no response, they knocked again with even more urgency, now yelling "Emergency, Emergency."

Like the telephone company, the cable television company kept one employee onsite when the business office was closed. Their job was simply to oversee the computers and automated components that ran the cable systems. The young woman who was working the weekend day shift was the mother of three. She was a fulltime employee of the cable company who worked the weekends and holidays because it paid a little more and her husband was home on those days so she didn't have to worry about child care.

Company regulations absolutely forbade opening the door after business hours. However, after hearing the knocking for the second time, the woman peered out the closed mini-blinds to see two soldiers standing at the front door. She could also now hear the word emergency.

There is something in the American mentality that trusts a person in uniform. Whether it's a policeman, a postman, or a meter reader from the gas company, Americans drop their guard a little when the person they are dealing with is in uniform. These were two soldiers in uniform and they were yelling something about an emergency. The woman unlocked the front door without hesitation.

She had no more than opened the door when one of the soldiers pushed his way into the office and smashed her in the face with his fist, knocking her to the floor. Dazed and confused, the woman saw the soldier draw his pistol and fire two rounds into her chest. It happened so fast she didn't even have time to think about her husband and children.

While the first man was murdering the woman, the second, with pistol in hand, made a quick search of the rest of the building. Finding no one, he was returning to the front of the building when the front door opened.

An elderly man appeared in the open door with an envelope in hand and upon seeing somebody inside the building said, "I thought you were closed today?"

The second man didn't quite understand what the elderly American said, but it made no difference. Raising his pistol, he fired one round into the old man's forehead killing him in mid-stride as he walked into the office.

The appearance of the elderly man was inconvenient, but not an insurmountable problem. While one of the men checked to ensure there were no other people outside, the other dragged the two dead bodies behind the front counter of the business office. Seeing no one else outside, the first man left the building and retrieved his equipment bag from the motor home.

The process of disabling the cable communications system was the same as it had been at the phone company. Once the men identified the master control systems they were smashed with rifle butts. Chain saws were again employed to sever cables and computer control wiring. The whole process, from the time they arrived at the cable company until they were done, had taken only seven minutes. They radioed Emil Lagare they too had completed their assigned task and were heading back to the armory.

With the exception of some cellular-to-cellular service between those using the same cellular company, all communications using traditional land line type telephones in Crescent City and the surrounding county had been eliminated. The time was 8:57.

After learning both the telephone and cable systems in the town had been destroyed, Emil Lagare felt confident all security alarm systems had been disabled. He now directed the explosives team to penetrate the closed Cal-Trans yard. Working in the back part of the armory parking lot, out of sight of the highway, four of the six men from the explosives team quickly cut the chain link fence separating the armory from the maintenance yard by using another pair of large bolt cutters. Once in the Cal-Trans yard, they rapidly made their way to the back of the office where, unseen from the street, they forced the rear door open and entered the office.

The interior of the office was small, about the size of a motel room. It was obviously a working office as there were books and papers piled on two of the desks, heavy work boots on the floor, and various radios, hard hats, and other tools on chairs or hanging on the walls.

A small door at the rear of the office was double padlocked and displayed an orange Federal Department of Transportation placard for explosives. The door was armed with an electronic alarm system and an audible intrusion alarm. Even though the telephone lines for the alarm system had been disabled, the audible alarms were still active because of their electrical power. One of the team members quickly cut the wires to the audible alarm while another used the bolt cutters to cut the shanks on the two padlocks. Because the Cal-Trans facility was state property, responsibility for its security fell to the Highway Patrol. With the city's phone system disabled, no alarm triggered at the Highway Patrol Communications Center in Eureka, eighty miles to the south, when the door was opened.

The supply of dynamite in the room was only twelve sticks, plus a like number of blasting caps. During the summer months the supply on hand was intentionally kept low as it was needed infrequently. In the winter months, with the constant rain weakening the mountainous hillsides, rock slides were common and a greater supply was kept readily available.

Nonetheless, the explosives team quickly gathered up the dynamite and blasting caps and began to fashion explosive devices. Using electrician's tape, they secured two sticks of dynamite together and inserted a blasting cap. From their individual bags of equipment, they rapidly attached triggering devices to the dynamite and blasting caps. The triggering devices were simply two nine volt batteries attached with wires to a cheap sports watch. The backs of the watches had been removed and the wires from the batteries attached to the audible wakeup alarm feature. When the preset wakeup time was reached, a circuit would close sending a current to the blasting cap. The current would fire the blasting cap which would in turn detonate the dynamite. The two nine volt batteries had been added to ensure there was sufficient electrical current to fire the blasting cap. All that remained was to set the alarm for a designated time. It took less than five minutes to construct three time bombs.

With the remaining six sticks of dynamite, they fashioned three more homemade explosive devices. These three were similar to the others except, instead of timers for triggers, they had remote controls. The firing mechanisms were simply transmitters and receivers taken from automatic garage door openers purchased at various hardware stores in the Oakland area. The receiver was wired to batteries which would provide the electrical current. The batteries were then wired to blasting caps and could be detonated by simply pushing the open button on the transmitter. Tests conducted by the team using similar equipment at the training camp in Syria indicated the transmitters had a range of about one hundred fifty feet.

By 9:15 the two motor homes with the communications teams had returned to the armory after destroying the telephone and cable systems of the town. Emil Lagare now used one of the returning motor homes to send the men who had assembled the dynamite bombs armed with sport watch timers on their mission.

In developing the plan, Qassim Saleh knew the towers on which the antennas for cellular phones were mounted were in locations open to public view and any time consuming attempt to disable these antennas would draw a considerable amount of unwanted attention. Although disabling the telephone and cable systems had more than likely eliminated most of the town's communication ability, destroying the antennas towers would ensure all communication via any type of telephone was impossible.

Locating the towers had been a simple matter of driving around the town and looking for satellite dish receivers and multi-pronged radio antennas. Three had been found. The explosives team drove to each of these locations and by using the motor home as a shield, one of the team members climbed the chain link security fence around the antenna tower and attached an improvised bomb to each. The process took less than a minute at each tower. The alarm on each of these devices was set for 10:30.

Emil Lagare sent the motor home from the armory to plant the explosives at the cellular telephone towers at 9:25. He could still hear the sounds of the high school band which told him the parade was still in progress. He knew up to this point they had, through a combination of training, discipline, and luck, avoided detection. Gathering up the remaining members of his team inside the armory, he praised them for their skill and daring thus far. It was time he told them to leave the armory and begin their mission. The next time they met he said would be in front of Allah.

To shouts of Allah Akbar, the twenty-five men quickly gathered the weapons they had obtained from the armory and piled into their designated U.S. Army vehicles. They had taken with them a small arsenal of weapons, four machine guns, twenty-five M-16 rifles, eleven 9 Millimeter pistols, plus over twenty thousand rounds of ammunition, and three homemade explosive devices. On this Fourth of July, at that moment, there was not a heavier armed band of men anywhere in the nation. It was 9:41.

The vehicle procession left the National Guard Armory at the same time. To any citizens who cared to notice, the vehicles looked like a normal army convoy, four Humvees and two trucks, all full of soldiers in uniforms with rifles. Weekend maneuvers no doubt.

When the last vehicle cleared the gates, they were pulled shut again and a new padlock attached to the chain which held them together. If any of the soldiers returned to the armory unexpectedly, they would find the gate closed and their keys unable to open the lock.

When the telephone lines in the town went dead, they also went dead at the sheriff's office dispatch console. The dispatcher was a long time veteran and had seen it happen before. Not only were all of her regular lines down, so were her emergency 911 lines. The last time something like this happened, the phones in Crescent City were inoperable for almost eight hours. That time it had been caused by an air conditioner failure at the phone company which overheated the line switching equipment.

As a matter of routine, she used the radio to notify all sheriff and police department units the telephone lines were down, and consequently, so were all security alarm systems. She also dispatched one of the city police department units to the telephone company office to do a routine check.

The telephone company office was within blocks of the parade route and one of the city police officers who was observing the parade took the call. Driving by the building, the officer noted the air conditioners were all functioning, and the back gate was locked as usual. The officer parked near the front door and used the after-hours push-to-talk speaker at the entry. After several tries with no answer from inside the building the officer used his radio to call dispatch to report everything looked okay outside, but he could get no response from within the office.

Standard protocol in this type of situation was to contact a phone company supervisor and request they respond. Using her computer, she easily pulled up the telephone company emergency callout list, the name of the contact person, their phone numbers and address. Lacking the ability to contact anyone via telephone, however, the dispatcher had to send a unit by the supervisor's home to make personal contact. In this case the supervisor lived in Smith River, a small village near the Oregon border, twenty miles north of Crescent City.

Because Smith River was in the county area, she used the radio to call the sheriff's patrol unit assigned to the north county to make contact. The deputy assigned this sector acknowledged the call but said he was tied up taking a burglary report and it would be about a half-hour before he could respond. The deputy suggested she try calling the Highway Patrol.

The sheriff's dispatcher touched the CHP icon on the screen of her computer-aided-dispatch system and the internal software automatically dialed the Highway Patrol Communications Center in Eureka, to see if a CHP unit could make contact with the telephone company supervisor. Within seconds the screen flashed a message back indicating the telephone line was inoperable.

Although she was increasingly frustrated by the situation, the sheriff's dispatcher was an old hand at emergencies. She calmly used the radio to call the on-duty sheriff's sergeant. The sergeant, who was at the park as part of the security for the Governor, told her he would pass the information on to the sheriff who was there preparing to participate in the awards ceremony. He also told her to keep trying to contact the phone company supervisor.

———

While Emil Lagare was sending a team to plant the timer armed explosives at the cellular antenna towers, Red Wolff and the six Crescent City officers, along with the four officers from the Governor's Protection Detail, were leaving the Highway Patrol office enroute to the airport. There were three black and white Ford Crown Victoria patrol cars, and three unmarked dark colored Jeep Libertys.

Mike Waters, the protection detail supervisor, had explained to Red Wolff that the Highway Patrol supplied whatever type of vehicles the Governor wanted, and that there were about a dozen stationed at various locations around the state. He went on to tell her every Governor had their favorite type of vehicle. Some previous Governors preferred large passenger type cars, others wanted luxury SUVs. This Governor wanted something that projected the grandmotherly image she cultivated. The Jeep Liberty was perfect for that "I'm just like you image," not too big, not too flashy, not too expensive.

It was quiet at the airport, with no commercial flights due until early evening. There were about a dozen local residents of the town at the airport to get a glimpse of the Governor when she arrived and another two or three who were working on their private planes. Parked on the tarmac was an olive drab twin engine Beechcraft King Air. The presence of this aircraft indicated the commanding general of the California National Guard had arrived for the ceremony. The army pilots were standing by their aircraft drinking coffee.

After the Highway Patrol vehicles parked, Red Wolff got out of her car to talk to Mike Waters, but her officers stayed in their vehicles. McNamara Field sits along the ocean, and even though the sun had finally broken through, the slight breeze off the Pacific was chilly. Normally the Crescent City officers would be wearing long sleeved uniform shirts with dark blue dickeys, and their dark blue nylon jackets rather than the formal green wool "Ike" jackets and blue neck ties. The officers from Sacramento stayed in their Jeeps also as their lightweight summer suits, ideal for the one hundred degree central valley summer weather, were of little protection against the wind and the fifty-two degree temperature of Crescent City.

———

Also at the airport was a green and white van with call letters painted on the side from the television station in Eureka. KHUM was a Fox Television affiliate. It was the only television station on the north coast between Santa Rosa and the Oregon border.

Patricia Dodge was drop dead gorgeous. She had jet black hair, finely chiseled facial features, and what those in the broadcast news industry called a great on-air personality. She was one of five members of the KHUM broadcast news team. She'd been hired by the station about nine months prior, right out of college. She'd been given the assignment to cover the Governor's visit to Crescent City, she assumed, because she was the junior reporter at the station. In reality, none of the other reporters wanted to do it.

Patricia Dodge didn't mind the assignment one bit. She was not happy working at what she considered a Podunk station in the sticks, and she saw any chance to increase her exposure as an opportunity to be discovered by one of the Fox flagship stations in Los Angeles or San Francisco. The chances, however, that Patricia Dodge would make it big in broadcast journalism were about the same as the chances a pig had at a luau. Patricia Dodge was rock stupid.

A graduate of the University of Southern California School of Journalism, she had completed her academic work without any problems and had interned at the Fox flagship station in Los Angeles. Upon graduation, Fox offered her a chance to hone her broadcast skills in Humboldt County at KHUM in the city of Eureka. While it wasn't an ideal job offer, it did give her the opportunity to become an on-air personality. Her problems started almost from the first day she first went on-the-air.

As the junior person on the station's team, she began by doing the late night weekend news broadcasts and after a few months moved to doing the local six a.m. news on weekdays. Patricia Dodge's problem was that, although she was book smart, she had almost no real life experience. Names of famous people, political figures, worldwide historical events, and geographic places were like a foreign language to her.

During the winter months, when the salmon make their annual run from the ocean up the many rivers in Humboldt County to spawn, local fisherman tune to the early morning news to hear the latest fishing report. What they got was Patricia Dodge telling them about what she called Sal-mon. Or when President Bush visited Omaha Beach in Normandy to lay a wreath at the cemetery, she pronounced it Nor-Mandy. Patricia Dodge didn't have a clue. Every time she committed one of these verbal faux pas, the station's switchboard lit up with calls from irate viewers. The local people may not have been as sophisticated as those in the big cities, but they didn't like their news delivered by an airhead. Unknown to her, the station was not going to renew her contract when it expired in three months.

For today, however, Patricia Dodge was on assignment. She, her cameraman and a technician left the station about 7:00 a.m. in one of the news vans. Since the story on the Governor's visit would be picked up by the larger stations in Los Angeles and San Francisco, they took the van with satellite capability. It took them almost a full two hours to make the eighty mile trip due to the fog and the volume of traffic already using the mostly two lane Highway 101. Pulling into Crescent City just before 9:00 they first scouted out the beachfront park where the ceremony would be taking place, then headed for the airport.

Patricia Dodge's idea was to get footage of the Governor arriving and try to interview her at the airport. On the trip to Crescent City she had been framing questions to ask the Governor about withdrawing troops from Iraq. When the Governor left the airport they would lower the boom mast satellite antenna on the van and go back to the park to film the Governor reviewing the troops and making her speech.

She was putting the final touches on her makeup when the procession of CHP cars arrived at the airport.

When Emil Lagare and his team left the armory they headed in different directions as planned. The two trucks, driven by the Oakland Muslims, with Emil Lagare in the passenger seat of the lead truck, headed north on Highway 101 through the city and pulled into the Wal-Mart parking lot. There, in the back of the large mostly empty parking lot, was the motor home containing the three men who had planted the timed explosives at the cellular telephone antennas. As soon as the lead truck pulled adjacent to the motor home, the three men jumped out and into the truck. Just as quickly as they had entered the parking lot, both trucks were back on Highway 101.

The four Humvees, each with a driver and passenger, headed south on Highway 101. Three of the military vehicles pulled up to the closed gate at the entrance to the local fuel farm. After they stopped, the six men began visually observing the large oil storage tanks in the back of the lot that held diesel fuel and gasoline. From their location on the street they could also see ten, three-axle tanker trucks parked in the lot, along with several large tank trailers. The fourth Humvee turned toward the center of town and was now slowly driving south on a mostly deserted side street toward the beachfront park.

At the same time Emil Lagare and his men left the armory in their military vehicles, Mary Jean Snider and Julie Bradley were setting up their chairs at the beachfront park. They found a great location about twenty yards from the podium from which they would be able to see and hear the ceremony.

From their vantage point they could see the soldiers standing in formation. One of the things that struck Julie Bradley was the number of women in the unit. To her eye it looked like out of a hundred soldiers about twenty of them were women. They were in the rest position, so they could talk to each other, but could not leave formation. At the front of the unit they could see what Mary Jean explained to Julie was the company commander, the company's sergeant major behind him, and behind them both, held by soldiers, were the American flag, the California state flag, the United States Army flag, and the unit flag. The company commander was talking to a person that Mary Jean explained was a major general, probably the Commanding General of the California National Guard. Unlike the local soldiers who were in their camouflage desert fatigues, the general was in his green dress uniform.

Sitting in chairs next to Mary Jean and Julie was a father with two small children, one a boy about six, the other a girl about four. The father had a large picnic basket and was rummaging through it to find something for the kids to drink.

"Momeee!" the little girl yelled as she waved to the formation. In the formation Mary Jean and Julie could see a woman of about thirty waving back.

"That's my mommy, she's a sol-idger," the little girl said proudly to the two women sitting next to her.

Both Mary Jean and Julie talked to the father and the little girl for several minutes and then turned their attention back to the formation.

Although they could not hear the conversation between the general and the company commander, it was obvious by watching how they checked their watches and gestured that something was going on. The company commander signaled the sergeant major to join him and within a few seconds the sergeant major turned back to the formation. The sergeant major now said a few words to one of the soldiers who promptly left the formation and headed to where the companies vehicles were parked. Julie and Mary Jean saw him roar off in a Humvee seconds later.

The soldier driving away in the Humvee was Specialist Four, Ralph Silva. A lifelong Crescent City resident, he was Ray Silva's nephew.

Ralph Silva had done a combat tour in Iraq with the rest of his company and had distinguished himself in several firefights with insurgents. He was slated to be awarded a Bronze Star in today's ceremony. Right now, however, he was on his way back to the armory. The "Old Man" would be helpless without me Ralph Silva thought to himself as he drove. How could he have forgotten to bring the medals with him?

As he drove northbound on Highway 101, Ralph Silva saw three Humvees heading south. He knew no other troops were going to the ceremony, so his first thought was the vehicles were from another unit. As they passed each other in opposite directions, Ralph Silva checked the unit identifier numbers painted on the front bumpers. 47 BGD-CNG. No, they were from his unit the numbers and letters told him, 47th Brigade, California National Guard. Although he didn't recognize the men in the vehicles, he waved as they passed each other and they waved back. Oh well, Ralph Silva said to himself, more important things to worry about right now.

———

The Governor's aircraft went "wheels down" at 9:53. The flight had taken about ten minutes longer than estimated and as a result, the protection detail would have to hustle to get her to the ceremony by 10:00.

The aircraft pulled to a stop about seventy-five yards away from the small terminal building and Red Wolff could hear the sound of the engines as they were winding down. As soon as Sergeant Mike Waters was sure that the aircraft was stopped, he signaled the motorcade to drive onto the tarmac. The lead black and white, driven by a Crescent City officer, was followed by Red Wolff in her patrol car. The first Jeep stopped directly adjacent to the aircraft's front door, followed by the two other Jeeps for the Governor's staff, and Ray Silva in his black and white at the rear.

At the terminal Patricia Dodge was outside the news van while her cameraman shot footage of her narrating the arrival of the Governor's plane. When the aircraft parked far away from her location, she had to abruptly stop that shot and with her cameraman in tow, run to the stopped aircraft.

133

The Governor and her staff, including the head of her protection detail, Highway Patrol Captain Aimee Gardner, were off the aircraft within a minute. There was a brief conversation between the Governor and her press secretary and then they were in the Jeeps and headed toward Crescent City.

"Shit," Patricia Dodge said in frustration to her cameraman as the motorcade snaked its way out of the airport. All she could do now was hurry up and get to the beachfront park before she missed everything.

Running back to the van, she and her cameraman stowed their equipment while the technician was lowering the satellite antenna mast. As soon as the antenna was secure, he jumped into the driver's seat and turned the ignition key. The metallic click-click-click of the Bendix Gear on the starter as it tried to engage the flywheel told the driver the battery was dead.

The tirade from Patricia Dodge was worthy of a longshoreman. "God-damn, cheap-ass, Podunk station, can't even afford a new battery," she yelled at no one in particular. Her cameraman and the driver technician looked at each other and shrugged.

CHAPTER TEN

When he was charged with developing the plan for an operation in the United States, Qassim Saleh had been instructed to ensure the level of devastation would be such, that all across America, people would live in fear another attack might occur in their town.

The planners of 9/11 had succeeded beyond their wildest dreams. Three of the four hijacked aircraft successfully crashed into their targets, the World Trade Center Towers had been brought down, and several thousand people had been killed. It had shown the Americans they were not immune from attack and that even within their own borders, they were not secure. As horrific as the events of 9/11 had been, however, the planners of the attack did not get the one thing they wanted most, gory scenes of countless dead in the street, hundreds of bloody injured people, mass panic, and fear. Scenes such as those were an everyday occurrence in the Middle East. Qassim Saleh had been charged with making them occur in the United States.

The plan he developed was to be an Islamic version of "Shock and Awe." Nobody, except the media, was considered off-limits. All Americans, men, women, and children were enemies of Allah and, therefore, equally responsible for supporting Israel and bringing western decadence to Islamic countries.

It was these thoughts that went through Emil Lagare's mind as he watched the crowd grow at the beachfront park through his binoculars. From his vantage point in the front seat of one of the two trucks carrying eighteen of his men, he could see the National Guard unit standing in loose formation, numerous dignitaries and city officials gathered around the podium area, and although his view was partially obscured, hundreds, perhaps as many as a thousand, ordinary citizens standing and sitting around the perimeter of the park. With the trucks parked along the curb of one of the city side streets, they were perfectly positioned to observe the ceremony without being seen by any of the National Guard troops in formation who might question what they were doing there.

It was 9:59, and according to the local paper, the ceremony was to begin at 10:00. It did not appear to Emil Lagare, however, that it was ready to start within the next several minutes. Sitting there watching the park, he let his mind wander back to his parents and the events of the day they were killed by Israeli helicopters. The image of his lifeless parents, covered with blood, haunted him everyday. Hate was a powerful motivator. It was hate that allowed him to be drawn under the spell of Yusef al-Mashtal, and hate that had pushed him to undergo the indoctrination in radical Islam. That same hate gave him the strength to withstand the harsh and demanding training in the Syrian Desert. It was hate that would now make him unmerciful as he sought his vengeance.

The blur of the first black and white police car as it passed from right to left in front of him on the street leading to the park, snapped Emil Lagare's mind back to the present. A second black and white police car followed within a few feet of the first, followed by three dark colored vehicles he knew were called SUVs, and a final police car. The entire procession was moving very fast and passed his location in less than two seconds. Emil Lagare rightly surmised the Governor of California was in one of those vehicles. He keyed his radio and told his men it would not be long now.

An area along the curb on the street at the entrance to the beachfront park had been blocked off by the local police for the Governor's motorcade. The first black and white pulled well forward along the curb and stopped, leaving plenty of room for the other vehicles. As soon as the Governor's Jeep came to a stop, Captain Aimee Gardner was out of the front seat as were her officers in the other vehicles. The officers assumed positions around the Governor's vehicle and faced outward, scanning the crowd and the surrounding area. Within a few seconds the right rear door opened and the Governor emerged.

Her Chief of Staff was already out of his vehicle and had made his way over to the group of local dignitaries by the podium. Within a few seconds he returned, with several of them following behind. Introductions were made, and within a minute, the Governor was escorted from the sidewalk to the grassy area where folding chairs were set up.

While the Governor was doing the "grin, greet, and grip" with the local people, Red Wolff was directing two of her officers to assume a position on the left side of the VIP seating area behind the

Governor and two others to the right side. Assuming positions near the uniformed Highway Patrol officers were two of the three plainclothes protection detail officers. Captain Aimee Gardner stood on one side of the VIP seating area, Sergeant Mike Waters on the other.

Red Wolff, Ray Silva, and the third plainclothes officer remained near the vehicles, about twenty-five yards from the podium.

"How long do you figure she'll speak?" Ray Silva asked the officer from Sacramento, more in a manner of making conversation than any real interest.

"She's not a long speech giver," the officer replied. "I think she'll want to keep it short and get back to Sacto."

"That's better for us," Red Wolff joined the conversation. "There must be fifteen hundred people here. They'll create a real traffic mess when they leave."

Looking at the podium, Red Wolff could see the Mayor of Crescent City getting ready to speak. The commander of the National Guard unit called his troops to attention. The noise of the crowd began to dull as the mayor asked the assembled crowd to stand while the high school band struck up The National Anthem.

Two blocks away Emil Lagare watched and listened as the hated song reverberated in his ears. As the last note played, the crowd cheered loudly, then resumed their seats on the ground, or in the folding chairs they'd brought with them.

It was the moment Emil Lagare had been waiting for. Bringing his radio to his lips, he gave the go signal to his team of men at the fuel farm and the other two men who were three blocks away. It was 10:12.

It took Specialist Ralph Silva about five minutes to drive from the beachfront park back to the armory. When he got there he thought it strange the gate was closed and locked. The guard, Hal Stephenson, was always supposed to be at his post when the armory was open for a drill weekend.

Normally he didn't carry his cell phone when he was in uniform during a drill weekend, but this parade and award ceremony was a little different situation so he'd stuffed it in his pocket when he put his uniform on that morning. Knowing the company clerk stayed behind when the rest of the company left for the parade, he punched in the number for the company office. Within a few seconds an automated voice told him his call could not be completed. He tried several more times and each time the message came back the same.

Weighing his options, Ralph Silva thought he could return to the park and explain the situation to the sergeant major, or he could find another way into the armory. Dealing with the sergeant major was never a pleasant task, but the only other way into the armory was over the fence with its barbed wire top. Ralph Silva decided on the fence. Pulling his Humvee as close to the fence as possible, he climbed on top of the vehicle and began to carefully pick his way over the barbed wire.

While Ralph Silva was attempting to climb the fence at the armory, Emil Lagare's team of six drivers, plus three men from the explosives team, sprang into action at the fuel farm as soon as they received the go signal.

Using large bolt cutters, they easily snapped the shank on the lock that secured the gate. They pushed the gate open and drove their four Humvees inside the large parking lot of the facility. The five men who would drive the fuel trucks were out of the military vehicles in a flash and sprinted to the row of parked trucks.

The local fuel company used three-axle fuel tanker trucks rather than the longer semi-truck and trailers in the Crescent City area because their shorter length made it easier to get to many of the homes located on mountainous roads or down narrow lanes off the paved highways when they were delivering home heating oil. They also had several trucks that carried diesel fuel for servicing the fishing boats in the harbor, and automotive gasoline for the several remote gas stations in the county.

The men scrambled to the top of the trucks and opened the vent caps on the tanks. Using flashlights they each carried, they peered into the tanks to assess how much fuel each contained. Every tank was full, ready for the company's drivers to begin their routes the following morning. Once they were satisfied the tank contained sufficient fuel, the men jumped into the cabs of the vehicles.

Every driver had the tools and wire in their equipment bags needed to hot-wire the vehicles. It was not necessary. The vehicles in the yard all had keys in the ignition. This was standard practice at the fuel company, as no one ever dreamed somebody would break into the yard to steal a truck.

The two trucks assigned missions on Highway 101 had the farthest to go and left the fuel farm immediately. Each was followed by a Humvee. The other three trucks and the remaining two Humvees left less than a minute later to take up positions near their targets.

———

At the beachfront park the mayor was introducing the dignitaries to the crowd. Besides the Governor, the list of VIPs was a who's who of government in Crescent City and Del Norte County. In attendance this day were all the members of the county council, the city council, the district attorney, the judges of the superior and municipal courts, the Crescent City Chief of Police, the Del Norte County Sheriff and Undersheriff, the Commander of the CHP, the Commander of the Coast Guard detachment, the city and county fire chiefs, and the state assembly representative. Anybody who was anybody was there to honor the troops and get a chance to meet the Governor.

The mayor kept his comments brief, then introduced the Commanding General of the California National Guard.

Emil Lagare watched intently through binoculars from his position several blocks away. When the general rose to speak, he told his men to dismount the trucks and prepare the last of their equipment.

Standing on the sidewalk next to the trucks, Emil Lagare inspected his men, and the equipment they carried. He then directed them into formation.

At that moment one of the four Crescent City Police cruisers on patrol slowly passed by, the officer looking at the formation of armed men standing on the sidewalk.

Although the presence of the officer was unexpected and sent an initial shudder of fear through Emil Lagare, he quickly regained his composure.

"What's up?" the officer said from inside his vehicle as he stopped next to the curb. It wasn't so much a question as it was a friendly comment to acknowledge their presence.

Emil Lagare smiled at the officer and said, "We are getting ready to march over to the park."

"Okay, you guys take care," the officer replied as he slowly pulled away from the curb and continued on patrol. The officer was young and had never been in the service. He didn't notice anything unusual about the soldiers he saw, and it seemed logical to him they would be marching the two blocks to the park.

———

Patricia Dodge was beside herself. Not only had she not gotten to interview the Governor, she was now stuck at the airport in a van with a dead battery while the ceremony was kicking off at the park.

While she might not have been the sharpest knife in the drawer when it came to history, geography, and world events, she was also not one to give up easily. She gave her personal Triple-A card to the driver of the news van and told him to call for road service. Once he got the van started he could hook up with her at the park.

She then approached the three men who were working on their private airplanes on the tarmac. She picked the one who appeared to be the youngest. Introducing herself to the man, she batted her big blue eyes at him and used the same charm that helped her through college to plead for a ride to the park for her and her cameraman. The man was reluctant to stop what he was doing and about to refuse, when she "accidentally" brushed her left breast against his arm. Within a minute they were in his pickup truck headed for the park. Men were so easy, she smiled to herself as the young man drove.

Ralph Silva didn't know why, but the whole feel of the armory was eerie. He'd managed to scale the fence and drop into the parking lot without cutting himself on the barbed wire. As he jogged across the lot toward the armory building, he could see three white motor homes parked in back. He didn't remember them there when the company left for the parade a couple of hours before. It also seemed to him there were a bunch of the unit's vehicles missing.

The feeling didn't go away when he opened the main door to the armory building. The overhead lights were out and the only illumination came from the company office. He saw the company clerk in a pool of blood on the floor as soon as he walked into the office. Ralph Silva had seen plenty of death during his tour in Iraq. The clerk was definitely dead. He immediately picked up the phone to call 911. There was no dial tone. Moving into the captain's office he tried another phone. No dial tone there either. While he was trying the phone, his eyes wandered to the open key box on the wall. Lots of keys were scattered around the inside of the box and many more were on the floor.

Ralph Silva grabbed a set of keys to a truck and ran from the office. He had the presence of mind to run to the Weapons Room where he found the door unlocked. Pushing the door open he could see all the M-16 rifles, and all the M-249 machine guns, were gone.

There were magazines all over the floor and hundreds of rounds of 5.56 caliber ammunition were scattered about.

Ralph Silva sprinted to the parking lot and jumped into the cab of a truck. The truck fired up immediately and he jammed the transmission into first gear. The two and a half ton truck groaned as he let the clutch out and pressed down on the accelerator. The truck lurched forward. It was about twenty yards from where the truck was parked to the gate. Ralph Silva had the gas pedal to the floor, but because of the low gear ratio in the trucks differential, it only got to about fifteen miles per hour as it approached the closed gate. Turning the steering wheel hard to the right, he made a U-turn and drove to the far rear of the parking lot where he made another U-turn, heading back toward the gate. Without letting the truck stop, he accelerated again, gaining speed enough to shift into second gear. Ralph Silva wound the engine up as tight as it would go, then shifted into third. By the time the truck reached the front gate it was traveling nearly forty-five miles an hour. The reinforced steel front bumper of the truck hit the spot where the two swinging gates were chained and locked together, snapping the chain, and knocking one side of the gate off its hinges.

The distance from the gate to Highway 101, was about thirty feet. Ralph Silva didn't even try to slowdown after crashing through the gate. The front end of the truck bounced as it hit the rain gutter, then continued into the northbound lane. Whipping the steering wheel hard to the left, he headed for the southbound lanes, oblivious to the southbound passenger car he side swiped. Ralph Silva was on a mission. It would take him less than five minutes to reach the park.

The stolen fuel truck reached its target at the junction of Highway 101 and Highway 199 ten minutes after it left the fuel farm.

The driver slowed to about forty miles per hour as he scanned the intersection of these two highways and the flow of traffic as it merged Highway 199 onto southbound Highway 101. Selecting his location, the driver pulled to the right shoulder and let a half-dozen cars pass on northbound 101. When he gauged the highway to be clear of traffic, he cranked the wheel of the thirty foot truck to the left and pushed the accelerator to the floor. The truck jumped forward and was now at right angles to the highway blocking the southbound lane. Stopping briefly, he put the truck in reverse and backed up enough so that the truck blocked both the north and southbound lanes.

Because the shoulders in this location were only three feet wide on each side of the highway and were bordered by dense undergrowth, giant ferns, and numerous Redwood trees, there was no way for traffic to pass in either direction.

Jumping out of the cab, the driver ran to the back of the truck and rapidly opened the fuel control valves. Fuel heating oil flowed from the tank truck onto the asphalt.

The affect on traffic was immediate. Vehicles were beginning to stack up on both sides of the truck, and within a minute there were no less than fifty cars, trucks, and motor homes stacked up on the north side of the fuel truck. In short order there were at least as many on the south side. Most of the drivers and passengers stayed in their vehicles. Drivers on the north coast are used to construction delays during the summer and assumed the road would be reopened soon. Only a few people made the connection that it was a holiday and there wouldn't be construction going on.

Had the tanker truck contained gasoline it would have been a simple matter of dropping a lighted match on the ground to ignite the fuel. Heating oil, however, is a less refined petroleum product than gasoline. As such it has a higher ignition point, or temperature where it will continue to burn once an ignition source is introduced. Qassim Saleh had planned for this contingency.

While the driver of the fuel tanker was jockeying the truck to block the highway, the driver of the Humvee that had followed the truck made a U-turn to head south back into town and parked on the right shoulder. As soon as he parked, he grabbed two ordinary highway warning flares from his equipment bag and ran back to the fuel truck. The two men spoke briefly then each struck their flare against its striker cap. The two flares burst to life. The sulfur compound in the flares emitted a low hissing sound as it burned. Within seconds the flares were burning at over five hundred degrees. Each man dropped his flare into the liquid pooling on the highway.

Unlike gasoline, the fuel oil did not roar into a fireball as soon as it came in contact with the flame. Instead, it began to burn and immediately created a dense black smoke. Both men ran toward the parked Humvee knowing within a minute the flame would work its' way back to the fuel tank control valve where it would find its' way inside the tank. Only when the fuel oil reached the proper temperature within the tank would the entire truck explode.

Motorists on the north side of the truck could not see what was happening on the south side. Those on the south side watched in disbelief as the two men lit their flares and dropped them on the ground. It was only when the flames began to encroach on the vehicles nearest the truck that any of the drivers reacted. While the two men were running toward their escape vehicle, the drivers of the closest cars quickly got their passengers out and ran from the approaching flames.

One man had the presence of mind to use his cell phone to dial 911.

In California, all cellular 911 calls are routed to the Highway Patrol, then rerouted to the proper city or county agency to handle the emergency. Once the man was connected to the Highway Patrol Communication Center in Eureka he excitedly related the burning fuel truck blocking the highway and the actions of the two men. The communications operator acknowledged the call and began to contact the appropriate resources.

Her first call was to the Highway Patrol beat unit responsible for that location.

"95-1, Humboldt, 95-1," she called on the radio.

"Humboldt, 95-1 at Lake Earl Drive," the voice of a male officer replied.

"95-1, a truck fire at 101 and 199, possible arson involved, the suspects fled southbound in a military style Humvee. Suspects described only as male, possibly Hispanic, early twenties, dressed in army fatigues.

"Humboldt, 95-1 copies, enroute," the officer acknowledged the call.

"95-1, I'm contacting the S.O. and fire," the communications operator concluded the conversation.

As soon as she finished talking to the officer, she punched up the Del Norte Sheriff's Office on her computer and waited for the direct connection phone to ring. After several seconds with no connection, she tried again. She then tried the county fire department and again found her call would not go through.

Unphased, she called the Highway Patrol unit assigned to the area around Crescent City and asked the officer to "10-5," or relay, the information about the possible arson suspects and the need for a fire truck to the sheriff's office dispatcher.

Knowing the S.O. dispatcher would be scanning the CHP radio, the female officer transmitted the information on the CHP frequency. The dispatcher responded on the S.O. radio frequency knowing the officer was listening on the scanner in her patrol car. It was an awkward way to communicate, but it worked. Unfortunately, the phone lines were still out and the sheriff's dispatcher could not call for a fire truck.

She did, however, put out a B-O-L, or "Be-On-the-Lookout," to all police and sheriff's units for two possible arson suspects, dressed in army uniforms, driving a military Humvee heading south into Crescent City.

It took the fuel truck designated to block the highway south of Crescent City about three minutes longer to get to its' target area than it had taken the other truck to get in position north of town.

The location selected for the southern roadblock was called "Last Chance Grade." In this location, Highway 101 travels from within yards of the ocean up the side of a mountain for about a mile. The highway had been cut out of the side of the mountain with numerous switch backs and curves. On one side of the highway the mountain loomed above the road. On the other it was a sheer drop off to the Pacific Ocean four hundred feet below. The entire one mile stretch was posted thirty-five miles per hour because of how dangerous the road was in this location.

Driving south from Crescent City, the fuel tanker truck reached the top of the grade and slowed, as did the Humvee that was following. The driver studied the roadway for a few seconds, let several northbound vehicles pass, then turned the wheels to the left. The front of the truck nosed across the northbound lane at a forty-five degree angle and came to rest against the side of the mountain. The rear one-third of the truck was still in the southbound lane. Because there were no shoulders of any kind along the grade, the whole highway was blocked in less than ten seconds.

Just as the men north of town had done, the southern roadblock team opened the tanker's fuel control valves and repositioned their Humvee. The content of this tanker truck was diesel fuel rather than fuel oil. As soon as the liquid started to flow, the air was full of the kerosene type smell associated with diesel.

Mirroring what happened north of town, the southern roadblock immediately caused traffic to backup in both directions. Drivers on the south side of the truck could see the diesel fuel flowing down the six percent grade in the roadway, and within a minute the first three cars in line were surrounded by the smelly liquid.

The driver of the first car in line did not comprehend what was happening when the two men, dressed in army fatigues, lit the highway warning flares. He watched as molten sulfur spewed from the flares as the flame burned red hot. It wasn't until the men dropped the flares and the diesel fuel ignited, that he yelled to his wife to run.

Now having an ignition source that would sustain itself, the diesel fuel burned both down the grade toward the vehicles trapped in the queue, and north back to the fuel tanker itself. Although not as refined as gasoline, the diesel fuel was more combustible than the fuel oil in the other tanker truck. The liquid burst to life and flame now followed the fuel source while creating rolling clouds of black smoke.

The two men ran back toward their Humvee as soon as they were satisfied the fire would perpetuate itself.

The occupants of the second and third cars in line on the south side of the tanker could only partially see what was happening ahead of them.

The second car was driven by an elderly man accompanied by his wife. They never had a chance. The burning liquid engulfed their car within seconds. Both died still wearing their seat belts. In the third car, a man and his wife watched in horror as the car ahead burst into flames. They yelled at the same time and were out of their car in an instant. On the driver's side, the man tore open the back seat and feverously tried to undo the safety harness that held his two year old daughter in her car seat. On the passenger's side, the mother quickly opened the rear door and had the regular seat belt off of her eight year old son in an instant. Grabbing the boy by the shoulders, she physically jerked him out of the back seat and clutched him to her chest as she ran down the road away from the encroaching flame.

The five way restraint system on his daughter's car seat had always been a struggle to fasten and unfasten. She was still asleep in the seat as her father yanked on the straps. She did not awaken even when the flames incinerated them both.

Several citizens dialed 911 and reported the fire and the circumstances involving the two men in army uniforms. Just as she had done in the previous incident, the Highway Patrol communications operator notified the beat unit that patrolled the Last Chance Grade area, and because her phone lines to Crescent City were still down, she used the same officer in the town area to 10-5 the information to the sheriff's office.

Although she wasn't a cop, the "comm-op" was an eighteen year veteran with the Highway Patrol. She took her job deadly serious, and believed it her responsibility to tell "her officers" things they might not know otherwise. Two fuel truck fires in less than ten minutes, same descriptions of the possible arson suspects, same vehicle type. She could smell something wrong.

145

At the beachfront park, Red Wolff was watching the Commanding General of the California National Guard wrap up his comments to the assembled crowd. She had the volume on her radio turned way down, but her subconscious mind could hear what she thought was a lot of radio traffic and something about a truck fire. Even though she was on a special detail to escort the Governor, she was still the only on-duty CHP supervisor. She casually walked back to her patrol car and sat behind the wheel just as the radio came to life.

"95-S-3, Humboldt, S-3," the radio called. Red Wolff could detect a sense of urgency in the comm-op's voice.

"S-3 at the park with CHP 5000, go ahead," Red Wolff answered.

The communications operator laid out the events of the past ten minutes north and south of town, and the fact that the phone lines were down to Crescent City. Red Wolff acknowledged the information and sat in the car for several moments digesting what she had just been told.

She rejoined Ray Silva as he watched the Governor rise to speak.

"What up Red?" he asked.

"Weird stuff," she replied. "Tanker truck fires north and south of town, possibly arson related by a couple of guys in army uniforms, phone lines aren't working either."

"The Governor in town must be bad mojo. The quicker we get her back on the plane, the better," Ray Silva said matter-of-factly.

Red Wolff didn't say anything, her mind still working to sort out what the comm-op had reported.

———

As the Governor rose to speak, Emil Lagare radioed the three remaining fuel tanker trucks and the two men who were positioned three streets away, telling them to proceed on their missions. He then gave his formation of men the command "Forward March." Just as they had done for countless hours at the training camp in the desert, the eighteen men, nineteen counting Emil Lagare at the head of the formation, began to march down the street. It was 10:28.

Behind Emil Lagare came three men carrying flags on highly polished heavy wooden staffs. The flags of the United States, the State of California, and the California National Guard had been easily obtained over the internet. There were no fewer than two dozen companies selling every conceivable type of flag, in every size, on the web. Just as he had done with other items he'd purchased, the imam ordered the full-sized four by six foot flags with decorative gold trim fringes, and the wooden poles, from different companies. The flags were top quality, and were in fact, better quality than the ones the National Guard unit troopers were holding at the park.

The three men who carried the flags were also carrying M-16 rifles. The rifles were slung on their shoulders with the muzzle down. Flag bearers did not carry weapons at the same time they carried flags in a parade situation, but the planners of the operation had reasoned by the time somebody noticed, it would be too late.

Following the flags came five rows of men in columns three abreast. In the formation the men who carried rifles had them on their right shoulder. The four machine guns were carried in the sling arms position.

In drill field perfect step, Emil Lagare's small formation made its' way the two blocks down the street, and made a column right turn that headed it directly into the park. Marching from the street onto the grass of the beachfront park, they were heading right between the microphone where the Governor was speaking, and the front of the one hundred soldiers of the National Guard unit standing at attention in company formation. Fifty more yards, Emil Lagare thought to himself.

So many things happened in the next two minutes nobody could be sure in what order they occurred.

At the northern city limits, one of the on-duty city police units was positioned so the officer could observe southbound traffic. Having monitored the call of the truck fire north of town and possible arson suspects headed south on Highway 101, he knew they would have to pass his location. Within a few moments the olive drab painted Humvee passed the officer. As it did, the officer could see two males in the vehicle dressed in camouflaged army uniforms. At the same time both men in the vehicle saw the officer.

Following standard procedure, the officer began to follow the vehicle, while calling other units for back-up before attempting a traffic stop. One Crescent City police unit and the Highway Patrol unit assigned to the town area both monitored the call and radioed they would be in position to assist in less than a minute. As the officer continued to follow the suspect vehicle, he talked on the radio to the two other units devising a plan to use felony stop procedures. As soon as the other two units joined the first officer, he activated the patrol car's overhead lights and tapped the siren to gain the driver's attention.

The driver of the Humvee was one of the four young Muslim men from Oakland who joined the operation to provide logistical support and drive the motor homes. As soon as he saw the red lights in the mirror, his first thought was to pull to the curb. The vehicle slowed slightly, then accelerated rapidly southbound on Highway 101, with two police cars and the Highway Patrol unit directly behind. Following standard practice, the officer in the first unit focused on driving, while the officer in the second unit advised the dispatcher they were in pursuit. The female Highway Patrol officer trailed behind, knowing if the pursuit left the city limits, she would take over as lead unit. She advised Humboldt Dispatch she was involved in a pursuit with the city police.

At the park, Red Wolff and Ray Silva continued to watch the Governor speak as they monitored the pursuit on the radio. "Jesus Christ Ray, what the hell is going on today?" There was a tone of exasperation in her voice. Ray Silva just shook his head.

The Humvee, being pursued by three units was heading into the heart of downtown Crescent City on southbound 101. In this location the two north and two southbound lanes are separated by two city blocks of motels, fast food restaurants, and small businesses. Running perpendicular are city streets that intersect the main highway for nine blocks. The speed limit is a reasonable thirty-five miles per hour. The Humvee was doing over seventy.

The two teenage couples in the small compact car were having a great Fourth of July. They were headed to the Smith River for some swimming and a party with another group of kids. The eighteen year old driver of the car had just scored a couple six packs of beer, and was laughing with his friends as he pulled from one of the cross streets into the intersection. It was only when the girl in the left rear seat screamed that he saw the fast moving Humvee bearing down on him.

In a collision between a fast moving heavy vehicle, and a slow moving smaller vehicle, the smaller vehicle always loses. The front of the Humvee struck the little car broadside and virtually ran over the top of the compact vehicle. Both the male driver and the female passenger in the left rear were killed instantly. The boy and girl on the passenger side were crushed by the weight of the Humvee and pinned inside. They would live, but both would be paraplegics for the rest of their lives.

After rolling over the top of the smaller car, the Humvee spun one hundred eighty degrees, coming to a stop facing north in the southbound lanes. The two city police units, and the one Highway Patrol unit fanned out three abreast across the southbound lanes in a "V" formation and came to a stop thirty feet from the suspect vehicle. The city police officers exited their vehicles with handguns drawn, while the female Highway Patrol officer removed the shotgun from its' vertical mount in the front seat of her vehicle. All three officers took up kneeling positions behind the open doors of their cars.

The female officer racked a round from the shotgun's magazine into the chamber of the weapon. It made that distinctive harsh metallic sound as she pumped the slide back, then rammed it forward locking the breech. Following CHP policy, she left the safety on as required, a precaution against an accidental discharge, and took aim at the Humvee.

Traffic was backing up behind the officers as they prepared to execute a felony stop. Several citizens were already at the small compact car trying to help the victims of the crash.

Just as one of the city police officers began to yell at the suspects in the Humvee, the passenger's side door opened, followed within a second by the driver's door. Out of both sides of the vehicle came the barrels of rifles. All of the officers instantly knew they were M-16s by the distinctive arch shaped front sight on the barrel. Both of the men in the Humvee leaned out of their vehicle and opened fire.

The two city officers returned fire immediately.

As soon as the suspects fired their first round, the female officer drew the butt of the shotgun tight to her shoulder as protection against the weapons nasty recoil and pulled the trigger. Nothing happened. Muttering to herself, without taking the shotgun from her cheek, she moved her finger from the trigger, pushed the safety release button, and pulled the trigger again. The shotgun roared as she discharged the first round.

It was a firepower mismatch. 5.56 caliber rounds now filled the air as the men in the Humvee showered bullets on the officers. Each round traveled at 3,200 feet per second disintegrating anything it struck. The first rounds punctured the driver's side door of the city police car directly in front of the suspects. The officer behind the door was hit seven times in the torso and three times in the arms and legs. He crumbled to the ground dying within seconds.

Because the suspects stayed inside the Humvee, they presented very small targets for the two remaining officers. To the left side of the "V" the remaining Crescent City Police Officer was firing at the suspect in the passenger's seat of the Humvee as fast as he could pull the trigger of his 9 millimeter pistol. The "spray and pray" method of returning fire was not something police weapons instructors taught. It relied on the sheer volume of fire, and luck, to hit a suspect. In this case, however, up against an automatic weapon, the officer didn't have a lot of options. The officer's method paid off, not that any of the fourteen rounds he fired hit the suspect, but because his rate of fire kept the man with the rifle from being able to take aim at him. It also gave the officer time to reposition himself behind the engine compartment of his vehicle where the cast iron engine block would deflect incoming rounds, and the time he needed to reload with a fresh magazine.

On the right side of the "V" the female Highway Patrol officer was returning fire with the man on the driver's side of the Humvee. The Muslim from Oakland had been trained in firearms by the imam during one of his many weekend "religious" outings to the California delta country. He had not, however, fired an M-16 rifle before. Although he managed to fire several rounds at the female officer, he was wildly inaccurate. Part of his problem in firing accurately was that he was right-eye dominant, and needed to have his right cheek against the left side of the rifle stock to take proper aim. In his training by the imam, he had never fired any type of weapon using his left eye. Firing the M-16 from the left side of his head just wasn't working. Abandoning the cover of the military vehicle with its' steel reinforced doors, he stepped out onto the pavement where he had sufficient room to bring the rifle up to his right cheek.

It was all the opening the female officer needed. As soon as she saw the suspect's head appear in the space between the Humvee's body and the open door frame she fired a round. The twelve double-aught buckshot pellets spread out twenty feet after they left the shotguns barrel. By the time they traveled the thirty feet to the suspect, they had a spread pattern about two feet wide. Ten of the pellets missed, hitting either the Humvee's windshield or the open door. One struck the young Muslim man in the left shoulder causing him to drop his rifle. The last pellet hit him above the left eye, grazing his forehead. It was not a serious injury, but like all head wounds, it bled profusely. As soon as she fired the round that hit the suspect, the officer racked a fresh round into the chamber and fired again. This time she fired at the bottom of the open door. Because the Humvee sits high off the ground, the area between the suspect's knees and his feet was fully exposed. Seven of the twelve pellets hit the suspect in the front of his legs. He dropped to the ground screaming and writhing in pain.

While still seated in the passenger side of the Humvee and still firing at the city police officer, the suspect saw his driver exit, then fall to the ground after being hit by the shotgun blast. Alone now, and with no chance of help, the remaining suspect weighed his options. He could stay and shoot it out with the officers, or he could run in hopes of rejoining Emil Lagare at the beachfront park. Putting a new thirty round magazine into his rifle, the man fired four more three round bursts at the Crescent City officer still crouched behind the engine compartment of his police car, then ran south on Highway 101.

The city police officer's initial reaction was to run after the suspect, but when the man turned and fired another three round burst in his direction, he stopped in his tracks. The officer tried momentarily to start the engine on his vehicle but the M-16 rounds from the suspect had punctured numerous holes in the radiator and the engine block.

The female Highway Patrol officer saw the other suspect running and realized he was out of range for her shotgun. She quickly yelled for the city police officer to join her. Telling the officer to secure the suspect who was on the ground, she jumped back in her patrol car and roared off southbound after the other suspect.

He was about two blocks ahead, running hard, and looking over his shoulder at the same time.

The Ford Crown Victoria's engine whined as the female officer kept the accelerator to the floor, not giving the transmission a chance to shift into a higher gear. The patrol car was gaining speed rapidly, and the distance between the suspect and the black and white patrol car closed to less than a block.

Very few things in police work elicit spontaneous reflex reactions in cops. Most reactions are trained responses to specific situations. Being shot at, and seeing a fellow officer killed, however, are not events that can be trained for. Running on adrenalin, the female officer's primal instincts took charge of her actions.

The suspect, who was running down the middle of the highway, had not looked over his shoulder in the past several seconds. When he did, it took his brain a moment to comprehend what his eyes saw. The black and white police car was less than fifty feet away, bearing down on him at almost sixty miles an hour.

He tried to stop, turn, aim, and fire, all at the same time. He managed only to turn slightly and begin to bring the rifle up to his shoulder. The push bumpers on the front of the CHP car hit the suspect first. The force of the impact slammed his head into the pavement cracking his skull open, killing him instantly. The entire weight of the full-sized sedan then ran over his prostrate body.

Although she didn't know she did it, the female officer yelled, "Take that scumbag!" her adrenalin pumping, pulse racing, and sweat running down her face.

Once she regained her composure, the officer called the communications center to report what had just occurred. The comm-op called Red Wolff. Governor's detail or no Governor's detail, an officer involved shooting required a supervisor to respond.

"Ray, I've got to go, we've had a shooting, a city officer is dead, and multiple fatalities out of a pursuit. You take care of things here and let the L.T. know what's going on," Red Wolff told Ray Silva.

"No problem Red."

He had no more than gotten the words out of his mouth when a loud explosion in the distance ripped through the air, followed three seconds later by two more in rapid succession. Any cellular phone communications within fifteen miles of Crescent City ceased, as the pre-planted dynamite bombs brought down the antenna towers.

"Now what?" Red Wolff said out loud.

The explosions were close and loud enough that they caused the Governor to pause mid-sentence in her speech.

At the head of his formation of men, Emil Lagare did not miss a step as they marched closer to the podium. Twenty-five yards, he thought to himself.

Seated behind the Governor, the National Guard General saw the formation of marching men coming in from the street and across the grass, heading for the podium. From his seat, he looked inquisitively at the captain of the local guard company who was standing at attention at the head of the formation in front of the Governor. The general's eyes said to the captain, "Who the fuck are these guys?"

The captain saw the marching men about the same time the general did. He didn't know who the men were, or why they were marching right into the middle of a ceremony already in progress. Even if he wanted to do something, protocol dictated that with the Governor speaking, he could do nothing but stand there and watch. The captain's return look to the general told him, "I have no idea who they are."

When Red Wolff told Ray Silva she had to leave to take charge of the officer involved shooting scene, he was watching the formation of marching men as they turned from the street and onto the grass of the park.

"Hang on a second Red," he said to her with kind of a quizzical tone in his voice.

Red Wolff recognized that tone from years ago, and she knew, even now, he had great street instincts. "What's up?" she asked.

"Look at this," he said. "Anything look funny to you?"

With all the events that had happened in the last five minutes, the truck fires, arson, a pursuit and shooting, and then explosions just moments before, Red Wolff's brain was working overtime to process everything. She looked at the formation of men marching into the park and drew a blank. "Looks like another screwed up army parade," she said, jabbing Ray Silva with a dig about the army.

"Red, I know the air force is just a "semi-military" outfit, but even they don't march as bad as these guys. Look at the two in the last rank."

Red Wolff saw exactly what Ray Silva had seen. In the last rank of the formation, two of the former Iraqi soldiers had reverted to marching in the stiff, high-arc arm swing style that was unique to the Republican Guards. The two Iraqi's had been chastised numerous times at the desert training camp about marching in this manner, but in the excitement of the moment, they had unknowingly reverted to their training as part of Saddam Hussein's elite troops.

"I see them. American troops don't march like that. And look Ray, why do all of them have magazines in their weapons?" Red Wolff exclaimed.

"I don't know, but I don't like it," Ray Silva said, his instincts telling him something was terribly wrong.

Fifteen more yards, Emil Lagare whispered to himself.

CHAPTER ELEVEN

In the center of town, over a mile from the park, two fuel tanker trucks were moving toward their targets. The third truck was stopped a quarter-mile from its designated target while the driver said his final prayers in this life.

The first truck gathered speed as it traveled down the two lane street toward the Del Norte County Sheriff's Office. The driver knew the front of the office was three steps higher than the street, and there was a red painted curb that prohibited parking directly in front of the entrance. There was no other traffic on the street that would impede his progress, a sign he thought from Allah for the success of his mission. The driver had the heavy three-axle fuel tank truck going over sixty miles per hour as he turned the wheel slightly to the left and pressed the accelerator all the way to the floorboard. The truck now angled across the opposite lane and struck the raised curb at the sidewalk.

Loaded with diesel fuel, the truck weighed over eighteen thousand pounds, but the forward momentum of the vehicle easily carried it across the sidewalk and up the three steps. The front of the truck smashed through the double glass door entrance and continued across the lobby of the office. The truck had just enough remaining speed to crush the sheriff's dispatcher as she sat at her radio console. The fuel laden vehicle finally came to a stop when it struck the concrete wall that formed one side of the jail cellblock.

Yelling Allah Akbar, the driver brought his right hand off the steering wheel and up to his chest where the garage door transmitter was taped to the two sticks of stolen dynamite that had been fashioned into an improvised bomb. The driver had secured the bomb to his chest to ensure it would be immediately accessible after he crashed the truck into the building. Secure in the knowledge that he was only seconds away from meeting Allah, the driver pressed the button without hesitation.

The bomb detonated instantaneously, rupturing the truck's three thousand gallon tank, spewing burning fuel in all directions. Within thirty seconds, the sheriff's office became an inferno. The force of the explosion disintegrated the wall separating the business office from the jail cells. Flames, now fed by the burning diesel fuel, quickly spread into the cellblock sucking out the oxygen and filling the room with thick black smoke. The male deputy who was in charge of the jail was killed in the initial explosion, leaving no one to free the prisoners from their cells as the flames continued to march down the cellblock. Eleven male and two female prisoners died screaming, incinerated in their locked cells.

The flames also spread to the back of the sheriff's office toward the locker room, the roll call room, and the numerous other offices where everyday business was conducted out of sight of the public. Besides the dispatcher and the deputy in charge of the cellblock, only one other deputy was in the building. That deputy had just finished booking a prisoner and was completing some paperwork when the explosion occurred. He received a face full of flying glass when the bomb detonated, blinding him temporarily. Unable to see, he couldn't navigate his way out of the burning building. The deputy died when a portion of the burning roof collapsed on top of him. The Del Norte County Sheriff's Office ceased to exist.

Within moments of the explosion that decimated the sheriff's office, the driver of the second truck was careening across the parking lot of the Crescent City and Del Norte County government building. The building was home to all of the departments and offices that made a city and county operate. Located on the corner of the building, twenty feet from the edge of the parking lot, was the police department.

Unknown to the driver of the truck, no one was at the police department. Because there were only eleven officers on the department, it was not unusual that the office would be closed on weekends and holidays. A sign on the door directed people to contact the sheriff's office down the street in case of an emergency.

Like his fellow team member, the driver of the second truck was focused only on his mission. The truck did not lose any momentum as it rumbled over the concrete tire stops in the parking lot at almost fifty miles per hour and across the grass. The truck crashed into the old wooden building and penetrated almost to the rear of the police department.

Believing Allah would be pleased with his actions, the driver pushed the button on the transmitter attached to his chest. The resulting explosion destroyed almost half of the offices in the building. The fire from the burning fuel would destroy the rest. In an ironic twist of fate, the one officer that should have been at the police station, who would have been killed by the explosion, had just left to drive to McDonalds for his regular lunch, a Quarter-Pounder with cheese Value Meal, super-sized.

———

At the small boat harbor, the driver of the third truck finished his prayers. He started the engine of his vehicle and drove slowly to the point he had selected to begin his run. Saying out loud to himself over and over Allah Akbar, he accelerated the truck forward. It took almost a hundred yards to get the gasoline laden truck up to twenty miles an hour, but after that it began to gain speed more rapidly. Now doing almost thirty, he approached the right turn which would bring him on the direct course to his target. The truck groaned as he fought the wheel to the right but it slowly began to turn in the desired direction. The turning radius of the truck was much greater than the driver thought, and as he approached the end of the turn, the left front of the truck sideswiped a parked car.

The collision had no effect on his speed, and driver pushed the gas pedal to the floor. Completely fixated now on his target, the driver held the steering wheel tight in his hands. Allah Akbar, Allah Akbar.

The truck struck the closed chain link fence at the entrance to the Coast Guard pier at forty miles an hour, still accelerating. The fence exploded off its hinges and flew into the air coming down next to two Coast Guard enlisted men who were shooting baskets at the hoop against the side of the building. Seventy-five yards ahead, the port side of the cutter was snuggled tight against the pier.

Aiming for the gangway that provided access from the pier to the ship, the driver had the truck traveling over seventy miles per hour when it reached the end of the pier. Even though the truck with its full load of automotive gasoline weighed nearly ten tons, the speed it was traveling allowed the front wheels about two seconds of flight after they left the end of the pier. Because the pier was about a foot higher than the side of the cutter, the momentum of the truck carried it almost ten feet onto the vessel before it crashed into the side of the main superstructure.

When the truck crashed into the side of the vessel, the fuel tank ruptured immediately, filling the air with the distinctive smell of spilled gasoline. The fluid poured from a large gash in the tank and began running over the deck. Raw gasoline found its way down open hatchways and air vents on the deck. When the driver pushed the button on his bomb, the results were catastrophic.

The fireball shot thirty feet into the air and flames billowed outward from the truck. Gasoline made its' way into the vessel and ignited, catching anything that would burn on fire. The conflagration now took on a life of its' own as it began to consume the cutter. It took only minutes for the fire to reach the main communications center where it consumed millions of dollars worth of the latest communications equipment in the world. At the same time the flames reached the vessel's own fuel supply. The heat from the fire quickly brought the ship's twenty-eight hundred gallons of diesel fuel to an ignition point and it too began to burn, adding to the destruction. The cutter would be a burnt out hulk within ten minutes.

———

The explosions that destroyed the sheriff's office and the police department were far enough away from the park that the muffled sound in the distance could have been loud firecrackers. Within several minutes, however, black clouds of smoke could be seen rising over the center of Crescent City. Even the Governor took notice of them while still talking from the podium.

Locked in by protocol, neither the sheriff, nor chief of police, could leave their seats to try and find out what was happening. The county's undersheriff, seated in the last row of folding chairs, discretely left his seat, moved a few yards behind the other seated VIPs, and tried to make a cell phone call. The visual display on his phone told him there was no signal.

Near the podium, the officers of the Governor's Protection Detail began looking at each other and shifting nervously on their feet. Their new commander, Captain Aimee Gardner, heard the explosions, but didn't think anything about them.

Red Wolff, her senses now fully alerted, quickly moved back to her patrol car and called the communications center to see if the comm-op had any information on what the explosions were. Ray Silva moved near his patrol car at the same time, taking up a position from which he could react to whatever happened next.

Emil Lagare was ten yards from where he wanted to be.

Five blocks from the park, two men from the communications team used their rifle butts to break the glass in the upper half of the wooden door to the town's only radio station. Reaching through the broken window, they unlocked the dead bolt securing the bottom half of the door.

KDEL had been run by the same person for over forty years. While it was still a low power AM station that only broadcasted eighteen hours a day, it was the only game in town. It was a family business, and today, the owner of the station, who was also a city councilman, was an honored guest seated behind the Governor. The owner's son-in-law was on-the-air today, playing music, giving weather reports and reading commercials.

The station's business office on the first floor was dark, illuminated only by the light from the street. The broadcast studio on the second floor was about as big as an average sized living room, with a sliding glass door leading to a large balcony overlooking the park and the ocean beyond.

The two men charged up the steps and burst into the studio. Seated behind the console while music played, the owner's son-in-law saw the two men in uniform as they entered the room. He knew it was unusual anyone would be in the station when it was closed, but they were in uniform, and there was a ceremony honoring the town's National Guard unit going on only blocks away. He smiled at the men and gave them a casual salute. One of the men fired a three round burst into his chest.

Instead of smashing the broadcast console, the man who'd fired his weapon sat in the chair and began to study the switches, dials, and computer system that ran the radio station. Trained in broadcasting and electronics, it took him only a minute to figure out how the entire system worked. He flipped a switch on the console and the station went off the air. The other man began pushing furniture around in the studio to barricade the stairs.

———

When the third fuel truck exploded at the harbor, it was not only close enough to hear, it was close enough that the shock wave could be felt by everyone at the beachfront park.

Red Wolff looked at the rising smoke from the harbor and said, "Damn."

Still marching toward the podium, Emil Lagare could see the rising smoke also. Five more yards, he said to himself.

At that moment, two vehicles arrived on the street running parallel to the park. They came from opposite directions.

The first was the pickup truck driven by the young man Patricia Dodge had enticed into giving her and her cameraman a ride from the airport to the park. The man pulled to the curb and the cameraman, who was sitting on the right side, said thanks to the driver while opening the door and getting out of the truck at the same time. Seated in the middle, Patricia Dodge smiled and told the man how much she appreciated his help and started to slide across the seat toward the door, but not before she again "accidentally" brushed her breast against the man's arm. In his dreams, she smiled to herself as she closed the door.

From the curb they were about fifty yards from the podium. They would have to walk across the grass to get a good shot of the Governor and the troops in formation. Her cameraman was already getting some long range footage of the park, the crowd, and the National Guard unit in formation. From this angle he also got footage of a small contingent of men marching across the grass toward the podium. Patricia Dodge smoothed out the front of her dark gray wool pants suit. She couldn't wait to get out of Northern California and back to L.A. where she could wear real clothes from Nordstrom's.

From the other end of the street, Ralph Silva pushed the two and a half ton army truck as hard as it would go. Weaving past the traffic on the street parallel to the park, he muscled the steering wheel and turned into the park entrance. Honking the truck's horn and waving his arm out the open window as he drove, he spotted several black and white patrol cars.

Although his arrival had been noisy, it hadn't been loud enough that it stopped the Governor's speech, nor was it noticed by any of the dignitaries in the park.

Red Wolff and Ray Silva did notice his arrival. This was the kind of unexpected thing they were there to handle. Their guard up, they diverted their attention from the formation of marching men to the soldier running toward them.

"Uncle Ray, Uncle Ray," Ralph Silva panted as he ran toward them. He was fifteen seconds too late.

Emil Lagare gave his small formation of men the command to halt when he judged they were centered on the podium.

By this time, the Governor had stopped her prepared remarks and looked over her shoulder questioningly at her Chief of Staff, the general, and the Mayor of Crescent City. None of them gave her any indication they knew what was happening.

Emil Lagare now marched smartly up to the podium, stood in front of the Governor, and gave her a crisp salute.

The officers from the protection detail were on edge, their street smarts and experience telling them something wasn't right. While they didn't know exactly what wasn't right, they did know, no one, especially someone they knew had a weapon, should be that close to the Governor without an officer at her elbow. They looked to their commander for direction.

Aimee Gardner stood motionless. Her time in headquarters had taught her careers are made or ruined by making the wrong decision. If she directed her officers in, to protect the Governor, and it turned out this was something planned as part of the ceremony, the Governor would be embarrassed. The Governor would call the Commissioner of the Highway Patrol and chew his ass out. The Commissioner would in turn take a bite out of her butt, then transfer her to Death Valley for the rest of her career. Her decision was to not make a decision. Aimee Gardner remained motionless.

Twenty-five yards behind the Governor, Red Wolff listened to Ralph Silva as he hurriedly tried to explain the scene he'd found at the armory. Ray Silva heard all he needed to hear and was already removing the AR-15 rifle from the Electro-Loc of his patrol car.

"They're impostors, they're impostors!" Red Wolff screamed, as she drew her .40 caliber Smith and Wesson semi-automatic pistol and started running toward the podium.

Her screaming caused everyone seated in the VIP section to turn in their seats to see what the commotion was.

Moving to the side of the podium, Emil Lagare unholstered his stolen, army issue 9 millimeter Beretta pistol. Then grabbing the Governor by her arm, he pulled her toward him, while bringing the pistol up and pressing the barrel against her temple.

Once he had the Governor, Emil Lagare's men broke formation and began to bring their weapons up to firing position.

Not waiting for a signal from Aimee Gardner, the three officers and one sergeant of the protection detail reached for their weapons. Nothing in Aimee Gardner's experience had prepared her to react in this type of situation. She stood there transfixed.

Ten of Emil Lagare's men opened fire on the formation of National Guard troopers, while the remaining eight took aim at the assembled crowd of dignitaries and fired.

From only fifteen yards away they couldn't miss. It was a massacre on an unthinkable scale. The staccato of the M-249 machine guns, as they spewed out hundreds of non-stop rounds, was accented by the three round bursts from the men armed with M-16s.

Two of the officers on the protection detail managed to get their weapons out of their holsters before they were cut down by machine gun rounds. Aimee Gardner died before she even realized what was happening, her weapon still in its' holster.

When Emil Lagare dragged the Governor clear of the VIP area, his men raked the seating area with bullets. Most of the guests in this area were still in their seats when the bullets ripped into their bodies. Even as they died, they still did not comprehend that terrorism had come to their town. The sheriff, who had jumped to his feet when Emil Lagare grabbed the Governor, managed to get his weapon out and fire two wild shots at the men who were raining rounds all around him. A three round burst from an M-16 took his head off. The CHP lieutenant and the chief of police took a kneeling position, and both returned fire with their pistols. The chief hit one of the men twice in the upper chest causing him to stagger backward. The internet bulletproof vest stopped both rounds. Lieutenant Bob Collier, Red Wolff's boss, had always been a good shot. Taking careful aim, he put two rounds into the forehead of one of the men firing a machine gun.

The men behind Emil Lagare kept firing at the small group of VIPs and officers standing on the sides of the seating area. Within thirty seconds, the unending hail of bullets had killed, or seriously wounded everyone around the podium.

Red Wolff, who was still running toward the podium, saw three of her own officers, the sergeant and his two officers from the protection detail, and her boss, killed by the intense fire from Emil Lagare's men. Although they had all valiantly returned fire, they were simply outgunned.

Blind with rage, her pistol in hand, she continued running toward her downed officers. Had she not been tackled by Ray Silva, she would have been cut down as well.

"Red, we can't help them," he told her as he dragged her behind the cover of a large tree.

While eight of Emil Lagare's men were firing at the VIP section, the other ten were raking the soldiers who were still standing in formation with withering fire. Once they realized what was happening, many of the troopers hit the ground, and were crawling toward the edges of the park, while others ran in all directions to save themselves. Armed with rifles, but with no ammunition, the soldiers were defenseless.

It took the people in the crowd a few seconds to realize what was happening also. Many at first thought the gunfire, people falling to the ground, the screaming, and the noise, were all part of some sort of demonstration the National Guard unit was doing in conjunction with the ceremony. It wasn't until bullets starting ripping into the crowd that many started running from the park.

The initial firing by Emil Lagare's men lasted for about forty-five seconds. In that brief time four hundred-fifty people, soldiers, cops, politicians, and ordinary citizens were killed outright. Hundreds more had been wounded and lay bleeding on the ground.

One group of armed men now began walking from the podium area through the park executing wounded soldiers on the ground, and murdering the men, women and children that had not fled the park who were cowering on the ground. Screams of "no, no" from citizens lying on the ground were ignored by the men as they fired indiscriminately at anyone still alive.

While one group of Emil Lagare's men were executing the defenseless people near the National Guard formation, another group formed a perimeter around about eighty people who had been seated near the podium. The armed men quickly, and roughly, separated the men from the women and children.

Qassim Saleh's plan called for the taking of a small number of women and children as hostages to use as human shields during the next part of the operation. The men were expendable.

From their location behind a tree, about thirty yards from the group of captive women, Red Wolff and Ray Silva could see that among the hostages were Mary Jean Snider and Julie Bradley.

They both watched in horror and disbelief as two of the men, armed with machine guns, turned their weapons on the thirty or so captive men. Holding the triggers of the automatic weapons they raked back and forth into the crowd of men. Screams of agony came from the women as they watched their men die. Among those who were killed, was the father of the two small children who had been sitting next to Mary Jean and Julie. The two children had no way of knowing they were now orphans. Their "sol-idger" mother had been cut down as she stood in formation.

Once they had finished murdering the unarmed men, both of them casually reloaded their weapons with fresh two hundred round plastic box magazines. It was at that moment one of the men saw Red Wolff and Ray Silva behind the tree.

Realizing they had been seen and with no where to run for safety, Red Wolff, armed with her pistol, and Ray Silva, armed with both his pistol and the AR-15 he had taken from his patrol car, began firing at the two men with the machine guns and the three other men who were guarding the women captives.

Red Wolff was an expert shot with a pistol. At fifty yards away, however, hitting a target, even one as large as a man, was more a matter of luck than skill. Added to that, the men firing at her had high powered weapons, and their bullets were chewing up the tree she was using for cover, making it nearly impossible for her to take good aim. On the other side of the tree, Ray Silva was in a prone position firing the AR-15 at the three men he could see. His side of the tree was also being hit with numerous rounds, splintering tree bark and sending wood chips flying everywhere. He did manage to hit one of the approaching men squarely in the "X-Ring." The man he hit was wearing one of the bulletproof vests the imam purchased over the internet. Unfortunately for that man, the vest he wore was similar in type to the ones worn by cops all over the nation. While it was extremely effective against almost all types of handguns, it did little to slow down the high powered AR-15 round Ray Silva fired. If he would have had time to look, Ray Silva could have seen the spreading ring of blood in the center of the man's chest.

Their position was becoming more untenable by the second. It would only be a matter of moments until one of them was going to be hit by the fusillade of bullets being fired at them.

Ray Silva, never one to get overly excited about tight predicaments, chose that moment to quip, "Does this mean there won't be a picnic?"

Not seeing the humor in being pinned down behind a tree by gunmen with automatic weapons, Red Wolff told him tersely, "You might want to choose your next smart-ass remark carefully Silva, it could be your last."

The five men had closed to within thirty yards of the tree, and were using fire and maneuver tactics to get closer, when they heard the truck coming.

Bouncing over the curb at the sidewalk, the two and a half ton army truck growled as it rolled onto the grass of the park and right between the five gunmen. The men couldn't believe what they were seeing as it pulled up to the tree.

Red Wolff and Ray Silva were on their feet and in the back of the truck in an instant. When the armed men saw what was happening, they opened fire on the vehicle with everything they had. The steel sides of the truck bed deflected the incoming rounds as Red

Wolff and Ray Silva pressed themselves flat onto the heavy gauge metal floor plate of the cargo area.

The truck never really came to a full stop before it was rolling again, carrying its' cargo to safety. Without a weapon, the only thing Ralph Silva could do was extend his left arm out the window and defiantly flip the men off as he drove away.

————————

Qassim Saleh had his "Shock and Awe." In the park there were over five hundred people dead, and perhaps an equal number wounded. At least half of those wounded would die in the next twenty-four hours as there was no way to get medical aid to them, or for them to get to the one hospital in the county. None of the deaths were clean and clinical. High powered weapons inflict horrible damage to the human body, leaving ghastly entry and exit wounds. Huge pools of blood formed next to the dead and dying, staining the grass a shiny black color. Chunks of bone, human tissue, and body parts were strewn everywhere.

Hundreds of people had fled the park in panic or were cowered down behind whatever cover they could find from the men who continued to fire at anything within range that moved.

The unthinkable had happened. Terrorists had attacked an American town. The town they attacked was not just any town. It was a small town, just like tens of thousands of other small towns across the entire country. The attack was not an isolated bomb planted here or there, or a commercial jet liner crashed into a building. It was carried out by armed men wielding not weapons of mass destruction, but with weapons that killed close up, causing a gruesome and painful death. The attack was designed to bring to the American people all of the horror and devastation from which, except for the events of 9/11, they considered themselves immune. Thus far it had accomplished all of that.

The unthinkable had happened. The system of government and emergency services, so common in any American town that they are taken for granted, had ceased to exist. Emergencies happen. Floods, fires, major crime, petty crime, power outages and earthquakes, are all part of life in America. From New York City to Crescent City it is the responsibility of government to respond to these events by providing the leadership and services necessary to mitigate the emergency. In Crescent City, however, in less than three minutes, armed terrorists had virtually cut the head off the government structure in the county. Those persons in leadership positions, elected or appointed, charged with making the governmental decisions, were all dead. Likewise, so were the leaders of all the public safety agencies, law enforcement, fire services, military, and disaster response in the county.

The unthinkable had happened. When an emergency occurs that is beyond the capabilities of local government, the state government is first in line to provide additional assistance. Events requiring an even larger response involve the federal government. For small events, generally such responses occur within a few hours, or can take several days when massive assistance is needed. The scope and swiftness of any response, however, is predicated on accurate communication and logistics. The terrorists had chosen their target well. Using only basic equipment and vehicles, they had cutoff almost all communication from Crescent City to the rest of the world. They had also isolated the town from receiving any immediate assistance via the highway system by creating roadblocks that took on a life of their own as more and more traffic found itself piled up in long lines, unable to enter or leave the town.

The unthinkable had happened. When Thomas Jefferson wrote "The price of liberty is eternal vigilance," he probably didn't envision three-day weekends. Terrorists had taken advantage of a day when celebrations of our independence cause Americans to let their guard down a little. Military and civil resources that could be brought into play, were at their lowest level of staffing readiness. Across California and the nation, except for the personnel necessary to sustain minimal operations, everyone else, from the decision making leadership, to the officers who patrolled the streets, to the grunt who slogged through the mud, was off-duty celebrating Independence Day.

The unthinkable had happened. For all intents and purposes, a group of armed Islamic terrorists were in control of an American town.

It had been a master stroke of planning. Qassim Saleh had used his knowledge of America to plan an attack that was unthinkable. It was unthinkable because no one had bothered to think it. Americans have short memories. The events of 9/11, as horrific as they were, were fast fading from memory. Political races, the latest misadventures of movie stars, steroid usage by sports figures, and the price of gasoline, were on their minds more than the possibility of an attack in their own town.

Qassim Saleh had only made two mistakes in his planning:

The first mistake he made was not realizing how hard Americans will fight back when they are attacked.

His second mistake was pissing off Red Wolff.

CHAPTER TWELVE

At the makeshift command post she established on a side street three blocks from the park Red Wolff could still hear sporadic gunfire coming from the automatic weapons of the attackers. It was a command post more in name, than any real substance, as it consisted of only one Highway Patrol vehicle and two city police cars. She put out a radio call for all officers, from all agencies, to meet at her location.

She didn't know the full extent of what had happened around the county, or exactly who the armed men were, but she knew the first thing that needed to be done, was to let Humboldt Communications Center know what had occurred.

Using her cell phone, she tried calling the communications center in Eureka but couldn't get a signal. Standing on the sidewalk next to several small businesses, she asked the two city police officers to break the glass door of a flower shop so she could get to a land line telephone. The officers were reluctant to destroy private property just to gain access to a phone.

"Don't you get it?" she said impatiently to the two officers. "There are fifteen to twenty men with automatic weapons right around the corner. I'm not sure, but I think they're probably Islamic terrorists. They just killed a shit load of people, including six Crescent City officers and your chief, most of the government officials in the county, God knows how many of my men, a bunch of sheriff's deputies, they captured the Governor, and they have women and children hostages! Now get one of those damn doors open!"

The city officers looked at each other, but did not move.

"Stand back, I'll do it," said Ralph Silva in his army uniform, armed now with the AR-15 from his uncle's patrol car. Using the butt of the weapon, he smashed the full length glass door of the local florist shop into thousands of little glass shards.

Picking her way through the metal door frame, with pieces of glass still clinging to it, Red Wolff found the phone behind the

167

counter. The smell of gunpowder in her nostrils was a stark contrast to the fragrance of the fresh cut flowers permeating the shop. She put the handset to her ear. There was no dial tone. "Crap," she muttered to herself.

Although she didn't want to use the Highway Patrol vehicle's radio to broadcast what had happened, she was out of options. Picking up the microphone, she took a breath before she keyed the mike.

"Humboldt, 95-S-3, emergency traffic," Red Wolff said clearly.

"All units on all frequencies standby, 95-S-3, go ahead with emergency traffic," the comm-op replied, anxiety in her voice.

For the next several minutes Sergeant Erin "Red" Wolff carefully explained to the person eighty miles away what she knew about the situation in Crescent City. The comm-op asked clarifying questions of Red Wolff trying to get her thought processes around the magnitude of what she was being told.

"S-3, Humboldt copies, what assistance do you require?" the comm-op asked.

"Everything."

"10-4, S-3, beginning notifications immediately."

The radio went silent for several seconds until the comm-op called again, "S-3, Humboldt, who's in charge up there?"

There was an uncomfortably long pause as the radio remained silent for about five seconds.

"I am!" Red Wolff said, a defiant tone in her voice.

From various meetings, the comm-op knew all of the sergeants from the three different CHP commands she dispatched for. She also knew bad shit when she heard it. "Good luck Red," she said somberly.

In the big scheme of things, being a CHP sergeant doesn't put somebody very high in the pecking order of dealing with world shaking events. While the Highway Patrol trains its supervisors to deal with all sorts of emergencies, they are predominately related to managing large scale traffic incidents, officer involved shootings, and natural disasters. Dealing with attacks by armed terrorists in a small town in the boonies, was just not something they are trained for.

Still, the principles of leadership are the same. Although she didn't know it, Red Wolff acted instinctively on something she remembered from a class at the Air Force Academy. The class had to do with how people react in adverse situations, and the responsibilities of leadership. The instructor had quoted some long forgotten military hero who said, "There are no extraordinary people. There are only ordinary people, who, because of circumstances, are called upon to do extraordinary things."

Like it or not, Red Wolff found herself in charge. She had seen her commander killed, making her the ranking supervisor in the Crescent City CHP Area. Until somebody from the Highway Patrol that outranked her showed up, she was it.

By ones and twos, the city police officers, sheriff's deputies, Highway Patrol officers who had been on patrol, and those officers that had survived the massacre in the park, began arriving at Red Wolff's command post. Looking at the group gathering around her, she could see the anger, disbelief, fear, confusion, and shock in the faces of the cops from all three agencies. Some of the officers were yelling information at Red Wolff, others were talking in small groups, and some were staring off into space.

To Red, it was much the same type of confusion she'd dealt with thousands of times before as an officer and as a sergeant, at accidents, shootings, riots, hazardous material spills, fires, and earthquakes. It was on a different scale she knew, the stakes were a lot higher, as thousands of lives depended on what she did next. The stakes were also more personal, because she knew the person she loved was a hostage of the men who had already slaughtered over five hundred people.

She knew instinctively what to do.

Climbing onto the hood of a city police car, she stood for a long second looking at the officers below her. Bringing the forefingers of both hands to her mouth, she let out a long shrill whistle. Officers from all three agencies and a handful of National Guard troopers who trickled into the command post, all stopped talking and turned toward her.

"Okay guys, time to cowboy up," she began.

Almost immediately, the whole group began to talk at once, yelling started again, with excited gestures and pointing.

Holding up one hand, she got the group of officers and troopers quieted down again.

"First off, let's see if we can piece together what the hell's is going on. Here's what I know. There are at least fifteen men armed with military M-16s and some type of machine guns at the park. They're dressed in army uniforms. From what we can tell, they broke into the armory and stole the weapons they're using. Then they marched into the park while the Governor was speaking. I guess everyone thought they were part of the ceremony. From what I saw, they gunned down almost all the troopers in formation and killed all the VIPs in town. They killed the sheriff, the chief, and my lieutenant, and about a dozen other coppers from our three agencies. Then they turned their weapons on the crowd and slaughtered a couple of hundred innocent men, women, and children. They captured the Governor and took about thirty women and children hostage. They torched fuel trucks on the highway north and south of town, to set up barricades on 101. That means nobody will be coming to help us anytime soon, at least not on the highway. They also rammed fuel trucks into the sheriff's office, the P.D. and the Coast Guard cutter in the harbor. The jail and sheriff's dispatch are gone. Except for car-to-car radios, you P.D. and S.O. guys don't have any communications. The Highway Patrol radio seems to be functioning okay. Anybody got any other info?"

One of the city police officers spoke up, "The phone company switching station was smashed up and the technician on-duty was killed. We don't have land line phones."

"They also took out the cable company, no phone service from them, killed a woman and an old man there," a deputy added.

Another deputy reported the cellular phone antenna towers had been blown up.

"That's great, no communications other than our radio," Red Wolff said. "Anybody else?"

"Hey Sarge, the guys who did the roadblock north of town were involved in a pursuit and shooting, a city officer is dead, and so is one of the suspects. The other suspect was wounded and one of your officers took him to the hospital," a city officer spoke up.

"Okay, first things first. You National Guard guys, take those army shirts off so we don't mistake you for the bad guys. All of you, there are probably other troopers out there, some will be wounded, don't get trigger happy. Make sure who you are shooting at. I want you army guys to partner up with a cop. Officers, if you have a spare weapon, shotgun, or rifle, give it to the trooper." Red Wolff's confidence was growing by the second.

Flipping the keys to the CHP office weapons locker to Ray Silva, she said, "Ray, take your nephew and two of the army guys back to the office and clean out the weapons room. I want everything. You two army guys, I want you to drive two of the spare patrol cars at the office back here. Oh, Ray, get any spare radios you can find too, go!"

They were a long way in miles, and a lifetime away in experience, from their first graveyard shift together in Central Los

Angeles, Ray Silva smiled to himself, as he jogged to the Highway Patrol vehicle to head to the office.

"Anything else?" she asked.

"Listen to this," said one of her officers holding up a small AM / FM radio.

Over the flat tone of the local AM station, Red Wolff could hear the voice of a man speaking slowly and deliberately in clear English, with the syncopation and slight accent of the Arabic language. The man was extolling the righteousness of the Islamic battle with western decadence, the oppression of Muslim people around the world, and the virtues of Allah.

One more thing to worry about, Red thought to herself. Well, let him talk, maybe he'll tell us something useful.

"As soon as you're ready, I'll assign you a spot around the park. I want to establish a perimeter so we can try to contain these guys. If they try to move from the community center, fire a few rounds at them to keep them inside. Remember, they have high powered weapons and a bunch of our people as hostages. Stay under cover and use your radio to report what you see. No heroes," Red Wolff told the group of cops and soldiers assembled around her.

"Who are these guys sarge?" one of the National Guard troopers asked.

"Based on the crap the guy on the radio is spouting, I'm pretty positive they're Islamic terrorists. More than likely a suicide squad, but they may try to use the Governor to bargain for the release of terrorists somewhere in the world. If they are a suicide squad, they'll try to do as much damage and destruction as they can, then kill their hostages when they know they're gonna die. Listen up troops, when they know they're going to die, they've got nothing to lose, so watch your ass."

Looking at the men and the couple of women soldiers assembled before her, Red Wolff couldn't manage one of the half-grins that were her trademark during stressful times. She had too few people, and even fewer weapons.

A quick head count told Red Wolff that, personnel wise, the terrorists had her outnumbered. In front of her, she saw three Crescent City Police Officers. All that remained of the eleven officer department. There were three sheriff's deputies with her, and maybe two more alive, but caught on the wrong side of the barricades on Highway 101. From the Highway Patrol, she had five officers, and two more, like the deputies, unable to get to the town because of the barricades. Eleven officers, she thought to herself. If she was lucky, there might be a couple more off-duty from the S.O. and the Highway

Patrol who worked graveyard shift who would show up when they found out what was happening. She did have six National Guard troopers. Anyone who could shoot a gun helped. Eleven officers, she thought to herself again.

Keeping two of her own Highway Patrol officers with her, Red Wolff sent the remaining officers and their National Guard partners out to establish a perimeter around the community center.

While Red Wolff was trying to establish some organization at her command post, Emil Lagare surveyed the scene at the beachfront park. Before him, he saw hundreds of dead Americans, soldiers, policemen, civilians, women and children. Hundreds of others were wounded and screaming as they lay on the grass or in the street. He'd captured the Governor of California, and had thirty women and children as hostages. Qassim Saleh's plan had worked beyond all expectations. Emil Lagare's thoughts turned momentarily to his father and mother and he gave thanks to Allah for allowing him his revenge.

It was 10:42, time to regroup and prepare for the next phase of the operation.

Using his radio, he called his men who were still in the park executing the wounded and picking up weapons, directing them to the community center. As they had practiced, his assault team was the first to enter the structure. They used entry techniques they'd perfected in the desert, the first man raced into the building, followed quickly by another. Each man covered the other as they made their way into the large main hall of the structure, weapons at the ready.

As soon as the assault team entered the community center, they found almost a hundred civilians who'd fled to the building when the initial shooting began. There were also twenty or so National Guard troopers, all still holding their impotent weapons. Emil Lagare's men knew exactly what to do with the people they found. The men were quickly separated from the women and marched out of the building, while the women were herded into one corner.

Outside the building, the men, and three female National Guard troopers, were pushed and prodded to the rear parking lot next to the seawall. Fifty-four men, including all of the troopers, were machine gunned to death by the same two men who had earlier killed the group of men in the park.

The remainder of Emil Lagare's men shoved the women and children taken hostage in the park minutes before, into the building. One of his men drug the Governor unceremoniously by the arm, into the building. The rest of the men followed, using cover and withdraw movements, until they were all inside. Emil Lagare barked an order in Arabic and they moved to establish a defensive perimeter within the building.

The community center was actually one big hall with movable room dividers that allowed it to be split into a big room and a smaller room. The dividers were already in place. Emil Lagare directed the Governor and about twenty of the women to be taken into the smaller room on the east side of the building. Among the women who ended up with the Governor were Mary Jean Snider and Julie Bradley. They were told to sit on the floor.

Emil Lagare now used his radio to ascertain the status of the men who were not with him in the community center. He knew the three drivers who had blown up the police station, the sheriff's office, and the Coast Guard cutter, were dead. They had died glorious deaths and were now with Allah. The two men who'd captured the radio station answered immediately when he called. The station was securely in their hands and broadcasting as planned. Calling the team that had set the northern barricade, he received no answer. He called again, still no answer. Not a good sign, he knew. He then called the two men who had burned their fuel truck on Last Chance Grade. They advised their mission was successful. They were back in Crescent City, at the predetermined rendezvous point near the airport, with their solo teammate who had driven a Humvee from the fuel farm. No, he learned, the northern roadblock team was not there as planned. Emil Lagare considered them dead. He had no way of knowing whether they had been successful in their mission of establishing the roadblock barricade on Highway 101. He would have to pay more attention to the American's radio to determine if the roadblock had been set. He told the three men to proceed on their next mission.

Doing a quick count of his men in the community center, Emil Lagare found he'd lost two of them to return gunfire during the assault in the park. Peering out the glass door entry, he could see their bodies lying on the grass near the podium. Of his twenty-eight men, he was down to twenty-one. He had lost more men than he anticipated, but still had more than enough to continue his mission.

When Qassim Saleh planned the operation, he used not only his knowledge of America, but his knowledge of American history. Although he gave the outward appearance of a chubby, middle-aged, immigrant businessman just trying to make a living in America, there was much more to the man than met the eye. He was an avid reader of history, and possessed an almost photographic memory when it came to recalling political and military events in American history. He was also a fanatical Muslim.

History had been the driving factor in selecting Crescent City as the target for this attack.

Qassim Saleh had studied the Battle of Hue during the Tet Offensive of 1968 in the Vietnam War. The Viet Cong had taken over the city during the Tet holiday truce when the city's military defenses were at their lowest point. Thousands of South Vietnamese troops had gone home for the holiday, leaving almost no military to defend the city. The V.C. had killed thousands of Hue's citizens, including every political and governmental official in the city. They destroyed large portions of Hue before taking refuge in the ancient citadel. It took American Marines several bloody weeks to route them out and retake the city.

He had also studied the Rodney King riots that occurred in Los Angeles in 1992. What struck him most was the inability of local law enforcement to respond to a violent situation, especially in the first several hours when confusion was at its' greatest. He also realized while the American armed forces could launch a counterstrike within hours of being attacked abroad, it took them days to react to events in their own country. In the Los Angeles riots, even with several active and National Guard military bases within fifty miles, it took well over twenty-four hours for them to arrive and begin to restore order. He could destroy the entire town of Crescent City in twenty-four hours.

As soon as she got off the radio with Red Wolff, the comm-op in Eureka put a call into to her supervisor at his residence. Getting no answer there, she tried his cell phone. No answer there either. It was a holiday and everyone except those officers necessary to handle the highways was on a three-day weekend.

The Highway Patrol had fourteen communications centers scattered across the state. Those in metropolitan areas, needed dozens of people to handle the multiple radio frequencies, the phone system, freeway emergency call boxes, and 911 calls. In rural locations like Eureka, often times, like today, one communications operator did everything. While trying to make her first notifications, the phones started ringing and officers in the field were calling on the radio.

"Screw 'em," she said out loud. Following protocol, she put a call in to her captain. She doubted he would answer, he never had before. No answer. "Screw protocol," she said to the empty radio room. Jumping three or four links in the chain of command, she put a call in to the Headquarters Communications Center in Sacramento. She explained the situation to the supervisor there and within minutes was connected to the on-call deputy chief.

After completing that call, she breathed a sigh of relief, envisioning help would soon be on its way. She then turned her efforts toward calling in everyone assigned to the local CHP command in Humboldt County. Things were going to get busy and they were the closest help for Red Wolff in Crescent City. She also called the Oregon State Police district headquarters in Medford. Although they were ninety miles north of Crescent City, they needed to be in the loop.

It took the on-call deputy chief a few minutes to contact the Commissioner of the Highway Patrol. From that point, calls started going out to ranking officials in state and federal government and the military.

Calls being made, and action being taken, are two different things, especially on a holiday. Talking to the person who was unlucky enough to have the duty at places like the Pentagon, the White House, or a military base, only meant the call had been received. Getting the information to someone who could actually make a decision, or order some type of response, was another matter.

The President was at his ranch in Texas. His Secret Service detail immediately threw a cordon around the property and shuttled him off to the securest part of the ranch house. The phone lines between Crawford and Washington were in constant use as staffers tried to get information. It took well over an hour before any of the Joint Chiefs of Staff were informed. They were all, at that moment, dressed in their formal uniforms, attending the annual National Fourth of July Concert on the Washington Mall.

In California, notifications were made to every law enforcement agency in the state. Police chiefs and sheriffs that could be reached started heading for their headquarters. Likewise, Highway Patrol commanders left picnics, softball games, or their backyards, and headed for their offices. All over the state, the top officials in every public safety agency were making notifications and calling in personnel.

Unfortunately, heading for work and actually getting to work quickly, are different. Like many Californians, a large number of those who could make decisions lived in the suburbs and their work locations were in the cities. It was the third day of a three-day weekend. The freeways were packed, traffic moved along, but in places it ground to a crawl as thousands of families were making their way home. It would take almost two hours before emergency operations centers across the state began to function up to speed. Even then, it would take several more hours before there was sufficient information to act upon, and even longer to get personnel and equipment ready to move.

At military bases the situation was much the same. There were of course personnel on-duty, but hardly enough to function as an efficient unit capable of a rapid response. Just like their civilian counterparts, military commanders and personnel had to be called in.

When Emil Lagare's men opened fire in the park, Patricia Dodge and her cameraman had just gotten out of the pickup truck that had given them a ride from the airport. The cameraman had actually been filming the formation of marching men when they stopped and opened fire. Like almost everyone else, Patricia Dodge stood there watching as hundreds of rounds were fired into the VIP's and National Guard troopers. It wasn't until the armed men began firing at the civilians, and she could see people falling to the ground, others running, and heard the screams of the dying, that it registered she was watching an armed attack.

It only took her cameraman, sixty-two years old and the father of five, a split second to realize what was happening. He hit the ground immediately, but kept filming. After she figured it out, Patricia Dodge hit the deck too.

From their location, almost a hundred yards from the podium, they could see the armed men slaughtering scores of people. Bodies flew through the air after being impacted by the high muzzle velocity rounds spewing from their weapons. Hundreds of people were running in all directions, and she could see a woman, she believed to be the Governor, dragged off by one of the men in uniform. It took her a few seconds to realize what she was witnessing was probably an attack by terrorists. Her cameraman was getting it all on tape. She began narrating what she saw into the microphone she held in her hand.

"This is Patricia Dodge in Crescent City, California. As I speak, dozens of armed men, dressed as American soldiers, are firing automatic weapons into the crowd of people gathered here at a ceremony to honor the local National Guard unit. I see people running everywhere, scores of people have been shot, and I can hear the screams of women and children. I don't know for sure but I believe the armed men are Islamic terrorists. I just saw the Governor of California captured by one of the men and dragged off. This is an incredible sight. Nothing like this has ever happened on American soil."

Her cameramen kept filming.

Pausing to take a breath, she scanned the whole park, then continued her commentary.

"This is like a scene from "Dante's Inferno." I can see dead and dying everywhere. The armed men are continuing to fire in all directions. Lookout! They're firing our way." Rounds could be heard whistling overhead and clumps of grass shot up as bullets struck within a few feet of Patricia Dodge and her cameraman.

Patricia Dodge paused and watched the scene. She had never really read "Dante's Inferno," but she did attend the class on using colorful phrases when you report live events.

Although she didn't know much about history, she knew she was on the frontline of history being made. The biggest story since 9/11 and she was the only reporter there. She was also getting it on film. Screw the flagship station in L.A. she thought, this was her ticket to the top. She could visualize the honors, The du Pont Award for broadcast journalism, the Pulitzer Prize for excellence, honors from her peers. Her mind flashed momentarily on her future, Bill O'Reilly, Sean Hannity, Nancy Grace, Patricia Dodge. An M-16 round hit the tree five inches from her head and snapped her back to reality.

"God-damn, Podunk station, the biggest story of the decade and our satellite truck is sitting at the airport with a dead battery," she said out loud.

It didn't take the media long to pick up on what was happening in Crescent City. Like all television stations, Patricia Dodge's station in Eureka used scanners to monitor radio traffic on police frequencies.

When Red Wolff radioed the communications center in Eureka, people were listening. Because of the holiday it was going to be a slow news day. Only one of the regular technicians was working at the station, going through news reports from the wire and putting together little snippets for the local evening news. He did have two student interns from nearby Humboldt State University helping him.

One of the interns was listening to rock music on the local FM station while monitoring scanner traffic in the background. The intern muted his music when he heard the comm-op say "emergency traffic." Although the scanner couldn't pick up what the officer in the field was saying because of the distance to Crescent City, it could pick up the return transmissions from the nearby comm-op. The intern started hearing words like "automatic weapons," "how many dead," and "terrorists." The intern notified the technician who put a call in to the CHP Communications Center. He got no answer. Then he tried calling the Del Norte County Sheriff's dispatch. Again, no answer. A call to the Crescent City Police Department. Nothing. He then tried the cell phone number of his friend who owned the only radio station in Crescent City. If anything was going on, 'ol Denny would know. The mechanical voice on the phone told him his call could not be completed at this time. His last call was to that airhead, Patricia Dodge, who he knew was supposed to be in Crescent City to cover the Governor. No connection. In her case he figured she was lost.

It was probably no big deal, the technician thought to himself, but it was worth a call to the station's news director. The news director lived a couple of miles from the station. He told the technician he had to run into Eureka anyway to pick up a couple of things for his afternoon barbeque, so he would drop by.

It didn't take the news director long to smell a story. Words like "terrorists," "dead," and "emergency" registered with him. The inability to make any kind of contact with anyone on the phone also bothered him. Something was going on.

The news director was a private pilot, and he kept his own Cessna 172 at the Arcata Airport, ten miles north of town. Calling his wife, he told her he was going to fly to Crescent City. It would take him thirty minutes up, an hour on the ground, and thirty minutes back. It was only 11:15, he would be back in plenty time for the BBQ.

Following Qassim Saleh's plan Emil Lagare put the next part of the operation in motion. He had already directed the three men who were driving stolen Humvees to proceed on their mission. He now had five of his men recover the two army trucks and the Humvee they had used to travel from the armory. The vehicles were parked two blocks from the community center. Inside these vehicles was extra ammunition and supplies.

The five men set out on foot. Two of the five men carried stolen M-249 machine guns. Walking quickly and cautiously, they moved in a disciplined manner, across the grass and the street toward the vehicles.

It was at just that moment when one of the nine patrol cars Red Wolff had assigned to take up a perimeter position around the park turned onto the same street from the opposite direction. The armed men saw the sheriff's unit an instant before the deputy slammed on his brakes. The machine guns riddled the patrol car, cutting through the thin sheet metal doors and hood, shattering the windshield, and killing both of the men in the car before they could react. The car's radiator hissed, as a cloud of steam billowed from the engine. The men mounted their vehicles and drove them back to the community center.

Joining forces at the entry road to the airport, the two men who had set the southern roadblock, and the solo man who had helped at the fuel farm, proceeded on their next mission.

Blocking the airport's runway was an important part of Qassim Saleh's plan. He knew even under the best of conditions, a response by highway from San Francisco would take at least six hours driving time. On a three-day weekend, traffic would clog the roads further slowing any vehicles. Lastly, even when they neared Crescent City they would have to deal with the roadblocks. Any assistance coming to the town would have to come by air, he knew.

The three men talked for several minutes. They could hear gunfire in the distance. It was the sound of machine guns. Their teammates were attacking the town as planned, Allah Akbar!

With two men in one Humvee and one in the other, they drove into the airport. Ahead, they could see a few cars in the parking lot, and two larger planes parked on the tarmac. They drove directly toward the planes.

The two National Guard pilots were on their aircraft sitting in the large VIP seats in the middle of the plane. They saw the two Humvees pulling onto the tarmac and jumped out of their seats and off the aircraft. The general wasn't expected back this soon, but the plane was ready.

As soon as the Humvees stopped, a dark skinned man jumped out of the lead vehicle and pointed an M-16 at the pilots. They were unarmed. The man shot both the pilots with a three round burst each. The driver of the other Humvee skidded to a stop, jumped from the vehicle, grabbed his M-16, and ran into the small terminal building.

Inside he found the two pilots of the chartered Cessna Citation sitting in the row of seats that lined the wall, drinking coffee from a vending machine. They'd heard the gunshots outside but assumed they were Fourth of July firecrackers. Both died sitting in molded plastic airport terminal seats. The man now scanned the terminal building. Behind the United Express counter, he saw a middle-aged woman and a young man he guessed to be the combination baggage handler and ramp worker. The man cut them down without hesitation. There was nobody else in the building.

When the National Guard pilots were killed, the two local men who were working on their private planes saw what was happening and began to flee across the runway. One of them made it about halfway across before a .556 round severed his spine. The other man made it to the edge of the runway where he jumped off into the marshy underbrush. Up to his ankles in water, he moved deep into the thicket of brush and ferns bordering the runway.

The three men didn't waste time looking for him. One American more or less didn't matter. Their mission was to block the runway. Rummaging through the pockets of the local citizens they'd killed, they came up with four sets of keys. It didn't take long to match the keys to the correct vehicles and drive them onto the runway.

McNamara Field has only one runway. At five thousand feet long, and one hundred fifty feet wide, it didn't take much in the way of obstructions to render it unusable to even small aircraft. Placing one vehicle near each end of the runway and offsetting two others near the middle, the men created an effective deterrent to any aircraft attempting to land. They then shot out the tires and threw two highway flares into each vehicle. There were soon four burning wrecks on the runway. The field was unusable for fixed wing aircraft. As an afterthought, they opened the fuel drains on the two aircraft whose pilots they had just killed. The highly refined fuel for the turbo jet engines ignited as soon as the burning flare made contact.

Satisfied with their work, the three men climbed back into their vehicles and drove from the airport, enroute to rejoin Emil Lagare at the community center. One of the men used his radio to report success to their leader.

It was just past 11:30 when Ray Silva, his nephew Ralph, and the two troopers Red Wolff sent with them returned to the command post. Ray Silva brought everything he could find. In the trunk of his car were three additional AR-15s, nine shotguns, four .40 caliber pistols, smoke and tear gas grenades, gas masks, flash-bangs, and several unopened cases of ammunition for the weapons. He also brought three spare radios.

Red Wolff had heard the firing down the street and sent one of her officers to check it out. Several minutes later the officer called her on the radio to report the deaths of the deputy and the trooper.

"Let's get this gear handed out," she said to Ray Silva. "I've got eight teams spread out around the perimeter of the park and the community center. We're spread way too thin, and with the deputy and trooper getting killed, we're even thinner. I'll keep the smoke and gas here until we can figure out when to use it. Ray, you and Ralph get a long gun to every position. Make sure the person you give it to knows how to use it. Some of the P.D. and S.O. guys have probably never fired an AR-15 before, so put it in the hands of a soldier. The shotguns are great for close in stuff, but not worth a damn for the kind of thing we're doing. Give anybody that needs one a pistol."

Ray Silva and his nephew left and she kept the two troopers with her at the command post.

"95-S-3, Humboldt," the radio called.

"S-3," Red Wolff answered.

"S-3, notifications made. Assets mobilizing."

"Any idea of an ETA?"

"Nothing yet S-3," the comm-op replied.

"S-3 for info, 101 is blocked both north and south of town. Citizen reports indicate there are massive backups on both sides of the blockades and numerous accidents. Humboldt officers are responding to the southern blockage at Last Chance Grade to assist your unit. I'm trying to get OSP to respond to the northern blockage to help at that location, but they can't cross the border without the Oregon Governor's permission."

"Any good news?" Red Wolff asked.

"Not so far."

Inside the community center, Emil Lagare was watching the forty or so frightened women and children who were sitting on the floor huddled in the corner of the larger of the two rooms in the building. He walked to the smaller room and opened the door where the Governor and another twenty women were held hostage.

He had monitored the radio traffic between the two women talking about roadblocks and the possibility of assistance arriving. He didn't understand all of the numbers and codes they were using, but he understood enough to know the northern barricade had been successfully set by the two men he could not contact, that there were massive traffic jams north and south of town, and no help was on the way.

Good, he thought to himself. We'll have free reign for a while to continue the operation. His men who were watching the surrounding area reported ten to twelve local police and a few National Guard soldiers had taken up positions on the far side of the park. Using the binoculars they'd brought with them, they could see several of the police officers were armed with what appeared to be M-16 rifles, while others had shotguns and pistols.

Emil Lagare had been told to expect some form of resistance from local law enforcement, but it would be disorganized once their leaders were killed, and any weapons the local police did have, would be no match for the military weapons he would obtain from the armory. Thus far, the only resistance his men had encountered was during the initial take over in the park. Emil Lagare was not worried.

He now ordered his men to assemble into their teams and prepare to leave. He also called the two men who were in control of the town's only radio station. It was a few minutes before 12 noon.

At the radio station, the man who had been talking continually for the past hour paused as his companion told him his orders from Emil Lagare. Within a minute he was talking again.

"Residents of Crescent City, embrace Allah! Time is short. Soon the mighty forces of the jihad will rain death and destruction on you and your town. Embrace Allah, renounce your Christian god of war and greed, and join the millions of true believers around the world who have recognized the merciful and righteous one true God, Allah. Time is short. Death will soon pass among you. Those who do not believe will meet the same terrible fate as your soldiers did today. Come to the park and embrace Allah. You will not be harmed. Your decadent government cannot protect you. Your puny police are no match for the sword of Allah."

The man's diatribe went on non-stop for the next thirty minutes.

For the most part, Americans handle emergencies pretty well. In times of crisis, ordinary citizens often rise to the occasion and do extraordinary things to help each other. In other cases, Americans can be just plain foolish.

In a small town, word travels quickly from person to person. Many who had been at the ceremony when the initial assault began, had made it safely back to their homes. When they did, they told their neighbors about the terrible slaughter in the park and the armed men who were killing everybody. Neighbors told neighbors, and at each telling the scale of the situation grew in magnitude, and the events grew more and more gory with each retelling.

People turned to their televisions to see what was going on. Those who did not know already that the cable system was not working found a blank screen on their televisions. Hundreds made panicked calls to the sheriff's department and found only silence on their phones, instead of a dial tone. Likewise, their cellular phones were useless.

Turning on their radios, they did find information there. The voice they heard was speaking with a strange accent and was telling them about the greatness of Allah. Their fears were confirmed. Terrorists were in control of their town.

Their reaction was precisely what Qassim Saleh had hoped for.

Soon the streets were full of vehicles trying to flee the town. Hundred of cars and pickups flooded the streets driven by frightened people. Rules of the road, driving courtesy, and speed limits meant nothing. It was every person and family for themselves.

The results were predictable. Soon collisions occurred and streets became blocked with wrecked vehicles. Fights broke out between neighbors, as common sense gave way to the primal instinct to survive.

Those drivers that made it to the highway, found hundreds of other vehicles fleeing north and south. Those that fled north managed to go only a short distance before encountering a line of stopped traffic as far ahead as they could see. A fire raged in the distance and thick, black smoke filled the air. Some drivers attempted to make U-turns to go the other way, only to be struck by other vehicles. Soon both the north and southbound lanes were littered with wrecked vehicles and scared people milling around.

The scene was much the same for those citizens who fled south. The first eight miles driving south on Highway 101, traffic was heavy, but it flowed. Then, just at the point where the highway narrowed, it came to an abrupt stop. Two miles of vehicles sat without moving. Drivers were out of their cars pacing anxiously around. Other traffic that encountered the blockade on Last Chance Grade, turned around and was heading back northbound. Frightened drivers told of the fiery truck on the grade and the lack of any police presence. More drivers now tried to make U-turns and more collisions occurred.

The roadblocks had taken on a life of their own, causing panic and confusion.

In town, a different type of confusion reigned. Many people who had heard of the attack in the park actually came into town to see what was going on. The streets around the park were soon crowded with drivers slowly cruising down the street that fronted the park, and hundreds of people, some with children, were standing on the sidewalk watching the community center.

At her command post, Red Wolff was issuing orders and trying to coordinate her meager resources, when the owner of a business across the street actually came up and asked her if he was going to get a ticket for parking his car at the curb without putting money in the meter.

Another asked if she knew what time the fireworks show started that evening.

Ray Silva stepped in and scooted the people away from his sergeant and told two of the National Guard troopers to close the streets leading to the park. He directed another to get the people who were milling around, off the street. Red Wolff, he knew, had other things to think about.

———

At 12:30 Emil Lagare's men were ready to leave.

"Command post, City-5," came the voice of a city police officer over the scanner in Red Wolff's car.

"Go ahead City-5," Red spoke into the microphone of her CHP radio, knowing the city officer could hear her on his scanner.

"Sarge, there's something going on, they've taken the tarps off the back of two big army trucks and they're loading women on. Looks like about fifteen women and kids in the back of each truck. I can see five or six men getting into each truck with the women."

"What's your location City-5?"

"I'm in the parking lot west of the entrance. The trucks look like they're ready to roll."

"Copy, enroute," Red Wolff said.

"Come on, Ray," she said to Ray Silva, motioning for him to drive.

Ray Silva jumped behind the wheel of the patrol car and his nephew jumped in back.

Emil Lagare watched as the two trucks slowly began rolling away from the entrance to the community center. Each truck was driven by one of the Muslim men from Oakland, with one of his men riding shotgun. A frightened local woman sat between the two men. In the back of each truck, standing against the wooden sides of the bed, were another fifteen local women, several holding babies. Almost all of the women were crying and several of the babies were screaming uncontrollably. Standing behind the women, were six armed men in uniform.

The trucks gathered speed as they headed for the street.

The driver of the lead truck could see the police car at the end of the street with two men, one dressed in blue, who he assumed was a policeman, and the other in an army uniform, crouched behind it. Both men, he saw, had weapons. The passenger in the truck saw another police vehicle two blocks away, also with armed men nearby. He used his radio to notify the men in the back of his truck and the men in the truck behind them.

Red Wolff arrived near the police car at the entrance to the park just as the first truck was approaching. The armed men in the bed of the truck began firing at the police car and the two men behind it. M-16 rounds ripped into the car shattering the windows and shredding the car's body. One round hit the city police officer in the shoulder, driving him to the ground. The National Guard trooper raised the shotgun he'd been given and was about to return fire, when the city officer yelled at him to stop.

Red Wolff could see what was happening and immediately yelled into her radio for all units to hold their fire and take cover. With hostages in the cab and bed of the truck, she couldn't let her people return fire for fear of hitting the hostages.

Watching through binoculars from the community center Emil Lagare realized it was just as Qassim Saleh had predicted, the Americans would not return fire.

Part of the "Shock and Awe" plan Qassim Saleh developed required the ability for Emil Lagare's men to roam freely throughout the town without fear of attack from whatever local law enforcement remained after the initial assault in the park. How to accomplish this part of the plan had caused several sleepless nights before the solution came to him.

Qassim Saleh was living in San Francisco in 1995, when he saw a news story about a disturbed man who had stolen an army tank from a National Guard Armory in San Diego. For forty-five minutes, the man had rampaged down the streets, crushing cars and sending people scattering in all directions. Law enforcement had been helpless to stop him. While the police could shoot their pistols and shotguns at the tank, they were useless against the steel armor.

So, Qassim Saleh reversed his thought process. The solution was not in having a vehicle that would repel bullets fired by the police. The solution was in having a vehicle the police would not fire at. His idea of trucks loaded with hostages to act as human shields was brilliant, if not savage.

In the scenario envisioned by Qassim Saleh for the use of "Hostage Trucks," when Emil Lagare's men made their forays into town to continue their destruction, they could fire indiscriminately at any Americans they saw. On the other hand, American law enforcement and military personnel would be hesitant to return fire for fear of accidentally hitting one of the women hostages. This was a situation Qassim Saleh was sure the American's had not trained for. Inevitably, the American's would accidentally shoot a hostage. In the frenzy of finger pointing and analysis that would occur in the aftermath of the whole incident, the American public and American politicians, fanned by the media, would raise a huge outcry over the tactics of the police and military. Television pundits would question the training given to American personnel and the "Rules of Engagement" they were governed by. The furor would not die down for months, and would serve to keep the incident alive in the mind of the entire world.

The trucks roared out of the park, one turning left, the other right. As they drove by the parked police units, the men in the trucks unloaded several magazines at the officers and troopers who had taken cover behind anything that would stop a high powered bullet.

Now on the city streets of the town, the armed men began shooting at any people who were on the street. Dozens of men, women, and children who had come to the park to see what was going on, were shot and killed by the men in the passing trucks. More panic ensued. People were running everywhere, ducking under cars or behind buildings, to escape the fusillade of bullets.

Both trucks drove four to five blocks into the city's small business district and stopped. From the back of each truck, three armed men jumped to the ground, canvas bags slung over their shoulders. They fired three round bursts into the front windows or doors of the closed for the holiday stores. Then, using their rifle butts, they smashed out any remaining glass to create an opening large enough to walk through. Inside the stores the men quickly put the most flammable things they could find into piles. They looked for clothing, papers, carpet, furniture and cardboard boxes. In their canvas shoulder bags, they carried ordinary roadway flares. Striking the flares against the striker caps, they burst to life, and were dropped onto the piles. The flame and high temperature of the flares quickly ignited the material. The fire spread from the burning piles to shelves of clothes, to wooden furniture, to stacks of files on desks. Within minutes the stores were infernos. With three men working from each truck, soon there were dozens of fires. Most of downtown Crescent City consisted of older wooden structures. Almost all of them were built before fire codes required automatic sprinkler systems. Thick smoke rolled from the broken store front windows and soon flames began to shoot out toward the street. Within ten minutes, the first of the roofs caught fire. Shake roofs, hot cinders, and a light breeze, did the rest. Soon over three blocks of downtown Crescent City were aflame.

Citizens who had been hiding from the armed men, now ran from their hiding places near the burning buildings. More gunshots rang out as the armed men in the trucks cut down anything that moved. Another twenty plus innocent people were shot as they ran for safety.

Red Wolff had followed one of the trucks, keeping a safe four blocks away, staying out of sight of the men guarding the hostages in the trucks. Now on foot, she and Ray Silva, using the corner of a building for cover, watched the men as they moved from store to store setting more fires. Neither of them saw Ralph Silva, who had been in the back seat, get out of the patrol car, take aim at one of the men on the street with the AR-15 he was carrying, and fire. The terrorist fell to the ground, dead from a bullet to his temple. It was a great shot.

One of the terrorists holding the hostage women in the truck saw him fire the shot that killed his comrade. He didn't even think about returning fire at the soldier. Instead, he pulled the Berretta pistol from his holster and shot the woman standing next to him in the head. He pushed her lifeless body out of the back of the truck to the ground. He then grabbed the woman next to her and did the same thing. He shot and killed five of the women hostages in retaliation, yelling Allah Akbar each time he shot.

"God-damn it Ralph," Ray Silva yelled at him angrily. "What are you thinking?"

Ralph Silva looked perplexed. "I thought our job was to kill those guys?"

Red Wolff spoke up, "It is, but our first job is to keep the hostages alive."

Ralph Silva turned away, head down, realizing what he had done.

Downtown Crescent City, on the west side of Highway 101, is about nine blocks by six blocks. It took the terrorists about forty-five minutes to set most of it on fire. Smoke streamed from the burning buildings leaving a hazy pall over the city, darkening the midday sky. The smell of burning wood filled the air.

The Crescent City Fire Department consisted of one man, the chief. The rest of the city's firefighters were volunteers. The fire chief had been one of the VIPs seated behind the podium and had been killed during the initial assault by the terrorists. Many of the volunteer firemen were among the National Guard troops, or other citizens who had been at the park. Most were dead.

Three men and one woman had responded to the fire station when the sheriff's office had been destroyed, without waiting to hear the usual muster siren that sounded all over town, or for the telephone call telling them to respond for an emergency. They'd waited at the station for almost an hour for their chief to arrive and when he didn't, they took the department's one truck out and headed for downtown. They were fighting the blaze at the sheriff's office when the terrorists started burning the downtown businesses.

Four volunteers and one fire truck were no match for dozens of burning buildings. They ceased their efforts and began concentrating on helping the wounded people they found on every street.

By 1:15, Emil Lagare's men had destroyed about half of downtown. They had also killed another sixty or so people who either didn't know a group of terrorists had taken over the town and just happened into their way, or who had intentionally come into town to see what was happening. Either way they were just as dead.

Red Wolff continued to shadow one of the trucks until it returned to the community center. She felt helpless. They were out manned, out gunned, and out maneuvered. They were on the defensive, with a bunch of terrorists calling the shots. She was sure help was coming, but knew it would be several more hours until it arrived. Things were not looking good. Given the tactics the terrorists were using of shooting hostages, there was little she could do to protect the town, or its people.

By 1:30 p.m. both sides paused to regroup.

In the community center, Emil Lagare took stock of his situation. The three men who had blocked the runway at the airport were back. His two teams of men who had set the fires in town had returned and were boasting to each other about their success. Cries of Allah Akbar could be heard. He had lost one man, killed, by a soldier in town, leaving him a total of twenty. His men still controlled the radio station and he still had over forty women hostages. His mission was proceeding according to plan.

The only part of the plan that had not gone according to expectation was the lack of media presence. Qassim Saleh had anticipated there would be at least one television station covering the event, and that their equipment could be used to broadcast the operation's success to the world. Demands would be made for the release of Islamic freedom fighters being held by the United States and other western countries, in return for the Governor and the other hostages. Qassim Saleh knew the United States would not accede to these demands, but the attention of the world would be focused on this small American town and the boldness of their attack. Every hour Emil Lagare's men held the town at bay would bring more glory to their cause. Live scenes of hundreds of dead, the town in flames, and America brought to its knees by a small group of Islamic warriors, would strike terror into people all over the world. If terrorists could attack America on American soil, how could people be safe anywhere in the world?

No matter, Emil Lagare thought to himself, if it is not broadcast while we live, it will be broadcast when we are all dead.

It was time to feed his men and the hostages, especially the children, if for no other reason than to keep them quiet. He directed four of his men to take a group of fifteen women and venture onto the grassy area around the podium to retrieve any food stuffs they could find. Picnic baskets and coolers littered the ground all around the park, and soon the men were back with dozens of containers with all the fixings of an American Fourth of July picnic.

Emil Lagare and his men ate first. They feasted on strange foods, sandwiches laced with mustard, potato salad heavy with mayonnaise, crispy, cold fried chicken, and a variety of fruits. The Muslims from Oakland had to explain to many of the men what some of the foods were. There was much laughter and praises to Allah. Once they finished eating, the remaining food was distributed to the hostages.

In the smaller of the two rooms in the community center, the Governor of California sat on the floor with a dazed look on her face. Nothing in her life experiences had ever prepared her for what was happening. A sixty's Berkeley liberal, she'd done the anti-Vietnam war protests, sat-in at the dean's office, and been arrested at Peoples' Park. It had all been a lark to her. She had always thought that being against war, was an insulator against actually having to experience war. Her rise to political power had always relied on people with the same liberal bent she had. Looking around, she didn't see any of those people with her today.

Sitting on the floor next to the Governor were Mary Jean Snider and Julie Bradley. There were about fifteen other women in the room. The smell of fear permeated the air. While they couldn't see what was happening outside, they'd heard the going and coming of trucks, and the gunshots in the distance. They could also smell the smoke from the burning town. Both the women were scared, but neither was catatonic like many of the others.

When the terrorists distributed food, Mary Jean ate ravenously. Julie Bradley said she wasn't hungry. "Eat," Mary Jean told her. "First, because you don't know when you might get to eat again, and second, to keep your strength up for when it might be needed." Her training in navy pilots' survival school was kicking in. Julie Bradley ate. Mary Jean also offered food to the Governor and told her the same thing. The Governor told Mary Jean to mind her own business and leave her alone. Fucking Democrats Mary Jean said to herself.

Back at her command post, Red Wolff considered her situation. She was down to ten officers and a handful of National Guard troops. Communications were difficult and the terrorists had free reign to ravage the town anytime they chose by using hostages as shields.

She knew from being a good sergeant that her first responsibility was to her people. "Keep them fed and keep them informed," were things she'd learned from experience.

She didn't have the option, like the terrorists, of picking up picnic baskets and coolers in the park. Putting Ray Silva in charge at the command post, she told Ralph to jump in her patrol car.

Two minutes later, she pulled up to the front entrance of the local Safeway store. Incredibly, they were still open, lights blazing inside, and there were scores of shoppers frantically filling their carts. "Panic buying," Red Wolff told Ralph.

"Grab a cart," she told Ralph Silva as she grabbed one at the same time.

Bursting into the store, she told Ralph to pick up a dozen loaves of bread, luncheon meat and condiments. She headed for the water section and picked up two large ice chest type coolers, ten bags of ice, and four cases of bottled water. She then grabbed chips, crackers, cookies, and candy bars. She wanted quick sugar rush foods that would keep her people awake. It was going to be a long night.

With both carts full of food and water, they headed for the exit.

"Excuse me officer," came the quizzical voice of the store manager. "What exactly are you doing?" he asked.

"I'm taking this stuff to feed my troops," Red Wolff told the manager.

"Well that's fine, but aren't you going to pay for it first?" the manager said with a slight smile.

The thought of paying for the things they took, had never crossed Red Wolff's mind. First, it was an emergency and she had no time for formalities. She needed to get back to her command post and get her people fed. Secondly, like most cops, Red never carried a wallet when she was working. She always had a couple of bucks in her pocket to buy lunch, but carrying a wallet was just something else to worry about losing.

"Listen," she said to the manager. "Do you have any idea of what's happening? There are terrorists burning up the town, killing everybody they see. They've already killed over six hundred people at the park, they've burned down most of the town west of 101, and God knows where they are going to strike next."

"Yes, I heard what's going on, terrible, just terrible. I understand your problem officer, still, I'll have to insist that you go through the checkout line and pay for the things you have," the manager said in his best "how can we serve you" voice.

Her patience gone, she turned to Ralph Silva and told him to start unloading the carts into the patrol car. She then turned back to the manager.

"You pompous fuck, get the hell out of my way. There are fifteen people a couple of blocks from here who are trying to save this little town. They are hungry and tired, and most of them will probably be dead in a little while. I'm going to feed them with your food, and I'm not going to pay you for it. If by chance we make it out of this thing alive, you can file a claim against the state. If you don't like it, call a cop."

With that, she jumped back in the driver's seat of the patrol car. The manager stood there looking at her, not knowing what to do.

As she started to drive away, Red leaned out of the open window and said to the manager, "If you were smart, you'd close this store and get all your employees to a place of safety. When the terrorists come again they very well could be coming to this side of town. If they do, they'll kill everyone they find here and burn this store down."

The manager watched her drive away. I'll have her badge he thought to himself. And besides, he couldn't just close the store.

191

Red Wolff got all of her people fed in just over an hour. She didn't eat until she was sure all of her troops had eaten first.

———————

About the time Emil Lagare's men were starting to set fire to downtown Crescent City, the first response by the American military was just under way. It came from the California Air National Guard. Two F-16 fighters from the Air Guard squadron in Fresno were scrambled at 12:39 with orders to do a reconnaissance fly-over of Crescent City.

Almost six hundred miles away, it would take the "Fighting Falcons" about twenty-five minutes to reach the area. Climbing first to thirty thousand feet, the fighters streaked straight north up the central valley to Mount Shasta, then turned west toward the coast. When they reached Eureka, they turned north again and followed the coastline and Highway 101, toward Crescent City.

The fighters slowed and began a gradual descent as they followed the coast. About fifteen miles south of the town, they saw the mouth of the Klamath River, and within a few seconds, the black smoke from the burning fuel truck on Last Chance Grade. The pilots could see several miles of traffic backed up on either side of what appeared to them to be an accident on the grade.

Continuing north for another minute, they were soon over the last mountain before the town. Once over the mountain, they saw the town nestled in against the ocean. From five thousand feet they could see thick black smoke everywhere. Ahead, they saw the harbor. The burning hulk of the Coast Guard cutter was tied to the jetty. Then immediately, the park came into view. The pilots could see hundreds of shapes lying on the grass, or in the street. Adjacent to the park, they could see dozens of fires in what they assumed was the downtown district of Crescent City.

Flying two abreast, the lead pilot's flight path took him directly over the airport where he could see burning vehicles on the runway. His wingman, several hundred yards to the right, flew almost directly up Highway 101, where he encountered another burning truck and hundreds of vehicles stopped in line.

Using his wingman's nickname, the flight leader called for a sweeping turn to the right.

"Spider let's go around and come in slow from the north. Steady up on one-eight-zero, I'm going down for a closer look," the leader said.

"Right behind you Hondo," came the reply.

Both pilots now did a slow banking turn, easing back on their throttles and descending to three hundred feet. Flying almost directly north to south, the pilots looked out both sides of their clear bubble canopies. At three hundred feet, they caught quick glimpses of men in uniform, armed with rifles, moving through the burning town. Flying over the park, the lead pilot realized that the shapes he had seen lying on the grass on his first pass were the bodies of other uniformed men and many, many civilians.

The flight leader had seen enough. Soon, both jets were climbing back to altitude.

Enroute back to their base, the flight leader radioed information on what they had seen. While it wasn't definitive intelligence of a terrorist attack, what they reported certainly indicated that something horrific was going on. Coupled with the scant information provided by local law enforcement authorities and the inability to establish communication with the town, it was a plausible assumption.

The closest military installation that could put "boots on the ground" was the Marine Corps Base at Camp Pendleton, nearly a thousand miles away. Located halfway between Los Angeles and San Diego, it was home to the combined air-ground assets of a Marine Expeditionary Force.

Even for the Marines, gearing up to deploy takes time. Ground troops need to be assembled, equipment issued, ammunition distributed. Ground transportation needs to be mobilized, and air assets need to be fueled and preflighted.

Then comes the planning and logistics. Crescent City was a long way. Helicopters could be used, but the distance is great and fuel stops needed to be planned. What intelligence did they have of the area? What precisely was their mission? It all took time. It would be hours before they were ready to move.

Red Wolff finished her sandwich while sitting on the curb at her command post. Nothing like a bologna and cheese on white bread, a bag of chips, and a bottle of warm water to make you feel better.

It was almost 2:45.

The terrorists hadn't made a move in almost ninety minutes. They're probably doing the same thing we are, Red said to herself, eating and resting. No, that's not right, she thought, more likely we're losing faster than they can win. They'll come out again soon, she knew, and she also knew there was nothing she could do to stop them, when they did.

She heard the small plane coming from the south before she could see it. By the sound of the single engine, she imagined it was a Cessna or Piper. Probably someone coming in for a fuel stop, or a local resident returning after a weekend away, she thought to herself.

The news director's plane was at five hundred feet when it made its first pass over the town. Flying low and slow, he could clearly see things the fast moving F-16 pilots had not. Not only were there bodies all over the park, but on the streets of the downtown district also. He was familiar enough with Crescent City to know the sheriff's department had been destroyed, and most of the government building was aflame.

He put the plane into a slow right hand turn and began to circle lower over the park. It took him a moment to see the police cars strategically encircling the park, with armed men near them. He also located three or four police cars parked together on a side street about four blocks from the community center. He could see there were three policemen in uniform and a couple of others in army uniforms. Several were carrying rifles. They were all looking up at him.

A veteran of many years as a street reporter in San Francisco, he knew a police command post when he saw it. He banked out of his turn and headed for the airport to land. The burning vehicles on the runway put an end to that idea. Something was happening in Crescent City. Something big. He needed to get back to Eureka to get more news people up here, and to tell authorities what he had seen. A national news story was happening and the only reporter there was Patricia Dodge, he thought to himself. My God!

As soon as the plane headed south, Red Wolff was on her feet.

"Ray is that guy still flapping his gums at the radio station?" she asked.

"Yeah, still going on non-stop about Allah and embracing Islam," he replied. "You think it's too late to take him up on his offer?" a sly smile on his lips.

"I think it's time we revoked his FCC license," she said.

"95-S-3, 95-7," came the female officer's voice over the radio.

"S-3, go ahead Jodie," Red Wolff replied, using her officers first name.

"S-3, can you 11-98 at the hospital?"

"10-4, in about ten," Red replied.

Turning to the senior sheriff's deputy at the command post, she said, "I've got to meet one of my officers at Sutter Coast, take charge here. Keep everybody down and call me if anything happens, especially if they start to come out again."

"No problem sarge," the deputy responded.

"Come on Ray," she said, gesturing to Ray Silva to drive the patrol car. "We'll worry about the guy at the radio station later."

Red Wolff knew the officer who called her had been involved in the pursuit and shooting with the two terrorists who had killed the city police officer. One of the other city cops told her that this officer had actually shot one of the terrorists, and killed the other one by running him down with her patrol car.

Jodie Castle was one of her better officers. She had twelve years on the job and knew how to take care of business. Like a lot of females on the Highway Patrol, she was married to another CHP officer. Thank goodness, Red Wolff thought to herself, that her husband was in Sacramento at the academy for in-service training. Had he not been, he would have probably been at the park guarding the Governor. A small bright spot in an otherwise terrible day.

Sutter Coast Hospital was on Washington Boulevard, just off Highway 101. It was actually within walking distance of the Highway Patrol office. For a small county, it was a good hospital, offering emergency and acute care. Patients that needed more intricate procedures, or had complicated medical problems, were sent to Medford, Oregon or south to Eureka. All-in-all, however, it served the community well, with a constantly rotating staff of new doctors who often came to Crescent City right out of medical school.

The circular driveway entrance was usually a no parking zone. Only the pick-up or drop-off of patients was permitted. Today, as Ray Silva guided the patrol car into the entrance, it was a scene of chaos. Cars were parked everywhere, making it almost impossible for him to squeeze through to a parking slot near the emergency room entrance. People were rushing about, panicked looks on their faces, dozens of wounded were on stretchers outside, with the hospital staff trying to administer aid.

As hectic as it was at the main hospital entrance, the emergency room was even worse. Designed to handle four, or in a pinch, as many as six emergency cases, there were almost a dozen gurneys crowded into the room. The din was almost deafening. Doctors and nurses yelled orders and scurried from gurney to gurney. Aides moved equipment and pushed patients in and out of the room. The floor was littered with blood soaked clothing, plastic and paper outer wrappings from sterile bandages, oxygen tubes, and masks. Discarded latex gloves were strewn everywhere.

Red Wolff saw Jodie Castle standing near the hallway leading to the patient rooms. The officer motioned for her sergeant to join her.

"How you doing, Jodie?" she asked the officer.

"Okay Red," she replied.

Red Wolff had worked enough officer involved shootings, pursuits, and other traumatic incidents involving cops to know her officer was not okay. Right now the officer was still running on the adrenalin her body was pumping into her blood in reaction to what she had just been through. She would be coming down soon, and the full impact of what she had done, or more rightly what she had to do, would send her deep inside herself. Unlike the movies, killing someone or seeing another officer killed, always took a toll on police officers. Whatever outward bravado she displayed, was just a defense mechanism. Red Wolff knew that under normal circumstances, she would get her officer out of there, into a quiet environment, and make sure she didn't have constant reminders of the incident. Within twenty-four hours, she would get the officer into a debriefing with a specially trained counselor that dealt with officer involved traumatic incidents. These weren't normal circumstances.

Red knew there were a few things she could do to help the officer. Foremost, among these, was to reassure the officer that her actions had been proper and necessary.

"Jodie, one of the city officers told me you did good. He said the two guys would have killed everyone there if you hadn't taken them out."

Jodie Castle just looked at her sergeant.

Standing at the partially open door of one of the private rooms, she said, "Sarge, I took this guy out with a shotgun round to his legs." There was no emotion in her voice.

Jodie Castle pushed the door to the room fully open revealing a young, dark skinned man, lying on his back, with both hands handcuffed to the rails of the hospital bed. Because of the wounds to his legs, he was on top of the sheet. He was wearing a short white hospital gown which did nothing to protect his modesty. He looked to be about seventeen or eighteen years old. He had intravenous tubes flowing into his left arm, and another in his right arm attached to a plastic bag of blood. His legs were wrapped in heavy bandages, and there was a large gauze pad taped to the wound on his forehead. The man's eyes were open, and he was staring at the three Highway Patrol officers standing in the door.

"Sarge, these are his clothes," the officer said, pointing to the army uniform she'd put into a large clear plastic garbage bag. "I've gone through everything, nothing unusual. Just his wallet, a little money, some matches, a pack of smokes. Here's his license. Says he's from Oakland. The guy I ran over didn't have anything on him except this little book. I think it's like a bible in Arabic."

It took Red Wolff a second to realize what Jodie Castle had said. Nothing unusual! His license! From Oakland! A Quran! Of course, Jodie Castle had been at the hospital all day. She didn't know they were dealing with Islamic terrorists.

"Also, both of them had these radios. They're expensive programmable ones. They have built in scanners. I've been listening to traffic from our radio, the P.D. and the S.O. on it."

Crap, Red Wolff said to herself. These guys are listening to everything we say. Okay, we'll deal with that later. "Have you talked to him yet?" she asked her officer.

"Yeah, a little, he's pretty arrogant right now, keeps screaming Allah Akbar, whatever the heck that means. I gave him his rights, but he won't talk."

"Okay, let me see what I can do. You go get something to eat. I'll get somebody else to guard him," Red Wolff told her.

The officer turned and started to walk away.

"Hey, Jodie," Red Wolff said.

She stopped and turned toward her sergeant.

"Good job."

Jodie Castle gave an almost imperceptible nod and walked away.

Red Wolff keyed the remote mike attached to her uniform shirt epaulet and called the command post requesting that the deputy she'd left in charge send an officer to the hospital. Knowing now that the terrorists were monitoring her transmissions, she didn't mention anything about a prisoner. She then studied the driver's license of the man in the bed.

According to the license, the man, well more like a boy, in the bed was Abdul Abbas.

He had just weeks before turned eighteen, and graduated from high school. The son of Egyptian immigrants, he had been in the states since he was nine. His parents ran a small local grocery store in downtown Oakland, specializing in ethnic foods from the Middle East.

Growing up in Oakland had been tough on Abdul. Living in the poorer part of the city, he'd grown up a member of a small minority group, in a city of larger minority groups. Physically, he was rather small in stature compared to the black, Hispanic, and Asian kids he lived among and with whom he went to school. He had done fairly well in school and gotten pretty good grades. He went to the very tough McClymonds High School, where he was constantly getting beat up by the black and Hispanic kids who traveled in packs.

By the time he was sixteen, he found his only refuge at the local mosque, and had fallen under the spell of Imam Nasr Ahmed. Although he didn't understand everything the imam espoused, he eagerly embraced the camaraderie the imam's weekend trips to the delta provided. By his senior year, he was fully indoctrinated into radical Islam and did not hesitate to participate in the mission to Crescent City.

Red Wolff locked eyes with the boy lying on the bed. She put the driver's license in her pocket and walked over to the side of the bed. The boy's eyes never broke contact with hers. He was puffed up with himself, she could see. She knew the best way to approach an interrogation with someone like that was to attack his ego.

"Abdul, my name is Sergeant Wolff. I know my officer has read you your rights. I want to ask you a few questions," she said in a calm slow voice.

"I will tell you nothing!" Abdul Abbas said loudly in reply. "We have brought you to your knees. Through the righteousness of Allah, we have destroyed your town and killed hundreds."

"No, Abdul, your comrades have murdered some people, and burned some buildings. Many of them are dead also. Soon the American military will be here and the rest of your friends will die."

"They will die glorious deaths and be with Allah, just as I will."

"Wrong again Abdul. All you did is set a fire with a truck, and then run over a couple of kids in a car. Your partner is dead, and you got shot by a woman. Your friends may die, but you'll live and go to prison for the rest of your life."

Abdul Abbas struggled against the handcuffs which restrained his hands as the words sank in.

"How many men in your group Abdul?" Red Wolff asked.

"I will tell you nothing!"

"Where are they going to attack next?"

"The cause of Allah is just!"

"What are they going to do with the Governor and the rest of the women hostages?"

"Nothing can make me betray my comrades or Allah!"

"Unless you talk to me you're going to die in prison Abdul."

"No, Imam Nasr Ahmed promised I would be with Allah. I will be rewarded with seventy-two vestal virgins."

"Did your imam tell you what it's like in prison for a boy like you?"

Red Wolff could see she was starting to get to him. Keep working on his ego, and his manhood, she said to herself.

Ray Silva stood with his back against the wall, watching.

Again Abdul Abbas struggled against the handcuffs attached to the side rails of the bed. This time he thrashed around, his back arching and legs flailing. The short hospital gown rode up to his navel.

Like almost every other cop in the United States, or most Americans for that matter, Red Wolff knew almost nothing about Islam. But, she was a good street cop and she knew how to play hunches.

"Okay Abdul, you want to go to Allah? You want to have seventy-two virgins? I'll help you."

Although it wasn't part of the regulation issue equipment officers were required to carry on their Sam Browne belts, like lots of other Highway Patrol officers, Red Wolff had long ago taken to carrying a Buck knife in a basket weave leather pouch. It was handy to have a knife to cut seat belts, pry open containers, and touch things without using your fingers.

She moved slowly and deliberately so Abdul Abbas could see what she was doing. Using her right hand she slipped the folded six inch knife from its pouch on her gun belt. Most people held the knife in one hand and used the other to open the blade and lock it in place. Red Wolff had mastered the technique of flicking her wrist to let centrifugal force open the blade.

Her eyes never left Abdul's as she flicked her wrist. The blade clicked into place.

Ray Silva watched in silence.

"Did your imam tell you when you get to Allah's side you have to be a whole man in order to enjoy the seventy-two virgins? I'm going to kill you Abdul, put first I'm going to fix it so you'll have no need of the virgins."

Abdul Abbas's eyes bulged in their sockets, revealing white all the way around.

With that Red Wolff grabbed his scrotum and yanked. Abdul Abbas let out a yell of shock and pain.

"You're getting into some unfamiliar territory Red. Sure you know your way around?" Ray Silva quipped, his back never leaving the wall."

She turned and gave him a "Screw You Silva" look.

Red Wolff moved the knife toward the boy's stretched out scrotum. He was thrashing and kicking while yelling at the top of his voice. His screams reverberated around the room and could be heard down the hallway.

At just that moment one of the doctors heard him screaming and burst into the room. He saw what was going on and yelled, "What the hell are you doing?"

As he tried to rush to the bedside to stop the woman cop from castrating the boy, an arm wrapped around his neck.

Ray Silva was about six inches taller and fifty pounds heavier than the doctor. Without choking him, Ray backed up, pulling the doctor on his heels out into the corridor.

"That man is a patient. You can't torture him, he has rights," the doctor yelled. "I'll have you arrested."

"Assuming we live that long, you can do all of those things," Ray Silva said looking down at the doctor. "Until then, there are lots of people here that need your help. You take care of them and we'll try to keep you from getting anymore business."

The doctor was young and idealistic, but he knew a "Don't fuck with me look" when he saw one. He turned and walked back into the chaos of the emergency room.

Ray Silva stayed outside the door. About ten minutes later, the deputy sent to guard the prisoner arrived. Ray briefed him and they both waited outside the room.

Within another minute or so the door opened and Red Wolff came out. Through the open door, Ray Silva could see the young boy from Oakland still handcuffed to the bed. He was sobbing, but otherwise looked okay.

He then turned his attention to Red. For the first time today she had her trademark half-smile. He knew things were going to be okay.

"Let's go get some payback," she said to Ray Silva.

CHAPTER THIRTEEN

Ray Silva drove the patrol car back from the hospital toward the command post. Red sat in the passenger's seat staring out the windshield, obviously mulling over the things Abdul Abbas told her.

The scale of the attack, the planning that had gone into every detail, and the viciousness of the terrorists, told her she was up against a formidable adversary. No, she thought to herself, they weren't up against her. They were up against the whole town. She just happened to be the one in charge of whatever meager defense they could put up.

"So what did Abdul tell you?" Ray asked.

"Well it's a suicide squad alright. They intend on doing as much damage, and killing as many people as possible before help gets here. According to Abdul, they figure they have twelve hours. Then, they'll kill all the hostages, before going out in a blaze of glory," Red Wolff replied, her eyes never leaving the windshield.

"Why didn't they kill the Governor right off the bat?"

"They're hoping for press coverage. They want to broadcast to the world that they can operate in America with impunity, kill and burn when and wherever they like, and even capture high ranking government officials."

"So far they're batting a thousand," Ray Silva said matter-of-factly. "Speaking of press coverage, wasn't there a TV reporter at the airport? I'm sure I saw that woman from the station in Eureka, the young one who does the morning news. She's kind of pretty." He had a fake, sly, lecherous smile on his face.

"Yeah, now that you mention it, I saw her too. She is kind of pretty, but dumb as a box of rocks. And you need to put your tongue back in your mouth. About the only thing an old guy like you could do with a young thing like that is adopt her," Red Wolff said sarcastically.

Ray Silva chuckled, her on-going digs about his age always made him laugh.

"I wonder what happened to her when the shooting started?" Red asked.

"Reporters and lawyers, they always seem to survive. What did Abdul say they're going to do next?" Ray asked.

As they drove Red Wolff detailed out what Abdul Abbas had told her about the terrorist's plans for their next attack, and for disposing of the Governor and the other hostages.

"Maybe we can do something to upset their plans, Red. How many of them are there?""The kid told me there were twenty-nine total, including the guy in charge. He's French-Lebanese, speaks perfect English, about twenty-five years old."

"Well, we've killed three or four, and witnesses report the three guys who drove the fuel trucks into the P.D., the S.O., and the Coast Guard cutter all blew themselves up. Jodie killed one on the highway, and Abdul is in the hospital. Means there are twenty or twenty-one left," Ray Silva said.

"And we got ten cops and six National Guard troopers. They've got at least four machine guns, and probably eighteen M-16s. We've got two M-16s we took from them, a half-dozen AR-15s, ten shotguns, and a bunch of handguns," she replied.

"Makes it just about even don't you think, Red?" Ray Silva said, looking her dead in the eye.

The half-smile came back as she nodded and replied, "Yeah, just about even."

Driving through the town, the scene was surrealistic. The west side of Highway 101 was a fiery inferno. Fires burned everywhere as large portions of the downtown area were still ablaze. Smoke rose from business structures, flames leapt into the air, and black soot, driven by the freshening afternoon wind, floated inland.

In stark contrast, the side of Crescent City east of 101 was untouched. Incredibly, some stores were still open for business, and except for the frantic vehicles still scurrying north and south on the highway, it could have been another lazy summer day on the North Coast.

They pulled back into the command post about 3:45.

The deputy she'd left in charge met her as she exited the patrol car.

"Nothing new here sarge. The terrorists haven't moved. The guys on the perimeter report they can see occasional movement inside the building, but no one has come out," he told her.

"Okay, good job, go relax a while, but stay close, we'll be moving soon," she told him.

"Oh, one more thing, some woman reporter from the station in Eureka showed up here looking for whoever was in charge. When I told her you weren't here and she needed to leave, she started yelling about the First Amendment, freedom of the press, and lawsuits," the deputy told her.

Swell, she thought to herself, another thing to deal with. "Okay, no problem, I'll handle her if she comes back," she said to the deputy. Red Wolff had more important things to think about. From Abdul, she'd learned the terrorists would be coming out again soon to start another round of destruction and wanton murder. She had the rough outline of a plan in her mind to deal with them when they did.

"Ray, work your way around to every post and pull out all of the National Guard troops. Get them back here. Bring all the long guns too. Tell everyone to limit their radio traffic to emergencies only. The terrorists are scanning everything we say. And hurry back."

Ralph Silva was keeping watch on the community center from the corner of the building next to the command post, one of the two captured M-16s in his hands, and an A.M. radio by his side. He watched his uncle get his orders from the female sergeant, then drive away. He motioned to Red Wolff to join him.

"What's up Ralph?" she asked, crouching down beside him.

"Hey sarge, this guy on the radio is still spouting off about Allah, and the glory of Islam. Can't we take him out?" he asked.

"We'll get him later," she said calmly. "Right now I want you to go back to the armory and see if there is anything left we can use. Weapons, ammo, explosives. Take one of the patrol cars."

He was gone in a flash.

Once Ralph left, Red Wolff paused for a moment. She was physically tired. She knew that tired people make mistakes and bad decisions. She needed a couple of minutes to rest and think through the problem she had with communications.

The terrorists had done a good job in cutting off all communications with the outside world. The phones didn't work, internet communications weren't possible, and the only radio she could communicate on was being monitored by the bad guys.

Like so many things in police work, the solution to her problem had been in front of her the whole time. She mentally kicked herself for not seeing it before.

Reaching into the back seat of her patrol car she found the bag of equipment Jodie Castle had taken from Abdul Abbas at the hospital. She pulled out the radio he'd been carrying. She studied it for a couple seconds then began to manipulate the switches on the radio control console in her patrol car. Satisfied she had it programmed correctly, she picked up the patrol cars hardwired microphone and pressed the transmit button.

"Humboldt, 95-S-3, on the blue," she spoke into the mike.

There was no response from the communications center eighty miles away.

"Humboldt, 95-S-3, on the blue," she tried again.

"Unit calling Humboldt on the blue, identify and go ahead," the comm-op's voice was clear and strong.

"Humboldt, 95-S-3, wait fifteen seconds, then give me a ten count on the blue," Red Wolff said.

"S-3, 10-4," the obvious tone of confusion in the comm-op's voice at Red Wolff's request.

Grabbing the radio taken from Abdul Abbas, Red Wolff jogged about fifty feet from the patrol car to ensure there was no feedback, and waited for the comm-op to call. Within a few seconds, she heard the voice of the comm-op calling on her CHP radio, but not on the radio taken from the young terrorist. Keying the mike clipped to her uniform shirt, she asked the comm-op to repeat the test. Again, nothing came over the captured radio. Red Wolff had found a way to communicate without the terrorists hearing her.

What Red Wolff had done was activate the alternate frequency built into every CHP radio. The "Blue" frequency was for statewide use. By switching to the blue, she could now talk with the communications center without the terrorists hearing their conversations.

Qassim Saleh had made a mistake. Well, not so much a mistake, as the fact he simply didn't know about the CHP's blue radio frequency. When he downloaded the page from the internet that had the frequencies for all the public safety agencies in Del Norte County, the local CHP frequency, the "Green" was listed. The statewide blue frequency was not.

"Humboldt, 95-S-3 on the blue," Red Wolff called.

"Go ahead S-3," the comm-op responded.

Over the next several minutes, Red Wolff explained to the comm-op the reason for using the blue frequency, and the status of situation in Crescent City.

"S-3, Humboldt copies," the comm-op replied.

Feeling comfortable her transmissions were not being overheard by the terrorists, Red Wolff asked the status of any assistance enroute to Crescent City.

"S-3, a Marine infantry company left Camp Pendleton about forty-five minutes ago via helicopter. They'll need to stop enroute at least once for fuel. Their ETA to Crescent City is about twenty-hundred. The FBI Hostage Rescue Team left San Francisco about an hour ago on an Air Force C-130 from Travis Air Force Base. They'll land in Eureka and transfer to helicopters. Their ETA to your location is seventeen-thirty. Aerial reports indicate traffic north and south of Crescent City is grid locked. Units from here are trying to work their way up to the roadblock at Last Chance Grade to clear the highway, but they are encountering numerous collisions and abandoned vehicles blocking their way. The Oregon State Police is enroute to the Junction of 101 and 199, but they're finding the same traffic conditions. Best estimates on having the roads open is tomorrow morning."

The comm-op's voice was clear and professional, but Red could hear a hint of exasperation in her tone.

"Humboldt, S-3 copies, stay on the blue," Red Wolff answered.

Ray Silva was just arriving back at the command post with five of the National Guard troopers. Red took him aside and explained the situation with the radios, and that help was coming. The FBI team would get there by 5:30, the Marines by 8:00. If they could hold on for a couple of more hours things might be okay, she thought to herself.

Almost simultaneously, Ralph Silva returned from the armory. He'd found several thousand rounds of M-16 ammo, a case of fifty 30 round magazines, two night vision goggles, but nothing else. He explained to Red Wolff that all of the armory's firearms were gone and there was nothing else usable there.

She was disappointed there was nothing in the way of weapons at the armory they could use. The ammo would help of course, but for now she had other things to worry about.

For the first time since the early morning, Red Wolff felt a chill. It was only a few minutes after four, but already she could feel the moisture in the air. It had been a beautiful day in Crescent City, weather wise. The skies had been clear, a high of fifty-seven. On the other side of the mountains, only five miles inland, it had been a scorcher. Temperatures climbed to well over ninety. It was a typical summer weather pattern. Looking out to the ocean, Red could see the fog bank forming. Within a few hours the heat radiating off the ground inland would suck the fog bank onshore and up against the mountains. Even though the sun would not set until after eight, and twilight would linger until after nine, the town itself would be cloaked in a thick blanket of cold, wet fog.

That could create a problem for the marine helicopters she thought to herself. Well, one thing at a time. Abdul Abbas had told her the terrorists would be coming out again at six o'clock. It was going to be another "slash and burn" mission. The terrorists would come out in two trucks, female hostages being used as human shields. They would attack two different sites this time, again killing everyone they saw and setting the buildings on fire.

They only had about ninety minutes to get ready Red Wolff told the small group of people around her at the command post. She had the five soldiers Ray Silva had taken off the perimeter, plus Ralph Silva, giving her six National Guard troops. She also had one of the three remaining Crescent City Police Officers, and one of the remaining three sheriff's deputies, plus three out of six of her own Highway Patrol Officers. Counting herself, eleven people to confront the terrorists when they moved again. It only left seven officers to hold the perimeter around the community center, but it would have to do.

She divided them up into two groups. She put Ray Silva in charge of one group, herself in charge of the other. She hastily explained where Abdul Abbas told her they were going to attack, and how they were going to do it. She laid out her plan, then looked into the faces of her people to see their reaction. Each of them remained stone faced.

Police work for the most part is a reaction to the actions of other people. A traffic stop is a reaction to an errant driver. Responding to a crime in progress is a reaction to the actions of the perpetrator. Dealing with a hostage situation, is a response to the hostage takers actions. Even in situations where specially trained officers are deployed with sniper rifles and assault weapons, their actions are in response to the criminal actions of the bad guys.

What Red Wolff was planning was an offensive action. It was not something she was trained to do, nor even remotely close to anything she'd ever done in the past. She felt certain none of the officers with her had ever been involved in an action of this type before. She was flying by the seat of her pants, but there was nothing else she could do.

"Any suggestions from you army guys?" she asked. "Any of you ever done anything like this? Any questions from anyone?"

No one said a word.

While she may not have ever done an operation like this before, she was a good enough supervisor to know she had to project absolute confidence to her people. If she had any self-doubts, none of them saw it in her mannerisms or leadership. Ray Silva was the only one in the group that recognized the half-smile on her face.

"Okay guys, grab your weapons. One M-16 in each group. The rest of you troopers take the AR-15s. Remember, the AR-15 fires exactly like the M-16, except that it's single shot. I want every cop to have a shotgun and a pistol. Ray, you and I will take one "Flash Bang" and one CS grenade each. You guys get going and get set up. I'm going to wait for the FBI and try to get them in position in time. Be careful guys, and good luck."

It was 4:42.

As soon as the news director for the Eureka television station got back into town, he was on the phone to the network. A major event was happening in Crescent City. No, he didn't know exactly what it was, but there were dead bodies everywhere, half the town was on fire, and cops were carrying rifles.

In San Francisco, network news teams were mobilizing. They, however, had the same problems the government and the military had, everyone was scattered around for the three-day weekend. It took time to get reporters, technicians, drivers, and pilots called in. People were responding, but they faced the same traffic nightmares everyone else had to contend with, as the afternoon traffic got heavier, and more and more people were headed home.

On the national level, the media was confronting the same problems. Programming was being interrupted as special reports were being aired about some type of incident in Crescent City. Most of the big name "talking heads" were on a long weekend and the second stringers were manning the news desks. Staffers hurriedly prepared graphics. Where the hell was Crescent City? At one station, a staffer remembered that besides being known as the "Big Easy," New Orleans is also known as "The Crescent City." The New Orleans Police Department was flooded with calls from the media asking about the emergency in that city.

News reports, some factual, and some wildly inaccurate, caused an immediate jump in telephone usage across the nation as relatives called relatives, friends called other friends, and neighbors called neighbors. Was it a natural disaster, a terrorist attack, some type of police action?

Nationwide vehicular traffic, already extremely heavy due to the long weekend, increased dramatically. The three hour time difference between the East and West Coasts added to the confusion. In the

West, it was around two p.m. when the first reports hit the air. People began cutting their day short and headed for home earlier than planned. On the East Coast, it was five in the afternoon, and the already packed interstates were flooded with tens of thousands of additional cars.

Speculation ran rampant. Police agencies across the nation began calling in officers. People made emergency trips to their local markets to stock up on water and staple food. When the Joint-Chiefs-of-Staff, attired in their dress uniforms, all unexplainably left the National Fourth of July Concert on the Washington Mall, the reaction of the tens of thousands of spectators was predictable, they began to leave also. By the millions people tuned into their radios and began to pick up news reports of some type of incident in California.

It wasn't panic yet, but it was getting close.

When the California Air National Guard pilots returned to base in Fresno after their flight over Crescent City, they were immediately shuttled off to a video conferencing link with the National Security Agency in Washington.

The report by the pilots took only five minutes. Yes, there were bodies everywhere. Half the town was on fire, the runway at the local airport had been purposely blocked, as had the highways north and south of town. The Coast Guard cutter had been sunk while tied to the pier, and there were no communications with the town.

It had all of the earmarks of a terrorist attack.

In Washington, the NSA's command center had an entire wall of television monitors tuned to all the major networks. By now every network had preempted regular programming to cover the escalating, yet unknown situation occurring in a small California town on the Oregon border. For the decision makers at NSA, almost nothing they heard from the media was of any help. Because the media had so little information, they just kept repeating it in different ways.

The one thing the government could do was establish a "No-Fly" zone over the small town. The call went out to the Federal Aviation Administration and a twenty-five mile buffer was created in the skies over the town which prohibited all civilian aircraft from entering. Whatever was happening in Crescent City wouldn't be helped by hundreds of planes and helicopters clogging up the airspace.

Orders were given to reposition a spy satellite to get "real-time" intelligence. It would take almost three hours before the satellite could be brought into position. In the meantime, the President was aboard Air Force One heading back to Washington.

Not everyone in the news media was guessing what was going on in Crescent City. After the initial attack in the park, Patricia Dodge and her cameraman found themselves on foot and wandering the streets of Crescent City. They had hundreds of feet of video of the fires burning all over town and the hundreds of bodies lying in the street.

When the two trucks of terrorists made their first attack into the heart of town, they had been hiding in one of the buildings that had not been set ablaze. They videoed the carnage and the terrorist's rampant shooting of civilians as they fled the burning buildings.

Almost by accident, they stumbled upon the makeshift police command post. She approached a sheriff's deputy who seemed to be in charge, stuck a microphone in his face while her cameraman videoed, and began to pepper him with questions.

The deputy was less than helpful. He didn't want to answer any of her questions, and in fact, he was downright rude when he told her to "get the hell out of here." She'd tried all of the buzzwords like freedom of the press and First Amendment that she remembered from college when it came to dealing with the police but none of them seemed to work.

They'd continued to wander around the town on foot when they encountered an abandoned car in the middle of a deserted street with the engine still running. Her cameraman jumped behind the wheel and told her to get in.

"But it's not our car," she told him.

"So," he replied.

"But we could get arrested for stealing it," she said to him.

He shook his head in disbelief. "Look, Patty, my feet are tired, I'm lugging this thirty pound camera and fifteen pounds worth of batteries, I'm sixty years old and I don't need to be walking all over Crescent City. A bunch of terrorists have just shot the hell out of this town and killed hundreds of people. Not to mention that they've been shooting at us too. The few police that are left are trying to deal with them. Do you really think anyone gives a shit about this car? Now either get in, or get out of the way."

"Where are we going?" she asked as she got into the passenger's seat.

"The airport," he told her.

209

It took them five minutes to get to the airport. Their news van was still there, the hood open, their technician driver working on the battery cables. When he was done, he moved to the driver's door, reached in and turned the key. The van's engine roared to life.

The driver explained that when he couldn't get a call through to get a tow truck, he'd hitch-hiked to Wal-Mart, where he bought a new battery. He was just leaving the store when he heard the shooting from downtown. Within a few minutes people began racing by in their cars. One man stopped and told him that a bunch of soldiers had gone crazy and were killing people at the park. Nobody would give him a ride back to the airport, so it had taken him almost two hours to walk the three miles carrying the heavy battery. When he got back, he found the planes on fire and dead people everywhere.

The cameraman quickly explained to him what was occurring in Crescent City, and their close brush with death as the terrorists began firing at them as they filmed from the street next to the park.

"Now that the van is running, let's get back into town and get some more shots," Patricia Dodge said with a tone in her voice that made it seem like she was in charge.

"No, let's see if we can get the remote feed working first," he said to her. There's no sense in driving around in this big target if the transmission equipment isn't gonna to work."

The driver now switched hats and became the technician. Jumping into the back of the van, he electrically raised the satellite transmission mast mounted on top of the van and powered up the equipment. It took the antenna a couple of minutes to locate and establish contact with the communications satellite in geo-synchronous orbit two hundred miles in space off the West Coast of California. Once a link was established, he inputted the stations access codes, and the transmission link was established.

"Give me a test Patricia," he said into his microphone headset.

"This is Patricia Dodge, K H U M reporting live from Crescent City," she said into her wireless microphone.

"Perfect," he told her, his voice resonating in the partially covered receiver in her left ear. "We're ready to go live."

The radio in her patrol car crackled once, then went silent. A few seconds later Red could hear the sound of the comm-op's voice. "95-S-3, Humboldt, on the blue."

"Humboldt, S-3, go ahead," Red Wolff replied.

"S-3, the FBI is requesting you meet their helicopter at the airport in ten."

"10-4, S-3 copies."

She left one officer at the command post and drove toward the airport.

She got to the airport a couple of minutes before five. As she was driving in, the news van was just pulling out in the opposite direction. She could see the pretty young reporter sitting in the passenger's seat. The van slowed momentarily, but then continued out of the airport.

With everything else she'd been doing, Red Wolff had been unaware of what the terrorists had done at the airport. Sitting on the tarmac, she saw the burned out shells of two aircraft and the bodies of the two National Guard pilots. She could also see the smoking hulks of four vehicles on the runway. The vehicles had burned to the ground, their rubber tires still smoldering. Drawing her service pistol, she made a cautious approach to the terminal building. The door was open and she peered inside. The bodies of two men, dressed in ties and suit coats, were slumped in the plastic chairs of the waiting area. She rightly assumed they were the pilots of the Governor's aircraft.

Jesus, she thought to herself, whoever planned this attack covered all the bases.

The helicopter came in from the northeast rather than the south. That, she assumed, probably meant it was already getting foggy along the coastline and the copter's pilot had veered inland to maintain visual flight references. It was a sleek Bell 427. Painted jet black, it was fast and could seat eight.

Red Wolff was excited. The arrival of the helicopter meant the whole FBI Hostage Rescue Team was here. For the first time in nearly seven hours she felt like they might get the upper hand on the terrorists.

The helicopter circled around McNamara Field once, then flared for a landing near the terminal building. As it did, she could see the pilots. Both were dressed in black flight suits with matching black helmets. She had worked with an FBI team once before when she was a sergeant in L.A. They were really good and knew their business. Dressed in black uniforms, they were a fearsome sight when they deployed on a mission. This team, she knew, was from the San Francisco FBI office. She assumed they would be dressed the same and would be just as good. She eagerly waited for the sliding door on the passenger cabin to open.

When it did, her heart sank.

Out of the cabin came a single man. Dressed in the FBI work uniform, a dark suit, white shirt, and subdued tie. He looked to Red Wolff to be about the same age as Doogie Howser, M.D.

The man bent over slightly as walked calmly away from the helicopter's still turning rotor blades. Red Wolff could hear the jet engines throttling back as the pilots began to shut them down.

When the man was clear of the helicopter, Red Wolff greeted him with a handshake.

"Erin Wolff, CHP," she said loudly to be heard over the engine noise, omitting her rank that would have been obvious to him by the stripes on her uniform shirt.

"Douglas Newsome, Special Agent, Federal Bureau of Investigation, San Francisco," he replied formally, returning her handshake.

She escorted him away from the helicopter far enough so they could communicate normally.

"Where's the rest of the hostage rescue team?" she asked, an obvious questioning tone in her voice, looking back at the empty cabin of the helicopter.

"What rescue team?" he replied.

"The team I was told you guys were sending to help us," Red answered, her voice unable to hide her exasperation.

"There's no hostage rescue team coming."

"Not coming, why?"

"The Bureau is concerned that too many times we have to respond to minor incidents you local's blow all out of proportion. Our policy is to verify we are needed, and local resources can't handle the incident, before we deploy," he said, an obvious air of "we're the FBI, and we know best," in his voice.

Red Wolff had learned self-control from many years of working the streets. Minor incident! Blow out of proportion! It was all she could do not to deck him on the spot.

"Do you have any idea what's going on here?" she asked. Not waiting for him to respond she gave the agent a two minute rundown on what had happened.

"Well, if you don't mind, the Bureau likes to make up its own mind on this type of thing," he answered, again with an air of FBI superiority in his voice. Douglas Newsome was twenty-four. He'd been an FBI agent eighteen months.

"The Bureau." He was one of "those" FBI agents. Red Wolff now knew who she was dealing with.

Like most street cops, Red Wolff had a love-hate relationship with the FBI, mostly hate. Broken down in to five distinct operations, the FBI had sections that dealt with everything from terrorism to computer crime. All FBI special agents had a college degree, mostly in computers, foreign language, law, or accounting. Most of its agents were recruited directly from college, private industry, or other government agencies, and had no practical law enforcement experience. There were some agents who'd been former street cops with other police departments who switched to the FBI, but most of its agents had little or no actual real time on the street.

Red Wolff knew if Douglas Newsome had been a former street cop, he would probably have used the term "we" when talking to another cop about the FBI, rather than "The Bureau," like it was some omnipresent being.

"Have it your way Doug. You want a ride into town to see what's going on, or are you staying here with your thumb up your ass? I've got a bunch of minor incident terrorists with automatic weapons to deal with," Red said to the agent, looking him squarely in the eye. She made no attempt to hide her disdain for the arrogant young man.

"Please call me Douglas," the agent responded, using the FBI tactic of staying superior to the local cops.

"Okay Douglas, fuck you, and the helicopter you rode in on!" she said with a half-smile on her face as she turned and walked back toward her patrol car.

She was already in the driver's seat when Douglas Newsome yelled for her to wait and ran toward her car. Obviously, some of the things he learned at the FBI Academy in Quantico, Virginia, about dealing with local cops didn't work real well in Northern California.

"If you're going with me, get in," she said. "But you better tell your pilots to get that copter out of here. The terrorists could show up here again anytime."

Once he warned the helicopter pilots, Douglas Newsome jumped in the passenger's seat of her patrol car. Red Wolff smashed the accelerator down, and the patrol car leapt forward, its' rear wheels spinning for several seconds on the slick tarmac of the airplane parking ramp before biting in. As she maneuvered the patrol car toward the exit, she could see the white news van coming back into the airport toward them.

The driver of the van had his arm out the window, waving for her to stop. Her senses alerted, she stopped quickly, opened the patrol car door, pulled her service pistol, and took up a defensive position behind the door. She knew it was probably that ditzy reporter and her crew, but better to be safe. In the passenger's seat, Special Agent Douglas Newsome sat perplexed. It took him a few seconds to realize that whatever was going on in Crescent City was for real. He promptly got out with his pistol drawn.

Red Wolff signaled for the van to stop, as she did not want it to come any closer. If it was the bad guys, she wanted room to maneuver. The van stopped about twenty feet in front of the patrol car and the passenger's side door opened. Out came Patricia Dodge, microphone in hand, her cameraman coming out of the sliding side door.

She walked directly up to Red Wolff and pushed the microphone into her face. She was non-stop questions.

Red held her hand up to indicate that the reporter should pause for a second.

"Ma'am, I don't have the time to answer your questions right now. I'm not trying to be uncooperative, but I have more pressing things to deal with," Red Wolff's tone was matter-of-fact.

The cameraman was standing behind Patricia Dodge's left shoulder, filming. He was using the camera's built in light unit to illuminate the female sergeant's face, as the sky was already darkening from the approaching fog.

The light from the camera was blinding. Red Wolf had to squint and divert her eyes. The light was so powerful it actually generated enough heat to warm the air.

"Officer, the public has a right to know what's going on and what steps are being taken to protect them," Patricia Dodge said in her best Nancy Grace like tone.

It had been a long day for Red Wolff. She'd just dealt with the moron FBI agent, and now this reporter. She nodded her head as if agreeing with the reporter, then motioned for her to come closer.

Smugly Patricia Dodge thought to herself, that's right, you have to take a firm stand when dealing with cops. Let them know in no uncertain terms about the power of the media.

When Patricia Dodge was about eighteen inches away, Red Wolff bent forward and whispered something in the reporter's ear. She then jumped back in the patrol car and drove away.

The cameraman filmed the patrol car for a few seconds as it pulled away, then stopped his camera.

"What'd she say?" he asked.

"She told me to fuck off," the stunned reporter replied.

Red Wolff drove the patrol car very fast back into town. It was almost 5:30 and she had to get back to her squad of men to ensure everything was ready for the terrorist attack that, according to Abdul Abbas, would come in less than thirty minutes.

As she drove, she talked to the FBI agent in the passenger's seat telling him in greater detail about how the terrorists had marched into the park during the Governor's speech and how they'd opened up on the formation of National Guard troopers and the crowd.

She drove him through the west side of town amid the burning buildings and the dozens of bodies lying in the street. When they arrived at the command post, the sole CHP officer reported he could see increased movement inside the community center, but as of yet, no movement outside the building.

She directed Agent Douglas Newsome to the corner of the building facing the park and gave him a pair of binoculars. The agent squatted down by the side of the building, careful to not dirty his suit, and began to survey the park and the community center. He wasn't ready for what he saw. The streets around the park, and the park's main grassy area, were littered with hundreds of bodies. The area that had served as the VIP section was a jumble of overturned chairs and dead bodies. At the entrance to the community center he could see several army trucks, two Humvees, and dozens of dead men on the ground.

Douglas Newsome pulled back from the corner and shook his head in disbelief. His instinct was to vomit, but he summoned up the strength to choke it down.

"My God, we didn't believe the reports we were getting in San Francisco from the Highway Patrol," he said to Red Wolff, his head and eyes downcast so he didn't have to look the female sergeant in the eye.

"You think maybe we could get that hostage rescue team now?" Red Wolff said, a hint of sarcasm in her voice, knowing it would take them hours to get to Crescent City.

"I'm calling the helicopter now, they can relay the request to San Francisco," the agent said pulling out his small portable radio.

"By the way, who's in charge here?" he asked Red Wolff.

"I am."

"Not any more, this is now an FBI operation under the provisions of the Patriot Act, and the National Security Act," he said, reverting to his "we're the FBI" mode.

Red Wolff had to laugh. The agent glared at her with his best twenty-four year old "I'm serious" look.

"Get a life, Dougie, there's only one of you, you have no idea what the hell's going on in this town, you don't know your way around, and the cops here don't give a damn who you are. They've been shot at by these assholes, and seen their friends and families killed. Some of my troops have hemorrhoids older than you, and they sure as hell won't follow your orders. You've probably never even been in a bar fight before, on-or-off duty," she said to him. Red Wolff could be articulate when she needed to be.

Agent Douglas Newsome didn't know what to say. They didn't cover this type of scenario at the FBI Academy. And, she was right. He'd never been in bar fight.

When the agent didn't respond, Red Wolff spoke again, "Right now I've got my troops setting up to handle the terrorists when they come out again in about twenty minutes. You want to help, or do you want to argue about jurisdiction?"

"What do you want me to do?"

Inside the community center, Emil Lagare ordered his assault teams to prepare to move out. It was quarter to six, and he wanted them ready to drive away precisely on the hour. Ten of his men picked up their weapons and reloaded their ammunition pouches with full thirty round magazines. Those that would be doing the actual assault checked their shoulder bags to ensure they had an ample supply of emergency road flares to start fires. It had only been seven hours since the assault began, but already they had the haggard look that comes with physical and mental exhaustion and being the dealers of death. The prospect of another mission to rain death and destruction on the hated Americans, however, had the affect of wiping away their tiredness and infusing them with spirit. As they readied themselves, there were many Allah Akbars and mutual hugs among the men.

Emil Lagare watched as they readied themselves. Counting the two people at the radio station, he still had twenty men, twenty-one counting himself. Ten would depart on the mission to destroy another portion of the town. They still had an abundance of weapons and ammunition, sufficient food and water for several more days, and thirty-five American women and children hostages.

The police radio had been strangely silent for over two hours. He interpreted that as a good sign. His men reported seeing occasional movement from the ring of police around the community center, but they had made no attempt to rescue the hostages or maneuver for an assault on the building. This he believed was because his men had superior firepower, and because the initial attack had decimated the American police, who were content now to wait for their military to arrive.

He had heard and seen the two fighter jets as they passed over the town. Qassim Saleh had told him the first response from the Americans would probably be a reconnaissance flight. He could expect ground troops within six to twelve hours after that. Good, Emil Lagare said to himself, at least another four to five hours with only the few remaining local police to deal with.

When his men were ready, he called them together and told them Allah was watching over their actions, and they would be rewarded for every infidel American they killed. The ten men gave a collective Allah Akbar and turned toward the twenty-five or so women and children hostages in the back corner of the room.

Yelling, prodding with rifles, dragging, cursing, and hitting, the ten men forced the women to their feet and out the front door of the building. They were forced to climb into the open beds of the army trucks. Those who didn't move fast enough were clubbed with rifle butts, others were physically picked up and thrown into the trucks. The crying and screaming from the women, some of them holding children, was ear-piercing. It took almost five minutes to get the women loaded.

Just as before, one terrorist drove, another rode on the passenger side. Between them, was a single woman hostage. In the back of each truck twelve women were forced to stand up, facing outward, holding onto the side rails of the bed. Behind the women stood three terrorists, each with an M-16 rifle. Emil Lagare decided for this mission, all of the M-249 machine guns would remain at the community center, lest they fall into the hands of the Americans should his men be attacked. As soon as the trucks were loaded, they pulled away from the entrance heading toward the street.

Emil Lagare watched them go. He had no doubt they would be successful. Qassim Saleh had told him he didn't believe either target would be guarded and if they did meet opposition his men should shoot hostages as a way of making the Americans cease their resistance.

He looked around the main room of the community center. Except for six of his men who were stationed to keep watch from the doors and windows, the room was deserted. Trash littered the floor, and dozens of empty plastic water bottles and aluminum beverage cans were strewn about. In the corner, where the women hostages had been, there were numerous pieces of clothing, purses, backpacks, and blankets.

Walking across the room to the movable partitions that divided the large conference hall into two rooms, he opened the door and peered in. Two of his men stood guard. One was looking out the window next to the exit door leading to the back parking lot, while the other watched the fifteen or so women hostages seated on the floor. Among the hostages he could see the Governor of California. She was sitting with her back against the wall, head lolled to one side. Her eyes were open, blankly staring at the floor. Next to her, sat two women who were looking back at him. Neither of them diverted their eyes when he made eye contact with them. Shameless he thought to himself. These American whores have no manners or respect. Well, no matter, soon they too would be dead.

He looked back at the Governor. It was really too bad, Emil thought to himself that there had not been any television coverage. Scenes of the Governor of California as a hostage in her own state would be worldwide news. People all over the world would have a new respect for, and a healthy fear of, Islam. If Muslim martyrs could capture the Governor of California in her own state, where in the world would any politician be safe? Governments would be forced to increase security around their leaders and those same leaders would not feel free to travel even in their own countries.

It was 5:46 when Red Wolff, with FBI agent Douglas Newsome as a passenger, stopped at the hospital. The scene was much different than it had been only a few hours before. There was still plenty of daylight left, although the fog was rolling in, darkening the skies. She could see that Ray Silva had done his job well.

Almost all of the cars that had crowded the semi-circle driveway main entrance were gone. Patients that had been lying outside on the concrete entrance had been moved out of sight. Instead of the throng of people who'd crowded the entrance several hours before, there were only about a dozen civilians sitting in the waiting room. The glass doors to the main entrance were locked open and the entire interior was lit with every light available. Dozens of cars had been double and triple parked in front of the emergency room entrance and it was completely blacked out. Even the large red directional arrow on the street that pointed the way to the emergency room was covered over. To anyone not familiar with the layout of the hospital, it would look like there was no emergency room or emergency room entrance. There were lots of cars in the main parking lot, and about ten larger

SUV and van type vehicles were parked along the edge of the driveway leading to the arch covered portico entrance.

As she pulled under the portico, Ray Silva emerged from the entrance.

"All set Ray?" she asked.

Her career long friend nodded, but uncharacteristically, did not speak.

Red Wolff picked up on the fact he didn't say anything, but let it go. She remembered what she had been told about Ray Silva by other officers when she was a brand new rookie in Central Los Angeles so many years ago. It was a play on the old Jim Croce song, "*You Don't Mess Around With Jim.*" In his case, the way it went in Central was, "You don't sword fight Zorro," "You don't draw on the Lone Ranger," and "You don't fuck with Ray Silva." She knew the hospital was in good hands.

"Good luck, Ray," she said as she wheeled out of the entrance.

She drove less than a half-mile to the expected second location of the terrorists attack. As she'd directed, the building was completely blacked out, and except for some night lights, the entire structure was dark. Likewise, the large parking lot was dark, as her officers had extinguished the dozens of lights that sat atop the long metal poles in the lot. There were a few civilian cars still parked in the lot here and there, but for the most part, the entire building and grounds looked deserted.

Pulling the patrol car to the rear of the building she and FBI Agent Newsome entered through the back door. Inside she was met by Ralph Silva who told her that everything was ready.

Red Wolff took a deep breath and slowly let it out. I hope this works, she thought to herself. She would know in just a few minutes.

CHAPTER FOURTEEN

When she'd been unable to get the female Highway Patrol officer to answer her questions at the airport, Patricia Dodge and her crew drove back into Crescent City and set up near the command post to do a live feed. Once they were in position, the technician again raised the boom mast and reestablished contact with the satellite.

Now, with direct communications to the station in Eureka, the technician hurriedly explained to the news director what had happened in Crescent City over the past eight hours. The news director contacted the flagship station in San Francisco, who in turn alerted Fox News headquarters in New York City. All Fox affiliates across the nation were notified to prepare for a live feed from Crescent City.

"This is Patricia Dodge, Fox News, reporting live from Crescent City, California. This small town on the Pacific Ocean, just twenty miles south of the Oregon Border, has been taken over by terrorists. Early this morning, during a Fourth of July celebration, heavily armed terrorists opened fire with automatic weapons on a large crowd of National Guard soldiers and civilians gathered in a park near the ocean. As you can see from the videotape we obtained at that time, terrorists can be seen randomly shooting people."

As Patricia Dodge spoke, the network played the blurry tape shot that morning by her cameraman showing hundreds of people running, others falling, and armed men spraying the assembled crowd with bullets.

"At the time of the attack, the Governor of California was giving a speech honoring the local National Guard unit that had just returned from a twelve month deployment in Iraq."

The anchorman in New York interrupted her to ask the status of the Governor.

"We're not sure if the Governor was killed, or was taken hostage by the terrorists. We did see several dozen women forcibly taken into the building to my rear. I can tell you that several hundred people have been killed and the terrorists have burned large sections of this small town. I have been in contact with the local police agency, but they have been reluctant to tell me how they intend to deal with this crisis situation."

"Patricia, have the terrorists made any demands?" asked the anchorman in New York.

"We are not aware of any demands thus far," she replied."And do you think this is an isolated attack, or the start of attacks all over the nation?" he asked.

"We have no way of knowing at this point," Patricia Dodge responded.

Across the nation, millions of viewers heard and saw the live feed from Crescent City. The reaction was almost instantaneous. Switchboards at police stations all over the country were flooded with calls. Public safety agencies activated their emergency action plans, local governments began emergency meetings. At the national level, all commercial airlines were warned of the attack and all further outgoing flights were cancelled. The Federal Aviation Administration issued a warning to all flights in the air, and all incoming international flights were ordered to return to their country of origin, or to divert to the closest non-United States airport.

The Department of Homeland Security immediately raised the national threat level from orange to red. Military personnel were put on full alert, leaves were cancelled, and all American embassies across the world put on heightened security.

Everything was done in response to the brief news report from Crescent City. It was a logical common sense reaction to a situation of still unknown proportion. In Washington, the President and his key advisors were moved to secure locations.

In Crescent City, Patricia Dodge continued her live report from the police command post with the community center in the background.

It was at just that moment when the first of the two trucks full of female hostages being held at gunpoint by the terrorists as human shields, passed by on the street not one hundred yards behind the reporter as she broadcast live to the nation.

As the trucks passed by the reporter and her cameraman standing in the street, the men in the back of the trucks had ample opportunity to open fire on them had they wished to do so. They were, however, under strict orders not to intentionally shoot at the American media.

Up to this time, neither Emil Lagare, nor any of his men, had seen any indication that the American media was in town. In the lead truck, the passenger used his radio to advise Emil Lagare of the television reporter's presence in town.

Excellent, Emil Lagare said to himself, thanks be to Allah. The presence of the broadcast media gave new impetus to the entire operation. He could now implement another portion of Qassim Saleh's plan. He would focus on this, as soon as his men returned from their current mission.

Patricia Dodge's cameraman saw the trucks pass by through the viewfinder of his camera as he filmed her live broadcast. He spoke into his remote mike on the camera and told the female reporter what he had seen. Patricia Dodge could be seen bringing her right hand up to her ear to capture the sound of her cameraman's voice through the ear piece hidden by her hair. As soon as she heard the information she abruptly signed off her live feed, and she and her cameraman ran back toward the nearby broadcast van.

"Let's go," she excitedly told her combination technician and driver.

"Go where?" he asked.

"Follow the terrorists!" she almost screamed at him.

"Not till we lower the mast, and secure everything, otherwise the vehicle movement might damage the transmission equipment," the technician told her.

"I don't give a shit, we have to go now, or we'll lose them!" she said with a force in her voice that surprised the man.

"Okay, but if it breaks, it comes out of your pay," he replied.

Within thirty seconds they were moving, turning north on Highway 101 as the road made its' way through the almost deserted town.

In the lead truck, the American Muslim driver ground his way through the gears of the large unwieldy army truck. Designed for use on dirt roads and rough terrain, the truck had a very low gear ratio making it slow to pick up speed. The second truck lumbered along behind.

By now, eight hours after the initial attack, almost all the townspeople knew what was happening, as did all of the tourists who had been trapped when the terrorists had blocked the highways north and south of town. They wisely stayed in their homes, armed themselves as best they could, or gathered with friends for mutual defense. The streets were deserted except for the inevitable ten percent who never get the word, or who are oblivious to the signs of something disastrous going on around them. They went about their business in spite of the smoke from the burned out buildings, the dead bodies they encountered in the street, and the Islamic propaganda being broadcast on the town's only radio station.

It was 6:07 p.m. when the trucks got to the north end of town and took the turn-off for Washington Boulevard. They drove past the cable television office they had attacked early that morning, and the dark and deserted Highway Patrol office.

About a half-mile past the Highway Patrol office the first truck turned off Washington Boulevard into the entrance of its' target, Sutter Coast Hospital. The second truck continued on.

During the development of the plan, Qassim Saleh had reasoned that following the initial attack the local hospital would be flooded with the dead, dying, and wounded. As such, it would be crowded with emergency medical personnel, and hundreds of people either seeking aid, or bringing others in for treatment. He also believed that local law enforcement authorities would have scant resources to spare to defend a hospital. It would be an easy target, what the Americans called "shooting fish in a barrel." Besides being an easy target, attacking a hospital would be righteous revenge for the American and Israeli bombings of hospitals in Palestine and Islamic countries.

The driver fought the wheel as he turned the truck and headed directly for the covered portico entry. From the cab and the bed of the truck, the terrorists could see the well lit entry, and about a dozen people sitting or standing in the waiting room. They could also see several people, dressed in white, sitting behind the two counters in the spacious hospital entrance.

As soon as the truck began to pull close to the front doors, the people in the room all began to point at the vehicle. There was much frenzied movement, men yelling and women screaming. The terrorists could clearly see all of the people in the room through the mostly glass walls of the entry as they ran to the rear of the room and down a parallel hallway.

As the truck passed underneath the covered entrance, the terrorists and the female hostages in the bed of the truck actually had to duck down to avoid striking their heads. When the truck was directly adjacent to the front doors it stopped, and two of the three men in the back jumped to the ground, as did the passenger in the cab.

Once the three terrorists were on the ground, they stood shoulder to shoulder for a brief second, then began running through the glass entry doors in pursuit of the people they'd seen running from the waiting room.

While their comrades on the ground ran into the hospital to wreak death and havoc, the driver remained behind the wheel of the truck, pointing a Beretta pistol at the frightened female hostage seated next to him in the cab. In the large bed of the truck, another man, armed with an M-16 rifle, held a dozen women as human shields against any unforeseen attack.

Although none of the terrorists knew it, they had less than a minute to live.

———————

Ray Silva, the three National Guard soldiers, and the other two cops on his team of six, had set up a classic ambush. They counted on the terrorists reacting impulsively and arrogantly, when they attacked the hospital.

The entrance to the hospital was fairly spacious. There was a waiting room to the right with thirty or so chairs, several low tables, magazine racks, a small children's play area with a few toys, and the ever present television set. Directly to the front of the entrance sat the check-in station, a long counter with several computers, desks and chairs, and volumes of paperwork stacked everywhere. A hallway led from the right of the counter to the main portion of the hospital. To the left side of the entrance, directly opposite the waiting room, was a smaller counter, a sign on the wall behind the counter read "Information."

What the terrorists didn't know was that the people who'd fled from them had been solicited by Ray Silva to act as human bait to draw them in.

Setting the ambush had not been easy. When he first got to the hospital with his team, they began moving vehicles, moving wounded patients from the entry, and trying to make the emergency room entrance disappear.

Almost as soon as he arrived, Ray Silva was confronted by the same doctor he had restrained when Red Wolff was dealing with the wounded terrorist, Abdul Abbas.

"You can't move those patients," he screamed at Ray Silva as his men as gently as possible moved all of the wounded from around the main hospital entrance.

"Those people are in need of medical care, this is a hospital, you can't bring your war here," he yelled, as Ray Silva and his team continued to make their preparations, ignoring the doctor's ranting.

When his team's preparations were completed, Ray Silva finally turned to the young doctor who had been verbally chipping at him and his men for the past half-hour, grabbed him by his shirt with one hand and pushed him against the wall of one of the corridors. He then brought his face directly down to the shorter man's and said, "Listen you little shit, everyone else here gets it but you. In less than twenty minutes, a truck load of armed men are coming to this hospital to kill as many people as they can, then they're going to burn it to the ground. It doesn't matter to them that the people here are injured, or sick, need surgery, or that you're trying to give them medical attention. It also doesn't matter to them whether you are against the war on terrorism, or hate the President. And by the way, I'm not bringing the fight here, they are." It was more words than Ray Silva had said in a long time.

When Ray Silva released him, the young doctor said, "What can I do to help?"

"I need about a dozen volunteers," Ray Silva told him.

"Okay, I'll see what I can do, but I'm still against guns and killing," the doctor said.

"Me too," replied Ray Silva as he turned his attention to the outside portion of the ambush.

In five minutes the doctor returned with about fifteen people, mostly men.

"Here are your volunteers, officer, I'm volunteering also."

"Thanks doc, but you're too valuable. You go back and help those people that need you. I'll brief the others," Ray Silva said to the doctor, a tone of genuine appreciation in his voice.

As the doctor turned to go, he extended his hand to Ray Silva and said, "Good luck."

The doctor then returned to his patients and Ray Silva briefed the volunteers on what he needed them to do.

———————

As they ran through the open glass entry doors, the terrorists, weapons at the ready, were so intent on pursuing the people who'd fled from the waiting room and from behind the counters, that they did not pause to look for any signs of danger. The entry was deserted, but they could hear the sounds of yelling and screaming from the hallway to the right of the check-in counter. The terrorists picked up their pace as they ran toward the sounds.

The entry, waiting room, and the first twenty feet of the hallway were brightly lit with every light available. As they ran around the corner from the waiting room and down the hallway toward the examination and patient rooms, they encountered different conditions. While the first twenty feet of the corridor were illuminated, the rest of the long hallway was not. Ray Silva's team had removed the fluorescent tubes from the overhead fixtures making the hallway dark. It gave them the effect they wanted, the terrorists were brightly silhouetted, but could see nothing down the darkened corridor.

What they couldn't see, seventy feet down the hall, were five metal gurneys turned on their sides, covered with numerous mattresses. Kneeling behind the gurneys were two National Guard soldiers, rifles leveled.

Once they rounded the corner and started down the corridor, the terrorists saw the darkened hallway before them and realized that something was wrong. With their forward momentum, however, it took just a second longer before they could stop, or reverse direction. Not that it mattered. One of the two kneeling soldiers had an M-16 taken from the terrorists who'd been involved in the high speed pursuit and shooting earlier that day. The other soldier had a CHP issue AR-15.

The soldier with the M-16 opened fire on the three terrorists with a constant string of three round bursts, while the other pulled the trigger on the AR-15 as fast as he could. The first three round burst from the trooper with the M-16 was high and whistled down the corridor toward the opposite end of the hospital. The second burst caught one of the terrorists full in the chest. The blast completely stopped the man's forward motion, lifted him upright, and slammed him backward. The terrorist to his right was struck six times by the other soldiers AR-15 fire. He died, standing against the wall, his blood staining the bright white painted wall with streaks of red.

Hazy, white smoke, trapped by the eight foot ceiling in the corridor, hung in the air, as did the acrid smell of gunpowder.

The third terrorist, who had been a bit slower in rounding the corner, was shielded from the soldiers' fusillade of bullets by the bodies of his two comrades. He actually had time to return fire at the two soldiers, although hidden as they were in the darkness, he could never get off an accurately aimed shot.

As the remaining terrorist was returning fire, he was also backing up toward the check-in counter and waiting room. He successfully made it back to the check-in counter, turned, and began to run toward the entry door.

He was taking his second stride when he heard someone say in English, "Happy Independence Day, mother-fucker."

Looking up, the terrorist saw the third National Guard trooper standing behind the information counter, twenty feet in front of him, with a police 870 Winchester shotgun leveled at his chest. Carrying his M-16 in his right hand by the pistol grip on the stock, the terrorist tried to bring the weapon up to a firing position. The last thing he heard and saw in this lifetime was a loud boom, and two feet of flame that came from the barrel of the shotgun.

The round left the barrel at 1200 feet per second. At a range of less than twenty feet, the sixteen steel pellets did not have enough distance to spread out. Remaining in a tight group, they all hit the terrorist squarely in the chest, stopping him dead in his tracks, shattering his sternum and ripping into his heart. Blood spurted out of the gaping wound as the terrorist fell forward and died.

When the three terrorists who made the assault into the hospital dismounted the truck, the two who remained, watched them as they ran into the entry, disappeared around the corner, and down the hallway. Their attention should have been focused on their surroundings.

When they heard the sounds of the M-16 rifle being fired, they assumed, wrongly, it was their comrades shooting and killing Americans in the hospital. They both yelled, Allah Akbar and smiled as they pictured the killing that was occurring out of their sight. The screaming and crying of the women they held as human shields only increased their complacency.

Unseen by the terrorist in the bed of the truck, Ray Silva slipped from behind one of the SUVs parked on the opposite side of the driveway, while a sheriff's deputy and another Highway Patrol officer emerged from behind a large decorative hedge that separated the parking lot from the entry portico. All three had their service pistols in hand and were wearing the U.S. military type gas masks used by the Highway Patrol.

Ray Silva was three feet from the bed of the truck when he pulled the pin on the tear gas grenade. The weapon was about the size of a softball, painted an olive drab color, with a small detonator on top. After pulling the pin, he moved his fingers off the spring loaded safety spoon, which caused the detonator to activate the two to five second delay fuse. The terrorist in the truck, still intent on trying to see what was happening inside the hospital, did not see him reach up through the wooden slats on the side of the cargo bed and drop the hard plastic grenade onto the steel floor.

The grenade made a dull sound as it hit the bed of the truck, not loud, but enough for the terrorist to hear. He turned and his eye caught a small trail of gray smoke coming from a round object on the cargo bed. He'd seen the American smooth, egg shell sided fragmentation type grenade before, but this object was bigger. Whatever it was, he was sure it wasn't good. He was contemplating whether to jump from the truck, yell at the driver, or begin shooting the female hostages when the object activated itself.

When the grenade activated, it did not explode like a fragmentation grenade, instead it started spinning rapidly in small circles much like a top, and began to spew out a grayish white vapor. The spinning effect was caused by the high pressure of the tear gas inside the grenade as it vented into the air. As the spinning increased in speed, the grenade began to move around in the cargo bed causing it to bounce off the steel sides of the truck, and the feet of the women hostages. The women now began to scream and tried to climb up the wooden side rails of the truck.

Within a few seconds, the entire bed of the truck was engulfed in a thick cloud of eye-stinging, choking, Chlorobenzalmalononitrile gas. More commonly known as CS, the chemical compound inside the grenade was the favorite choice of law enforcement and the military for riot control because of its' almost immediate effectiveness in neutralizing large crowds of unruly people. The effects on the terrorist and the female hostages in the back of the truck were almost instantaneous, as the chemical agent began to irritate the sensitive mucous membrane tissues in their eyes and nose. Their eyes began to water, and noses began to run, they all started coughing as they breathed the gas into their lungs, and several of the women vomited. When they could manage a breath, several of the women cried and others screamed. The terrorist, try as he might, was not immune from the effects of the gas. As the cloud of noxious gas grew, it was moved by the slight breeze toward the cab of the truck. Within five seconds from the time he dropped the grenade into the bed of the truck, all of its' occupants were incapacitated. It was exactly the effect Ray Silva wanted.

Ray Silva and the other two officers moved quickly. Wearing the gas mask made movement a little harder, but thanks to the big army truck's high ground clearance, he was able to crouch, and half-crawl under the truck, emerging on the hospital entrance side. Simultaneously, while he climbed up one side of the truck bed using the wooden slat side rails as hand holds, the other officer climbed up the opposite side. Standing now on the outside of the truck bed, a thick cloud of whitish gas still hanging over the cargo area, the officers saw the lone terrorist bent over retching, long streams of snot hanging from his nose.

As incapacitated as the terrorist was, when he saw Ray Silva standing on the outside of the truck bed, one hand holding onto the wooden side rails, and a pistol in the other, he began to raise the rifle he held in his right hand to shoot the officer. His training in the Syrian Desert had made him physically tough and his fanatic belief in radical Islam meant he would never give up.

Ray Silva was already pointing his pistol at the terrorist who was bringing his rifle up. He was just starting to squeeze the trigger when one of the female hostages, recognizing him by his uniform as a Highway Patrol officer, lunged at him and threw both her arms around his neck in a gesture of relief at being rescued. The woman's action caused Ray Silva to lose his grip on the side of the truck bed. In a reflex action, he dropped his hand holding the pistol down to grab the wooden side rail. He still had the pistol in his hand, but could not bring his arm up to fire at the terrorist.

Ray Silva watched in what seemed to be slow motion as the terrorist straightened, while at the same time bringing the M-16 rifle up to fire at him. What a crappy way to die he thought to himself, teetering on the edge of a truck, a sobbing women with her arms wrapped in a vise like grip around his neck, and no way to defend himself.

The sound of a pistol being fired and the resulting splatter of brain tissue, bone, and blood were the next things Ray Silva heard and saw.

The .40 caliber, controlled expansion, half-jacketed round, entered the back of the terrorist's head just below the knot at the base of his skull. In a microsecond, too quick for the human eye to see, the power in the round caused his head to balloon to twice its normal size, then contract just as fast. The round continued into his head, shattering his cranium and blowing out a large portion of his frontal lobe. He was dead instantaneously, but his body continued to stand upright, his right hand still holding the M-16 on Ray Silva. Two seconds later the terrorist crumpled to the bed of the truck in a lifeless heap.

Covered in the terrorist's blood, with grayish vapor from the CS grenade still hanging in the air, Ray Silva looked across the eight foot wide truck bed to see Officer Jodie Castle holding her service pistol. While he'd been climbing up one side of the truck bed, she had been climbing up the other. In his rush to fire on the helpless Ray Silva, the terrorist had not seen her.

"Thanks, Jodie," he yelled to her, although his voice was muffled by the gas mask.

Jodie Castle, who had just killed her second man in eight hours, made no acknowledgement.

While Ray Silva and Jodie Castle had been attacking the terrorist in the truck bed, the sheriff's deputy had stealthily crept up on the truck's cab. The driver, another of the American Muslims, was holding a pistol on the woman hostage in the cab when the first of the CS gas cloud made its' way into the driver's compartment. He immediately began coughing and his eyes begin to sting. He was nineteen years old, and was less of a true believer in an afterlife with Allah and virgins. The gas was too much for him. He dropped his pistol to the floorboard and opened the driver's side door.

He took one step out of the cab onto the truck's frame rail so he could jump the four feet to the ground, when his left arm was grabbed by the deputy. In one motion, the deputy pulled and twisted on his arm, causing him to do a complete flip in the air and crash to the pavement on his back with a loud thud. Looking up, he found himself staring into the barrel of a pistol held by a man wearing a gas mask.

The young Muslim man was in the process of bringing his hands up over his head into the "I surrender" position, when three rapid fire pistol rounds hit him in the center of his chest, killing him instantly.

The deputy reacted to the sound of the shots, swinging his body, and pistol around toward the open driver's side door of the truck. Looking upward, he saw the woman who had seconds before been the driver's hostage in the cab of the truck. Half-standing, half-sitting in the open door, she held the terrorist's 9 millimeter pistol in both hands. She had mucous running from her nose, and a blank, far away look in her red and watery eyes. The woman was fifty-four years old, with three grown children and five grandkids. She had never before in her life fired a gun, but she knew instinctively what to do when she picked up the pistol dropped by the man who'd held her hostage. Eight hours ago, she had seen her husband of twenty-eight years, gunned down by the terrorists in the park.

In less than a minute, all five of the terrorists were dead. None of the six people on Ray Silva's team, or civilians at the hospital, were injured. The twelve women hostages and three children were rushed into the hospital for medical treatment. They had been through a terrible ordeal, but were physically okay.

Ray Silva and his team quickly gathered up the terrorist's weapons, radios and equipment. He knew they would be needed if the situation in Crescent City continued much longer.

Leaving Officer Jodie Castle and one of the National Guard troopers at the hospital to provide security against another unforeseen terrorist attack, he directed the remainder of his people into their patrol cars. Red Wolff might need his help, he thought.

———

After the first truck of terrorists turned off Washington Boulevard into the hospital, the second truck continued westbound. A half-mile down the road, it made a left turn into the Wal-Mart parking lot.

Qassim Saleh had told Emil Lagare that Wal-Mart was a symbol of American imperialism and exploitation of people all over the world. Attacking and destroying the Crescent City Wal-Mart store, he said, would send a symbolic message to the entire world.

As the truck turned into the parking lot, the terrorists could see the store was deserted. There were a few cars scattered around the parking lot, an odd shopping cart here and there, a couple of overturned large shiny metal garbage cans half-full of trash rolling around, and a few night lights around the store's entrance, but otherwise, there were no signs of activity.

The driver maneuvered the truck up to the glass front of the building and stopped in the large, white-line painted, twenty foot wide crosswalk that led from the store's entry to the parking lot. As soon as it came to a stop, repeating the actions of the terrorists at the hospital, two men jumped from the cargo bed, and one man exited the passenger's side of the cab. One terrorist remained in the bed with the women hostages, and the driver stayed behind the wheel.

Wasting no time, the three men on the ground, each with a bag of roadway flares in a canvas bag slung over their shoulder, made their way to the double sliding glass door entrance. They paused for a second when they began to hear the sound of gunshots in the distance. Their comrades at the hospital, they said to each other, Allah Akbar.

One of the men fired a burst from his M-16 into the glass doors shattering them in to thousands of small pieces. Another man used his rifle butt to finish the job by knocking out any large pieces of jagged glass that remained in the door frame. The three men ran into the store.

Qassim Saleh's planning up to the point of attacking the hospital and now Wal-Mart, had been flawless. Everything Emil Lagare's men

231

had done thus far had been unanticipated by the Americans. Every time they attacked they had the element of surprise, superior firepower, and the ability to move quickly. His plan to destroy Wal-Mart, like the attack on the hospital, would have been a simple matter of killing any people found there, and using the roadway flares to start fires, had they not been expected.

In setting up an ambush at Wal-Mart, Red Wolff was confronted with a different set of problems than Ray Silva faced at the hospital. Whether or not the terrorists burned the Wal-Mart store to the ground was not important to her, the chance to kill five terrorists and rescue a truckload of women hostages, was. She set up her plan accordingly.

She anticipated the terrorists had never been inside a store as cavernous as a Wal-Mart before, and it would take them a few seconds to get oriented. The lack of overhead lighting inside the store would create numerous shadows and places for her people to hide. Ralph Silva, and two of his National Guard buddies, were assigned inside the store. Red Wolff, another Highway Patrol officer, and FBI Agent, Doug Newsome, would take care of the truck with the hostages.

Using his military training, Ralph Silva set up an "L" shaped ambush just inside the store where there was a wide aisle in front of the row of thirteen checkout registers. Like most Crescent City residents, he knew the layout of Wal-Mart very well. He anticipated the terrorists would come through the main entry doors, pass the registers, and head directly for the merchandise laden aisles. It would be at that point when they would be most vulnerable to an ambush.

The "L" shaped ambush was basically simple. The idea was to be able to fire at your enemy from two different directions, without worrying about hitting your own people. Ralph Silva and another trooper took up prone positions at one end of the wide main aisle in front of the registers, using floor displays for concealment. Made of cardboard and wood, the displays would provide no protection if the terrorists started returning fire, but they were perfect for an ambush. He stationed the third trooper atop one of the seven foot high metal aisle dividers. Normally a storage place for large bulky items, the top of the divider was a perfect spot to lie down and take aim. The trooper stacked a few cardboard boxes around his position atop the divider for additional concealment.

When the three terrorists ran through the door, one of them stopped near the storage area where all the large shopping carts were stacked together, the other two continued past the registers. Just as Red Wolff predicted, they stopped momentarily when they reached the wide main aisle to get their bearings. They were in the "kill-zone."

From the far end of the aisle, Ralph Silva and the other trooper both opened fire at the same time. Both terrorists heard the loud report of the weapons, followed by the immediate intense pain of bullets ripping into their bodies. One of the terrorists died immediately, the other less than a minute later.

The terrorist who had paused by the shopping carts froze when the first gunshots rang out. The sound of the weapons he heard firing was the same as the sound made by the weapons he and his comrades were carrying. His initial thought was that the other two men had spotted someone inside the store and were firing at him. When the firing stopped, he called out to his comrades. When he received no answer, he hastily turned and ran the ten yards back toward the entry doors.

From atop the aisle divider, the trooper waited until he had a clear shot at the running terrorist. Armed with a CHP issue AR-15, he took careful aim through the round peep sight and squeezed off one round. The terrorist fell face down in the broken glass of the entry door, a large red stain growing on the back of his uniform shirt. Outside the store, Red Wolff bided her time until she had a clear shot at the terrorist standing in the back of the truck surrounded by a dozen women hostages. Unlike the ambush set up by Ray Silva at the hospital, she did not have the advantage of numerous cars parked in the lot to provide cover that would allow her and her team to sneak up on the truck. The vast parking lot was almost empty of cars, and completely devoid of large trees, out buildings, or anything else she could use for cover. Scattered around the parking lot were several areas used to corral shopping carts, and a half-dozen covered wooden trash can bins.

Unlike their comrades who had remained with the truck at the hospital, the terrorists in the truck at Wal-Mart were diligently watching in all directions for the possible arrival of local law enforcement or military. When they heard firing coming from inside the store, they reflexively diverted their attention momentarily to the sound of the shots.

It was the moment Red Wolff had been waiting for. The terrorist stood erect in the back of the truck, peering into the store, fully a head taller than the closest women he held hostage around him. He never saw the barrel of the AR-15 rifle that appeared from inside the covered trash bin in the parking lot.

Red Wolff had always been a crack shot with a rifle. She'd learned to shoot from her father who took her to the indoor ranges on the military bases where he was stationed. By the time she was ten, she'd won numerous shooting competitions with a .22 rifle. Her skills improved as a cadet at the Air Force Academy and continued onto the Highway Patrol where she annually qualified expert.

The shot was less than seventy-five yards. Taking aim at the side of the terrorists head, she gently pulled the trigger. The bullet actually went in the terrorist's right ear canal, where, when it hit solid tissue, it split into five jagged fragments that cut their own separate paths into his brain. He slumped forward, his head and torso hanging over the truck's wooden side rail, his legs and feet still in the bed of the truck. As soon as she was sure of a clean kill, she keyed her radio mike and said, "Go."

Now that the terrorist with the greatest field of vision had been eliminated, the most dangerous part of her plan was set into motion. With no cover anywhere around the truck, she needed a diversion to focus the driver's attention long enough for someone to creep up on the cab of the vehicle.

The sound of a siren began to pierce the cool, and now increasingly wet, early evening air. A second later, from behind the far end of the store, came a Highway Patrol car, red and blue rotating lights flashing as the siren continued to wail. The patrol car, over a hundred yards away, crossed directly in front of the truck, sped across the empty parking lot, and out onto Washington Boulevard. As quickly as it had appeared, the patrol car was gone.

It happened so fast that all the driver of the truck could do was watch. It was long enough, however, for Doug Newsome to emerge from the bushes at the opposite end of the building and make his way toward the back of the truck.

As the agent approached the truck from the rear, he tried to keep himself in the blind spot so the truck's rearview mirrors would not pick him up. He was almost to the back end of the truck, when a bright light illuminated him from behind.

Nobody had seen or heard the news van as it pulled into the parking lot. Still concealed inside the wooden trash bin, Red Wolff looked to her left and there, standing less than thirty yards from the back of the truck and the fully exposed FBI Agent, were Patricia Dodge and her cameraman.

The reporter had her back to the truck as she calmly spoke into her handheld remote microphone, the camera's built in floodlight brightly illuminating her face, the truck, and the FBI Agent in the background.

The terrorist driver of the truck was one of Emil Lagare's original drivers trained in the Syrian Desert, not one of the American

Muslims from Oakland. He was a skilled shot with a pistol and committed to his mission. In one fluid motion, he flung open the driver's side door, swung himself out onto the frame rail, and fired three rounds from his Beretta pistol at the man approaching the truck from the rear.

After firing the shots, the driver didn't wait to see the results. He knew he'd hit the unknown man at least twice. He swung himself back behind the wheel of the truck, slammed it into gear, and smashed down on the accelerator.

"As you can hear, there are gunshots behind me," Patricia Dodge said as she looked into the camera, oblivious to the FBI Agent who had just been shot and who was now lying on the ground behind her. Turning slightly toward the truck in the background, but still in the cameraman's picture, she continued. "I believe the terrorists are now attacking this Wal-Mart store, yes, you can see their truck now as it is driving away."

Let's see Geraldo top this, she said arrogantly to herself.

The truck lurched forward and slowly began to pick up speed. Several of the women hostages in the cargo bed, now unguarded, were in the process of climbing over the side rails to escape. The motion of the truck caused one of the women to lose her grip and fall to the pavement directly in front of the dual back wheels of the heavy vehicle. She was crushed to death as the tires rolled over her body. Two other women jumped to the ground, cut and scraped from sliding on the asphalt, but otherwise okay.

Emerging from the wooden trash bin, Red Wolff took a bead on the driver of the truck with her rifle, but could not get a clear shot because of the hostage he held next to him.

"Crap," Red Wolff yelled, as the truck gathered speed, realizing there was nothing she could do to prevent the truck from escaping with nine hostages still onboard.

An instant later her eye picked up the black and white blur of the Highway Patrol car. The vehicle roared by her at about forty miles an hour, at a right angle to the truck. It was her officer who had been the diversion to distract the driver of the truck. The officer slammed the front of the patrol car into the right front wheel of the truck.

The force of the impact activated the patrol car's front air bags. Between the restraint of the shoulder harness seat belt he wore and the cushioning of the air bags, the officer was more shook up than injured by the collision.

The impact shredded the truck's right front tire and bent the steering rods. The truck ground to a halt, fifty yards from the entrance.

The driver again opened the door and stepped out onto the frame rail, this time with one arm around the neck of the woman hostage, a pistol in his other hand. From his position on the truck, the terrorist could see Red Wolff standing exposed in the middle of the parking lot, the FBI Agent he had shot lying on the ground behind the truck, and in the distance, what looked to be a television news crew filming him.

The terrorist began yelling at the people in the parking lot in Arabic and gesturing wildly with his pistol. Three seconds later a shot rang out and his pistol flew into the air. The terrorist, his arm still wrapped tightly around the hostage's neck, fell lifeless to the ground.

Red Wolff was not the only expert rifle shot that day. Ralph Silva stepped out of the entrance to the Wal-Mart store, ready to fire another round at the terrorist, if needed.

CHAPTER FIFTEEN

From the time the terrorists left the community center to the time they were all dead, was less than eighteen minutes.

Red Wolff and her small band of officers and National Guard troops, had killed ten terrorists, but it had been costly. FBI Agent Doug Newsome had taken two 9 millimeter rounds, one in the left shoulder, another grazing his neck. He was going to be alright, but he was out of this fight. Tragically, one of the woman hostages had been killed also.

Ray Silva, one of the local cops, and two National Guard troops got to Wal-Mart just after the last shot was fired.

He watched as Red Wolff quickly checked on the FBI Agent, the women hostages, and the rest of her team.

"Everything is Code Four at the hospital Red, no injuries to the good guys, what can I do to help?" he asked.

"I think we're pretty much under control too, Ray. Your nephew did great, so did everyone else. We lost a hostage, and the "Feebie" took a round in the arm. Neither of those things had to happen, it was that dammed ditzy-ass reporter who showed up and started filming," she told him.

As soon as she was sure the situation at Wal-Mart was Code Four and Agent Doug Newsome was enroute to the hospital, Red Wolff headed for the reporter. The cameraman saw her coming, and by the look on her face and way she was walking, he thought there was going to be trouble. He started filming immediately, the bright light on the camera illuminating a large area around her.

Ray Silva saw her start toward the reporter too. He knew what was coming. Quickening his pace, Ray Silva got to the cameraman about three steps before Red Wolff got to the reporter. Ray Silva made eye contact with the cameraman and shook his head, no. The cameraman turned off the bright floodlight and stopped filming.

There had been many times in her career when Red Wolff had been so angry at the callous actions of someone, especially someone whose senseless act injured another person, that she felt like cracking them over the head with her baton. There were even times when just shooting them seemed like a good option just to rid the world of someone the world would be better off without. During those times, her self-control, discipline, and training had always kept her anger in check. This was not one of those times.

When she was about four feet from the reporter, Red Wolff started bringing her clenched right fist behind her. She timed it out perfectly so her forward momentum, the speed she was walking, and the force of her swing when she uncocked her right arm, all added power to her punch.

Patricia Dodge saw it coming, but was powerless to move. Red Wolff's punch hit her squarely on her left jaw, snapping her head to the right, lifting her slightly off the ground, and depositing her on her butt.

Standing over the stunned reporter, Red Wolff yelled down at her, "You dumb stupid bitch, what in the hell were you thinking by turning on that camera light and doing a report right in the middle of our operation? Your little stunt got a woman killed and one of my troops wounded. If you ever do another thing that endangers one of my men or a civilian, I will kill you deader than shit!"

Red Wolff then turned sharply on her heels and told her troops to head back to the command post.

Patricia Dodge, still on the ground, watched her go, then indignantly said to her cameraman and the driver technician, "I'll sue her, I'll have her badge, I'll have her thrown in jail for assault, and for interfering with the media!"

The cameraman looked down at the reporter, shook his head and said, "Shut up, Patty."

"But you saw it, she hit me, and then she threatened to kill me."

"Looked to me like you slipped and fell," the cameraman answered.

Then the driver technician chimed in, "Oh, by the way, I told you we would damage the antenna if we didn't secure it before we left our last location, well we did. We can't transmit anymore, so none of the stuff you just did with the terrorists and the truck went anywhere."

Both men turned and walked back toward their van, leaving the reporter on the ground.

Patricia Dodge was fuming, first she gets cold cocked by that psycho female Highway Patrol sergeant, and then, her incompetent crew lets her down. I can't wait to get out of the boondocks and work for a real station, she thought to herself.

Red Wolff jumped into the passenger's side of Ray Silva's patrol car and they headed back toward the command post.

She sensed his quietness as they drove.

"Don't even ask, Silva, I learned a long time ago that sometimes Lady Justice needs a little nudge to do her job. A guy I used to work with called it Career Decision Number Two. That reporter got a hostage killed, the FBI agent wounded, and put all of us at risk by what she did. The little tap on the jaw I gave her was all the justice she'll get."

"No harm, no foul," he replied.

It was a few minutes before seven as they drove into the main part of town. The fog had come in thick and wet. Although it was at least an hour until the sun went down, in downtown Crescent City it was cold, damp, and dreary.

"95-S-3, Humboldt," the comm-op called.

"Humboldt, go ahead for S-3," Red Wolff answered using the hardwired microphone from the radio in Ray Silva's patrol car.

"S-3, status check?" the comm-op asked.

Over the next minute, Red Wolff relayed to her only link to the outside world, the events of the past two hours. She then asked the status of the Marines who were enroute to Crescent City.

The radio was silent for an uncomfortably long time.

The comm-op chose her words carefully. She'd been on-duty since six that morning. Her shift would have normally been over at two in the afternoon. And although her relief was at the communications center, along with a half-dozen other people from various state and local law enforcement agencies, she refused to relinquish the radio console. What was happening in Crescent City started on her watch, and Red Wolff and the other officers confronting the terrorists were "her troops." She would stay with them until the end.

"S-3, there's been a change in plans. The entire coast is socked in with fog from just north of San Francisco to Coos Bay, Oregon. There is zero visibility extending inland for twenty miles in some places. The Marine helicopters had to take the inland route through Redding. It was the only place they had visibility and could refuel. They're in the air again, headed for Grant's Pass. They'll stop there for the night, and attempt to get into Crescent City as soon as the fog clears in the morning." The comm-op's voice was businesslike and deliberate.

Red Wolff sat in silence for a moment, then asked, "What about trucking them in from Grant's Pass?"

"The Oregon State Police reports Highway 199 is like a parking lot from the intersection of 101, almost the entire eighty miles to Grant's Pass. Numerous accidents and abandoned cars blocking both the north and southbound lanes. No chance of them coming by truck," the comm-op replied.

"Humboldt, S-3 copies," Red Wolff said, with a finality in her voice the comm-op understood to mean their radio interchange was over.

"So, it looks like we're doing a solo, Red," Ray Silva said to her.

"Yeah, but the odds are a little better now, there's only ten or eleven of them left and sixteen of us."

"Only they still have a bunch of hostages and four machine guns. If they come out with the hostages and their automatic weapons, we'll get our clock cleaned, the hostages will get killed, and the terrorists will be able to run wild all over town until the Marines get here," Ray Silva told her.

"Ray, what's better than a company of Marines?" she asked.

"Half a company of soldiers," he dead panned, the age old who's the best, the Army or the Marine Corps rivalry in his voice.

Even in the face of everything that had happened in the past nine hours, she had to laugh.

"I was thinking we need a couple hundred volunteers," she said as the patrol car pulled into the command post. "Come on, I've got an idea." There was a half-smile on her face.

Inside the community center, Emil Lagare was starting to worry. Even though the hospital and Wal-Mart were over three miles away, he'd still been able to hear the sound of shots being fired from that direction. He assumed they were from his men. He imagined his two teams of men had been able to wreak havoc at these locations and had expected them back already.

It was now almost 7:30, and they weren't back yet. He tried several times to call them on their individual radios, but had gotten no response. He now called his two men at the radio station to see if they had heard from either of the teams. They reported no contact from either team, and their calls had likewise gone unanswered. They also reported that, except for the occasional sighting of a local police officer, there was nothing unusual going on in town. They continued their non-stop exaltations of Allah and Islam over the air to the local population. They were somewhat surprised that nobody had as yet taken up their offer to embrace Allah by coming to the park to convert to Islam.

Emil Lagare, now almost certain that neither of his teams would be returning, took a quick check of his situation. Besides the two men at the radio station, he had eight men, plus himself in the community center. Weapons wise, he still had the four machine guns and more than enough M-16 rifles. He also had fifteen women hostages, including the Governor of California.

The thick blanket of fog that had descended on the town was something he had not expected. The fog blotted out the ample sunlight that had filled the community center all day, making the inside of the large hall dark. He instructed his men to maintain the state of darkness to preserve their night vision, and to make it harder for anyone on the outside to observe activities inside the building.

He was concerned that the failure of his two teams to return meant there must be more in the way of local law enforcement resistance in Crescent City than he was led to believe, or there was a military presence in town he was not aware of. No matter, he thought to himself, he still had the upper hand because of the hostages he held. What he needed to do now was take advantage of the American media to broadcast to the world the striking power of Islam. He had the makings of a plan in his mind.

———

Red Wolff finished discussing her plan with Ray Silva and three other Highway Patrol officers. They'd already gathered the equipment they would need from a quick trip back to Wal-Mart. Ralph Silva pleaded to go along, but Red Wolff told him he was needed to coordinate security around the perimeter of the community center to cover their backs in case the terrorists came out unexpectedly.

He acknowledged Red Wolff's orders, but couldn't help making one more attempt to go along with a shot at his uncle. "You're a pretty old man to be climbing around like that Uncle Ray, want me to take your place?" he jabbed at Ray Silva.

That drew a collective "oooh" from the other three highway cops who laughed and turned to see Ray Silva's response.

"How'd you like to write home and tell your mama that an old man kicked your ass?" he said with a half-funny, half-menacing tone in his voice.

Everyone had a good laugh, Ralph Silva took off to check the perimeter, and Red Wolff's people grabbed their gear.

The local radio station was three city blocks from the command post. The entrance was on Front Street facing the park. Capturing it had given the terrorists not only the ability to broadcast their propaganda to the local residents, but also an observation post to report on the movements of the town's law enforcement to Emil Lagare, a half-mile away in the community center.

In Red Wolff's mind, the terrorists holding the radio station had been, up to this point, an inconvenience. She had much more important things to do in organizing her scant resources, and trying to react to the terrorist's forays into town, than worry about the station. Now, however, she needed the ability to communicate with the people of Crescent City.

She'd been to the station numerous times to do on-air interviews, and to give safety tips on driving over holiday weekends. She knew the station's business office was downstairs and the broadcast studio was the only thing upstairs. The studio was a single room about twenty feet by twenty feet, with a sliding glass door opening onto a small balcony that hung partially over the sidewalk below. The broadcast console sat in the middle of the room, facing the glass door, which allowed the on-air personality to give constant updates of the town's ever changing weather. When she did a quick scouting of the station as part of developing her plan, she noticed the terrorists had the sliding glass door open, probably to hear anything going on outside, she surmised.

Logic told her there had to be at least two terrorists at the station, one on the radio, the other to provide protection. The trick, she knew, would be in overpowering however many terrorists there were in the station, without having to resort to using their weapons. The longer the leader of the terrorists didn't know the radio station had been recaptured, the better, Red Wolff thought to herself.

It was just about sundown, around 8:10, when everyone was in place around the station.

Red Wolff assigned two officers to handle the distraction, while a third would provide cover fire if necessary. The officers, each armed with an M-16 captured from the terrorists after their failed assault at the hospital and Wal-Mart, moved slowly and quietly from around the corner of the station, and arrived at the front entrance coming from the west. Red Wolff and Ray Silva approached from the east, carrying an aluminum ladder already extended to its full sixteen foot length. As soon she could see everyone was in position, Red Wolff keyed her mike and quietly whispered, "Go."

The two officers on the west side of the station began to loudly bang on the wooden door and yell gruff commands to each other. They made no attempt to actually enter the door, but kept up a steady stream of banging and noise.

As soon as the terrorist, whose job it was to provide security, heard the noises from downstairs, he rushed to the makeshift barricade he'd erected at the top of the stairs and took up a defensive position to repel the attack he knew would be coming from below. The other terrorist, who had been broadcasting the glories of Islam, stopped talking, grabbed his M-16 and joined his comrade.

It was all the distraction Red Wolff needed. As soon as her two officers started making noise at the front door, she and Ray Silva hoisted the ladder up against the wooden side rails of the station's upstairs balcony. With Red Wolff leading the way, they were both up the ladder in seconds and over the railing.

Kneeling behind the barricade of desks and tables at the top of the stairs, both the terrorists caught the movement on the balcony out of their peripheral vision. As they swung their weapons toward whatever threat was out there, they both saw a black cylindrical object fly into the broadcast studio through the open sliding glass door.

The "flash-bang" Red Wolff had thrown, detonated before it hit the floor. Instantaneously, there was an extremely loud explosion and a blinding light. Designed for use in hostage or barricaded suspect situations in confined spaces, the "flash-bang" worked as advertised.

The roar from the explosion was deafening. The blast immediately disturbed the fluid in the semi-circle ear canals of the two terrorists. The sensation they felt was as if they had been rapidly spinning in one direction and suddenly stopped, but the room they were in continued to spin. At the same time, the blinding light from the explosion, caused by the manganese powder in the device, activated all of the photosensitive cells in the retinas of their eyes. It was as if their eyes were on "freeze-frame" seeing the same thing until their retinas returned to normal.

Red Wolff knew the twin effects of the noise and the light would incapacitate both the terrorists for at least five seconds. It was more than enough time for her and Ray Silva to charge into the room from the balcony, while the other two officers vaulted up the stairs.

Neither terrorist could offer any resistance. They were both roughly forced to the ground on their stomachs and handcuffed before they fully recovered from the blast.

"Good job guys," Red Wolff told everyone.

"Yeah, but now what do we do with them? There's no jail anymore, and we don't have the people to spare to guard them," one of her officers said.

"You two take them to the hospital and drop them off with Jodie and the soldier that Ray left there to guard the place. Tell her to handcuff 'em to a bed, and hurry back here," she told the two officers.

Turning to Ray Silva, she said, "Ray, find your nephew and see if any of the National Guard troopers know how to operate this radio."

Within ten minutes, Ray Silva returned with a trooper who was about thirty-five years old. "Sergeant, I'm a communications specialist," he told her. "Give me a couple of minutes and I think I can figure this system out." True to his word, the soldier figured out the radio console in short order and was ready to broadcast.

"Good, now here's what I want you to say. Keep broadcasting it for the next hour," she told him.

Assigning her last remaining officer to stay with the trooper, she and Ray Silva headed back to the command post.

Retaking the radio station had eliminated two more of the terrorists. By her count, there were maybe seven or eight left, all in the community center. The sun had set by now, and although there was fading twilight inland, Crescent City was dark, thanks to the heavy blanket of fog that had descended on the town. Street lights were coming on, casting long shadows from the trees in the park and the buildings along the street. The pungent smell of burned wood and rubber hung in the air and mixed with the salt smell from the ocean.

Back at the command post, Red Wolff wandered about fifty feet away from the two officers and one soldier who were there. She was mentally exhausted. For the past eleven hours she had been in non-stop motion. Everything that had happened today seemed to be a blur. She needed a couple of minutes to let her mind digest the day's events and clear her head.

The town and its' people had taken a real beating. There were hundreds, maybe even as many as a thousand dead, half the town burned down, limited communications with the outside world, and no help in sight until sometime tomorrow. She knew a heavy fog, like the one that had come in this night, sometimes did not clear until around midday. She also knew her little group of cops and soldiers would be no match for the terrorists when they made their next move.

Red Wolff's big concern now was for the hostages. As much as she would have liked to mount some type of rescue mission, she knew instinctively she did not have the personnel or the equipment to do so. She also knew if she did attempt a hostage rescue and failed, there would be almost nobody left to defend the people of Crescent City. Conversely, according to what she'd learned from the captured Muslim from Oakland, Abdul Abbas, the hostages were to be killed anyway. It was what people who have to make life or death decisions called "The Devil's Alternative." No matter what she did, or didn't do, someone was going to die.

Within fifteen minutes, they started to come. The first few came by ones and twos, then groups of five or six. Over the next hour, well over two hundred came, both men and women.

The citizens of Crescent City responded to the trooper Red Wolff had left at the radio station who broadcast a call to arms. They came dressed in dark clothes, heavy jackets, boots, and with gloves to protect against the cold, damp night air. They brought with them every conceivable type of gun that could be found in any American small town, high powered hunting rifles with scopes, shotguns, pistols of every caliber, and many weapons that were illegal to possess.

The people who came were a cross-section of the town. Old men, young men, married, single, Black, White, Native American, and several young Hispanic males who were in the country illegally. Some were clean shaven, while others had scruffy beards and shaggy hair. Lots of women came also. Some of the women came because they were every bit as proficient with a firearm as their men, others to provide support. Other people came without weapons, but were there to do anything they could to help. They also brought with them food, barbeques, medical supplies and ice chests.

The rallying point was the playground of the elementary school, four blocks from the beachfront park. It was a big enough area to handle the volunteers and their vehicles, but still far enough from the park that the activities there could not be seen by the terrorists at the community center. By 9:00 the school parking lot was a beehive of activity.

Red Wolff, Ray Silva and his nephew, Ralph, got to the school at about that time. With the help of two other National Guard troopers, they quickly began to organize the local volunteers into three units. Red Wolff assigned one of the soldiers to command each of the units, while she and Ray Silva walked around.

If she would have had the time to think about it, Red Wolff would have pondered the scene before her. It was a scene from a part of America that is seldom heard about on television, or read about in the newspapers. It is certainly a part of America that is unknown to most Europeans and totally unknown to Islamic radicals. What brought these people to a school parking lot on a cold foggy night was something inside each of them that only those who have lived in America can understand.

The volunteers represented everything that was right, and wrong, about America. They were Democrats and Republicans, they supported the War on Terrorism and they opposed it. Among them were many "haves" and a larger number of "have-nots." There were professional people and laborers, some highly educated, while others were high school dropouts. The differences between them were as vast and varied as America itself. There were ultra-conservatives who had bumper stickers on their cars that read "My Country - Right or Wrong," and no small number whose vehicles had stickers that supported everything from "Free Tibet" to "Legalize Marijuana."

Unlike the volunteers standing in the damp, cold night air of Crescent City that July Fourth evening, what those who have never lived the American experience have always mistakenly done, is to confuse their differences in ideology, politics, and social standing, with an unwillingness to defend their country.

Yes, they knew their country had problems, and everything wasn't perfect. But the problems were their problems and they would deal with them as best they could. For now, however, they would put their differences aside, and defend their homes and their families.

In the big scheme of American holidays, the Fourth of July is probably not even in the top five anymore, and there is only a passing connection of the calendar date to Independence Day. That somewhat apathetic appreciation of the day, however, was simply another of the differences that bound the volunteers together. Tonight the significance of the day was a rallying cry. The terrorists had chosen a bad day to pick a fight.

Ray Silva had been born and raised in Crescent City and had worked there for a large part of his adult life. As he and Red Wolff walked among the quickly swelling ranks of volunteers, he recognized people he saw on a daily basis. Many he knew by name, others by where they worked, or through social activities.

"Hey Jimmy, thanks for coming," he called to a middle-aged man standing in one of the formations.

"Mike, Jorge, don't shoot one of the good guys by accident," he joked with some friends he went to high school with.

Red recognized the manager of the Safeway store she had the run in with several hours earlier. He was bundled up in a nylon ski jacket, holding an expensive custom bolt action deer hunting rifle. She nodded at him as she walked by.

"Holy shit, where did you get that?" Ray Silva exclaimed, as he stopped dead in his tracks in front of one of the men. He recognized him as the manager of the local Napa Auto Parts store. He'd seen and dealt with the man when he needed to buy spark plugs and tune-up parts for his vehicle so many times in the last ten years he couldn't remember.

"I sent it back from Vietnam, one piece at a time," the man replied softly.

"Red, do you know what this is?" he asked Red Wolff excitedly.

She shook her head to indicate no, as she stared at the large weapon the man was holding and the two military issue metal ammo boxes by his feet.

"It's a friggin M-60 machine gun. It was the standard automatic weapon used by all the services in Vietnam. It fires a big caliber bullet that can kill the shit out of you, and it can fire a lot of them very fast!" Ray Silva told her, with excitement in his voice.

"Where were you man?" Ray asked in a way that the auto parts store manager understood he was talking about Vietnam.

"Marines, around Da Nang, '69," the man told Ray. "And you?"

Army, Central Highlands, '69 and '70." Ray Silva responded.

"How did you manage to?" Ray Silva was going to say "get it out of the country?" when the man raised his hand and cut him off.

"Don't ask," he said.

Ray Silva understood, and then asked, "Where did you get the ammo and how much do you have?"

"Mostly from gun shows, some from the internet, a little here, a little there. I've got two boxes, five hundred round belts each," he responded.

"Can you use it?" Red Wolff asked.

The almost sixty year old, semi-balding, and a little overweight man looked at her and said casually, "Is the pope Catholic?"

Ray Silva laughed. He hadn't heard that expression in years.

As they continued to look over the assembled crowd, Ray Silva told Red Wolff he had an idea about how to deploy their newly swollen ranks.

"Red, we captured eight more M-16s at the hospital and Wal-Mart, plus the two we already had. Let's put four each in two of these groups. We then put the guy with the M-60 and two of the M-16s in another. That will give us pretty balanced firepower no matter which direction the terrorists try to go from the community center."

"Okay set it up with Ralph and the other two troopers. I've got to get back to the command post. When they have all of these people organized and briefed, move them out on foot. Tell Ralph to get them deployed like we discussed," she told him.

"Right. Say Red, does this guy having a machine gun bother you?" he asked as she turned to walk away.

"What machine gun?" she replied with a half-smile on her face.

Career Decision Number One, Ray Silva thought to himself.

Red Wolff was about to get in her patrol car when she saw the television news van pull into the parking lot. The passenger's door opened and out came Patricia Dodge. She walked hurriedly up to Red Wolff, although her gait was not quite as arrogant and confident as it had been earlier in the day.

"Excuse me sergeant, do you mind if we film what's going on here? We'll stay out of the way," she added, her voice had a subdued tone.

"Sure, just don't interfere with them," Red Wolff told her. "Say, can you transmit live with your equipment?" she asked the reporter.

"Not anymore, the antenna got knocked out of calibration, so we can't link to the satellite," Patricia Dodge replied.

Patricia turned to the van and signaled it was okay to her cameraman, just as Red Wolff opened the door to her patrol car. At that instant the radio came to life.

"95-S-3, Command Post," the radio called. It was one of her officers she'd left at the beachfront park.

"Go ahead to S-3 Command Post," Red Wolff said into her mike.

"S-3, there's something starting to stir in the community center, you better get back here." There was a sense of urgency in the officer's voice.

"Be there in two minutes," Red Wolff replied.

Whistling loudly, she got Ray Silva's attention and waved for him to join her. He jogged over and jumped into the passenger's side of the vehicle.

Patricia Dodge heard the whole radio exchange. She tried to whistle to her cameraman and the technician who were by this time already filming the assembly of men and women as they were being briefed by Ralph Silva. What came out was a weak chirp. She did a half-run over to her crew, quickly said something to both of them, and they all rapidly piled back into the van.

Emil Lagare looked as his watch. It was just after 9:30. The town was dark. The thick fog swirled around the trees in the park and the yellow sodium lights along the street. The effect was kind of like a scene from an old black and white Jack the Ripper movie. Using the night vision goggles obtained by the imam over the internet, he could get an occasional glimpse of American police officers scattered here and there around the perimeter of the park. Aside from the policemen, there were no other people to be seen.

About an hour earlier, he'd heard a loud explosion coming from one of the buildings across the street from the park. He immediately tried to contact his two men at the radio station, but could not raise them. They had functioned all day as his eyes and ears to tell him of any movements by the Americans. Their constant barrage over the radio about the righteousness of Allah, the glories of Islam, and the description of the destruction that was being inflicted on Crescent City, he was sure had unnerved many of the town's residents and served to keep them from any organized resistance.

Emil Lagare cursed to himself when he realized that as meticulous as Qassim Saleh's planning had been, everyone had overlooked including a simple A.M. radio. The radio would have told him if his men at the radio station were still broadcasting. He directed his men in the community center to search through the belongings of the female hostages to try and locate a radio. They found i-Pods, digital cameras, cell phones, and a variety of other electronic equipment, but no radio.

Trying one last time, Emil Lagare attempted to contact the radio station. Again getting no response, he came to the conclusion his men were lost. He also realized, whoever was in charge of the American resistance, was slowly tightening the circle around him.

For the past hour, Emil Lagare had been considering his options. He'd been told by Qassim Saleh an American military response could be expected about eight hours after their initial attack. It would take them at least that long to assemble their assets, mobilize, then travel the long distance to Crescent City. It was now going on twelve hours, and so far, he had seen no indicators the American military had arrived in town. The roadblocks his men created north and south of town, blocking the airport runway, and the thick, wet fog that had descended on the town all had something to do with that, he suspected.

He was also told that every hour he and his men could hold the community center and American hostages, increased the credibility of their cause around the world. It was imperative, therefore, that the world see first hand what was being done on American soil by a small group of men determined to die for Allah.

Qassim Saleh had devised three possible scenarios for Emil Lagare and his men to follow in order to accomplish this goal. All of them, Emil Lagare knew, ended the same way.

In actuality, Qassim Saleh devised only one of the possible endings. The other two had already been used, with deadly results, by Islamic terrorists, numerous times.

In the scenario devised by Qassim Saleh, when the American military arrived, he and his men would use the hostage trucks. They would charge into town, killing as many Americans as they could. Unfortunately, his only two trucks had failed to return from their missions to destroy the local hospital and the Wal-Mart store. This option Emil Lagare, knew, was now not feasible.

The second possible ending would be to remain barricaded in the community center until the military made an assault on the building. When that occurred he and his men would execute the hostages and engage in a pitched battle with the American forces. Qassim Saleh told Emil Lagare before the Americans attempted an assault of this nature they would first try to negotiate the surrender of he and his men. The negotiation process could take hours, even days, time in which media from around the world would descend on the town and broadcast the situation endlessly over every possible channel. People all over the world would be glued to their televisions, the world economy would grind to a halt as millions watched, the American stock market would tumble in a wave of wild selling, and everyone who watched would tremble. This option would accomplish the goal of showing the striking power of Islam and instill fear in people all over the world. This was looking to Emil Lagare increasingly more and more like the final outcome.

The last option involved using the American media to broadcast live pictures showing Emil Lagare and his men holding American hostages while having them plead for their lives, begging the American government to accede to any demands their captors made. Qassim Saleh told Emil that if the opportunity arose, he should demand the release of all Islamic freedom fighters held by American forces at Guantanamo Bay, Cuba, in exchange for the lives of the hostages. This process, he knew, would also take hours, with the same media coverage taking place. He also told him it was highly unlikely the American government would agree to this demand and he should then execute all of the hostages on live television.

How he proceeded, Qassim Saleh advised Emil Lagare, was his decision, based on the situation he faced, the length of time he believed he could prolong the incident, the number of men he had, and the amount of media coverage he was receiving. It would become, Qassim Saleh said, a giant high stakes chess game.

When she arrived back at the command post, Red Wolff popped the trunk on her patrol car and grabbed her own set of night vision goggles. They were military surplus, obtained in the late nineties, equipment police agencies across the nation got at the end of the "Cold War" from the military when it began to downsize. Part of the Clinton Administrations "peace dividend." They were old, but they worked fine.

Focusing on the glass doors of the community center, she could see the outline of a man standing off to the side, a rifle cradled in his arms. The rest of the building was blacked out.

"What did you see?" she asked the officer who'd called her back to the command post.

"All the lights came on inside about twenty minutes ago. The whole place was lit up. I could see a bunch of the terrorists walking around, rummaging through boxes and backpacks, like they were looking for something. Then everything went dark again," the officer told her.

Red Wolff exhaled deeply. Whatever it was they were doing, she thought, it looked like they were finished. She started to walk away.

"Red, the lights are coming on again, the whole place is lit up," the officer said hurriedly.

Red Wolff discarded the night vision goggles in favor of regular binoculars. She could clearly see into the front of the community center. Standing just inside the glass doors, off to one side, she could see the terrorist who had only been an outline moments before. He was wearing a gas mask.

"What the?" she said to her herself.

She watched as he turned and momentarily disappeared from sight. When he came back into view, he held a woman by the arm on each side of him. Red Wolff worked the focus wheel on the binoculars until the women became crystal clear.

"Crap," she mumbled. With his left hand, clamped firmly on her upper arm, the terrorist held a young woman of about twenty. She was crying, her hair disheveled, and the look of fear on her face. With his right hand he held the Governor of California.

Quickly, Red Wolff turned to Ray Silva and told him to get on the radio and tell everyone to hold their fire. She then went back to watching the drama unfolding three hundred yards away. Dozens of thoughts ran through Red Wolff's mind. Was showing the Governor a warning to back off? Were they going to execute her right in front of them? Where were the rest of the hostages? What did the gas mask mean?

The terrorist continued to hold both women roughly by their upper arms. Red Wolff could see the women as they struggled against the terrorist's grip. He held them firmly in place in front of the glass door in plain view. It was almost like the terrorist was daring someone to shoot at him.

A second later, another terrorist appeared, grabbed the Governor by her free arm and drug her out of sight. The terrorist in the gas mask now pulled open one of the glass front doors and roughly pushed the other woman out the door. The woman fell to the ground, tried to get to her feet, slipped, then rose completely. Unsteady on her feet, the woman began to half-run, half-stagger away from the building.

Red Wolff was on the radio immediately. "Hostage coming out, everyone hold your fire, everyone hold your fire!" Her voice on the radio was loud and assertive. Running back to her patrol car, she reached into the vehicle and flicked the emergency light switch which caused the roof mounted, rotating red and blue lights to activate. The darkness was filled with bright rotating lights as they bounced off the buildings on either side and cast long red and blue shadows into the night.

Red Wolff also grabbed the hard wired microphone attached to the radio console. Using the button on the microphone, she keyed the public address system speaker. "Come toward the red and blue lights," she spoke slowly and clearly into the microphone. "Walk toward the red and blue lights. Keep your hands over your head!" she repeated. While she had no doubt that this was a hostage, safety demanded she and all her men treat the woman as a suspect until they were sure.

While she was watching and talking to the woman who was approaching her patrol car, Red Wolff saw the lights in the community center go out. The entire building was dark again.

The woman staggered out of the park and toward the patrol car, her hands half over her head, and half being used to keep her balance. Red Wolff could see two of her men were in a defensive position with their hand guns drawn, pointed at the approaching woman. When she got within fifteen feet of the patrol car, Red Wolff told her to stop. Ray Silva was on her in a flash. The woman was hysterical and sobbing uncontrollably. She didn't even notice Ray Silva patting her down for weapons.

Red Wolff was not naturally the most comforting person in the world. Crying, hysterical women didn't rate real high on her list. Yet over the course of her career, she'd found herself on countless occasions hugging people in exactly that condition. Putting down the microphone, she gathered the young woman in her arms and stroked her matted and dirty hair.

Unnoticed by Red Wolff because she was focused on the just released hostage, Patricia Dodge and her crew, positioned about fifty feet behind the patrol car, had filmed the entire incident.

It took about ten minutes before the woman was calm enough to talk. Wrapped in several blankets and seated in the back of the patrol car, the woman sobbed intermittently as she tried to answer Red Wolff's questions.

It was a torturously slow process. There was so much Red Wolff needed to know from the woman. How many terrorists were in the building, where were they located, what weapons did they have, where were the other hostages, why were they wearing gas masks, why did they let her go? Red Wolff used the same techniques she'd learned years before as a road patrol officer dealing with drivers involved in accidents, victims of crimes, and witnesses. All of her questions to the woman were asked slowly and calmly. When she had a general idea of the situation in the community center, she went back and asked the same questions again trying to elicit more specific information. It took about twenty minutes, but by the time she was finished, she had a good grasp of what was happening in the community center, and what the terrorists wanted.

Emboldened by being able to film the release of the hostage, Patricia Dodge had inched closer and closer to the patrol car where Red Wolff was questioning the woman. By the time Red was finished, Patricia Dodge and her cameraman were within a few feet of the car. As soon as Red Wolff opened the door to get out, the reporter started her own barrage of questions and tried to shove a microphone into the back seat of the patrol car.

"What did the terrorists want?" "Did they harm you?" "Is the Governor still alive?" "What do you think of the President's War on Terror?"

The woman, startled by the sudden appearance of the reporter, began to sob again.

Red Wolff angrily slammed the door to the patrol car and abruptly ended Patricia Dodge's attempt at an interview. She then got face-to-face with the reporter and told her to get back to her news van or she would be arrested for interfering with an active police investigation.

Patricia Dodge didn't know if Red Wolff had the actual power to arrest her, but she did know the Highway Patrol sergeant was violent. She and her cameraman retreated to their van.

Once she made arrangements for the woman to be cared for, Red Wolff got on the radio.

"Humboldt, 95-S-3," Red Wolff said.

"S-3, go ahead to Humboldt." It was the voice of the same comm-op that had been with her all day.

"Humboldt do you have contact with the "Feds?" Red asked.

"There are two FBI agents in the comm center with me, listening, S-3," came the reply.

"10-4, I need some information," Red Wolff told her.

Over the radio Red Wolff described the actions of the terrorists in the community center, the release of the hostage, and the appearance of the terrorist wearing a gas mask.

"Can you get me some information on similar terrorist hostage incidents?"

In the communication center, eighty miles away, the comm-op looked at the two FBI agents, who looked at each other. One of the agents nodded yes, but indicated it would take a while to contact Washington to get the information.

"S-3, affirmative on the information, it may take awhile," she told Red Wolff.

The radio exchange ended as Red Wolff began to consider her next move. The information on previous terrorist incidents would be important to know.

Emil Lagare was not the only chess player in Crescent City that night.

CHAPTER SIXTEEN

Ralph Silva moved the volunteers from the school toward the park on foot. In the great American tradition of having a name for everything, the volunteers began calling themselves the "Crescent City Militia." They moved more like a giant snake than an organized unit, but eventually arrived one block from the main street in front of the park.

Although they weren't happy about it, Ralph Silva halted the militia out of sight of the community center. It was 10:00 at night, and they and their town, had been getting their asses kicked for twelve hours by the terrorists. They wanted to get some pay back. Ralph Silva and the other two National Guard troopers had their hands full keeping the three, sixty person units, all of them carrying guns, contained and under control.

The Highway Patrol sergeant had a plan, he told the militia. For now, the plan was for them to stay out of sight. Ralph Silva hoped Red Wolff did indeed have a plan.

At the communication center in Eureka, one of the FBI agents was on his cell phone to Washington. Sitting at the radio console, the comm-op could tell from the parts of his conversation she could overhear he was getting nowhere in trying to get information on Islamic terrorist hostage incidents.

Calling one of her co-workers, the comm-op relinquished the radio to another person. She had to force herself to her feet. Except for a couple of bathroom breaks, she'd been sitting at the console for sixteen hours. Her legs rebelled against the strain of standing and she had to use her hand to steady herself on the console, before heading off to the supervisor's office.

The Humboldt Communications Center only had one supervisor and that person was on vacation for two weeks. The office was dark when the comm-op unlocked the door, turned on the light, and fired up the computer. Once she was on-line, she brought up the Google search engine, and typed in the words Islamic terrorist hostage. The high speed connection responded in an instant with seventeen pages that matched her criteria. She began by clicking on the first story on the first page. It took her about ten minutes to get the information she was looking for.

What she found amazed her. Like most Americans, she had no idea of the number of terrorist hostage incidents perpetrated by Islamic militants around the world. Most of what she found involved Islamic Chechen rebels who had been fighting for independence from Russia since the break-up of the Soviet Union. She found incident after incident involving the taking of innocent hostages, political assassinations, retaliation killings, suicide bombings, and hijackings.

She was back in the radio console chair within a minute. The FBI agent was still on his cell phone.

"95-S-3, Humboldt," she called.

"S-3, go ahead," Red Wolff answered.

The comm-op spent the next minute briefly telling Red Wolff what she had found. Two incidents in particular had eerie similarities to the situation in Crescent City. In 2004, in the southern Russian town of Beslan, nineteen Islamic Chechen terrorists had taken over a school holding hundreds of children hostage. The incident had drug on for two days as Russian authorities tried to negotiate with the terrorists. When negotiations failed, Russian Special Forces, the Spetsnaz, stormed the school. All of the terrorists were killed, along with over two hundred fifty school children. In another incident, thirty-three terrorists from the same group invaded a Moscow theater during a live performance, taking over eight hundred people hostage. That incident went on for over two days and ended when the Russians pumped an anesthetic gas into the theater's air conditioning system. The tactic worked to partially incapacitate some of the terrorists. Unfortunately, it also killed one hundred twenty of the hostages.

"That would explain the gas masks," Red Wolff said to the comm-op.

"Anything else S-3?" she asked.

"Keep me updated on the Marines, and if the Feds have any bright ideas, let me know," she answered.

It's all starting to make sense, Red Wolff thought to herself. The terrorists were working on a timetable. They had allotted themselves a certain number of hours to take over the town, kill as many people as they could, and destroy as much property as possible, before they thought the American military would arrive. Prior to the anticipated arrival time of the military, they would barricade themselves in the community center with their hostages and see how long they could drag the situation out, all the while attracting worldwide media coverage. That, Red Wolff thought to herself, explained why they'd made only two assaults into town, then retreated back to the community center each time. Their goal was a prolonged hostage situation, not the total destruction of the town and its' people.

They had done such a good job in cutting off all of the town's communications, however, it had taken longer than Qassim Saleh anticipated in getting word of the attack to the outside world. This had, in turn, delayed any organized response to Crescent City. They had also not foreseen their roadblocks would cause such massive traffic back-ups that when assistance was mobilized, it could not use the highways to enter the town. Then, added to all this, the totally unexpected heavy fog, which made assistance coming from the air an impossibility. All of these factors had combined to throw off Qassim Saleh's carefully plotted timetable for the arrival of the American military and the all important American media.

Combining what she'd learned from the woman hostage about the situation inside the community center, the demands from the terrorist leader, together with what she knew of the terrorists' plans from Abdul Abbas, and the historic information from the comm-op, Red Wolff could see what was going to happen and what she needed to do.

It would be dangerous and she would probably end up getting killed, she told herself. She didn't hesitate.

Ray Silva had just returned from taking the woman hostage to the hospital. When he got out of his car he approached Red Wolff.

"Red, the woman told me Julie and Mary Jean are okay. The terrorists have them, the other women, and the Governor, in the small room on the east side of the community center. They're being guarded by two terrorists. The leader guy pops in to check on the guards and the hostages every once in a while. She also said she told you they want a television crew to come into the building to do a live report and if they don't get one they'll start killing hostages."

"Yeah, that's what she told me too. And here's what I found out from Humboldt," as she began to explain what the comm-op had told her about other Islamic terrorist hostage incidents.

"None of those endings sound real good to me," Ray replied after she finished.

"Me either. Go get Ralph, and a couple of our guys, I've got an idea," she told him.

It took her about five minutes to explain the plan to the four men. Ralph Silva and the other two Highway Patrol officers took off immediately when Red Wolff was finished. They had prep work to do.

Looking at the man who had been her training officer, her mentor, and closest friend for many years, Red Wolff said, "Ready?"

"Well, it's too late to call in sick and we don't have much choice," Ray Silva said looking back at the person he considered the best partner he'd ever worked with. He noticed she didn't have the half-smile on her face.

They both turned and walked toward the nearby news van.

Inside the community center, Emil Lagare saw the lights begin to flash on all the police cars spread around the perimeter of the park. Red and blue lights revolved, sirens blared, and the headlights on the vehicles were flashing. This display lasted for one minute, then all of the lights were extinguished. It was exactly the signal he had told the woman hostage he'd released to tell the American authorities to give, if they agreed to his demands.

Standing just to the side of the glass doors of the blacked out building, Emil Lagare put all of his men on heightened alert and stared into the night.

The news van came slowly from the east, turned up the street leading to the community center, and stopped about seventy-five yards in front of the entrance to the building. The passenger side door opened and Emil Lagare could see the woman he assumed was the reporter step out of the vehicle. The television stations in the Middle East used an abundance of women as reporters, and although the imams denounced the practice of women being on-air personalities, the practice was tolerated, especially by those stations sympathetic to The Cause.

The woman walked slowly to the front of the news van and stopped, illuminated by the vehicle's headlights. After a few seconds, she began to walk toward the community center entrance with her hands held away from her body.

Emil Lagare watched the woman as she approached. She had long hair, a little over five and a half feet tall and was dressed in a dark colored pants suit. When the woman was about ten yards from the entrance, the lights inside the building came on. Emil Lagare stepped from the shadows of one of the glass doors, pushed it open and told the woman to stop.

"You are a television reporter?" he asked the woman, his English a little rusty. The woman responded that she was.

"And you can broadcast from your truck to other stations?" The woman reporter acknowledged she could.

"And in the van, how many other people?" he asked, his hand pointing to the van still stopped many yards away.

"My cameraman, and one technician to operate the broadcast equipment," the reporter told him.

"By the grace of Allah, I will allow you to interview your Governor, and to see the other women my men and I have as hostages. You will then broadcast my demands on the American government. If you do or say anything other than what I permit, it will result in the death of hostages," Emil Lagare told her.

The reporter nodded she understood, and told him she needed to signal her cameraman and the van to come closer to the entrance.

"Wait, how do I know there are not American soldiers hiding in the van waiting to attack us?" Emil Lagare asked.

"The camera we are using can transmit to the van even when it's five hundred yards away. I will have it back up to the street where it will not be a threat to you," the reporter responded.

"Yes, have the van pull away. Only you and your cameraman will be allowed in the building," Emil Lagare said. Another chess move made to his benefit, he believed. He didn't notice the female reporter had given an almost imperceptible sigh of relief.

The reporter and Emil Lagare stood by the entrance to the community center and watched as the side door of the van opened and the cameraman emerged with his large camera. As the man approached, Emil Lagare could see the camera was the large commercial type he had seen news crews use in his own country. It was designed to be held on the shoulder for filming, with a large light mounted on top, and a small antenna. As soon as the cameraman began to approach the entrance, the reporter motioned for the van's driver to back away. Within seconds the van had backed onto the main street and disappeared in the fog.

"As soon as you enter, my men will search you for weapons," Emil Lagare said. It was a statement, not a request.

Emil Lagare stepped out of the open door and motioned for the reporter and her cameraman to enter. As soon as they did, one of the terrorists roughly grabbed the female reporter and started rubbing his hands across her chest and back, up and down her legs, and into her pelvic area. When he lingered too long there, the reporter slapped his hand away which caused him to start to hit her. Emil Lagare barked an order at the man in Arabic, and he ceased his motion. The terrorist now turned his attention to the cameraman where, rebuffed once by his commander, the man did only a pat down.

The door to the community center closed, and the lights went out.

Sitting in the patrol car, Patricia Dodge and her cameraman were bundled up in blankets and the blue nylon Highway Patrol cold weather coats given to them by that lunatic female sergeant and the old officer with silver hair. She was still fuming, but deep in her heart she knew she'd done the right thing. For now, all she could do was watch and wish them good luck. It didn't mean, however, when all of this was over, she wouldn't have that sergeant's badge, and for good measure, that smart-ass other officer's too.

When the female sergeant had first approached her and told her what she wanted to do, Patricia Dodge was shocked. How could she contemplate impersonating a reporter! This was the biggest story in years, and it was her's alone. Absolutely not, there was no way she was going to let this cop pretend she was a reporter.

She'd used every argument she could think of, the First Amendment, the rights of a free press, and the trust of the American people. None of those dissuaded the two cops standing in front of her. When she switched gears and tried to claim "journalistic integrity," the old male cop laughed and told her that journalistic integrity was an oxymoron. She wasn't quite sure why he thought it was an oxymoron, but by the way her cameraman had laughed, she knew it wasn't good.

It was her cameraman that finally persuaded her to go along with the Highway Patrol sergeant's plan. She could stand on her principals, her ethics, her integrity, or even the ghost of Edward R. Murrow if she wanted to, but unless they helped, people were going to die, innocent people. "Time to choose up sides Patty, it's either more important to save those people, or more important for you to get a story," he told her.

As little as she liked letting the wacko female sergeant impersonate her, she liked even less giving her the clothes she had on. In the end, Patricia Dodge and the female Highway Patrol sergeant stepped behind the news van and changed clothes. Getting half-naked in the cold wet night air was just another of the indignities she had suffered this day at the hands of this woman, Patricia Dodge fumed to herself.

Amazingly, Red Wolff and Patricia Dodge were close enough in size that the reporter's clothes fit reasonably well. Even the reporter's shoes were close, although they had a two inch heel, something Red Wolff had not walked in since the Air Force Academy. After she got into the reporter's clothes, Red Wolff unpinned her hair and shook her head. Her long hair cascaded down around her shoulders and she used her fingers to smooth it out as much as possible.

Ray Silva slipped easily into the cameraman's well worn blue jeans, long sleeve wool shirt, and running shoes. Once they finished changing, the cameraman wished the officer good luck and shook his hand.

It took the cameraman about two minutes to explain the functions of the camera and the over the shoulder external battery pack to Ray Silva. He also showed him the function button for the floodlight atop the camera. Likewise, in the spirit of, "If you can't beat 'em, join 'em," Patricia Dodge coached Red Wolff on some techniques she might need to get the terrorists to move to different positions, or to change locations.

The functions of the technician, however, were not something that could be so quickly taught to somebody else. Even though the boom mast was out of calibration and could not link with the satellite, pushing the right button at the right time to keep the terrorists' confidence was important. If, in the opening moments of the ruse, the terrorists insisted on seeing the equipment function, his expertise would be essential. He agreed to go along.

———

Once inside the community center, it took several seconds for Red Wolff and Ray Silva's eyes to adjust to the dark. Soon, they could make out the figures of five terrorists within the main room of the community center. Four of them held machine guns and the fifth an M-16. Each of the men was strategically placed to view the area around the exterior of the building. The terrorists were each alternately looking at them and then back out the window or door they were positioned next to. Red Wolff and Ray Silva could see the look of hate in their eyes and the fact they had already resigned themselves to death.

After being outside for most of the last twelve hours, Red Wolff could detect the pungent odor of sweat, the peculiar odor like wet canvas given off by the military web gear the men wore, and the smell of old food from the many ice chests and picnic baskets taken from the park earlier in the day. As their eyes continued to adapt to the darkness, Ray Silva spotted several cases of canned food and bottled water in one corner of the room. They had planned well, he thought to himself, bringing enough provisions for what they assumed would be a multi-day siege.

"There are more reporters outside?" the man Red Wolff assumed was the leader, asked.

Red Wolff knew from the information she'd gotten from Abdul Abbas, that having lots of media coverage was an important factor in the terrorist's plans. "Yes, many more, but they were all afraid to come inside the building. Another news crew just arrived in town. When they are ready to come in the building, the police cars outside will turn on their lights and sirens just as before. Also, what we film in here will be broadcast to our van. My technician will link our broadcast to the other reporters who will broadcast it to their stations." By the look on his face, Red Wolff judged he was buying the line she was feeding him.

"And it will be broadcast to other countries?" the terrorist leader asked her.

"Of course, it will all be broadcast live around the world," she said with a confidence in her voice that was more than convincing.

"The American military, where are they?" he questioned her again.

Red Wolff was ready for this question too. She didn't want the terrorists to panic and start executing hostages because they thought the military was going to make an assault immediately. She also didn't want them to know that there was no military in Crescent City yet, as they might think it was safe to make another assault into town.

"The first units of military were just arriving when I came in here," she said. Her manner and tone did not give away the fact that she was lying through her teeth. She watched the terrorist leader's eyes to gauge his reaction. The man's face was expressionless. He bought it, she said to herself.

Red Wolff knew things were happening outside and she didn't have time to keep answering the man's questions, "Can I see the Governor and the other hostages," she said to the leader.

There is a tone and manner to this woman I do not like, Emil Lagare told himself. She was less than respectful and pushy. He put the thought out of his mind, non-Islamic women were all that way.

Emil Lagare led the reporter and her cameraman to the door in the movable partition that opened into the smaller second room in the community center.

Once inside, the first sensation that greeted Red Wolff and Ray Silva was the smell. In addition to the same smell of sweat, wet canvas, and decaying food, there were two other smells. One was that of urine, as the single toilet in the small room had been overworked for the last twelve hours by the fifteen women hostages. The other smell, was more subtle, but both of the Highway Patrol officers detected it immediately, it was the smell of fear.

The door to the small toilet was open and the light was on, throwing enough illumination into the room Red Wolff could make out the shapes of women on the floor. Some were sitting up, while others were stretched out flat. One terrorist could be seen crouched near the single window in the room, an M-16 by his side, as he watched the outside through a pair of night vision goggles. Next to this man was a metal door which led to the parking lot on the east side of the community center. The other terrorist was standing across the room, an M-16 cradled in his arms, watching the women.

Red Wolff and Ray Silva saw Mary Jean Snider and Julie Bradley sitting on the floor about twenty-five feet from them. Seated to their right was the Governor of California.

In the darkness Mary Jean Snider could just make out the shapes, but not the faces, of the two news people who had entered the room. Julie Bradley, who was seated next to her, hunched over in a half-sleep, looked up at the new arrivals momentarily, then put her head back down between her knees.

The terrorist leader led the reporter and her cameraman closer to the group of women on the floor.

"You may begin your interview with the Governor now," he told Red Wolff.

"Ah, okay, but let us get some distance shots first to film the whole group," Red Wolff told him as she panned her arms around and pointed like she was giving directions to her cameraman.

When she heard Red Wolff's voice, Mary Jean Snider nudged Julie Bradley with her elbow. The move was so subtle that none of the terrorists saw. Julie Bradley was instantly out of her sleepy state and fully alert.

"Very well, but your time is limited. Do you require more lighting in the room?" he replied.

"No, our camera has a special low light, high resolution, photo-optic filter. It will automatically amplify the available light in the room," Red Wolff told the terrorist leader. She had only a basic knowledge of cameras and had no idea what she was saying, but it sounded believable.

Ray Silva, the camera hoisted upon his shoulder, now stepped to the far corner of the room and pushed the record button on the hand grip of the big camera. Through the eyepiece he could see a digital display that told him the camera was recording and transmitting a signal to the van outside. On the front of the camera, a small red light illuminated.

"Do you see that red light? It means the camera is sending a signal to our van outside." Red Wolff told the terrorist leader.

Emil Lagare nodded at the female reporter. Finally, he told himself, my mission is being broadcast to the outside world. Mentally he breathed a sigh of relief. Unknowingly, he also relaxed his vigilance.

Ray Silva stopped filming, lowered the camera from his shoulder, and spoke for the first time since entering the community center. "Okay, I got that shot. We're ready for the interview now." He then stopped, looked around, and said to the terrorist leader, "Say, would it be possible to have one of your men, or maybe even you, in the picture when we do the interview?"

Emil Lagare thought for a moment and then said something to the man standing in the back of the room. The man quickly moved next to him and waited. "This man will be in your picture," he said to the cameraman.

"Thanks, okay, now move over and stand behind the Governor," Red Wolff made a big show of positioning the terrorist behind and just off to the side of the Governor who was still sitting on the floor.

Red Wolff was making it up as she went. It was cold in the room, condensation had formed on the single window, but she was sweating so much she was afraid the terrorist leader would notice.

——— ——— ———

Ralph Silva sat in the news van next to the technician waiting for the signal. It seemed like an eternity, and he was afraid something had gone wrong inside. He and the technician stared at the blank monitor in the van looking for some indication Red Wolff and his uncle were still alive in the building. Finally, the monitor flickered to life. The technician pressed his right hand against his earphones. "That's it, they're broadcasting," he said.

Ralph was out of the van in a flash and sprinting toward the small group of cops, National Guard troopers, and militia he had pre-positioned well east of the community center. "Let's go," he told them while still on the run. The small group took off after him and soon they had disappeared into the darkness and fog.

It'll be a miracle if we pull this off, Ralph Silva thought to himself. The whole plan Red Wolff came up with sounded crazy to him and he'd told her so. Trying to free the hostages by pretending to be a reporter and cameraman was a suicide mission. When Red Wolff invited him to come up with a better plan, Ralph lowered his eyes and the debate ended.

While Red Wolff and Ray Silva were changing clothes with, and being briefed by the female reporter and her cameraman, Ralph and the other two Highway Patrol officers had moved one of the units of the Crescent City Militia stealthily into the perimeter. From one of the other units, they took the guy with his own personal M-60 machine gun and two other citizens who had former military experience. It was these six men who were now circling around to the east side of the community center.

Using cover provided by the numerous trees and parked cars on the street, they'd inched their way as close as they dared to the building. The swirling fog helped hide their movements. They could get no closer. There was almost a hundred yards of grass and an empty asphalt parking lot between them and the east side of the community center. Somebody, Ralph knew, was probably watching from the lone window on that side of the building, and they probably had night vision goggles. Ralph positioned one of militia guys, one of the Highway Patrol officers, and the guy with the M-60 among the trees where they had clear lines of fire at the door and window. Then he and the two remaining members of his small group climbed over the top of the man-made breakwater that separated the park from the ocean. Now out of sight on the ocean side of the barrier, they began to move closer to the community center.

Positioned with the help of a giant crane years before by the Army Corps of Engineers, the huge rocks and concrete blocks formed a pyramid shaped breakwater almost twenty feet high. Most of the time the waves within the crescent shaped bay were fairly tame and the breakwater kept the ocean from flooding the beachfront park. Tonight, thanks to a combination of a high tide, and what was becoming a brisk wind, the waves lapped high onto the breakwater, soaking the three men as they crept along. The darkness, the slippery algae growing on the rocks, and the waves coming from the darkness of the ocean all made the footing treacherous as they moved closer to the community center from the one direction the terrorists would not expect.

It took them about five minutes to work themselves into what Ralph judged to be the right position. He had a clear view of the back corner of the community center, the door to the parking lot, and the window. All he had to do now was wait for the signal from inside.

———

Red Wolff made eye contact with both Mary Jean Snider and Julie Bradley. She gave them an almost imperceptible nod. The

Governor looked comatose, her eyes were glazed and she looked like she was drugged. She had barely moved since they'd been in the room and there was no sign she even acknowledged the presence of a reporter or cameraman. Scanning the remaining women in the room, Red Wolff could see most were fully awake now and focused on what was happening.

Several of the women tried to ask questions about what was happening outside and when they were going to be released. Emil Lagare yelled at them to be silent, accentuating his command with a backhand slap to the face of one of the seated women.

"You will begin now!" the terrorist leader told Red Wolff in a loud and commanding tone.

Red Wolff nodded to the man.

"Wait, I need to recalibrate my white filter," Ray Silva said, pulling a white lens cap out of his pants pocket.

"What is this for?" Emil Lagare asked the cameraman impatiently.

"It resets the camera's internal computer so the colors are correct. I need to do this so I can get a close-up of the Governor, it will only take a few seconds," he told the man.

When the terrorist leader did not object, Ray Silva brought the camera up to his shoulder, held the white plastic cover in front of the lens, and made a show of pushing the many control buttons on the hand grip. The lens whirled as it tracked from wide-angle to close-up. In reality Ray Silva had no idea what he was doing, but it looked good to the three terrorists in the room who were now intently watching him.

"One more test," he told them as he pointed the camera on his shoulder toward the window and flicked the switch which activated the floodlight mounted on top of the camera. Just as quick he turned it back off.

"All set," he announced to the terrorist leader.

It was the signal Ralph Silva had been waiting for. As soon as he saw the bright, white light come on, then immediately go back out, he keyed the transmit button on the portable Highway Patrol radio Red Wolff had given him. "They're ready," he said. Bringing the radio up to his ear so he could be sure to hear the acknowledgement of his transmission over the sound of the ocean behind him, Ralph Silva waited. Within three seconds he heard the word "copy."

Emil Lagare was tired. It had been a long day for him also. His patience was wearing thin, and having this news crew in his building was occupying too much of his time. He angrily told the reporter to begin.

Red Wolff got down on one knee about three feet in front of the Governor, she extended the microphone in her hand after asking, "Governor, how are you being treated?"

Behind her, Ray Silva remained standing with the camera on his shoulder.

Standing off to one side, Emil Lagare could again see the red light on the camera was on, telling him this interview with his hostage, the Governor of California, was being broadcast around the world.

Behind the Governor stood one of his men, M-16 held at port arms. The world was seeing America being humbled by Islam. Allah Akbar, he said proudly to himself.

It took three tries before Red Wolff could get even a sound out of the Governor. She finally mumbled a few incoherent words, then, almost like someone turned on a switch, she was completely lucid, speaking into the microphone and looking directly up at the camera.

Before the reporter could ask her next question, Emil Lagare heard the sound of sirens from outside the building. Seconds later, one of his men from the main portion of the community center came through the door in the partition and spoke excitedly to him in Arabic.

"Why are the lights flashing and the sirens going, and a news truck approaching the building?" he asked the female reporter, an anxious tone in his voice.

"I told you, when another television crew wants to do an interview, the police will use the same signal we did," she explained.

At that instant, the same man who had reported the approach of the news van to Emil Lagare seconds before was back, again rapidly speaking in Arabic.

"Another news reporter is approaching, this time a man," Emil Lagare said to her.

The woman reporter shrugged, "Probably from some other network. Can I continue my interview?"

She has that same pushy tone in her voice that I do not like, Emil Lagare thought to himself. He nodded yes, said something in Arabic to both of his men, and turned to leave the room to deal with the new reporter outside. He closed the door in the movable partition behind him when he left.

His mind, like his body, was tired. The events of the day had taken a toll on his ability to think clearly and make good decisions. Yes, he knew it was important to have more media coverage, but with the limited number of men he had remaining, he dared not allow too many news reporters into the building.

Back in the main room of the community center, Emil Lagare looked out the glass doors and saw a man standing seventy-five yards away, illuminated by the headlights of a dark colored van. The van had large words written on the side in white letters and a graphic design on the door. From the angle the van was stopped and because of the darkness and fog, he couldn't make out what was written on the side of the van or the logo on the door. The man made no attempt to approach the building.

What Emil Lagare couldn't tell because of the darkness and weather, was the man outside wasn't a reporter at all, but one of the three remaining Del Norte County Sheriff's Deputies. He also couldn't tell that what looked to him to be a news van, was in reality, the commandeered delivery van of the local beer distributor who was one of the Crescent City Militia.

Emil Lagare waited to see what the man was going to do. If he'd been thinking clearly he would have had one of his men fire a few warning shots at the uninvited reporter outside and gotten back to where the female reporter was doing her interview.

Inside the small room, Red Wolff, still crouched on one knee, continued her interview with the Governor of California. She knew she didn't have much time. Playing the odds, she gambled that it was unlikely either of the terrorists in the room would know the Governor's first name.

Looking directly at the Governor as if she was asking a serious question, Red Wolff said, "Julie, Mary Jean, will you be ready when the light comes on to negotiate your release." The Governor got a quizzical look on her face not understanding the reporter's nonsensical question.

The terrorist standing behind the Governor spoke so-so English. It got better when he was exposed to speaking and hearing it, but it had been awhile since he'd been around English speakers, so he was only able to pick up a word here and there. He may not have understood it all Red Wolff noticed, but he was intently watching her and the Governor.

Mary Jean and Julie both picked up on the signal from Red Wolff. Neither of them had a clue of what was coming, but they were both ready to react.

"The light of freedom will be coming on soon," Red Wolff said to the Governor who had a totally confused look on her face.

Julie Bradley and Mary Jean Snider braced themselves, ready for anything.

Ray Silva shifted the camera off his shoulder slightly so that he was no longer looking through the viewfinder. He looked directly at the terrorist who was watching the Governor and said in an angry, clipped, guttural voice, the only Arabic sounding name he could think of, "Hey, Omar."

Red Wolff heard the way Ray Silva said, "Hey, Omar." He'd said it with exactly the same tone and inflection in his voice as when he said, "Hey, Asshole."

When the terrorist heard Ray Silva speak, his natural reaction was to look up at the camera. As soon as he did, Ray Silva flicked the switch activating the camera's powerful floodlight. From less than six feet away, it was like looking directly into several suns. The bright white light burned at his eyes and caused him to flinch. He turned his torso away and brought one hand up to protect his face. Ray Silva kept the light pointed straight at him.

Julie Bradley moved first. Seated just to the left of the Governor, the terrorist was almost directly behind her. She twisted and drove her clinched left fist into his balls with all of the force she could muster. The effect was not instantaneous, but within a second the man doubled up in pain and dropped the M-16. Mary Jean Snider was on him before he could cry out in agony, her hand clamped tightly over his mouth.

At the instant Ray Silva activated the camera's light, Red Wolff pivoted and started toward the terrorist who was kneeling by the window on guard duty. He was less than fifteen feet away and had been slow to react. Five steps and she would be on him, before he could pick up his rifle, or yell out to the other terrorists. If she could disable him without making a lot of noise, all they had to do was move the hostages out the side door and into the night. They would be gone before the terrorist leader returned.

Red Wolff took three quick steps before her left ankle twisted as she lost her balance because of the high heeled shoes she was not used to wearing. She stumbled, but did not go down completely. It was enough, however, to give the terrorist time to pick up his M-16 from the floor, and squeeze off a wildly aimed three round burst as he struggled to his feet in front of the window.

Before he got the chance to release the trigger and pull it again, three M-16 rounds shattered the window he was now standing completely exposed in. All three bullets ripped into his upper torso. The impact of the rounds lifted him off his feet and threw him to the shiny hardwood floor. Even though he was wet from the occasional wave that broke over the top of the breakwater where he was hiding, Ralph Silva was still a hell of a marksman.

Everything that happened next was a blur of shouts, arms and legs moving in every direction, pulling, pushing, screaming, and gunshots.

Ray Silva grabbed the M-16 dropped by the terrorist he'd momentarily blinded, who was now lying on the ground writhing in pain, and holding his crotch, as he was being pummeled by Julie Bradley. Using the butt end of the rifle, he brought it straight down and smashed the man in the side of his head. It probably didn't kill him, Ray thought to himself, but he would have a terrible headache when he woke up.

Red Wolff grabbed the other M-16, kicked open the side door, then started yelling at the women to get out. Both she and Ray Silva then focused their attention on the yelling coming from the main room of the community center. They would be coming through the door any second now, she thought to herself, and we'll be on the wrong end of a lop-sided firefight.

Without thinking, she yelled for Ray Silva to grab the Governor, then fired two, three round bursts in the direction of the door in the movable partition. That will keep their heads down, she thought.

Ray Silva grabbed the Governor by the arm and yanked her to her feet in one motion, while at the same time pulling her toward the open door. Red Wolff fired three more rounds. She knew the M-16 bullets would easily tear through the cloth and wood partition and still be powerful enough to kill anyone on the other side.

Ralph Silva and the other two men who'd been hiding on top of the rocks on the breakwater now appeared at the door. Weapons held in one hand, they pulled and pushed the women hostages out the door and told them to run.

Ray Silva was already out the back door with the Governor in tow. Seeing another Highway Patrol officer, he pushed her into his arms and told him to get her out of there. He then turned and ran back into the small room.

The room cleared out quickly, Ray Silva was backing up toward the parking lot door when he saw her. Lying among the coats, sweaters and shoes on the floor, was Mary Jean Snider. She was face down, a large pool of blood on the floor underneath her, and a spreading blood stain on the back of her lightweight blouse. One of the rounds fired wildly by the terrorist at the window had found a target.

"Red," he yelled, as he pitched his M-16 to her. In one motion he had Mary Jean Snider turned over and scooped up in his arms. Her head was lolled back, her arms and legs dangling lifelessly, as he carried her toward the door.

Red Wolff caught the M-16 by its upper stock in mid-air. She saw he was carrying a woman, but in the darkness of the room she couldn't tell who it was.

Ralph Silva let go with two more quick bursts from his M-16 at the partition door as his uncle carried the unconsciousness woman out the back. It was then Red Wolff realized who Ray Silva was carrying.

"Oh my god!" she screamed out loud. Her natural instinct was to try to help Ray Silva, to hold the woman she loved, and to talk to her all at the same time. Red Wolff fought those instincts down and emptied the magazine of her M-16 into the partition.

By now the terrorists on the other side of the partition had begun returning fire blindly through the flimsy divider. Not having specific targets to shoot at, their fire was inaccurate, but there was a lot of it. The partition began to disintegrate in a hail of high velocity bullets.

Ralph Silva was the last one to leave the room. Kicking the door shut with his foot, he turned and ran as fast as he could. He could hear the sound of bullets impacting the metal door behind him.

The women hostages were strung out for fifty yards in the parking lot. Some of the younger ones, who could run faster, were almost to the safety of the trees, while the older ones struggled to move at much more than a fast walk. The officer who was pulling the Governor, had another twenty-five yards to go. Ray Silva was even further back, his legs moving in a half-running, half-walking, shuffling motion caused by carrying Mary Jean in his arms.

The back door of the community center burst open and one of the terrorists, holding an M-249 machine gun at his hip, opened fire on the running figures. When he pulled the trigger the weapon spat out twenty rounds in less than a half-second. Firing from the hip, however, especially at a moving target, is a very inaccurate way to shoot a machine gun. All of the terrorist's rounds were high and to the right.

Bringing the machine gun up to his cheek, the terrorist was sighting in on the man he recognized as the cameraman who came with the female reporter, when the pavement began to explode all around him. He watched fascinated as he saw little geysers of asphalt begin to jump up in a straight line, heading right toward him. It wasn't until his brain connected the sound of a heavy caliber bullet being fired, with the exploding asphalt, that he realized somebody was firing a machine gun at him, a very large caliber machine gun. The terrorist leapt back into the building and down behind the concrete block wall for protection.

The machine gun fire continued unabated for the next thirty seconds. The 7.62 millimeter bullets chewed big hunks out of the concrete block sides of the community center.

From his position in the trees, the Napa Auto Parts store manager was unhappy with his shooting. He used to be a pretty good machine gunner, he said to himself. He should have been able to blow the crap out of that guy. It had been almost forty years since he fired an M-60.

CHAPTER SEVENTEEN

Safely behind the cover of the trees and cars at the far end of the parking lot, Red Wolff did a quick check on the women hostages and the men who'd helped them as they ran from the community center. Thanks in no small part to the covering fire provided by the Napa Auto Parts store manager and his illegal M-60 machine gun, everyone was okay.

Many of the fifteen women were sprawled out behind the trees on the wet grass, simultaneously sobbing uncontrollably, and panting for breath. Others were still on their feet, but were doubled over retching. One of the National Guard troopers, and one of her own men, were puking. The hundred yard run from the community center, across the parking lot to safety, had taken its toll on everyone, she thought. Well, almost everyone. Standing next to her was Ralph Silva, breathing normally and unaffected by what had just moments before, been a run for his life.

After looking around and counting heads, Red Wolff got everyone to their feet, and started moving them away from the trees. It was dangerous to stay this close to the community center. The terrorists still had them outgunned, and were probably really pissed off about having the hostages snatched right from under their noses. As if to accentuate that point, the M-60, twenty feet away, barked out another string of twenty-five or thirty rounds.

"He's just keeping their heads down," Ralph Silva told her, referring to the Napa store manager.

She didn't see Ray Silva, or his girlfriend Julie. She knew they'd made it safely at least to this point. They must have kept going she thought, getting Mary Jean to the hospital. The Governor was on her feet, but looking dazed and disorientated. She'd deal with her when she had time. Right now they had to get moving.

"Ralph, you and the guy with the machine gun stay here. Give us enough time to move everyone back to the command post, then get the hell out of here. The guys on the perimeter can keep an eye on this side of the building," she instructed the young part-time soldier.

"No prob, sarge," he responded nonchalantly.

"Oh yeah, and by the way, thanks for taking out that terrorist with the through-the-window shot," she added, acknowledging that his timely shot had saved her life and probably that of all the hostages too.

Ralph Silva nodded, but didn't say anything. Depending on how you scored it, he'd just killed his fourth or fifth terrorist.

All of the women were on their feet and slowly moving away. Red Wolff took one more look around, turned, took three steps, stopped and came back.

The guy with the M-60 was flat on his stomach in the wet leaves under a tree, sighting over the barrel of his weapon at the side door of the community center. Red Wolff could see there was still steam rising from the entire length of the machine gun's barrel from the intense heat generated by the several hundred rounds he'd just fired.

She got down on one knee next to the man as he lay on the ground and extended her hand toward him. "Great shooting man. We would have all been killed without the cover from you and your gun," she told him, sincerity in her voice that was truly genuine.

"I'm a little rusty," is all the man said to her as he squeezed her hand.

Red Wolff then disappeared into the darkness.

She walked hurriedly to catch up with the women hostages and their escort officers. She got about ten yards when she noticed for the first time she was barefoot. Thinking back she realized that sometime during the firefight in the community center, or during her sprint across the parking lot, she'd lost both of the shoes she had borrowed from the reporter. She kept on walking, now aware of the pea gravel and debris on the street that made her wince with each step.

Red Wolff caught up to the others at the same time several SUVs and passenger vans, driven by militia volunteers, arrived. Always the supervisor, she immediately started directing the women into the vehicles and giving orders to the drivers to get them to the hospital. She told the Highway Patrol officer who still had the Governor in tow to stay with her no matter what, and she would be at the hospital as soon as she could.

As she continued to orchestrate caring for the hostages, one of her own officers cut her off. "Red, we can handle this, go check on Mary Jean," he told her.

Too tired to argue, all she could do was nod her head. Barefoot or not, she took off toward the command post at a slow jog. She needed to check on things there, get back into uniform, grab a patrol car, and get to the hospital. The staccato sound of the M-60 filled the night air. A final parting shot before Ralph Silva and the machine gun withdrew, Red Wolff said to herself.

She was about two blocks from the command post, still jogging, an M-16 slung over her shoulder, when she noticed how bright the area was ahead of her. What the hell she thought, as she continued jogging.

"Halt!" came the voice out of the darkness.

Red Wolff froze! Her first thought was the Marines had arrived. "Thank God," she muttered, not moving a muscle.

From behind a parked car on the street separating the beachfront park from the business district where the command post was, a man stepped out, an over-and-under shotgun in his hands, pointed right at her. "Who are you?" the man asked with a snarl.

Red Wolff could hear the partial sound of fear and the partial sound of uncertainty in the man's voice. She could see his outline in the shadows, but not his face. She could also catch the reflective glint off the blue steel barrel of the man's shotgun, still pointed at her.

"It's Sergeant Wolff, California Highway Patrol," she said with authority.

"That you Red?" the man asked, lowering the shotgun.

Red Wolff breathed a sigh of relief and started walking toward the man. As soon as he moved out of the shadows she recognized him instantly. It was Indian Joe.

"Joe, you scared the crap out of me," she told him.

"How'd I know who you were, Red? You come running out of the dark like that, I could have killed you," he said, slapping her on the back.

"What the hell's going on over there, the Marines get here?" she asked, pointing in the direction of the lights coming from the command post.

"Nah, some people just started doing things. All of a sudden there are lights, tents, and tables. Some army guy told me to come over here and stand guard," Joe told her.

"Joe, it's kind of dangerous being out here all by yourself isn't it?" she asked.

"Nope," he replied, pointing behind her.

From behind a tree, fifteen yards away, stepped two other men, both with hunting rifles.

"Thanks guys," she told them.

Turning back to Indian Joe she asked, "Have you seen Ray Silva, did he come this way?"

"Yeah, about five minutes ago. He was carrying a woman. She looked in really bad shape, lots of blood. He was running when he came up the street. I yelled at him to halt and he yelled back, fuck you, Joe, and kept on running."

Red Wolff started jogging again toward the command post. When she turned the last corner she was amazed at the scene before her.

When she left an hour before, dressed as a reporter, the command post consisted of one Highway Patrol car, one city police car, and a couple of officers. Now, at 11:05, the whole scene was changed. There were dozens of cars, pickups, and vans parked against the curbs on both sides of the street. In the middle of the street were two large motor homes, positioned so their side entrance doors faced each other. The whole street was lit up by portable floodlights. There were several small tents, five or six picnic tables, and no less than three portable barbeques. Red Wolff could count twenty to thirty people in the immediate area, each of them busily doing something, setting up chairs, cooking, or checking their weapons.

Red Wolff found the officer she'd left in charge, "What happened?" she asked.

The officer just shook his head. "Once some of them got deployed around the edge of the park, then gunfire coming from the community center, there was no stopping 'em. They all want to get involved. Look around the perimeter, there must be close to two hundred of them, all armed, and everyone ready to fight if the terrorists stick their heads out."

"Where'd the motor homes and lights come from?" Red Wolff asked.

"A couple of snowbirds who were over-nighting at the RV park just showed up and parked them here. They're pouring coffee as fast as they can make it. The lights are from the guy who owns the local lumber yard," he told her.

"Where's Ray?"

"He and his girlfriend ran in here a couple of minutes ago carrying a woman. They put her in a patrol car and tore out of here headed to the hospital. It was Mary Jean, wasn't it Red?"

"Yeah," she responded, her eyes still scanning the amazing scene around her.

"Red, she looked really bad, you better get to the hospital," the officer said solemnly.

"Where's the reporter? I need to get my uniform."

"She's in that motor home. But your uniform and Sam Browne are in this patrol car."

Opening the back door of the patrol car, Red Wolff spotted her uniform, boots, soft body armor vest, and gun belt. There was no time for modesty. Standing in the middle of the well lit street, she tore off the reporter's clothes, threw them in the back seat, and hurriedly got back into uniform. She was just putting on her gun belt when she heard the reporter call her name.

"Sergeant Wolff, what happened? We heard a lot of gunfire." Patricia Dodge was standing right next to her.

Looking up, Red Wolff could see the cameraman standing about four feet away, a small camcorder in his hand, the viewfinder on the side open, as he held the camera up recording the reporter talking to her. Both Patricia Dodge and her cameraman, she saw, were dressed in an odd assortment of somewhat ill-fitting clothes.

"Well, we got all the hostages out, the Governor's safe. One of the hostages got shot," she told the reporter, not mentioning the hostage was her pregnant life partner.

"Where's the Governor?" Patricia Dodge asked.

"All the hostages were taken to the hospital to get checked out. Say, where did you get the clothes and the camera?" Red asked.

"The clothes are from the couple that brought their motor home over. They're really nice, from Arizona, here on vacation. The camera is theirs too," Patricia Dodge told her.

Red Wolff just nodded while the reporter talked, pulling her pistol from its holster, ejecting the magazine, checking to ensure it was fully loaded, then slapping it back in her weapon.

"What do you think the terrorists are going to do next?" the reporter queried.

Red Wolff thought for a second, then spoke, "Without the hostages, there's not much reason for them to stay in the community center. Their leader knows without the hostages, he doesn't have any bargaining chips. He also knows the military will be here sooner or later and they don't stand a chance against them. My guess is they'll try and break out of there before the cavalry gets here and see how much more destruction they can do."

"What are you going to do if they come out sergeant?" the reporter asked.

"If they come out, there are a couple of hundred really pissed off American citizens who are going to shoot the shit out of them," Red Wolff told her.

"Aren't you going to try and stop the local people from killing the terrorists?" Patricia Dodge was back in her liberal media bias mode.

"You did see what those bastards did to this town and the hundreds of people they killed didn't you? If you want to try and stop the citizens from getting some revenge be my guest," Red Wolff told her, the tone and volume in her voice now starting to show impatience at the reporter's questions.

"We're going to the hospital," Patricia Dodge told her, sensing it was a good time to leave.

After the reporter left, Red Wolff took stock of what was happening. Grabbing her binoculars and night vision goggles, she went to the corner of the building where she could get a view of the community center and the perimeter. Through the night vision goggles she could see the community center was still blacked out, and she couldn't detect any movement inside the building.

Scanning the perimeter she saw a different scene. The entire street was ringed with armed men and women. Most were hidden behind cars or trees, while others were lying in the street, using the raised curb as cover. The scene almost brought tears to her eyes. Earlier in the day she had only ten or twelve cops and National Guard troopers to try and contain the terrorists, now there were several hundred ordinary citizens. Things were looking up.

By the time she finished checking out the perimeter, Ralph Silva and the machine gunner were back at the command post.

"Nice digs, sarge," he chided Red Wolff, referring to the motor homes, barbeques and tables set up at the command post.

Red Wolff didn't respond to his comment. "Thanks for covering us while we got away," she told him. "Any more movement from inside after we left?"

"No. I think my friend's M-60 persuaded them to stay put," Ralph responded, pointing to the Napa Auto Parts store manager and his weapon.

"Ralph, I need to get to the hospital. You and my officer take charge here. Get to the troopers who are in charge of the militia and make sure everyone stays put. No heroic attempts to charge the community center, no taking pot shots at terrorists. The Marines will be here in the morning. Enough good people have died today, let's not lose anymore. If the terrorists come out, it's open season. It's going to be a long, cold, wet night. Get half those people off the line and out of the weather. Get them food and coffee, and rotate them every couple of hours."

Ralph Silva told her they could handle it. Satisfied everything was under control, she was in her patrol car and gone.

Inside the community center Emil Lagare was livid. That female reporter had somehow overpowered his men and escaped with all the hostages. Not to mention that one of his men was killed and another had a severe head injury from being clubbed by a rifle butt. Then, to top it all off, when they tried to pursue the escaping hostages, someone had opened up on them with a heavy caliber machine gun.

This was not the way Qassim Saleh had planned the attack to go. The end game was to come after stringing the hostage situation out as long as possible. Without the hostages, Emil Lagare knew he only had two options left. The first option was to wait for the American military to come and overpower them. This would lead to he and his men dying, something they all accepted, but would not result in any more killing of the hated Americans. The second option would be to charge out in some fashion and engage in a gun battle for the town. He knew this option would also lead to their deaths, but it could also result in the deaths of more Americans. This, he knew, was the way for a true martyr to die.

Finding his night vision goggles, Emil Lagare moved to the side of the glass doors and began to scan the scene around the edge of the park. Once his eyes adjusted to the green display of the goggles, he could make out people all around the perimeter. There were well over a hundred that he could see, behind cars, behind trees, or flat on the ground. He moved from the glass doors to several of the large picture windows in the room and looked out at the three sides of the park. Everywhere he looked, he saw armed men. He saw something else, armed women.

Emil Lagare knew, from his training at the hands of the former U.S. Army sergeant at the camp in Syria, that women were integrated into many facets of the American military. But, he had been told women still did not serve in direct combat roles. If this were true, then what type of military unit was surrounding the building?

Emil Lagare began to scan the scene outside with more intensity. He had looked before, but he had not seen. The men and women around the park were not military at all! They were all dressed differently, they wore no helmets, and their weapons were of all different types. The reporter had lied to him, the American military had not arrived in town, these were the people of Crescent City, come to defend against any further attacks.

There may be a way to capitalize on the fact that the armed people outside were not soldiers. Perhaps with enough firepower, his men could cause panic among these citizens giving them a chance to escape into town. He and his men could hide in buildings or houses, killing more Americans. Such a thing could drag the situation out for several more days. All the while the American media would be in town, keeping the story alive across the world.

Emil Lagare put down the night vision goggles and began to plan his next move.

———————

It was just before midnight by the time Red Wolff got to Sutter Coast Hospital. She went directly into the emergency room entrance. Inside the scene was little better than organized chaos. There were dozens of people working, some in traditional hospital white, but a larger number in street clothes. Gurneys with patients were everywhere, and the noise was almost deafening.

Not seeing Ray Silva, she walked down the hall out of the emergency room into the main entrance area. There she spotted Ray and Julie standing near the information counter. He was still dressed in the blue jeans and wool shirt that belonged to the cameraman. The clothes were stained with blood.

The rest of the main entrance lobby was full of people. Many she recognized as the hostages she'd just helped free, others were family members, and a few other people patiently waiting to have their injuries from earlier in the day tended to.

When Julie Bradley saw Red Wolff, she ran toward her and threw her arms around her neck. "Oh, Erin," is all she said.

"Where's Mary Jean?" Red Wolff asked, bracing herself for the worst.

"In surgery, she took a round in the left side of her belly. She's lost a lot of blood," Ray Silva told her, his words matter-of-fact.

"Did you tell the doc she's pregnant?" Red Wolff asked.

"Yeah, he knows. He said the surgery will take at least a couple of hours," Ray replied.

Red Wolff let out a deep breath, at least she was alive.

She then looked at Julie Bradley and asked, "You okay?"

"Sure, I'm fine," she replied.

Julie Bradley then turned to Ray Silva, who stood a full ten inches taller then her, and slapped him hard across the face. The sound of the slap could be heard even over the considerable noise in the waiting room.

"What was that for?" he asked with a stunned voice.

"For taking so damn long to get us out of there," she said angrily.

She was about to slap Red Wolff for the same reason when Ray Silva grabbed her arm. He pulled her to him and wrapped his arms around her. For the first time since being captured over fourteen hours before, Julie Bradley let herself cry.

"Where's the Governor?" Red asked.

"In one of the private rooms down the hall, one of our guys is with her, and so is the reporter," Ray Silva said.

"Okay, let's go talk to her," Red Wolff said, indicating he should accompany her.

The door to the Governor's room was open and Red Wolff could hear voices inside. When she walked in the door she could see the Governor was sitting on the bed, still in the clothes she wore when she got to Crescent City over fourteen hours ago. Her hair was disheveled and her face dirty, a look she intentionally wanted to portray for the reporter and her cameraman with his handheld camcorder. Her political mind was racing. The pictures of her, looking as she did, talking about her ordeal, facing terrorism first hand, was not the kind of political advertising you could buy. It would be worth millions of votes if she chose to make a presidential run.

The Governor continued to talk to the reporter after Red Wolff and Ray Silva entered her room. Patricia Dodge was feeding the Governor big softball questions about terrorism, the president's war strategy, and the events of the day. The Governor was in political heaven, using this once in a lifetime opportunity to espouse her agenda.

"Who are you and where is my protection detail?" the Governor asked Red Wolff, the tone in her voice typical of the way children of the sixties Democrats talked to law enforcement officers.

"Governor, I'm Sergeant Erin Wolff, California Highway Patrol," Red Wolff told her. She'd included California Highway Patrol, even though her uniform clearly indicated who she worked for. Red Wolff had been around enough politicians to know most of them had no concept of the difference between a city police officer, a sheriff's deputy, or a CHP officer. "And this is Officer Silva," she added, pointing to Ray who was in civilian clothes.

"I asked you where my protection detail was," the Governor said curtly.

"All dead, Governor," Red Wolff replied.

The cameraman continued to record the exchange.

"How did I get away from the terrorists?" the Governor asked.

"There was a rescue operation that got you and the other women hostages out," Red Wolff told her, not mentioning that she was one of the rescuers.

"I need to get back to Sacramento as soon as possible," the Governor stated.

Red Wolff was starting to boil, "And the other hostages are safe also, one of the women was shot by the terrorists during the escape." She wanted to add, you cold, unfeeling bitch.

"Who's in charge here?" the Governor asked.

"Right now, I am," Red Wolff told her.

"Very well sergeant, since you're in charge, I want you to arrange for me to leave here and get back to Sacramento. I want a full security detail to protect me," there was an arrogance in the Governor's voice.

"Ma'am, perhaps it would be better if I first gave you a briefing on the situation," Red Wolff said calmly.

"Sergeant, I don't want a briefing, I want you to get me safely out of this town," there was a tone of superiority in her voice.

Ray Silva was standing by the door, watching and listening. He gently, but firmly pulled on the cameraman's arm and guided him out of the room. Then, using his bulk, he nudged the reporter out the door, and closed it behind her.

The Governor watched, somewhat uncertain of what had just happened. "What do you think you're doing?" she demanded.

Red Wolff saw the look in Ray Silva's eyes, she knew what was coming. "Don't Ray, let it go," she told him, knowing she was wasting her breath.

"Shut the fuck up you political hack, and listen. First of all, there is no way out of this town. The terrorists blockaded the highways north and south. The airport runway is unusable, and the fog outside is so thick, nothing can fly, in or out. The terrorists that took you hostage have killed hundreds, maybe even a thousand people, and they burned half this town to the ground. Right now, several hundred ordinary California citizens are risking their lives, trying to keep the terrorists bottled up in the community center until the Marines can get here tomorrow morning. A lot of people, led by Red here, put their lives on the line to get you away from the terrorists. We can't spare one person to get you out of town, even if there was a way to do it. So right now you have two choices, Governor, you can shut up and let us do our job, or you can keep demanding, in which case I will kick you in your bony ass and give you back to the terrorists."

The way Ray Silva pronounced Governor, he made it sound like a dirty word.

The Governor of California sat there, her ears not believing what they had just heard. Nobody had talked to her in that manner since she was a freshman congresswoman twenty-five years ago when the Speaker of the House had ripped her apart for not voting the way he had told her to on a certain bill.

However, it didn't take her long to recover. "You can't talk to me like that," she stammered. "Sergeant, he can't talk to me like that," pointing at Ray Silva.

"Yes he can Governor, he's exactly the kind of person who can talk to you like that," Red Wolff told her, a half-smile on her face.

"I'll fire him," the Governor snorted.

"You can't fire him Governor, he's civil service. Besides, he has thirty years on the job and could retire anytime he wants. And, it's your word against ours. You've just been through a traumatic ordeal, who do you think they're going to believe?" Red Wolff said.

The Governor sat on the hospital bed silent, but Red could see her mind working. Red Wolff launched a preemptive strike. "Or maybe we should just tell the media that in the midst of this crisis, with armed terrorists still a danger to the people and the town, you demanded to be taken to safety, leaving the citizens to fend for themselves."

She knew she'd hit a nerve.

The Governor of California stared back at Red Wolff. She may have been a cold, unfeeling bitch, but she was a shrewd, cold, unfeeling bitch. She could see the votes fading away with the headlines she'd fled Crescent City rather than staying to provide leadership. Who the hell was this female Highway Patrol sergeant anyway, she thought to herself?

After a long silence the Governor spoke, "Perhaps I should visit some of the people in the hospital to give them support. Sergeant, can you arrange for an officer to escort me, and later drive me around town so I can view the situation first hand?"

Red Wolff told the Governor she would make all the arrangements.

They stood in the hallway outside the Governor's room and Red Wolff looked at Ray Silva. "Kick you in your bony ass and give you back to the terrorists. Couldn't you think of anything better to say than that?" she said, shaking her head and laughing.

"Fucking Democrats," he replied.

They walked back into the waiting room to rejoin Julie Bradley. Almost at the same time the doctor came from the direction of the operating rooms.

Red Wolff could see it was the same young doctor she had the problem with when she interrogated the captured terrorist from Oakland.

The doctor spoke first, "She's a tough lady, and she lost a lot of blood. Most people would have died before they got to the hospital. The round was a through-and-through, didn't splinter or lodge in the body. I had to take out a bunch of intestine, but she'll never miss it. The baby is okay. If she can fight through the next twenty-four hours, I think she'll make it. In truth, it's less than fifty-fifty."

"Can I see her?" Red Wolff asked.

"She's out cold, but you can see her," he replied.

"Thanks doctor," she told him, tears now streaming down her cheeks, making tracks in the dirt on her face.

Turning to Ray Silva and Julie Bradley, Red Wolff told them she wanted to do this alone.

Mary Jean Snider's room was dark, with only two small night lights for illumination. Normally a single patient private room, there were three other beds crammed into the small space. Red Wolff assumed the other patients were from the initial incident at the park. How many hours before was that, she asked herself looking at her watch. It was just after 1:30 in the morning, almost sixteen hours ago.

Red Wolff sidestepped between the tightly packed beds. Mary Jean had several IVs in her left arm, a tube down her throat, and an oxygen hose under her nose. She was sleeping, her respirations shallow, but regular. The glow from the digital readouts on the various vital sign monitors mounted on the wall cast a red tint on her face, and the constant beep-beep of the heart monitor indicated her pulse was steady.

Bending over, Red Wolff took Mary Jean's hand in hers and spoke slowly to the woman she loved, "Mary Jean, I know you can hear me. The doctor says you're going to be fine and the baby's okay too. You need to be a fighter now, for all of us. We have a lot of things to do yet and I don't want to do them alone. I have to go back to work now, but I'll be back soon. I love you, don't you die on me damn-it."

Red Wolff kissed her on the cheek and walked out of the room. The heart monitor continued its' steady beep-beep.

———————

Inside the community center, Emil Lagare evaluated his options. He had decided he and his men would attempt to break out of the park and try to create more havoc in the town before the military arrived. How to best accomplish this was the issue he was grappling with.

He was down to seven men, eight including himself. They still had plenty of firepower with the four M-249 machine guns, plus the M-16s, and thousands of rounds of ammunition. Although his men were silent, he knew they were all looking to him to provide the leadership that would bring them the glorious deaths they desired. Even though the mission had not gone entirely according to plan, none of them found fault with Emil Lagare. He took the time to speak to each of his men and offer words of encouragement, and talked to them about the rewards they would soon be receiving from Allah.

It was two in the morning. All of them were going on a full day without sleep. Part of his training as commander had dealt with the effects on the human body of extended periods without sleep. His training had taught him the most vulnerable time for the human body was always between the hours of four and six in the morning. It was during these hours the body's internal clock most wanted to sleep. Even people who normally worked during these hours were always less than one hundred percent ready to react.

He went back to using the night vision goggles to observe the people around the perimeter who had the community center surrounded. It did not appear to him that the Americans were guarding the perimeter in the same strength he had observed earlier. No doubt some of them were off-line, sleeping or eating. It occurred to him that the same lack of sleep that he and his men were facing, would also be affecting the Americans.

The plan slowly developed in his mind.

———————

At the Humboldt Communications Center, the comm-op finally relinquished her chair. She'd been on-duty since six the previous morning. The radio to Crescent City had been silent except for the hourly status checks between her and 95-S-3.

285

The last major report she had was several hours ago when she received the news that the Governor and the hostages had been rescued, and things had settled into the police work equivalent of a barricaded suspect situation. S-3 told her with the help of the militia they were just going to keep the terrorists contained until the Marines arrived.

The comm-op headed for the supervisor's office where she promptly fell asleep on the couch. She slept fitfully, her mind not able to block out the sounds from the radio, or the voices of the half-dozen people in the other room.

Throughout the evening and early morning, Highway Patrol officers from the Humboldt CHP command and deputies from the Humboldt County Sheriff's Office had been working to clear Highway 101 south of Crescent City. It was a hard, time consuming process, complicated by the darkness. Hundreds of cars were stopped in the northbound lane. An equal number of drivers had crossed into the southbound lane and continued driving northbound. This resulted in both lanes being clogged with vehicles. When drivers in the northbound lane attempted to turn around, they were often broad sided by other cars driving north in the southbound lane. For the officers, it came down to walking the highway, turning around one car at a time, and directing it back southbound. Every time they encountered an accident, and there were over fifty of them, they had to call for tow trucks and often ambulances. This meant stopping all traffic so the emergency vehicles and wreckers could drive north in the southbound lanes to reach the scene. It took hours.

It was after midnight when they finally got to the blockade the terrorists had made by torching the fuel truck on Last Chance Grade. That scene was a nightmare. The fiery fuel from the truck ran down the grade almost a quarter-mile. Fifteen cars had burned down to their rims, and eight people burned to death still in their vehicles. In an effort to expedite clearing the road, the officers used the push bumpers on their patrol cars to simply shove the unoccupied vehicles over the side of the embankment and into the ocean hundreds of feet below. There would be repercussions later from environmental groups, the Environmental Protection Agency, and countless other government agencies for this action. To their credit, the on-scene supervisors didn't worry about the need for an Environmental Impact Study and ordered the vehicles dumped anyway. Those cars with victims still inside were towed away, so the bodies, or what was left of them, could be removed.

Moving the burned out cars took several hours, and it was close to three in the morning when they finally got to the charred hulk of the fuel truck. Moving this vehicle would take a heavy duty tow truck, the type especially designed with a boom that could lift the truck onto a flat bed trailer. Although they had the equipment, the steepness of the grade, and the narrow roadway made trying to remove the truck a slow tedious job. The officers at the scene advised Humboldt Communications Center it would be close to dawn before the truck was removed. Even then, they still faced all the vehicles on the north side of the blockade that were abandoned in the roadway, or had been involved in accidents. They had no idea how far the backup extended on that side.

A similar scene was playing itself out on the north side of Crescent City. In this case, the Oregon State Police and the Josephine County Sheriff's Office were trying to clear the intersection of Highway 101 and Highway 199. They faced almost the identical problems being dealt with by those trying to clear the road south of Crescent City. Their problems were compounded, however, by the greater distance assistance had to travel from Grant's Pass or Medford, the fact their radios did not work so far from Oregon, and because those agencies were considerably smaller, personnel wise, than their counterparts in California, and could spare fewer resources.

———

Red Wolff was sitting in the passenger's seat of her patrol car, the door open, engine running and heater on, her head tilted back against the top of the seat. She was asleep. Not a deep sleep, her mind still aware of the noise and comings and goings around her at the command post.

Ray Silva was standing outside the open door of the motor home that had become the de facto command post headquarters, talking to two other officers and his nephew. In the last several hours, they'd gotten the names and personal information from every member of the Crescent City Militia, and those of the citizens who had come to help in any way they could.

Between Ralph Silva and the other National Guard troopers, they had refined the militia into three companies of seventy people. Each company was split into two equal squads. They also redistributed the available automatic weapons to ensure they could counteract any attempt by the terrorists to breakout at any point around the perimeter.

It was 4:30 a.m., the sun would be up in another hour and if the fog had not been so thick, the first traces of dawn would be visible in a little over thirty minutes. Ray Silva was drinking coffee from a Styrofoam cup, his ninth in two hours.

"Ralph, let's tour around the perimeter and make sure everyone's on their toes. We only have to hold 'em another couple of hours," he said to his nephew.

They had no more than started out on their inspection tour when they heard the first shots coming from the west side of the community center.

Emil Lagare had planned well. He and his seven remaining men all came out of the door on the west side of the community center at the same time. It was still dark, and the fog seemed to have thickened over the last hour, providing some degree of concealment.

With the four machine guns in the lead, the plan was to run the seventy-five yards to the three highway patrol cars and the three jeep Libertys that had formed the Governor's motorcade the previous morning. Emil Lagare and his men would use these vehicles to crash their way out of the ring of Crescent City townspeople and local law enforcement encircling the park.

Once in the vehicles, they would drive toward the extreme west end of the park where there were fewer people on guard and where the weapons from those in the center and east side of the perimeter, could not be brought to bear.

They had actually made it almost all the way to the parked vehicles before the first of the militia saw what was happening. Even then, the several townspeople on guard on the west side perimeter held their fire, summoning the National Guard troopers and local cops to report what they saw. By the time it fully registered on everyone what was occurring, two of the terrorists were already in the driver's seats of the two black and white Highway Patrol cars. The others, including Emil Lagare, were standing outside, weapons at the ready, waiting for the vehicles to start.

On the west side of the perimeter, the National Guard trooper opened up with an M-16 on the terrorists standing by the police car. As soon as he fired his first three round burst, over thirty other weapons were fired by the citizens on that side of the park. The sound of the militia weapons being discharged was not the rapid fire of automatic weapons, but that of single shot hunting rifles, pistols, and shotguns. It may not have been fast, but it was continuous. From the time the National Guard trooper fired his first shots, over three hundred rounds had been fired at the fleeing terrorists within ninety seconds. More firepower was coming, as those citizens who had been off-line ran to join their fellow townspeople manning the perimeter to stop the terrorists attempted breakout.

Emil Lagare and his men could hear and see the effects of the incoming rounds. The first Highway Patrol car took over fifteen hits in the body, the passenger side windows were blown out, and the right front tire was flattened. Two of his men armed with machine guns, returned fire immediately. The rapid firing machine guns spit out hundreds of rounds each at the unseen citizens on the west side of the park, two hundred yards away.

For the first time, the terrorists were at a disadvantage. Their rapid firing weapons were capable of a high rate of sustained fire, but in the darkness and fog, they had no discernable targets to concentrate their fire on.

The terrorist in the first Highway Patrol car managed to start the big V-8 engine in spite of being showered with glass as the passenger side windows were shattered by the intense fire from the citizens around the perimeter. Emil Lagare yelled for three of his men to get in the car. Two men armed with machine guns and a third with an M-16, jumped in the car.

The driver pulled the transmission into gear and pushed down on the accelerator as soon as the last man was in the back seat. The patrol car lurched forward, wobbling badly from the flat, right front tire as it moved ahead. As it pulled away from the curb, one of the men in the back seat yelled Allah Akbar. The vehicle drove across the wet grass directly for the edge of the park and ring of people on the west perimeter.

Had it not been a life or death situation, what happened next might have been almost "Keystone Kops" comical. The first thing that happened was operator error. The patrol car had been sitting in the elements for over eighteen hours. The outside was wet from the moisture in the heavy fog, making the windshield impossible to see through. Between the stress of trying to escape and being shot at, the terrorist driver simply could not find the right switch to activate the windshield wipers. Nonetheless, he continued driving, trusting in dead reckoning and an occasional lean of his head out the window to get his bearings. The second thing was a phenomenon familiar to almost every American driver. The temperature inside the vehicle was approximately the same as the outside air temperature. Now, with four excited, heavily breathing men in the vehicle, the inside of the windows began to fog up, further impairing the occupants' visibility.

The terrorist driver's last mistake was fatal. He chose to try and drive as fast as he could toward the edge of the park, thinking the quicker they could breakout, the quicker the intense gun fire they were taking from the citizens would end. The result, however, of trying to drive fast on a flat tire caused the right front of the vehicle to bounce up and down. This in turn made it impossible for the three men in the vehicle to take accurate aim at the people who were firing at them. Each time they tried to aim and fire, the bouncing of the front end caused their rounds to go high over the heads of the defending townspeople, or low into the ground.

Conversely, the rounds being fired by the Crescent City Militia became more accurate as the car came closer. One of the militia on the west side perimeter was an avid hunter. He watched as the vehicle bounced its' way across the grassy park, the head of the terrorist in the right front seat centered in the cross hairs of the scope on his rifle. He timed the up and down motion of the vehicle perfectly and squeezed the trigger. The high powered hunting round caught the terrorist just behind the right ear. The bullet exploded the man's head.

Inside the Highway Patrol car, the entire passengers' compartment and its occupants were showered with bone, brains, and blood. The blood splattered on the windshield further decreased the driver's ability to see where he was going. The two passengers still alive in the backseat were loudly yelling at each other and giving directions to the driver, none of them now firing at the people outside.

Even as bullets from the citizens of Crescent City continued to impact the vehicle, the driver pushed ahead toward the edge of the park and the street beyond. Another round found its' mark, hitting the terrorist in the left rear in the arm, completely pulverizing his upper right arm bone. Almost to the street, the driver looked for an opening between the trees ringing the grassy park and the cars parked on the street. Without the ability to look straight ahead through the windshield, the driver misjudged everything and slammed the left front of the patrol car into a Redwood tree.

With rounds coming in from three different sides, the driver opened the door and rolled to the ground. On his knees, he reached back into the patrol car for his M-16. On the other side of the tree he'd just hit, stood the twenty-three year old night manager of the local video store. As the terrorist reached into the car, the local man fired one round from his shotgun. At point blank range, the shotgun round tore out a section of the terrorist's back about the size of a pie pan.

The final act of this comedy of errors occurred as the two terrorists in the backseat tried to get out of the vehicle. The patrol vehicle they'd commandeered was called a "cage car." Not every Highway Patrol car was equipped with a cage. In the Crescent City command about half of the patrol vehicles had cages. They were ideal for transporting combative prisoners as the heavy gauge steel screen formed a protective barrier between the prisoner in the backseat and the officer in the front. The back doors of cage cars could only be opened from the outside.

The two terrorists in the backseat now clawed desperately at the door panels searching for the handle. In the darkness and with their adrenalin pumping, they began to pound on the doors, then ram them with their shoulders. The doors stayed closed, the patrol vehicle rocking side-to-side as they tried to force open an escape route. In desperation, the terrorist on the right side began to climb out of the vehicle through the space left by the gunshot shattered window. It was already too late. From three sides, twelve men and three women cautiously approached the car. One of the terrorists was halfway out the window when the first of the militia opened fire. A hail of bullets ripped into his body from pistols and single shot hunting rifles. On the opposite side of the patrol car, other members of the Crescent City Militia, two National Guard troopers, and a city police officer, all fired through the left rear window into the vehicle. Trapped in the backseat the last terrorist was riddled by twenty-seven bullets.

While the first patrol car was making its ill-fated escape attempt, Emil Lagare and the other two terrorists were waiting for the driver of the second Highway Patrol car to get the vehicle started. Unfortunately for the terrorists, the officer who'd driven that patrol vehicle had taken the keys with him when he parked the previous morning. It took precious seconds for the terrorist to realize the keys were not in the ignition, to feel around on the floorboard, and to communicate back to Emil Lagare that the keys were missing.

More shouts and orders from Emil Lagare moved everyone back toward the first of the Jeep Libertys. The keys were in this vehicle and soon everyone, except Emil Lagare, was inside.

Red Wolff was awake and instantly alert when the first gunshot was fired. She immediately headed for the sound of the firing, Ray Silva by her side. The firing had also brought all the militia who were not on-duty, running back to the perimeter from their resting places.

As soon as she saw what was happening, Red Wolff yelled for half of the available citizens to shift their positions to assist those on the west side of the park, and the other half to take up posts near the center of the line. The terrorists were making their breakout. It was time to end the nightmare of the last eighteen hours.

Before Emil Lagare could get in the vehicle with the three remaining members of his team, it came under a heavy volley of fire from behind. It was that damned heavy caliber machine gun again and several M-16s, he told himself. His men in the vehicle were returning fire, but with it still being dark, their rounds failed to silence any of the over fifty weapons spewing rounds at them.

The combined fire from a half-dozen law enforcement officers, three National Guard troopers, and nearly forty citizens from the Crescent City Militia, shredded the Jeep and killed the three terrorists inside. Not one of the town's defenders was even wounded.

Emil Lagare dropped to the pavement when the first bullets began striking the Jeep. He could hear the cries of his men as they were hit by the seemingly endless fusillade of rounds fired by the Americans. His mind flashed on Qassim Saleh's statement that the Americans would not be organized enough to put up any type of viable resistance.

Emil Lagare crawled to the front of the all but destroyed Jeep. Surrender never crossed his mind, but survival did. He had long ago resigned himself to dying. Being cut down, however, in the middle of a wet grassy park, on a foggy morning, without having the ability to kill at least one more enemy of Islam was not a martyr's death.

His only safety was back in the community center. As soon as the gunfire stopped, he was on his feet and sprinting back to the building that had been his stronghold for nearly a day. The first strains of daylight were lightening the sky, although the heavy blanket of fog held on to the grayness.

He was halfway back to the building when rounds began kicking up tuffs of grass around his feet. Suddenly it sounded as if every gun the Americans had was firing at him. Ten yards to go, a round ripped through the baggy legs of the American Army uniform pants he was wearing. He didn't think it was possible, but he actually ran faster. He made it to the side door just as a burst from an M-16 tore into the door frame six inches above his head.

"Son-of-a-bitch," Ralph Silva cursed to himself. It was the first time today he'd missed.

Emil Lagare tore at the door handle. It was locked. When the terrorists came out of the building minutes before, they'd not considered ever having to come back. The heavy metal fire door was self-closing, and self-locking.

Knowing it was not worth the time to stand and pull on the door, Emil Lagare ran for the back of the community center. Safely behind the building, he paused for only an instant and looked around. To the east and west were armed, angry Americans waiting at the perimeter of the park. From the front of the community center, in less than a minute, would come more Americans, probably the one with the machine gun. Ten yards ahead of him was the twenty foot high rock and concrete breakwater and the Pacific Ocean beyond. It was his only chance.

Red Wolff, Ray Silva, and his nephew Ralph, saw the final terrorist run from the locked door and around to the back side of the community center. As much as she wanted to charge after him, she was a good cop, the guy she learned from, right next to her. Good police tactics and officer safety demanded they take it slowly and safely. Running blindly around the corner of a building after an armed suspect, was a good way to get killed. It took both of them to contain young Ralph Silva to keep him from doing just that.

As they came to the corner of the building, all three stopped and Ray Silva got down on the ground, flat on his face. Red Wolff and Ralph were standing behind him. He inched his way forward and did a quick peek around the corner, exposing just the part of his head needed to get a good look.

"He's on top of the breakwater, thirty yards down," Ray yelled, seeing the last terrorist silhouetted against the rapidly brightening morning sky

Emil Lagare had climbed up the rocks and concrete forms piled in a pyramid shape which formed the breakwater. He got to the top, just as Ray Silva did his peek around the corner of the building.

Ralph Silva's blood was up, and when his uncle yelled that the terrorist was atop the breakwater, he brought his M-16 up to this shoulder and stepped from behind the cover of the building. It took him only a second to visually locate the terrorist and sight him in.

It was a foolish move, one neither of the two experienced Highway Patrol officers would have made.

From his position on top of the breakwater, Emil Lagare fired a three round burst at the American who was now standing completely exposed thirty yards away. The man went down, the rifle he held, flying from his hands.

When Ralph Silva hit the ground, neither Ray nor Red Wolff hesitated. Both leapt from the side of the building and drug him back to safety behind the corner. Blood was pouring from the right side of his head. While Ray Silva used both hands to apply direct pressure to the wound, Red Wolff used her radio to call for other officers to reinforce the eastern perimeter around the breakwater to cut off that escape route for the terrorist.

Ray Silva's hands were red as the blood of his nephew oozed between his fingers. A patrol car drove up, skidding to a stop behind him as he knelt over the unconscious body. The officer driving the patrol car used the specially installed electric powered trunk release button to pop open the vehicle's trunk. Within seconds, he was next to Ray Silva, ripping open a gauze compress bandage from the vehicle's first aid kit.

While the two officers worked on Ralph Silva, Red Wolff peered around the corner of the community center trying to spot the terrorist who was last seen on top of the breakwater. It was light enough now that she could see about a hundred yards in any direction. From her position, she could see perhaps two dozen officers and militia covering the east side of the community center and another group of twenty covering the far west side perimeter. She could clearly see the breakwater, although the fog and the early morning grayness of the sky made trying to make out a person hiding among the rocks almost impossible.

Ralph Silva started to moan and within a few seconds was sitting upright. The compress bandage wrapped tightly around his head was soaked with blood, but had done its' job in stemming the flow.

"I'm alright," he said woozily, shaking his head side-to-side.

Ray Silva unwrapped the long ends of the compress encircling Ralph's head and gently removed it from the wound. There was a large gash along the right side of Ralph's head running from just above his eye to behind his ear. The bullet had cut a perfectly straight line as it ripped the skin and hair from his scalp. The wound was still weeping slightly, but the direct pressure had caused the blood to clot.

Red Wolff looked down at the young trooper and said, "Hard-headed Portugee."

Ray and the other officer both laughed. Ralph Silva tried to laugh also but his head hurt like hell.

Red Wolff told the other officer to get him to the hospital to get stitched up. "Then get your butt back here Silva, I need you," she added.

Using her radio to coordinate with the officers on the east side of the community center, Red Wolff directed everyone to climb the rocks of the breakwater, then pinch in toward the center. If the terrorist was up there, they had him trapped.

Working her way up the slippery wet breakwater, she made it to the top, crouched down to make herself a smaller target. Peering over the top she could see nothing hidden among the rocks. Staying on the inland side of the breakwater, just below the crest of the rocks, she worked her way toward the center, popping up every few yards to look over the top.

It took less than a minute for the two groups of officers, National Guard troopers, and militia to work their way to the center of the breakwater where the terrorist had last been seen. They found no one.

At the point where the two groups converged, Red Wolff stood atop the breakwater, looking east and west. One of the troopers found an M-16 rifle at the bottom of the breakwater where the waves of the bay gently met the base of the rock barrier.

"Crap, he's in the water," Red Wolff said out loud, to nobody in particular. Looking out to the ocean, the fog still hung low and thick on the water. She signaled for everyone to stop talking.

After the noise and confusion of the last twenty hours, the silence was eerie. The only sound she could hear was the soft, almost silent lapping of the waves on the breakwater and the distance moan of the fog horn from Battery Point lighthouse, over a half-mile away, at the entrance to the bay.

CHAPTER EIGHTEEN

It was completely light by 5:45, although the fog continued to hang low over the entire town, keeping the sky a dull gray.

Red Wolff was exhausted, but she couldn't stop. There was still one terrorist unaccounted for. It was possible she knew, he'd been wounded and died in the flat calm water of the bay, or he drowned. Until she closed that loop, the town and the safety of its' residents were still her responsibility.

She quickly gave orders to the troopers in charge of the militia companies and the few cops she still had left. One group would fan itself out from the community center, all along the coastline for the half-mile to the harbor. Spaced twenty yards apart, they would be able to keep anyone from slipping ashore unseen. Likewise, she ordered another group out from the community center toward the Battery Point lighthouse, almost three-quarters of a mile away in the opposite direction. She knew whoever the terrorist was, he would have to be an Olympic caliber swimmer if he ventured beyond the lighthouse where the protection of the bay ended and the open ocean began. If he got that far, the currents and the waves would smash him on the jagged rocks.

As soon as the troopers started giving orders to the citizen militia, the grumbling began. It had been a long night for them and everyone was cold, wet and hungry. The adventuresome part of the battle was over and now the boredom part of being a volunteer was about to begin. Complaints and excuses were heard everywhere. "I've got to get to work," "I need to get home and tell my wife I'm okay," and "They're all dead," were the comments heard most.

Red Wolff saw the breakdown immediately, and called the National Guard troopers and officers to her. "Listen, you guys need to kick a little ass here. Let your people know that until we can account for the last terrorist, nobody is safe. The Marines will be here in a couple of hours. We can't afford to let one person leave. They all volunteered for this, now get them deployed. Stay alert and keep them on their toes. I'll make arrangements for coffee and food to be brought out."

Everyone nodded or verbally agreed with her. Soon the militia was fanning out on foot, taking up posts along the coastline.

While the first group of volunteers was being deployed, Red Wolff sent Ray Silva to round up the remaining Crescent City Militia volunteers and move them to the harbor and Endert's Beach. Just south of the harbor, Endert's Beach was almost two miles of flat white sand, where the shape of the bay ensured that only small waves broke on the shore. It was a favorite beach for families and kids, and had the water of the northern Pacific not always been so cold, it would have been an ideal place for swimming.

By the time Ray Silva got back to the command post, about half the remaining volunteers had already left to go home. Those who remained were engaged in self-congratulation, with much handshaking and backslapping. From ice chests, beer started to appear and everyone was celebrating their victory over the terrorists.

"What the fuck are you doing?" Ray Silva bellowed when he saw what was happening. "There's still one terrorist on the loose and until we eliminate him, neither you nor your families are safe. Look over there, you're standing here drinking beer less than a hundred yards from the bodies of your friends and neighbors who were slaughtered yesterday," he said, pointing to the grassy park where hundreds of bodies still lay where they fell when the terrorists made their initial attack.

The festive mood among the citizen militia quickly changed to one of heads hung low and quiet mumbling.

"You want to drink beer, go home. You want to help, follow me," Ray Silva told the fifty or so volunteers around him.

Everyone stayed.

Ray Silva first poled the volunteers to see who had four-wheel drive vehicles. There were about fifteen of them. He doubled them up with another volunteer and sent them to Endert's Beach. The flat sand beach was fifty to seventy yards wide, most of it hard packed and could easily support vehicles. Given its' two mile length, having the militia patrol in vehicles was the best option.

He had the last twenty people drive to the harbor, where he and a Crescent City Police Officer deployed them on the pier and on the wooden walkways that formed the slips for the fishing boats and private pleasure craft.

The harbor that morning was a collection of different sights and smells. The always present smell of decaying fish, drying fishing nets, diesel fuel, and the ocean, were mixed with the heavy smell of the burned out Coast Guard vessel. It was still smoldering eighteen hours after having been demolished by a terrorist in a fuel truck.

None of the usual early morning harbor noises were heard either. Many of the fishermen, who normally would have been on their boats, had been among the first victims of the terrorists when they began their rampant shooting at the park. Others had simply chosen to stay home.

At any rate it didn't matter, had they tried to leave the harbor that morning they would have been stopped by one of Red Wolff's officers. With one terrorist still unaccounted for, no one was leaving Crescent City, by boat or vehicle.

By 7:00, the first signs of the sun starting to burn off the heavy fog were beginning to be seen. It was still thick over the bay and near the ocean, but it was clearing inland. Red Wolff was in her patrol car talking to Humboldt Communications Center. She reported the attempt by the terrorists to break out of the community center and the subsequent shootout that had left all but one of them dead.

The comm-op who'd been with her for the entire incident, was back on the radio. She'd catnapped for less than an hour, but was feeling the adrenalin rush that came from sensing the situation was about to play itself out.

"95-S-3, Humboldt," the radio called.

"S-3," Red Wolff replied.

"95-S-3, 101 south of Crescent City will be open in less than an hour. There are two hundred CHP personnel, a National Guard medical unit, a disaster response team, and a million media people waiting for the road to clear. North of town the road is still blocked. Oregon State Police advises it will take several more hours to get the roadway open. The CHP and National Guard commanders are inquiring how you want their personnel deployed when they get to Crescent City," the comm-ops voice was slow and deliberate.

"10-4, copy on 101 being open soon. Advise all incoming personnel there is still one terrorist at large. Last seen in the vicinity of the community center, probably escaped into the ocean about 0530. He was wearing military fatigue uniform and brown boots. Described as white male, twenty-five, dark hair, olive complexion. Considered to be armed and dangerous, probably has a military semi-automatic pistol. Also advise all in-coming personnel there are several local National Guard troops wearing the same uniform the terrorist was last seen wearing. They are all armed. Have the commanders meet at the command post. The medical units should proceed direct to Sutter Coast Hospital. The disaster team needs to get to the beachfront park and start the recovery process on dead bodies." There was tiredness in Red Wolff's voice.

"S-3 the commanders are being advised now. The Marines are airborne from Grant's Pass. Their ETA to Crescent City is less than thirty minutes, can you advise weather conditions?"

"Still heavy ground fog in town. Their best bet would be trying to land north of town on the highway. I'll arrange transportation using National Guard vehicles from the local armory," Red Wolff told the comm-op.

"Copy S-3, additional information, the FBI's Hostage Rescue Team helicopter is inbound your location. They intend to land at the airport. Can you assist?"

"I'll make sure they get everything they deserve," Red Wolff snorted.

"Humboldt, one more thing, the Highway Patrol personnel should set up roadblocks at both ends of town. Nobody but authorized personnel in and nobody, repeat nobody, out until we find the last terrorist," Red Wolff's voice had a tone to it that the comm-op could clearly convey to all responding personnel.

Her conversation with the comm-op complete, she headed back to the command post to coordinate the arrival of help.

Emil Lagare was a fairly strong swimmer but the weight of the army boots and wet uniform caused him to struggle to keep his head above water. He wasn't close to drowning, but he knew unless he did something soon, panic would involuntarily set in. First, he unfastened his army pistol belt. He then refastened it and looped it over his neck. Next, taking a deep breath, he dunked his head beneath the dead calm waters of the bay and worked at the laces of his boots. It took him three tries, but he got them both off. Next he stripped off the uniform shirt and trousers. Now, he could relax a little, tread water, and regain his composure.

He was a little over a hundred yards off shore from where he had slipped into the water. The fog was still thick enough that he could not be seen from shore, although he could make out the shapes of over two dozen people standing atop the breakwater. He knew soon the sky would be light enough for people on shore to see him, even with the thick fog cover. Silently he swam further away from shore using his best swimming technique, the breaststroke.

As he swam, he played the videotape of Crescent City in his mind. The bay was roughly half-moon shaped. At the northern end was an old lighthouse, now a museum. The harbor was roughly in the center of the deepest part of the curvature of the bay and there was a long sandy beach to the south. He estimated the harbor was less than a half-mile away, still a considerable distance for even a strong swimmer. If he could get there before the Americans were able to deploy guards, he might have a chance to escape, or at least hide. He turned and headed south toward the harbor. The water was cold, somewhere around fifty degrees. He knew he would need all of his strength to reach the harbor before the coldness of the water sapped his body heat and caused his leg muscles to cramp. He began reciting prayers to Allah in his head, both for the strength they provided and to keep his mind off the frigid water.

The Crescent City Police Officer positioned ten of the militia along the length of the fishing pier from where it began on shore for the seventy-five yards it extended out into the bay, where it ended at a small sandwich and chowder shop. He took the remaining three citizen volunteers into the marina and out on the wooden catwalks that provided access to the boats in their slips. He stationed one person on each of the three walkways. He gave everyone the same orders, "Keep your eyes open and no talking. You'll get relieved as soon as the Marines get here."

"This sucks," Lonnie Kincaid mumbled to himself as he slowly walked up and down the five foot wide wooden catwalk. He'd been stuck out here for what seemed to him to be an eternity. It had actually been less than a half-hour, but he was tired and bored. He'd been an eager volunteer the night before when there was a real danger to the town, but now, it was just boring, and besides, he hadn't even gotten a chance to shoot anybody. Crescent City born and raised, he'd just turned nineteen. Still living at home, his life for the most part consisted of partying with his friends, working part-time at Taco Bell, and little else.

He was walking from the far ocean end of the catwalk toward the point where it intersected with the main walkway when he heard the sound of water splashing and the loud thud of something plopping onto the catwalk behind him. Being out at the far end of the marina by himself, the noise scared him almost to the point of peeing his pants. Wheeling around, Lonnie Kincaid brought his father's shotgun up and aimed at the noise.

It was a bull California Sea Lion. Exhaling, he lowered the shotgun, while the shudder of fear he had just felt drained itself from his body. There were always sea lions in the harbor, cruising around the fishing boats for a free meal, stealing an occasional fish from the line of a fisherman on the pier, and generally making a nuisance of themselves. The catwalks, being only a foot or so higher than the surface of the water were favorite places for the large mammals to haul out and rest.

"You almost got yourself shot big guy," Lonnie Kincaid told the creature. "Better watch out, there's a big bad terrorist around."

As if understanding the words the youth said, the sea lion began barking back at him with a loud guttural "aarf, aarf."

Emil Lagare had made the swim to the harbor tired and his leg muscles almost to the point of burnout. He'd managed to conceal himself under the raised catwalk in the marina just as the three citizen guards were being deployed. The water under the catwalk was too deep for him reach the bottom, forcing him to hang onto one of the wooden cross members under the walkway. The underside of the catwalk was slick with algae and the slime of the marina, not to mention the dozens of small black rock crabs that crawled everywhere trying to bite his hands with their dual pincer claws.

Hanging on to the support under the catwalk, Emil Lagare felt his strength returning. When the sea lion hauled itself out at the far end of the catwalk, he saw his chance. Silently he pulled himself out of the water and crept up behind the young man.

"Aarf, aarf," the sea lion warned, Lonnie Kincaid now completely transfixed by the antics of the big mammal.

With several fishing boats blocking the view between Lonnie Kincaid and the next closest guard, no one saw Emil Lagare grab the lanky teenager from behind and snap his neck. Lonnie Kincaid died silently, one of Emil Lagare's hands over his mouth to muffle any death moans. He couldn't, however, catch the youth's shotgun as it dropped loudly onto the wooden planking of the catwalk.

From the next walkway over came the voice of another guard, "Hey kid, you okay over there?"

Emil Lagare froze.

"Hey kid, you alright?" the voice called again.

Summoning up his best English, Emil Lagare called back, "Okay over here."

Red Wolff was just leaving the command post to meet the Marine helicopters due to land on Highway 101 north of Crescent City in less than ten minutes when she heard the excited voice of the Crescent City Police Officer over her scanner.

The officer's voice was rushed and almost unintelligible.

"10-9, 10-9, and slow down, slow down," Red Wolff spoke into her microphone telling the city officer to repeat his transmission.

"One citizen down at the harbor, dead, stripped of pants, jacket, and shoes, his weapons gone too," the city officer explained.

"Any idea what the citizen was wearing?" Red Wolff asked.

"Negative," came the reply over the scanner.

"How long ago?" she asked the officer.

"No more than five minutes," the officer said.

"95-S-3 to all units, terrorist is in the town area, probably dressed in civilian clothes, he's on foot as far as we know. Set up a street search from the harbor toward the Safeway shopping center. Suspect is probably armed, type of weapon unknown," Red Wolff said into the microphone.

Ray Silva drove up next to Red Wolff as she sat in her patrol car calling out instructions on the radio to the three or four units in the town area. It wasn't nearly enough coverage, he knew. Given the confusion of the last day and number of armed people walking around town, the terrorist could blend in anywhere.

"Ray, you take 101 south, I'll take the northbound side. Work a grid east and west along the cross streets. The streets are starting to get crowded with people and cars," she told him. Ray Silva nodded and was gone.

It was 7:35, and Red Wolff could hear the sound of the heavy Marine transport helicopters north of town. She'd sent the stitched up Ralph Silva with five Army trucks out there to transport the Marines into town. Her original plan was to be there to meet them, but now they would have to fend for themselves. She had more important things on her mind.

As she pulled onto Highway 101 where it made its way north through town, she was amazed at the number of people who were out and about. Less than two hours before she and the citizens of Crescent City were involved in a vicious firefight with the terrorists as they tried to escape from the community center. It had been less than a day since the whole incident started. Yesterday the terrorists had burned half the town to the ground and killed somewhere around a thousand people. Hundreds had tried to flee Crescent City and those that didn't, had locked themselves in their houses. Now, there were dozens of people shopping at Safeway, the McDonald's was open for business, and scores of people were on the street. Amazing Red Wolff thought to herself, only in America.

Even though he was over fifty yards away and his back was towards her, she knew it was him. It was the way he was walking. Hands in his pants pockets, collar up, shoulders hunched, and a baseball hat pulled low on his head. He was trying to look invisible as he walked north on the sidewalk.

"Ray, I got him, walking north on 101 from Second Street," she called over the radio. Red Wolff slowed the patrol car almost to a stop in the right hand lane of Highway 101, staying a block behind the terrorist.

"I'm coming south from Fifth, I'll cut him off at Third Street," Ray Silva told her.

Emil Lagare could feel the presence of the patrol cars before he could see them. Glancing over his shoulder he saw the roof mounted lights of a police car, barely moving, almost fifty yards behind him. He quickened his pace.

He was at the edge of the Safeway shopping center parking lot when he saw the police car coming the wrong way down the street directly toward him, its' red and blue lights flashing. Looking behind he could see the other police car coming too, its' lights now flashing also.

After he'd changed into the clothes of the young man he killed in the marina, Emil Lagare slipped his victims shotgun silently into the ocean. He still had the stolen Berretta 9 millimeter and two extra clips of ammunition.

Now at a full run, he pulled the pistol from beneath his jacket, as he sprinted between the rows of parked cars in front of Safeway. Even at a full run he could see what he was looking for. Four parking rows away an elderly woman was just pulling into a parking stall. Saturday was her regular shopping day at Safeway and terrorists or no terrorists, nothing was going to change that.

She had just put her almost new Chevrolet Malibu into park when Emil Lagare ripped open the driver's side door. The engine was still running when he tried to jerk her from behind the wheel. He actually pulled the elderly woman's left arm from its' shoulder socket, but the women stayed in the seat. He pulled again before he realized she was still seat belted in. Cursing loudly in French, he reached into the car, across the woman's body, and unfastened the seatbelt. With one final pull, he jerked the women from the car and threw her to the pavement. In an instant he was behind the wheel. He tossed his pistol onto the passenger's seat, shifted into gear, and accelerated away.

The tires of the mid-sized American car screeched in protest as Emil Lagare accelerated and turned the wheel at the same time. He was headed for the second exit from the parking lot onto Highway 101. The two Highway Patrol cars were right behind him. When he got to the exit, Emil Lagare didn't slow at all. The front end of the Chevrolet's frame bottomed out as it crossed over the sidewalk and banged onto the asphalt of the highway. Both Highway Patrol cars did the same thing, metal from their low hung push bumpers grinding the pavement, sending a shower of red and white sparks into the air.

Emil Lagare didn't know where he was going, but his instinct to survive was pushing him on. He drove straight across the northbound lanes of Highway 101 onto Third Street for one block, then turned left, southbound on 101. The Highway Patrol vehicles right on his tail.

Highway 101 is a thirty-five mile per hour zone through town. As it nears the ocean, it makes a sharp ninety degree turn to the left and becomes one lane in each direction. Emil Lagare was going way too fast to make the turn to the left safely. He realized his error at the last second and didn't try to turn. His stolen car bounced over the raised curb, across a dirt field, and into the parking lot of a restaurant. Regaining control, he navigated back onto the highway and accelerated southbound.

Ray Silva was in the first patrol car behind the terrorist, Red Wolff only a few feet behind her in her vehicle. She handled the radio advising the communications center of the pursuit and coordinating the response of other units. Ray Silva drove. He was dead on the terrorist's bumper.

All three cars were doing over eighty when they crossed out of the city limits, just south of the harbor. The highway now became trees and ferns on both sides, the last buildings rapidly fading out of sight behind them. Ray Silva backed off and kept a thirty-to-forty foot space cushion between his patrol car and the terrorist's vehicle. They were doing nearly ninety when they approached the steep hill leading into the Redwood forest.

The grade on Highway 101 at Crescent Hill rises from sea level to about four hundred feet in less than three-quarters of a mile. The highway has one lane in the northbound direction for vehicles coming downhill and two heading south, which allowed slower moving traffic to use the right lane as it climbed the steep grade.

There were a few other cars on the road, some coming northbound, having been directed back into town by the officers clearing Last Chance Grade ten miles to the south. Others, unaware they were going to be turned around and sent back to Crescent City, were headed southbound toward Eureka.

As he started up the grade, Emil Lagare could see vehicles in both southbound lanes several hundred feet ahead. Still going ninety, he crossed into the northbound lane and passed them both before having to swerve back into the right hand lanes to avoid smashing head-on into a pickup truck coming down the hill.

With his overhead lights flashing, Ray Silva started to pass the same vehicles by using the wrong side of the road before seeing the truck. He backed off his speed and glided back into the southbound fast lane. Now doing only fifty, he was stuck behind a small passenger car directly in front of him, and a motor home struggling up the grade at thirty miles an hour in the slow lane. The terrorist vehicle was rapidly pulling away.

It took the driver of the vehicle in front of Ray Silva nearly ten seconds to comprehend there were red lights flashing behind him and to hear the wail of the patrol vehicle's siren. Trapped with the motor home right beside him, the driver didn't know whether to speed up to let the patrol car pass, or to slow down until he could pull into the right lane. The driver did neither. Instead he hit his brakes and started to stop in the lane.

Ray Silva cursed to himself as the driver's actions caused him to slow down even more. Red Wolff, still behind him, had to slow also. The terrorist vehicle was rounding the curve at the crest of the grade and would be out of sight in less than two seconds.

As soon as he saw an opening, Ray Silva swerved into the slow lane, punched the accelerator and was around the passenger car. He kept the pedal floored as he jogged back into the fast lane passing the motor home. Red Wolff was right behind.

Emil Lagare didn't know where he was going, but at least for the moment, he had eluded the two police cars pursing him. Now deep within the redwood forest, Highway 101 twisted and turned, undulated up and down slightly, and snaked its' way south. He encountered an occasional car traveling south and a few vehicles coming north. There were even several bicyclists on the road, tucked as far to the right as they could get because there were no shoulders or bike lanes. Every mile or so there were short stretches of two lanes which allowed him to pass easily, and other sections where he had to cross into the opposing lane to pass slower traffic. He hadn't seen the police cars behind him for several minutes.

The fog still clung to the tops of the towering redwoods, although the first rays of the sun were beginning to penetrate in thin streaks of gold through the branches of the trees. The asphalt of the roadway was still wet and in those sections where the sun could penetrate, it caused a blinding reflective glare.

Ray Silva negotiated the curves expertly, maintaining his speed as he and Red Wolff continued southbound. It took several miles, but soon he could see the taillights of the Malibu less than a quarter-mile ahead. The terrorist's vehicle appeared and then disappeared as the roadway curved and undulated.

It was one of those things that just happened. Nobody's fault really, just the confluence of many things happening at the same time.

Ray Silva was doing about seventy, with Red Wolff a hundred feet behind. The speed wasn't unreasonable given the section of roadway he was on, his red lights flashing, and the fact he was pursing the terrorist. He'd driven this highway ten thousand times before, often at a much higher speed.

Highway 101 was two lanes in both directions for several miles at this particular spot. The terrorist was a couple hundred yards ahead and Ray Silva was closing fast. Staying in the fast lane, he passed several slower moving cars in the right lane. Ray Silva had just pressed the accelerator down a slight bit more to pass a family passenger van in the right lane.

In this section of highway, there was a short stretch with no trees for about a hundred yards where the reflective glare from the sun on the wet pavement was terrible. The driver of the van squinted as the reflection momentarily blinded him. It was almost too late when he saw the two bicyclists in his lane. Although they were as far to the right as they could get, the road was not wide enough for him to pass them safely and stay completely within his lane. The driver steered to the left to go around the bicyclists first, then looked in his mirror second.

The right front bumper of the patrol car was less than ten feet from the left rear of the van when the driver moved six feet into the fast lane to go around the bicyclists. Ray Silva's first reaction was to steer to the left into the opposite lane to avoid the van. There were three cars coming from that direction. He swerved back to the right to avoid taking an innocent driver head-on. His only option was to brake and steer back to the right.

As soon as he hit the brakes, the weight transferred from all four wheels to the front tires causing the entire front end of the big Ford to dip. The backend, lighter now because of the weight transfer, began to slide to the left. The patrol vehicle was broadside as Ray Silva counter steered to the left. If the pavement had been a little dryer, the counter steer would have worked and he would have been able to control his skid. At the speed he was going, however, his momentum, centrifugal force, and vehicle dynamics were driving the car, not him.

Broadside in the lane, the right side tires of the patrol car came off the ground first as the vehicle rolled to the left. The dynamics of a side-to-side rollover are different than might be expected. As the vehicle came completely off the ground it was actually the passenger's side of the roof that hit the ground first. The entire right side of the roof was crushed down to the top of the door from the force of the initial impact. It was the second roll that crushed the driver's side. Now on its roof, the patrol car slid for over two hundred feet, across the northbound lanes and slammed into a tree on the edge of the road.

Red Wolff kept her foot pressed down on the accelerator. She was past the demolished patrol car in less than three seconds. The thought of stopping to help her lifelong friend was only in her mind for a fleeting second. First, she knew there was little she could do medically if he was seriously injured. Additionally, she was aware that more help was coming up behind her. Mostly, however, she didn't stop because Ray Silva would be pissed off if she did. She remembered his lecture from the very first night they ever worked together, God knows how many years ago that was, "If something happens to me, leave me, catch the asshole and cancel his ticket." In her rearview mirror, she could see several citizens already stopping near Ray Silva's upside down patrol car.

Red Wolff used the radio to advise the communications center of the accident and request other units to respond. Now in the pursuit by herself, she held the accelerator down and began to close on the terrorist.

The collision involving Ray Silva had opened up the distance between her and the terrorist to over a half-mile. There were brief stretches where she could catch a quick glimpse of his taillights as he continued southbound through the trees at speeds between sixty and eighty miles per hour.

Driving a high speed pursuit affected different people in different ways. For some officers she'd worked with it was just a routine thing. For others it caused them to hyperventilate from the stress it put on their bodies. The most common thing that happened, however, was called "tunnel-vision." It caused an officer's field of vision to narrow as they became fixated on the vehicle they were pursuing. The revolving lights, the wailing siren, the high speeds, and the radio calls all conspired to block out the officer's sense of what was happening around them.

In Red Wolff it caused another reaction. She began to relive the events of the last twenty-four hours. All the wanton killing, the panic, her being thrust into taking charge of the law enforcement resources in town, the ambush of the terrorists at the hospital and Wal-Mart, and the rescue of the hostages. She also thought about her lover and unborn child fighting for their lives in the hospital, and now her career long friend just involved in what very well could be a fatal accident.

It flashed in her mind that, after everything that had happened, it had come down to a car chase. Well, she thought to herself, she'd been forced by him to play at his game, now he was playing at hers. And she had home field advantage.

Emil Lagare had seen the patrol car rolling over in his mirror. At least there was only one of them still behind him, he thought. The road ahead was wide open now, for the moment no cars in front, and none coming the opposite way. He kept his vehicle traveling as fast as he dared given the curves in the road and his lack of knowledge of the terrain. He built up his speed in the straight-aways, then applied his brakes hard as he approached the curves. In the curves, he steered the car around the corners. He was driving as fast as he could.

Red Wolff was slowly gaining on the terrorist ahead of her. The Crown Vic's eight cylinder engine was obviously more powerful than the V-6 engine in the Chevy Malibu. The extra horsepower would have been useful had the chase been on an open freeway. On the twisting, narrow lanes of Highway 101, however, it was a matter of driving skill, not engine size.

As she approached each curve she slowed slightly, positioning the patrol car high on the outside of the curve, then turning the steering wheel slightly, she aimed for the inside apex of the curve. Locking her arms, she held the wheel steady and let the weight of the patrol car shift on its' springs. As the weight shifted, the springs on the outside compressed, and the patrol car powered through the curve. Then, as the curve ended, she turned the wheel an almost imperceptible amount, causing the springs to unload, transferring the weight back to all four tires. Using the dynamics of her patrol car she was gaining on the terrorist with every curve.

Emil Lagare was out of his element. He wasn't a bad driver. In fact, like most people, he considered himself pretty good behind the wheel. He'd driven in most of the major cities in Europe where driving was as much a survival skill as it was a method of transportation. As a youth, he'd often driven his father's Mercedes in the wide open desert flatlands of Lebanon at much higher speeds than he was driving now. There is a big difference, however, between racing from lane to lane in a crowded city, turning up side streets to get around stopped traffic, or going as fast as the car would go on a flat desert, and being chased by the police. He could see the police car was rapidly gaining on him.

The pursuit had been going on for over eight minutes now, and had covered nearly ten miles. Red Wolff knew the terrorist would be at Last Chance Grade soon where the road was still blocked, and there would be other officers to help. She kept her foot buried in the accelerator and continued to close the distance on the Malibu.

The officers working to clear the last of the traffic stopped behind the blockade caused by the burned out fuel truck, monitored the approaching pursuit on the radio. It had taken well over an hour and a half to remove the burned out hulk from the road, and the officers were now trying to clear the stalled and abandoned cars from the north side of the blockade. They were the last impediment to getting Highway 101 completely open so relief personnel could get to Crescent City.

The line of cars to be turned around and routed back to Crescent City, or towed away, stretched for about a quarter-mile, around a curve and back up into the redwoods. There were lots of people standing in the road next to their vehicles, and others who were sitting on the side of the road. The sound of a patrol car siren could be heard in the distance. The sound was getting louder.

Emil Lagare was sweating profusely. His palms were wet and he occasionally had to wipe the sweat from his forehead to keep it from running into his eyes. In his rearview mirror he could see the black and white police car growing larger. He drove as fast as he dared, hitting his brakes hard before every curve, punching the gas where the road straightened.

The road began to descend slightly as it approached Last Chance Grade. The Redwood trees started to thin out and the road cut through a gorge of solid granite rock.

Although he didn't know it, Emil Lagare was less than a quarter-mile from the place where the previous day two of his men had torched the fuel truck. As he came around the last curve in the highway before the start of the downgrade, he encountered the tail end of the line of stopped and abandoned cars in the road. He slammed on his brakes.

The Malibu responded sluggishly to the brakes being applied. The vehicle was slowing slightly, but wasn't stopping. Because of the way he was driving, accelerating, then braking hard in the curves, Emil Lagare had overheated the brakes. They had built up so much heat the brake pads could not apply enough friction to the brake discs to stop the vehicle. Emil Lagare pushed harder on the brake pedal, but the vehicle refused to stop.

At the last second before plowing into the rear end of a full-sized seventies vintage Dodge pickup truck, Emil Lagare turned the wheel to the left. The Chevy Malibu skidded in that direction, the right side of the car striking the left rear of the pickup. Like a pool ball, the Malibu caromed off the pickup, did a 180 degree spin, and came to rest facing to the north in the northbound lane. The impact with the pickup sent Emil Lagare's head into the steering wheel. A large gash over his right eye started blood streaming down his face, impairing his vision. Dazed and unsure how bad he was injured, he sat behind the wheel for several seconds. The sight of the police car rolling to a stop fifty yards in front of him, snapped him back to his senses.

Emil Lagare made one quick attempt to restart his car. The starter turned the engine over, but it refused to start. He had to run. Reaching to the passenger's seat, he groped for his Berretta pistol while watching the door of the police car open. The pistol was gone. The impact with the pickup truck had knocked it to the floorboard, and the spinout had slid it under the seat. Emil Lagare knew he had no time to search for it.

He was out the door and running toward the rocks and trees on the west side of the highway.

Red Wolff came around the last curve in the road just as Emil Lagare's car struck the pickup truck. She watched as it bounced off the truck, spun, and came to a stop facing north. She hit her brakes hard and the big Ford stopped on command. She advised the communications center that the terrorist had crashed and requested assistance.

She knew two other Highway Patrol units from Crescent City had joined the pursuit and were coming up behind her. They would be there within ninety seconds. She also heard the voices on the radio of the officers from the Humboldt Highway Patrol command who were on foot clearing the last of the cars from Last Chance Grade telling her they would be there within a minute.

As she was sliding to a stop, Red Wolff popped her seat belt loose, unlatched the driver's side door and kicked it open with her boot. The door sprung back at her as the car stopped and she pushed it open all the way again with her foot. Keeping her eyes on the terrorist as he was still seated in his vehicle, she reached for the hidden release button for the magnetic lock that held the shotgun in its' mount between the front seats. She'd just pulled the weapon clear and was racking a round into the chamber when the terrorist sprinted from his car toward the shoulder on the ocean side of the road.

"Leg bail, foot pursuit!" Red Wolff yelled into her epaulet mike, telling the communications center the terrorist was fleeing on foot and she was going after him.

"10-4, S-3, in foot pursuit," the comm-op acknowledged.

The comm-op's voice was calm and businesses like as she broadcast, "All units hold your traffic, 95-S-3 is in foot pursuit of terrorist suspect vicinity of Last Chance Grade, all units hold your traffic."

She waited for ten seconds, then called, "95-S-3, status?" She waited five more seconds and repeated her call. There was no response from 95-S-3.

Red Wolff was a good copper. She knew better than to go charging off by herself into the trees and rocks after a suspect, especially one with a gun. Help was only minutes away. They would organize a search along a broad front and move systematically into the forest to root out the suspect. There was nowhere for him to go.

The events of the last day, however, had taken much too high a toll on her. Good cop or not, right or wrong, this was the end game, and it was hers alone to finish. With the shotgun at port arms, a round in the chamber, and the safety on as a precaution against tripping and accidentally discharging a round, Red Wolff plunged into the woods.

Emil Lagare was breathing heavily, panting for air. His head ached and the blood would not stop streaming from the large cut on his forehead. The underbrush was thick and the ground soggy, making every step difficult. There was a thick mat of vegetation on the forest floor causing his feet to sink into the ground as he tried to run. Every step caused branches to snap under his feet and other low hanging branches blocked his way. He kept moving forward, away from the road.

As soon as she entered the underbrush, Red Wolff stopped. It was so thick the terrorist could be only feet away and she would not see him. Standing still she listened. She could hear the sound of sirens in the distance, her officers coming to help. She could also hear the sound of the ocean. More precisely she could hear the sound of waves crashing on the rocks. She had done suspect searches in this area before. Whoever the terrorist was, he'd made a bad mistake. Had he run east, there are miles of thick forest and underbrush so dense it would take dogs to flush him out. By running west, he'd entered an area where there was only about fifty yards of trees and rocks before they ended at the edge of a four hundred foot drop to the ocean below.

Snap, she heard the sound of a tree branch being broken, then the sound of rustling leaves. The sound came from her left, maybe fifty yards away. She began to make her way in that direction.

Emil Lagare broke out of the dense forest and into the now bright sunshine. He found himself on a flat ledge of rock ten yards from the edge the cliff. He quickly moved to the edge of the precipice and looked down. Below him was a sheer four hundred foot wall. He could see the waves pounding against the rocks below, sending twenty foot geysers of white water and foam into the air. He looked left and right for an escape route. He saw a large rock with several trees to his right.

Red Wolff was moving quickly through the underbrush and tree branches toward the sound she'd heard. She could see sunlight ahead as the forest was thinning out.

The two patrol cars skidded to a stop right behind Red Wolff's vehicle, just as the first of the officers were coming up from Last Chance Grade on foot. They looked around, then at each other. In the excitement, Red Wolff had not told anyone which way the suspect had fled. One of her officers called her on his portable radio, "S-3, are you east or west of the highway?" There was no response.

Emil Lagare secreted himself on top of the rock, about eight feet off the ground. The dense green branches of the two Redwood trees provided thick concealment. As he waited on top of the rock, he heard the static of a police radio, then the voice of someone talking, although he was too far away to make out what was being said.

Red Wolff came out of the trees and onto the rock ledge just as she heard her officer calling on the radio. She was reaching up to key the microphone clipped to her epaulet when the terrorist dropped on her from above.

Emil Lagare landed hard on top of Red Wolff causing her to fall to the ground, the shotgun she was carrying flying from her hands. The element of surprise gave Emil Lagare the advantage. He was on his feet in an instant and sent a hard full leg swing kick into her side as she lay on the ground. The force of the blow caused Red Wolff to recoil, although the wrap around soft body armor she was wearing dissipated the power in the kick and protected her ribs. She rolled to her left, away from the terrorist, and up on one knee as she drew her pistol.

Emil Lagare had the shotgun pointed right at her. From eight feet away, he couldn't miss. He hesitated. For the first time he realized the police officer was a woman. He looked closer at her, there was something familiar. Then it came to him.

"You!" he said incredulously to Red Wolff, recognizing her as the reporter he'd allowed in the community center who had freed the hostages.

Red Wolff had her pistol out of its holster, but it was still pointed down. She knew if she brought it up to shoot, the terrorist would fire. She might get a shot off, but so would he. It would be a tie at best, and they would both be dead.

She'd been in tight spots before, but this was as bad as it gets. Red Wolff had never contemplated her own death beyond the normal everyday hazards of her chosen occupation. She'd always known, as every cop does, that on any given day, something may happen that could bring about her death. Like most cops, she accepted that, but did not dwell on it.

The radio called again, "S-3, which way did the suspect go?" The other officers were searching for her.

"There are more police coming?" Emil Lagare asked, his breathing still heavy.

"You bet your ass they're coming," Red Wolff spit out a reply.

"Then I will kill you first and then the others, Allah Akbar," Emil Lagare said, a defiance returning to his voice.

"Yeah, you can kill me, and if you're really good, you might even kill the next officers who get here. But there are seven thousand of us, and sooner or later, they're all going to be here," Red Wolff told him, a defiance in her voice also.

"Women should stay at home and have babies," Emil Lagare told her, the shotgun still leveled at her.

Red Wolff got a half-smile on her face and said, "Not in this league, pal."

"Allah Akbar," Emil Lagare said, as he pulled the trigger.

Nothing happened. Red Wolff had left the safety on.

Red Wolff sprang as soon as she saw the terrorist involuntarily flinch milliseconds before he tried to pull the trigger in anticipation of the shotgun's tremendous recoil.

It took Emil Lagare a fraction of a second to realize the shotgun had not fired. By that time, she was on him. She used the side of her pistol to smash the left side of the terrorist's head as hard as she could, causing him to drop the shotgun. He went down to his knees, less than three feet from the edge of the cliff.

She was standing in front of him now, about four feet away, her right arm outstretched, the .40 caliber pistol aimed at his head. With her left hand, Red Wolff reached up to key her radio mike, the other officers were calling again, trying to determine her location. Once she responded, they would be with her in less than a minute. Still bleeding profusely from his forehead and now on his knees, the terrorist wasn't a threat to her anymore. She paused just before keying the mike, then brought her hand down, away from the radio.

Red Wolff could see the defiance and gloating in his eyes over the death and destruction he had wrought.

You are, what you do, when it counts, the words of Career Decision Number Three played in her mind.

"Allah Akbar, asshole," she said, as she pulled the trigger.

After they heard the gunshot it took the other officers less than a minute to reach her. She was standing at the edge of the cliff looking down at the water four hundred feet below. They could see the body of a man floating on the surface, face down. The motion of the waves drew the body out to sea and then pushed it in against the rocks. They watched for another minute before the body slipped beneath the surface.

It took her about half an hour to get back to Crescent City. Highway 101 was open now and there was a steady stream of military and Highway Patrol cars heading north. She drove toward the command post, but there were over seventy-five CHP cars, and maybe two hundred officers there. She had to park two blocks away and walk.

Marine helicopters were landing in the parking lots of the community center, their troops being deployed around town, while a National Guard disaster response team set up a temporary morgue in the tents they erected in the park

She stood in the background and watched the flurry of activity. The Governor was surrounded by media. There were at least fifteen television satellite trucks set up around the command post. She could hear the Governor talking about her ordeal at the hands of the terrorists and how, after her rescue, she'd remained in town to provide leadership.

Red Wolff worked her way to the center of the command post, found the ranking Highway Patrol commander and told him the last terrorist was dead. She gave him a brief run down on what had happened in the past twenty-four hours, and asked him to see that all of her cops and National Guard troopers were taken care of. She then told him she had to get to the hospital to check on some people.

Back in her patrol car, she was just pulling onto Highway 101 when she saw the FBI Hostage Rescue Team, dressed in their black jump suits, loaded down with weapons, walking in from the airport.

Red Wolff had a half-smile on her face.

EPILOGUE

In the week following the terrorist attack on Crescent City, the FBI took charge of the investigation into the incident. They quickly rolled up the mosque in Oakland, arrested the imam and his radical followers. The legal motions, trial, and subsequent appeals took many months. The imam received a life sentence. His young followers got lengthy jail time.

A month after the incident, the American ambassador to Syria received a strongly worded protest from the Syrian government. Fragments of American made "smart-bombs" had been found at a remote camp site in the desert where the Syrians claimed young men were attending a religious retreat. Among the dead was a naturalized American citizen and former U.S. Army sergeant, Muhammad Attiya. The American government denied any involvement in, or knowledge of, the bombing of the camp.

The FBI also conducted an hour-by-hour investigation into the events leading up to and during the attack on Crescent City. From the information they gained, changes were made in security at National Guard armories and local law enforcement procedures in dealing with terrorist attacks nationwide.

Part of the FBI's investigation dealt with the high speed pursuit of the terrorist leader on Highway 101 and the death of the man they were able to identify as Emil Lagare. According to their interviews with the female California Highway Patrol Sergeant, Erin Wolff, the terrorist had fired a round from a handgun at her while they struggled on the ledge at the edge of the Redwood trees. She stated she'd returned fire in self-defense.

The FBI is nothing if not thorough. In interviews with the other officers who were coming into the forest to help the female sergeant, none could positively say they heard a shot from the terrorist leader's 9 millimeter army Beretta before they heard the shot she fired from her pistol.

The FBI also conducted an inventory to account for all of the weapons the terrorists had stolen from the armory. When they added the army Beretta pistol they found under the passenger's seat of the vehicle the terrorist leader had stolen from the elderly woman in the Safeway parking lot, to the other pistols the terrorists stole, all the weapons were accounted for.

They were puzzled, therefore, as to exactly what pistol the terrorist leader had used to fire at the female Highway Patrol sergeant before she shot him. There were unsubstantiated rumors that political pressure had been applied to have the FBI limit their investigation into this part of the incident.

The FBI also picked up rumors that one of the citizens of Crescent City had an illegal machine gun. During their investigation, they questioned the manager of the Napa Auto Parts store and executed a search warrant on his house. No machine gun was found. Under the mattress in Red Wolff's bedroom was the last place anyone thought to look.

On the Fourth of July the following year, the Marine helicopters were again landing at the beachfront park in Crescent City. They were not the transport helicopters that had been there a year prior, but the Presidential helicopters of Marine Squadron One. Five of the shiny olive drab and white helicopters were parked on the grass. The President had come to honor the people of Crescent City for their heroic defense of their town, and to pin medals on a lot of brave people.

The Governor had returned also. Not that she had any fond memories of the place, but because it was her state, and she was the Democratic front runner in the next Presidential race. Her ordeal at the hands of the terrorists had thrust her into the national spotlight. It was the kind of national prominence you just couldn't buy.

The media came in full force also. The White House press corps was there, of course, not to mention the cable networks, and stations from up and down California and the Pacific Coast.

Covering the event for Fox News, was their newest on-air personality, Patricia Dodge. After winning the du-Pont award for excellence in journalism, and a slew of other honors from the industry, she'd gone on to become the darling of the "talking head" programs. She'd done all the late night shows, and commanded a healthy fee for giving speeches at colleges and national women's organization meetings. Her new cable network show, "Dodge City," was a cross between Nancy Grace and Geraldo.

This year, the annual parade in Crescent City was even better attended than it normally was. Thousands of people from Northern California and Southern Oregon poured into town to watch the parade, see the President, and get a chance to see real life American heroes. The parade route was the same as always, starting on Front Street, snaking through the businesses district, and ending up at the park. Much of the downtown area had been rebuilt in the preceding year. There were several buildings still under construction, their roofs not quite finished, or the framing not completed. Few scars of the terrorist attack remained on the landscape.

There was no parade Grand Marshal this year. Instead, the local National Guard Company led the parade, marching behind a saddled, rider less black stallion, with a pair of boots turned backward in the stirrups, to symbolize the loss of their comrades.

At the park, a large stage had been erected, and several grandstands rented to accommodate the crowd. The newly elected mayor of Crescent City opened the ceremony by introducing the dignitaries, the Governor, and then the President.

There was a moment of silence to remember all of the innocent victims of the terrorist attack, then a twenty-one gun rifle salute to honor fallen National Guard soldiers.

The President spoke first. It was a typical speech for the occasion, lots of words like heroic, sacrifice, bravery, and courage. Newly promoted army sergeant, Raphael Silva, received the Congressional Medal of Honor for his actions. It was the first time the medal had been awarded for bravery in combat against an enemy on American soil since the Indian Wars of the old west in the late 1900's.

The ceremony in Crescent City was carried live by all the cable networks. In Madrid, Spain, it was almost ten at night. In his hotel room, Yusef al-Masthal watched the ceremony with great interest.

Go ahead and celebrate, he said to himself, you won, and you earned your victory. But, he thought, don't celebrate too much, for you were always supposed to win this part of the battle. Plus, you paid a high price for your victory. Nearly eleven hundred people killed, another five hundred or so wounded, not to mention the destruction of half your town, while we traded the lives of less than thirty men.

Our victory came in other ways. Now, not only do you have to plan for and guard against future attacks in your big cities, but also in places like this insignificant little town. And, there will be future attacks. We are patient, and we have tens of thousands of men and women who are eager to martyr themselves for The Cause.

Yusef al-Masthal rubbed his cold lifeless black eyes. He was tired. It had been a long day, but he'd successfully recruited several new potential martyrs.

The seeds of a new plan were germinating in his mind.

The next time, hopefully, we will not attack a place where there is a "She-Devil" like the one in this town to spoil our plans, he thought to himself.

The Governor spoke next, reliving her harrowing ordeal, and thanking the people of the town for their bravery and for rescuing her.

The Governor's first award was not to a resident of Crescent City at all, but to a middle-aged, single mother of three, who lived in Eureka. The Governor didn't understand everything a Highway Patrol Communications Operator did, but her staff had told her that this woman's actions were instrumental in her being rescued.

What the Governor didn't relate to the crowd was that in the months following the incident she became more aware of how a gay female Highway Patrol sergeant had organized the resistance in the town and orchestrated her rescue. The Governor also learned this sergeant had been bypassed for promotion, something to do with her sexual preference.

The Governor contacted the Commissioner of the Highway Patrol and attempted to get him to reverse his decision not to promote the female sergeant to lieutenant. The Commissioner refused, telling the Governor she did not have the authority to override his decision. The Governor had her staff research the issue and confirmed that even as California's chief executive she could not circumvent Civil Service rules. Undeterred, the Governor told the head of the California Highway Patrol that while she may not have the authority to promote the female sergeant, she did have the authority to appoint a new Commissioner.

The Governor read the citation that accompanied the awarding of the State of California's highest honor for bravery, the Medal of Valor to CHP Officer Ray Silva. Seated in the front row of the VIP section, Julie Bradley almost couldn't contain herself as the Commissioner of the Highway Patrol slipped the ribbon and dangling medal around her man's neck. Ray Silva felt self-conscious standing on the stage in his dress uniform with everyone looking at him. He'd spent almost a month in the hospital after his rollover accident. His broken left arm had healed okay and was doing fine. The steel rod they'd put in to replace his shattered right femur, however, was still giving him fits. Probably time to retire, he thought to himself.

The Governor then read the citation for the second Medal of Valor being presented to newly promoted Highway Patrol Lieutenant, and new Commander of the Crescent City Area, Erin Wolff. Beaming at her partner from the VIP section, Mary Jean held their infant son, Raymond Raphael Snider-Wolff.

When the Governor finished reading the citation, the Commissioner of the Highway Patrol slipped the ends of the ribbon holding the medal around Red Wolff's neck. The Commissioner and Red Wolff were now face-to-face. As he bent forward to secure the ends of the ribbon behind her neck, she whispered in his ear, "Not bad for a Fucking Freak, huh Commissioner." There was a half-smile on her face.

ACKNOWLEDGEMENTS

Writing this was the easy part, fine tuning and trying to get it published was another story. So many people helped by reading the early versions, offering suggestions, helping with formatting, grammar, and punctuation that I can't express enough my gratitude for their help.

I would be remiss by not mentioning the names of Nancy Herrera, a former colleague who corrected my spelling and grammar. Melony Smith, Sandy Helmer, Tish Hunt, and Lori Wade whose input helped develop the characters. Suzanne Hancock for a critical proofread and edit. Scott Muttersbach for comments on the locales, and for shopping the manuscript around with his media friends. Thanks to Dawn Wooten for her expertise in computers and the patience to teach an "old dog" new tricks. Lastly, a special thanks to Kerri Hawkins, neighbor, friend, and Highway Cop, for her help with the cover design and formatting.

It's true what the *Beatles* said, you can get by with a little help from your friends.

CPSIA information can be obtained
at www.ICGtesting.com
Printed in the USA
FSOW02n1958120917
38706FS